Divas

About the author

Born in London, Rebecca Chance spent her twenties in Tuscany and her thirties in Manhattan before returning to London with a handsome American husband in tow. Rebecca's interests include gymnastics, trapeze and pole-dancing, watching *America's Next Top Model* and cocktail-drinking. *Divas* is her first novel.

Visit www.rebeccachance.net

Divas

Rebecca Chance

POCKET
BOOKS

LONDON • SYDNEY • NEW YORK • TORONTO

First published in Great Britain by Pocket Books, 2009
An imprint of Simon & Schuster UK
A CBS COMPANY

1 3 5 7 9 10 8 6 4 2

Simon & Schuster UK Ltd
1st Floor, 222 Gray's Inn Road
London WC1X 8HB

www.simonandschuster.co.uk

Simon & Schuster Australia
Sydney

A CIP catalogue record for this book is available
from the British Library

ISBN 978-1-84739-395-1

Typeset by M Rules
Printed by CPI Cox & Wyman, Reading, Berkshire RG1 8EX

Acknowledgements

With many thanks to my fabulous and always utterly supportive agent, Anthony Goff; to my editor Kate Lyall Grant, who is thankfully not at all a diva, but a total professional; to Caroline Harris, copyeditrix supreme; to Rob Cox and everyone in marketing and sales at Simon and Schuster, without whom this book wouldn't be in your hands right now.

Thanks also to Polepeople, who taught me a whole raft of pole tricks and whose classes are a ton of fun; to my trapeze teachers Natalie and Simone; to my gymnastics teacher Randy; and my trapeze partner Randon, who has never dropped me on my head yet. Thanks to my adorable husband Greg, who is always on my side, and who reaps the benefits of all my exercise classes . . .

And finally, thanks to Katharine Walsh and Kirsten Ferguson, two great hotel PRs who have kindly arranged stays for me in some of the most fabulous places in the world so that my heroines can live it up in the manner in which we would all like to become accustomed!

Prologue

Carin Fitzgerald was sitting naked in front of her dressing-room mirror, cutting her hair. It fell in white-blonde swatches over her shoulders, and as she cut, she shook each lock off contemptuously so it slid to the floor. She was using a big pair of scissors, impatient for it to be done, cutting it short to her head. Frédéric, her hair stylist – he was too expensive to be called a hairdresser – could tidy it up later today. But she couldn't wait for him. She wanted to do it now. Before she killed her husband.

She surveyed herself in the mirror. Her short fair hair, her translucent white skin, made her look eerie, otherworldly, especially with the gleam of intent in her pale blue eyes. The haircut suited her more than any she had ever had before. She'd always wanted to cut it this short, but when she was modelling, they'd told her no one would book her with boy-cut hair. And then her husband, that tub of lard, had insisted that short hair was unfeminine. She rolled her eyes and stood up, pushing back the upholstered stool, wiping off stray hairs from her shoulders as she crossed the room, pulling on a white velvet robe as she went.

She loved white. It was so simple, so pure.

Double doors connected her dressing room to her bedroom. She took hold of the handles and pulled them open, enjoying, as always, the drama of the doors soundlessly sliding apart. Barefoot, she strode through her bedroom and into the huge bathroom, with the sunken bath that her husband no longer used and the wet room, so large even his bulk could fit into it comfortably. She had chosen the Brazilian slate flooring and Carrara marble walls herself, but she might have it all stripped out later on today, just because she could. She might remodel the whole house.

She was smiling at the thought as she exited the bathroom.

Her husband was lying in his gigantic bed, snoring faintly. The heavy curtains had been drawn, but the perfect New York spring morning outside – bright sunlight, clear blue sky – had failed to wake him. She wasn't surprised. It took a great deal to wake him these days, apparently. The room, large and opulent, was the complete opposite to hers: brocade hangings, swagged velvet curtains, Oriental carpets. Everything that would catch and hide the dust. Revolting. She had never spent any time in here, so she had had no interest in redecorating it to be calm and serene like her own suite, with its white carpeting and blond wood furniture, its elegantly simple, though extraordinarily expensive, Japanese lighting.

Beside the bed stood Joe Scutellaro, the day nurse. He looked nervous, which didn't surprise her. In fact, she preferred it: had Joe been nonchalant, that would have indicated he wasn't taking this whole business seriously enough. As it was, his quivering lower lip, the frequency with which he was clearing his throat, showed that he had fully taken in exactly what they were about to do.

'He's still asleep,' he said unnecessarily of the snoring bulk in the bed.

'Good,' she said. 'Just as we planned. Is it ready?'

Joe reached down to the small metal trolley that stood next to the bed, and held up a syringe in a hand that was shaking a little. His dark eyes were wide with strain, his mouth taut, but he still looked very handsome. It had been his looks, as much as any other factor, that had got him the job as her husband's primary nurse. Italian men, in her opinion, should always be pretty. Some races – the

Celtic ones particularly – could be more stocky, more brutal-looking, which she liked just as much, in a different way; but Italians only worked if they were pretty. She surveyed Joe's long lashes, his carefully groomed dark curls, with great approval. Oh yes, it was definitely time to do this. She was tired of sneaking around, tired of pretending to be an ice queen so that her husband wouldn't pester her for sex because he thought she wasn't interested in the entire proceeding. She'd made sure he didn't suspect she had any passions at all, let alone how much she was enjoying herself with most members of the household staff.

She preferred to have sex with men she employed. She always had.

'I'll do it,' she said, taking the syringe from Joe.

His eyes widened still further.

'Are you sure?'

'Absolutely.' She smiled at him. 'My hand's much steadier than yours.'

Joe had already rolled up the sleeve of the pyjama-clad arm closest to them. The skin – mottled with ill health and faint fading needle marks – was so unpleasant to her that she could hardly bear to look at it, but she took the syringe from Joe, motioning him out of the way so that the daylight, pouring through the high window of their townhouse, illuminated her field of activity. In one swift, confident motion, she put the thumb and second finger of her left hand into the crook of his elbow, stretched the skin taut so she could see the old puncture marks, and inserted the tip of the needle into the centre of one, pressing the plunger down. As she slipped the needle out again, her task accomplished, she noted that she had left no new mark at all, nothing to indicate that an injection had just taken place.

She handed the needle back to Joe.

'Good,' she said, smiling at him. 'That was easy.'

He nodded, his eyes still wide, his hand still shaking a little.

This wasn't good. Joe would certainly be questioned, at least by the doctor, perhaps by others. Now that it had been done, she needed to take the edge off his fear. Some nervousness would be more than understandable, of course: but too much would raise a red flag.

Oh, who was she fooling? Certainly not herself. She was dying for it. That had been one of the most exciting things she had ever done in her life, and now she was on fire to celebrate.

Not that she'd ever needed much excuse for this kind of activity.

'Now,' she said to Joe. 'Take your clothes off, and fuck me.'

She slipped off her robe and stood there naked, slim and pale, almost six foot tall, her physique flawless. The sight of her nude body was all the encouragement Joe needed; he was already fumbling with the waistband of his trousers, his rising excitement making the task of unzipping himself harder than usual.

'And make it quick,' she said, turning away from the body on the bed. The last thing she wanted to see as she came was her husband's face. 'I've got a long list of things to take care of today.'

Chapter 1

'Miss Fitzgerald?' The receptionist was so apologetic it sounded as if she were about to cry. 'I'm really sorry, but your card's been declined.'

But Lola Fitzgerald wasn't listening: she was too busy examining her face in the huge gilt-framed mirror that hung in Dr Block's reception area. The mirror was tactfully placed so that Dr Block's clients had to take a few steps to approach it. This avoided them having to catch more than a glimpse of themselves if they didn't want to.

If you came in with a burgeoning spot that needed cortisone injected right into the middle of its nasty little swelling white cyst to kill it dead, or lines around your mouth that seemed to have deepened overnight and were desperate for some collagen to fill them up, you could swoop past the mirror without turning your head to see your shame. But if, like Lola, you had just had vitamin C injected all over your face in a stinging series of tiny needle pricks, you couldn't help wanting to see if this apparently miraculous new treatment did actually make you look like you had the glowing skin of a fourteen-year-old who had been brought up on a purely organic diet, gone for long healthy walks every day, and didn't even know what alcohol was.

Any observer would have been amazed at how critically Lola was staring at herself in the mirror. But though Lola Fitzgerald was twenty-nine and naturally drop-dead gorgeous, she was as obsessed with her looks as someone twice her age with a fraction of her own lucky genetic inheritance. Lola Fitzgerald was as beautiful as a shiny gold coin, new-minted and perfect. And it took a walletful of shiny gold cards to keep her looking that way.

Dr Block, the most famous and most expensive dermatologist in London, kept Lola's skin smooth and buttersoft, while glamorous blonde Abigail, the owner of BeauBronz fake tan, had visited Lola's dinky little Mayfair mews house earlier that afternoon to spray Lola from head to toe with a perfect gilded sheen. The golden colour, custom-blended for her by Abigail, matched Lola's hair, artfully highlighted by a colourist whose phone number was one of London's most closely guarded secrets.

Lola's eyes were big and dark and slightly slanted; her nose, while nothing special in itself, had been minimally straightened and shaved down so it was perfectly symmetrical. Her lower lip was markedly fuller than her upper one, but (a) that was actually very pretty, and (b) she had never seen anyone have a successful time with collagen-in-lip injections, so why fix something that wasn't broken?

Ditto with the breasts. Hers weren't large, but they were lovely, small and round, and because they weren't too big, she could wear anything she wanted. She could even wear a frock slashed right down to the waist and look elegant. Sexy, yes: vulgar, no. Which was important, because women envied you much more for looking elegant than they did for looking vulgar.

And Lola's aim was to be envied by every single woman in the world. Women on the street. Women in her social set. Women who bought weekly glossy gossip magazines, or monthly fashion bibles, thick and heavy with advertising, and thumbed through them for insights as to how the one per cent of really rich, beautiful people lived. Women who stopped at a picture of you and wished with all their hearts that *this* was how they looked, that they were inside

Lola Fitzgerald's shiny, golden body, tossing her mane of gilded hair, living Lola Fitzgerald's sun-kissed, charmed, beautiful life.

'Miss Fitzgerald?' the receptionist repeated, a degree of desperation entering her voice.

After her detailed survey, Lola decided that, to be utterly honest, it wasn't as if her face was really capable of that much improvement. Not after the peels and the fillers and the Botox. It wasn't that she *needed* Botox, but if you had it in your twenties as a preventative measure, you didn't need plastic surgery till your late forties, according to Dr Block. Almost everyone Lola knew Botoxed on a regular basis.

She glanced over her shoulder at the reception desk, the nervous tweetings of the receptionist having finally penetrated her consciousness.

'I'm *so sorry*, Miss Fitzgerald, but your card isn't going through! Do you have another one I could try?'

Sighing impatiently, Lola flipped out another card from the pink calfskin cardholder she'd just bought in a sweet little boutique in St Trop – it would be perfect for this summer, she'd throw it at her cleaning lady after that and get something a couple of shades darker for autumn. With a half-smile and a small bob of the head, the receptionist scraped the card along the desk with her long fingernails till it reached the edge and she could lever it up and insert it into the chip-and-PIN machine.

Lola tapped in her code with a perfectly manicured finger. Just then her phone beeped, and she fished it out of her bag.

'Lo? It's India.'

'Hi, darling! I'm just finishing up at Dr Block's.'

'Well, hurry up! We're all here waiting for you—'

The receptionist was saying something, which Lola found highly annoying. She had her regular appointments already booked in; she was fully stocked with Dr Block's skin wipes and cleansers and polishes, as the receptionist ought to know, as it was part of her job to send new ones out whenever Lola was due to be running low; so there was really *nothing* this woman with over-long fingernails needed to say to her at all, especially not in the middle of a very important phone conversation—

'Miss Fitzgerald?' The receptionist's face was screwed up into a tight little knot, as if she were carrying all the embarrassment on Lola's behalf. 'This card – it's been declined as well . . .'

'Oh, for God's sake!' Lola said impatiently. 'No, not you, India! Some stupid—'

But then, by complete accident, she actually caught the receptionist's eye.

Lola never looked directly at service people. Why bother? It made her feel awkward, because their eyes were always needy. They wanted to be her – they wanted some of her gilding to rub off on them and make them, for one brief moment, as shiny as her. Even if they resented her, even if they downright hated her, they still wanted that touch of gold. Poor things. As if, even if they had it, they'd know what to do with it.

This woman looked needy, of course she did, but she was visibly nervous, too. She suddenly reminded Lola of Devon's horrible husband's poor Labradors, who he kicked all the time while loudly announcing that they loved it. So Lola took a breath, changed direction, and continued:

'. . . Some stupid problem with my cards,' and, to be extra nice, she gave the receptionist a dazzling smile as she removed the card from her clasp and slid it back into the pink calfskin.

'Oh God, I hate that!' India was hugely sympathetic. 'I had that in St Bart's in February, there was some sort of transfer that hadn't gone through and it jammed me up so badly at this boutique – *so embarrassing*—'

'It's just some ridiculous mistake I don't have time to deal with right now,' Lola said to both India and the receptionist. 'Look, just bill me – I've really got to dash, it's my hen night—'

The receptionist nodded subserviently. She was more than happy to assume that this was a momentary glitch in the extremely well-oiled system that funnelled vast sums of money from Lola's father's bank accounts into Lola's own.

Lola clipped away from the desk, her white jeans so tight it was hard to walk fast in them. The floor of the office was marble, and the atmosphere in here was always reverentially quiet, church-like, every visitor a worshipper at the shrine of artificial beauty. Lola's Jimmy Choos clicked at the marble in fast, tiny little stabs, like the injections Dr Block had just dotted into her face.

'India? I'm literally down the street. Be there in five.'

After the respectful hush of the dermatologist's office, New Bond Street in early spring was bustling as always with rich old men, young men in suits who worked in galleries and auction houses, and perfectly groomed girls who dated both types of men at the same time. Lola wove through the crowds, drawing her customary more-than-appreciative stares from the men, and noticing, as was second nature to her, the quality of the brief glances the women gave her. Women wouldn't stare – that would be paying her too much of a compliment. But they flashed their eyes quickly, up and down, a razor-blade slice of assessment of their competition.

The nail salon was half a block down New Bond Street, one floor up. Lola managed to wiggle up the stairs – *God, these jeans had no give in them at all* – and entered to cries of her name. Her four friends were draped over white leather sofas in the antechamber, looking, inevitably, like one of those photoshoots for the glossies that brings together a group of young socialities and accompanies it with breathless captions about each girl. All of them were heiresses with fat trust funds, girls who were photogenic and loved by the gossip magazines because they dressed to the nines and partied hard. India was aristocratic, Devon had married a marquis, Lola and Madison were American, so it didn't matter that their money was new, while Georgia had already divorced a rackety Russian count and was on the prowl for husband no. 2. They all looked as if they had been styled by Italian *Vogue*: bright colours, sparkling jewellery, artfully mussed hair. There was only one brunette, and no one was wearing even a touch of black. You didn't starve yourself and spray on fake tan and work out to the point of collapse just to hide your trophy body.

'I love it! You managed to *be late for your own hen night*!' Georgia purred.

'I'm so sorry—' Lola clipped over to Georgia and gave her two enthusiastic air kisses. 'Dr Block was running late and the bloody receptionist buggered up my card or something—'

'Ooh!' Devon's eyes widened. 'You were having the vitamin C shots! Do they work?'

'You tell me,' Lola said, sitting down between Devon and Georgia on one of the sofas and presenting her face under the white-bright lights of the nail salon for detailed observation. The girls craned in, eyes narrowing as they squinted at her.

'I think you look a bit shinier,' Devon pronounced. 'In a good way,' she added swiftly.

'Yeah,' Madison agreed. 'Kinda glowier.'

'Needles in your *face*,' India whispered in horror. 'I don't know how you can *do* it.'

'India! Your eyebrows are going to *drop right on top of your eyes* when you're forty if you don't have Botox now!' Madison said passionately. As the only American in the group, she was naturally the most evangelical about plastic surgery.

'Crow's feet, India. Think about it. You blink too much as it is,' Devon added.

India's round moon-face pulled the kind of expression that every other girl present was incapable of making, the crucial facial muscles being temporarily paralysed by Dr Block's cunning needles.

'I just *can't*,' she said hopelessly. India was the poshest by birth, the sweetest by nature and the only one of the group who was plastic-surgery free. Everyone else thought she was a little slow, frankly.

There was a mass shrug from the rest of them. They had done what they could. Now India was alone with her incipient wrinkles.

'So!' Georgia announced. 'Pedi time! Shoes off, ladies!'

Naturally, Georgia had reserved the whole salon for them, so five minutes later, the anteroom resembled the most exclusive shoe shop in London. Pairs of Jimmys, Manolos and Ginas – all sandals, of course, chosen to show off the imminent pedicure to best advantage – nestled into each other, glittering and glistening, reflected in the floor-to-ceiling mirrors, catching extra light from the ironic mirrorball twirling slowly in the centre of the room. While each of their owners was ensconced in a state-of-the-art padded white leather chair with full massage system, their feet soaking in whirlpool baths of water filled with rose petals and gold leaf, about to have pedicures with real diamonds applied to their toes, drinking rose-petal martinis.

'Oh, *Georgia*. Best hen night ever,' Lola sighed happily.

'First of many!' Madison said, hoisting her glass aloft. 'And may you come out richer every time!'

'*Mad*,' India said a little reproachfully. 'You're so *American* some-times. You said that at Dev's hen, too, and Dev actually loves Piers, you know.'

'Oh, I didn't mind,' pretty blonde Devon said easily. 'Besides, I'm obviously never going to divorce Piers, because of the title.'

'I still can't believe you're going to be a *duchess*,' India sighed.

'Yeah, in twenty years' time,' Devon snapped. 'When I'm too old to look really fabulous in the coronet.'

Everyone tutted in sympathy. Devon *was* very unlucky that her father-in-law, the current duke, was a spry sixty-year-old with no degenerative diseases.

'Maybe he'll have a shooting accident,' suggested Madison hope-fully.

'I love you, Mad,' Devon commented, 'you're always so opti-mistic . . .'

'Ahem!' Lola, justifiably feeling that the focus had wandered away from her own nuptials, coughed loudly and wobbled her glass to call the attention back to herself.

'Oh God, Lo, I'm sorry!' Devon said. 'To Lola and Jean-Marc! First of many and richer every time!'

Everyone giggled, even Lola.

'I *do* love Jean-Marc,' she protested.

'Of course you do!' cooed India. 'We all love Jean-Marc!'

'Jean-Marc is the most lovable man in the whole of Europe,'

Devon pronounced. 'He just has to say *"Enchanté!"*, and smile at you, and you fall in love with him on the spot.'

'He is so lovely,' Lola agreed complacently. 'I do adore him.'

Plus, Jean-Marc was the man that every girl in Europe and New York had wanted to marry, but she, Lola Fitzgerald, had walked off with him without even flexing her perfectly manicured fingers to beckon him towards her. Jean-Marc had proposed within weeks of their first meeting. He was adorable. She loved him to bits. They were going to have the most wonderful life together. Already they were a staple of the upmarket glossy magazines . . . They had already received tons of requests to style and photograph the two of them smiling in pre-marital bliss . . .

'He knows all the best clubs,' Madison said.

'And all the best drugs,' Georgia chimed in.

'And all the best places to buy jewellery,' Devon added. 'Those earrings are *unbelievable*.'

'Yellow diamonds,' Lola said smugly, tilting her head so the girls could ooh and aah at the sparkle. 'He wanted them to match my ring exactly. He says they're the same colour as my hair.'

'*Divine*,' Madison breathed.

'You two are going to be so happy!' India exclaimed. 'I'm so jealous!'

'Jean-Marc could have had anyone,' Georgia commented. 'I went after him hard myself. He doesn't like redheads.' She sighed, flicking back her auburn locks.

'You *are* a specialised taste,' Madison said seriously. 'This complete whoremonger friend of my dad's – after his third divorce he only dates Russian prostitutes—'

'Bloody Natashas!' Devon exclaimed. 'They're everywhere! And they'll do *anything* for money!'

'Sluts,' Georgia agreed.

'Anyway,' Madison went on, 'he says that the madams don't keep more than one or two redheads on their books, ever. Because a lot of men just don't like them. But if they do, they go crazy for them.'

'I'm a niche market,' Georgia said. 'Matching collar and cuffs.'

'*Right*,' Madison said witheringly. 'Like any of us have any pubic hair left.'

That was so true that the conversation fell off for a moment, a natural pause as they all nodded in agreement and sipped their cocktails.

Lola adjusted her shoulders so that the knobs of the massage chair were kneading her just where she wanted them, and settled back, already blissed out. She gazed round the room. Here they were, five of the most beautiful, most socially successful, wealthiest girls in London, each with her own pedicurist in a white uniform kneeling before her, coaxing one pampered foot after the other out of the whirlpool baths for a long luscious massage. Five gorgeous examples of what happened when very rich men bred with very beautiful women and used their enormous fortunes to ensure that their daughters had the best of everything from the cradle onwards, from nutritionists to personal trainers to plastic surgery as soon as the doctors would agree to perform it. They were the girls everyone wanted to be friends with, the thoroughbreds who shook their manes and cantered through the best parties everywhere, jingling with the sound of tiny bells, shining like stars.

This was where she was born to be.

Georgia had organised the pedicure party – to perfection, everyone agreed – and Madison, who knew every fashionable restaurateur on three continents, had taken charge of dinner. Naturally, they had a private room in the Japanese restaurant, with a long table made from a single sheet of black granite with a black glass strip set into its centre, lustrous and smooth, the perfect surface for what Georgia was pouring out of a plastic bag, carefully, making one straight line all the way down the glass, from one end to the other.

'You look like you're icing a cake!' giggled India, who had had refills on the rose-petal martinis and was already, as Madison would say, lightly toasted.

'*Right*,' Lola drawled, 'as if any one of us would get near enough a cake to ice it—'

'Or even know *how!*' Madison exclaimed, horrified that anyone would think she would know one end of a piping bag from the other.

'Mmm, cake,' India said wistfully.

'Oh darling—' Georgia threw one slender, tanned arm round India's shoulders. 'You *can* have cake, just as long as you—'

'Bring it straight back up again afterwards!' Devon along with Georgia chorused.

Georgia set out five narrow, short-cut straws.

'Ooh!' Lola said, reaching for a straw. 'Exactly what the doctor ordered when you're trying to get into a size zero bias-cut satin Vera Wang wedding dress.'

With a practised gesture, she held one nostril closed with the thumb of the hand holding the straw while inhaling three inches of Georgia's long line of cocaine up the other nostril, her other hand sliding back to her nape to hold her hair out of the way.

'Whoo!' she said, straightening up and shaking back her mane of hair. 'Good stuff, Georgie!'

'Fresh off the plane,' Georgia said smugly. 'Only the best for us.'

'Darling! You look so pretty!' came a man's voice from behind them, and all the girls turned round, flicking their hair and flashing their best smiles.

'Jean-Marc! You shouldn't be here!' Lola said, shocked. 'It's my hen night – isn't that bad luck or something?'

'I'm sorry, darling!' Jean-Marc's smile was just as wide as the girls', his blond hair just as shiny. In a dark blue velvet jacket, white silk shirt, perfectly faded jeans and custom-made loafers, he looked like Lola's exact male counterpart, glossy and groomed, impossibly handsome, his teeth and the whites of his eyes almost blindingly bright. 'I just wanted to drop in for two seconds – Madison told me where you'd be.'

He was holding out a jewellery box to Lola, who cooed: 'Oh, you *shouldn't have . . .*' even as she took it and snapped the lid open.

'Oh my *God!*' exclaimed Georgia, who was standing close enough to Lola to see the contents.

'Just a little something to make you sparkle even brighter.' Jean-Marc smiled.

Lola slipped the yellow diamond bracelet out of the box and onto her wrist, where it rippled elegantly, catching the light. Jean-Marc fixed the clasp for her, and they admired the effect together.

'It's your stone!' he said. 'Gold diamonds for my golden girl!'

'I'm *so fucking jealous right now,*' India muttered, tipsy and honest enough to say out loud what every other girl was thinking.

'Thank you *so much*, darling!' Lola purred, leaning forward just enough to brush Jean-Marc's lips with hers. 'You're *so* sweet.'

'Anything for you!' he said. 'And now' – he looked round the room and mimed shock on seeing the cocaine-covered table – 'I see you have your appetiser all set out, so I mustn't keep you from dinner!'

A chorus of laughs greeted this, as Jean-Marc produced his own straw and took an extremely long pull of 'appetiser'.

'One for the road,' he said, wiping his nose as elegantly as he did everything. 'And now I love you and leave you.'

'You are *so fucking lucky*!' Georgia complained as the door closed behind him.

'I know,' Lola admitted smugly.

'Right then, time for dinner!' Madison announced. Over six feet tall in heels, her pale green silk jersey dress – the precise colour of her contact lenses – clinging to her Amazonian frame as if it were in love with her, she moved to the sliding doors at the back of the room and stood there, commanding everyone's attention. Her pale blonde hair glowed against the black walls. 'Everybody ready?' Her grin was wicked. 'It *is* a hen night, after all . . .'

She held up her free hand and tapped once on the sliding doors, still facing the girls, making the scene as theatrical as possible. The doors slid back, guided by unseen hands, and the four girls facing her gasped in unison, and then burst into titters of laughter.

'Oh, *Mad*, you are *amazing!*' Lola cried, teetering across the room to embrace her friend. 'Thank you *so much!* Best hen night *ever!*'

In the room beyond Madison was another long granite table with glass running down its centre, just like theirs. But this one, instead of being decorated with a long fat line of coke, was sporting an extremely buff, nude young man, lying on his back, with exquisitely prepared bite-sized portions of sushi and sashimi garnishing his long, smooth, heavily muscled limbs. Against his skin, which was almost as dark as the table, the raw fish glowed like jewels: coral salmon, cerise tuna, white mackerel translucent as moonstone against its jet background. The girls clustered round their dinner, their giggles deeper, dirtier, acknowledging the sexually charged treat that Madison had provided, the erotic charge of slowly, ritually stripping a gorgeously built hunk of manhood of the scraps of food that were partially concealing his nakedness.

'I'm not even hungry,' India announced, 'because of all that lovely lovely coke, but I'm going to have a bite anyway!'

And, with glee, she picked up a pair of ivory chopsticks and selected a glistening piece of yellowtail, framed by a couple of bright green leaves, nestling right on the centre of his stomach. As she lifted up the sashimi, she squealed in excitement, having revealed his belly button, a dark hollow swirl, mysterious and inviting, the start of a very faint line of black hair leading down to even more inviting places. There was a real gasp in the room, the first piece of real nakedness, of something that had been hidden that was now revealed, and the awareness, too, that it was in their power to strip this gorgeous young man of everything. Eyes widened, tongues flicked out to lick lips, and the girls closed in on the table. No one, after the coke, was hungry: but nobody cared.

'Is he *completely* starkers, Mad?' Georgia exaggerated her drawl to sound as if she didn't care one way or the other, but her eyes were gleaming with excitement.

'I think Lola should find that out, don't you?' Madison said, smiling wickedly. 'She *is* the bride-to-be, after all.'

'What will he do after we've eaten everything?' Georgia breathed.

'Oh, honey,' Madison said, 'it's a hen night! He'll do absolutely anything we want!'

And she reached out and flicked a piece of tuna off the swell of a pectoral muscle, revealing a plump little nipple so pink and pert that everyone sighed in unison, snatched at the chopsticks and dove into their dinner.

'Ugh, my head's *killing* me,' Lola mumbled, paying off the cab driver, and looking so pretty, even after a long night and morning spent partying, that he smiled at her sympathetically and waved her away when she started fumbling in her change purse for a tip.

Dying to climb into her cosy bed, don her cashmere eye mask, and take a super-strength sleeping pill to knock her out during the hangover and coke comedown that were well on their way, Lola teetered down the Mayfair mews street. She was pretty good at walking on cobbles in four-inch heels by now, but that didn't make the process any less painful. Just a few more steps – ow, she felt like the Little Mermaid when she got her feet, every step was walking on nails – yes, she was at her cute little white house, sliding the key out of her bag, in seconds she'd be inside and kicking off these instruments of torture she had strapped to her feet—

That was weird. Her key wasn't working.

She pulled it out, looked at it, tipping up her sunglasses to check it was the right one. Even the pale London sunlight hurt her eyes. But yes, it was the right key. Despite the pain to her retinas, she kept the sunglasses propped on top of her head as she re-inserted the key.

And then twisted her wrist uselessly, trying to force it to turn.

Oh! Was she so drunk and coked up still that she was at the wrong front door? How embarrassing that would be! She took a few steps back to make sure, raising a hand to shade her eyes from the almost non-existent sun.

No, she hadn't made a mistake: this was definitely her house. Her silver-beige silk curtains at the downstairs window, her pretty little topiary pots on the first-floor wrought-iron balcony. God, she was going to miss this place when she moved into Jean-Marc's Chelsea penthouse.

One more try with the key. It definitely wasn't working. And now that she looked closer – which of course aggravated her headache even more – she could see that the lock was really shiny. New-shiny. As if it had just been installed. Which wasn't possible, because she had never had the lock changed, and she'd been living here for three years now . . .

Through the drug-addled, martini-and-champagne-fuddled haze in her brain, Lola slowly began to connect the strange new lock on her front door to the fact that none of her credit cards had been working since yesterday afternoon at the dermatologist. With the first faint stirrings of disquiet, she fished out her phone and scrolled to her father's mobile number. It would be seven a.m. in New York – Daddy would be up by now. But frankly, even if he wasn't, she'd be ringing. This was an *emergency*.

'Hello, Lola,' came a voice.

Not her father. Her stepmother, Carin.

And for maybe the first time in her life, Lola Fitzgerald felt a faint cold tremor of fear slide down her spine.

'What are you doing answering Daddy's phone?' Lola blurted out.

'Ah, Lola. Always so polite,' Carin commented. 'I have some bad news for you, I'm afraid.'

'What? What is it?'

The headache was really beginning to clamp itself round Lola's temples now.

'Benjamin slipped into a diabetic coma last night,' Carin said as lightly as if she were announcing that she'd had steak for dinner. 'Apparently there's no chance he'll come out of it. God knows I tried to get him to diet, but he was always so stubborn. Well, you know what your father was like.'

Lola nearly dropped the phone.

'*What*? Daddy's in a *coma*?' she gasped.

'It was inevitable with his lifestyle, Lola. You know he refused to take care of himself.'

'You're talking about him like he's already *dead*!'

'Well, we must face facts, mustn't we? As I said, the doctors say there's practically no chance Benjamin will come out of the coma.'

Lola realised that she had never fully before understood the meaning of the phrase 'being unable to get your head round something'. It felt as if Carin's words were bouncing off the side of her skull, failing to penetrate her ears. Her beloved Daddy in a *coma*? He'd had Type II diabetes for years, of course, brought on by the huge amount of excess weight he was carrying, and the doctors had kept warning him how dangerous that was, but neither he nor Lola had ever believed that he was seriously at risk: how could a man as phenomenally rich as Benjamin Fitzgerald be seriously at risk of anything? Money would buy him the best healthcare, keep him safe, just as money had bought him and Lola everything else they could possibly want.

Money had bought him Carin, too, an ex-model who had put a very high price on her own head. Horrible, frigid Carin, with her white-blonde hair and icy, pale-blue eyes, as cold and frightening as the eyes of a Siberian husky, with a soul even more frigid than her eyes and an Ice Queen shard of glass for a heart.

'You can't be serious!' Lola managed to get out.

'Oh, I'm afraid I am,' Carin said.

'But you didn't – when did this happen? Why didn't you *ring* me?'

One of Lola's neighbours, a middle-aged divorcee who managed to look like Lola and her friends from behind, but whose face, despite all the surgeries, looked like a raisin stretched on a rack, walked up the mews, tutting at how loud Lola's voice had risen. Still, she couldn't hide the jealousy in her face as she snapped her eyes up and down Lola's perfect figure in the tight white jeans which would have revealed every imperfection, if Lola had any.

So it was with utter shock that Lola realised that the tables had just been turned. Because, watching Raisin-Face teeter along in overtight jeans tucked into high suede boots, shifting her Selfridges Food Hall shopping bag to reach for her keys, Lola was flooded with jealousy for her. Because Raisin-Face was about to go inside her own house, and Lola was locked out of hers, which meant she had to stand in the street hearing this appalling, unbelievable news about her beloved Daddy, unable to crumple onto a sofa in decent privacy and cry her eyes out—

'I didn't want to disturb you,' Carin said, distinct amusement creeping into her voice now. 'Weren't you on your hen night? I was sure you'd ring sooner or later. When you realised there was a problem with the money fountain.'

Lola swallowed hard.

'Did you do something to my credit cards?' she asked in a tiny voice. 'And my key isn't working—'

'Like I said, I was sure you'd ring sooner or later!' Carin wasn't even bothering to pretend not to enjoy this. 'I'm organising something of a financial restructuring, now that I have power of attorney—'

'You have power of attorney?' Lola realised that she wasn't quite sure what that meant.

'You *do* know that the house is owned by one of your father's companies for tax reasons?' Carin said. 'And your father made me a co-trustee of your trust fund. I've suspended payments from that too. I think your withdrawals from it have been unreasonably large for years.'

Lola's headache was like a vice now. She was literally unable to process all the information Carin was throwing at her. Grief was bubbling under the panic. She could sense it down there somewhere, far below, but it hadn't reached her yet. Could Carin truly be behind Lola being locked out of her own house.

But, according to what Carin had just told her, it wasn't her house at all . . .

'How could you *do this*?' Lola gasped. 'How could you think – Daddy's really sick and instead of looking after him, you actually got someone here to *change the lock on my house*—'

Carin's voice sharpened to a point.

'I think I just explained that it isn't your house, Lola! You have a fiancé – go and stay with him! Your father's supported you for long enough – it's someone else's turn now!'

'But I've got *all my stuff* in there!' Lola wailed, too hungover and spongy-brained to come up with any better riposte, though she was dimly aware that there must be hundreds.

'I'll make arrangements for you to get your things,' Carin said airily. 'Now I must go, I'm afraid. I have so much to organise!'

A click on the line signified that Carin had hung up, but Lola, unable to believe it, kept saying: 'Hello? Carin? *Hello?*' for at least a minute afterwards. Then, frantically, she searched her phone for Jean-Marc's number. Five minutes later, having left three frenzied messages begging him to call her as soon as possible, she slumped back against her pretty pale-green front door, which wasn't her front door any more, apparently. Her headache was pounding at her temples with a croquet mallet, and her brain was so overloaded she thought that if she had to take in one more unbelievable piece of information, grey ooze would start pouring out of her ears.

She was almost convinced that this was some awful joke Daddy and Carin were playing on her. It couldn't really be true. Her father couldn't really be in a coma! Maybe this was some kind of Swedish custom, messing with the bride the day after her hen night? Some awful, psychotic, evil Swedish custom, of course—

And why wasn't Jean-Marc calling her back?

Across the little mews, a front door burst open and Raisin-Face came running out, waving something. Having changed into slippers and velvet lounging trousers, she reached Lola in a matter of seconds.

'Do you *know*? Do you *know*? Have you *heard*?' she gasped, flailing with the paper.

'It's in the *Standard*?' Lola grabbed the paper. 'Daddy's in the *Standard*?'

But the headline that greeted her wasn't about her father.

'*PLAYBOY HEIR IN SEX SCANDAL OVERDOSE!*'

Lola's legs gave way under her. She sank down to the cobbled pavement, one of her Jimmy Choos twisting and snapping off a heel as she collapsed. But Lola was far, far beyond realising that her last pair of shoes had just broken. She was staring at the photograph on the cover of the *Evening Standard*, which showed someone being carried on a stretcher out of the nastiest-looking council estate stair-case Lola could imagine. His face was blurred, but the golden sweep of hair over his forehead was horribly familiar.

Lola realised why Jean-Marc's phone was going straight to voice-mail.

'*STEEL HEIR JEAN-MARC VAN DER VEER OVERDOSES IN TRANSSEXUAL LOVE PAD!*' the cover screamed. '*FIANCE OF "IT" GIRL LOLA CAUGHT WITH TRANNY LOVER!*'

And just then, from the main street, a woman came running into the mews, her face lighting up as she spotted Lola.

'Lola!' she yelled. 'Caroline Francis from the *Sun*! Am I the first to catch you? What are your feelings about Jean-Marc's overdose? Had you heard? Did you know he was seeing a transsexual prosti-tute?'

Raisin-Face grabbed Lola's arm and dragged her up.

'Run!' she said. 'Come on, *run*!'

And so, hopping grotesquely from a four-inch heel to a flat foot, her head feeling as if it were about to explode, her only refuge the house of a woman she didn't even know, Lola Fitzgerald ran from the home that wasn't hers any more, pursued by a *Sun* reporter yelling unbelievable allegations about her fiancé.

They barely made it back to Raisin-Face's house in time. She literally slammed the door in the eager face of Caroline-Francis-from-the-*Sun*, and turned to Lola, completely unable to disguise both her excitement at being in the middle of such a juicy tabloid story, and her joy at Lola's humiliation.

'*So!*' she said, her over-stretched face trying so hard to move that it looked as if it might pop at any moment. '*Did* you know about the transsexual prostitute?'

Lola did the only thing left to her. She burst into a flood of hys-terical tears. And then she fainted.

Chapter 2

$\mathcal{E}$ vie was halfway up her pole and contemplating what to do next. She hung there, head down, her ponytail a pale line of hair pointing towards the ground. Her ankles were wrapped tightly around the pole, her knees clamped one on either side in a double-lock that ensured she wasn't going anywhere.

Hmm. She tried a Caterpillar, holding onto the pole with both hands and levering herself up, rubbing her upper body along the pole so her bottom rose up suggestively, repeating it in a long slow sexy loop of movement that she knew would send anyone viewing it into an instant wash of desire, watching her taut buttocks lift closer and closer to her crimson stack-heeled shoes, then descend as the front of her body caressed the pole. After a couple of Caterpillars she checked her lock and changed her grip and pushed herself up and away from the pole into a Swan, gripping for dear life with her legs, using her considerable abdominal strength to hold her in a deep arch, arms out to either side, breasts pushed forward like a figurehead on a boat.

It felt good, but it was a little too gymnastic to be sexy. Evie crossed her arms in front of her chest. Was that better? No, too coy, a bit like a statue on a tombstone. . . She lifted her arms again and played with her hair, flicking it lightly, swaying her upper body fractionally from side to side, and knew she had the move now. Sexy mermaid. Cool. She could always sense it as soon as a move worked, as soon as it connected with her crotch, like someone pulling lightly on her G-string. Instantly she felt sexy, as if a hundred male eyes were on her and fifty men were breathing fast and deep, watching her play with her hair and twist her body into shapes that made their palms sweat and the blood rush to their groins.

Jesus, her ankles were killing her, and the muscles along her spine were burning up . . . Evie came out of the Swan, loosening the locks at knees and ankles just enough to slide gently down the pole till she could put her palms on the floor. Then she let the locks go completely, straightened her legs against the pole, and used it to kick herself over into a bridge. Careful not to bang her face into the pole – she'd nearly broken her nose once doing that – she stood up from the bridge, her back groaning after holding the extreme arch of the Swan for all that time. She dropped to all fours and did some cat stretches, pushing her lower back as high as she could, forcing it to round out, and finally it stopped complaining.

Then she looked at her ankles and winced. She was really working hard on all her extreme hanging poses, and it showed. Benny would freak. He was obsessed with her feet being smooth. He paid for twice-weekly pedicures, threw hissy fits if he ever saw her with bare feet – even in the apartment – and had bought her so many velvet slippers, marabou mules, softening foot lotions and pumice stones that even if those were the only possessions she owned, her bedroom and bathroom closets would have been bulging at the hinges.

It wasn't all she owned, of course. Benny had bought her plenty more than that. Which was why the spare bedroom had been converted three months ago into her walk-in closet. Evie loved that room, with its cedar panelling, its sliding drawers, its revolving clothes rails, its recessed lighting that switched from day to evening so you could assess the true colours of the clothes you were choosing, its shoe shelves reaching to the ceiling with the built-in stepladder for getting right up to the top.

Shoes. All those shoes. And the entire set of drawers right next to the shoe rack which were all for stockings, hold-ups and knee-highs. Benny loved that room even more than Evie did: he could spend hours in there pulling things out and selecting outfits for her. She was his little dress-up doll. With a special emphasis on the leg and foot area.

Evie grimaced, looking down at her ankles with the hard red lines running across the front of the bones, where the pole had bit in. She'd have to put on some opaque stockings for Benny this afternoon, or he'd have one of his tantrums. God. Benny was a wonderful guy – so sweet, so generous – but you'd think a guy as smart as he was could figure out that a girl he'd met hanging upside down on a hard metal pole by her ankles might have a few scrapes and bruises every so often as she pursued her art.

Benny didn't think that way, of course. He'd seen a girl who could do all those moves in a pair of flame-red patent heels, stacked six inches high, and fallen in lust in twenty seconds. Hard and fast, the best way. He'd had Evie out of the Midnight Lounge and into this Tribeca penthouse loft quicker than you could say 'billionaire tycoon'. And Evie, like every other girl she'd worked with in the Midnight Lounge, could get those words out pretty damn quickly. Benny saw Evie as a delicate, fragile creature, slender as a wand (years of gymnastics at high school, you needed to be skinny to compete), big dark doe eyes, slender wrists and ankles, small pointy breasts – his little gazelle, he called her sometimes.

Actually, Evie was lean and strong as a steel wire, tensile and hyper-flexible, with clearly defined muscles in her arms and back from all that taking her weight on her hands, and she needed to be that thin to do the pole moves she did. Curvier girls looked even better on a pole, those luscious breasts and asses wrapping round it seductively, but they could rarely do the hardcore flips and climbs, or hold the poses for long. They were carrying too much weight for full-on routines, it strained their arms and back too much and cut into their ankles really bad. Whereas slim light little Evie could haul herself up that pole in seconds and hang off it for what seemed like hours. She had the wiry build of an athlete. And for a Latina, she was pale, pale enough for her blonde hair to be plausibly natural.

But Benny, bless his heart, chose to see Evie as a frail soft-petalled naturally blonde orchid whose petals had been gently bruised by the cruel world. An orchid that Benny needed to put in water and cherish like a precious jewel. And Evie was more than happy to let him have his fun.

She undid the cruel stacked stilettos and took them off, flexing her feet. Other girls practised in bare feet, but not Evie. Nothing to do with Benny and his particularities on the subject; no, she'd always thought that if she started training in bare feet, she'd get too nervous to do some of the scarier moves when she put her shoes back on. If she always wore the wicked spiked heels, took them for granted, allowed herself no possibility of trying any move without them, then she eventually forgot the fear that comes with knowing you're kicking above your head in stilettos that could take your eye out if you aimed one wrong.

The clock on the wall said ten of twelve. Evie felt her lower body soften, melting down in pleasurable anticipation. Lawrence was always punctual to the minute. She hadn't realised how much she was looking forward to seeing him till this precise moment.

She stood up, suddenly half a foot shorter, and kicked her shoes across the room. They were just practice heels, banged up already, it didn't matter how scuffed they got. For the rest, she was already dressed for it; a black racerback sports bra and high-cut short shorts, covering the minimum amount of flesh possible. You needed bare skin on the pole: it gripped ten times better than any fabric you could ever find. Evie swivelled a tad to catch sight of herself in one of the full-length mirrors. One thing this apartment wasn't short on: mirrors. It was like a cross between a dance studio and a, well, a mirror showroom. You'd have thought Benny sold the things for a living. He sure did like to watch.

And so did Evie, though in an utterly different way. Benny looked at her and saw fantasy: Evie, merchandise. As she did several times a day, she stared at herself now with narrowed, assessing eyes. With the shoes off and her hair tied back, she could be taken for a gymnast still, her stomach flat, her small breasts pretty little points flattened slightly by the sports bra. She was short-waisted, which meant she had to work really hard on keeping that stomach flat, as there wasn't much space for all her internal organs, and that tended to make your tummy bulge out, even without any fat over it. But the plus side of being short-waisted was that you got lovely long legs. Even though Evie wasn't that tall, in her heels it looked as though her legs went on for days. All the women in her family had good legs, but hers, after all the exercise and stretching, were perfect now.

Almost perfect. She bent down, critically pinching at a small swell of flesh on the inside of each knee. It wasn't fat, of course not, it was solid muscle, but it needed to go just the same, so her line was totally smooth. Well, that was what she had Lawrence for. And at the thought of his name, her lower body softened again. Lawrence, her personal trainer, who would be here any minute, and who would gaze into her eyes and make her sweat from every pore of her body . . .

Just on time, the buzzer went. Evie crossed the floor to the intercom and said:

'Yes?'

'Miss Lopez, it's your noon appointment,' said Henry, the doorman.

'Send him up,' Evie said, and disconnected. She used to be all polite with Henry and the other doormen and the cleaning staff and the delivery men and everyone else she had working for her since Benny had established her here, high in the air at the bottom tip of Manhattan, where all the action was. Only, after a few weeks, she'd started realising that everyone else in this building, where one-bed apartments went for millions of dollars, was short with the staff, if not downright rude. And that the staff seemed to give them a hell of a lot more respect than they gave Evie.

Evie was a fast learner. From that moment on, she cut the staff dead if she didn't have anything to say to them, and was curt with them when she did. And guess what? Way more deference and politeness now than before, when she was all nice and friendly. It sucked, but that was New York for you. She should have known already. Be nice to people, they'll kick you in the face and laugh at you. Be rude to them, they'll take you seriously.

She'd once seen a girl knocked over at a newsstand by a guy pushing past her to get cigarettes. The girl was a tourist: you could tell by the fact that she had been approaching the newsstand slowly, getting her purse out, rather than marching up to it, money already out, good to go. The guy who'd bumped into her didn't even look down to see her sprawled on the big stacks of newspapers piled up by the side – lucky for her they'd broken her fall. Another guy leaned over to help her up, and she smiled at him gratefully, till he snapped at her brusquely: 'This is New York, baby. You better toughen up if you wanna stick it out here,' and the girl's expression went from grateful to appalled in a single beat.

Only in New York. But what could you say? It was Evie's town, she was born and bred here, it was in her blood. You had to hustle to get along. And yeah, that guy had given the girl good advice, if she'd only had the sense to listen. You did need to toughen up to stick it out here.

The elevator pinged, announcing Lawrence's arrival. The doors opened at the base of the long, long room, and there he was, smiling at her, his pale brown hair loose around his face, slightly damp from the heat of the street, a small kitbag over one shoulder, wearing a shabby T-shirt and a pair of sweats hanging off his narrow hipbones.

'Hey,' he said.

'Hey.'

Evie smiled back at him. She had all these work smiles, running the gamut from bright innocence to full-on sultry seductress, but with Lawrence her smile was so natural she didn't even think about it. Lawrence was as clear as water in a glass. His eyes were the colour of a lake in winter, pale grey, and when she looked into them she saw nothing but sweetness and clarity and straightforwardness. Total oddball. It was a miracle he survived in this town.

'Been doing some pole work?' he asked, walking across the floor towards her.

He had the sexiest walk, and he didn't even realise it. Evie had read, in the kind of bosom-heaving, princesses-and-pirates kind of book Evie's sister was literally addicted to, descriptions of heroes who 'walked like a panther', and she'd always thought it was just a dumb cliché. But Lawrence really did walk like a big cat. He was so in tune with his body that he moved like the big animal that he was, that all humans were, only they forgot it when they put on clothes and stood upright and started cutting their hair. Lawrence's DNA hadn't forgotten, though. He moved so lightly, so effortlessly, the slight roll to his shoulders like a cat's when it puts down one paw after another, his feet padding the ground rather than hitting it, that Evie had taken one look at him the first time she met him and thought, *if he makes walking look that easy, I bet he makes everything else look that easy too*, and then her mind was on sex with him and she couldn't get it off again.

'Uh-huh,' Evie said, reaching her arms up to the ceiling and taking a long stretch, partly because she felt like it, partly to make completely sure that Lawrence couldn't take his eyes off her.

'So you're nice and sweaty already?'

She nodded, her lips slightly parted. And she reached one hand down behind her back to massage her shoulderblades, which had the effect of making her breasts swell under the sports bra.

Lawrence was in front of her now, smiling down at her. She could smell him, a light musky, manly scent, fresh sweat from the street. Lawrence never wore aftershave, not even scented soap: it was all him and his Tom's of Maine natural deodorant. Mmm. She got what they'd called at the Midnight Lounge a girl hard-on: her nipples tightened. And he hadn't even touched her yet. She wanted to reach up and push back his hair, stroke along those high cheekbones that he'd got from his Russian mom.

'Well, now let's *really* work up a sweat,' Lawrence said, taking off his bag and putting it on the floor. Evie watched him bend over. His bottom was small, but round, and the sweats slid down it an inch or so as he leaned over, revealing a tantalising glimpse of pale skin lightly dusted with soft blond hair. Lawrence straightened up, produced an elastic from his pocket, and pulled his hair back into a scrappy little ponytail.

'Rolling sit-ups and obliques first,' he said firmly. 'Lots of them. We're trying to sculpt your waist, remember? And then leg pushes for here.'

He reached round her and touched her lightly just above her bottom, an area she had to target like a sniper to make sure she didn't build up a tiny roll on it. And then he opened one of the built-in cupboards and extracted an exercise mat, unrolling it and flipping it down on the wooden floor. With a theatrical sigh, she lay down on it, reached back for her pole, gripped it firmly and started pulling her lower body up into a ball. Knees to chest. Roll up, roll down, as slowly as she could. It hurt like hell. It also, as Lawrence knew perfectly well, was the best thing for putting her back into alignment again after the extreme arches of her pole work. Plus, it made her abs strong and flat and flexible. Win-win.

Evie loved to work out. It was her hobby, her profession, her vocation. If Lawrence hadn't been her trainer, she would be lying down right now doing sit-ups on her own. But Evie's life had been so much about self-discipline, about driving herself to higher and higher heights of physical excellence, that it was the biggest treat she could imagine to give over that discipline for an hour to someone whose job it was to take responsibility for her exercise. It was the supreme pleasure to be able to whine and protest and have Lawrence make her do a hundred sit-ups anyway.

Well, maybe not her supreme pleasure. That would come afterwards, when he massaged out all her kinks.

Evie did sit-ups for twenty minutes. Then Lawrence supported her on the pull-up bar, his hands steady at her waist, taking only the bare minimum amount of weight that he needed to, letting her struggle with the effort of chinning herself up and down. Then she lay down again, this time on her stomach, with her legs in what Lawrence called a figure 4 – the right one straight out, the left one bent to the side, foot back in, touching the knee of the right leg – and then she bent her right leg so her foot was parallel with the ceiling and pushed it up and down, hard and fast, with Lawrence kneeling next to her and holding down her lower back in just the right place, so all the painful muscle work focused into one exact spot above the right buttock, targeting that infinitesimal swelling which she needed to punish with regular leg pushes . . .

She did two hundred on each side and then collapsed, face down, puffing into the mat. This was another luxury she only allowed herself with Lawrence present, this theatrically exaggerated exhaustion. On your own you had to suck it up and keep going. When Benny watched her on the pole, she had to make everything look easy, as if she were floating, as if she were a fairy made of tinsel and moonshine, and then she had to float down off the pole and come over to him and go to work and make that all look easy too. But with Lawrence, she could let go and show the effort: he was a trainer, for God's sake, he knew how hard this shit was. So she lay there, groaning, and he knelt there, laughing at her, and finally said:

'I guess all this puffing and panting means you want your massage now?'

And she nodded, pretending she didn't even have the energy to talk any more. She heard him stand up and go over to his kit-bag for the massage cream, and all the breath really did go out of her in one long delicious exhale of release, because there was nothing more for her to do now, Lawrence was going to put his clever hands on her and work out every single knot and leave her all loose and stretched and happy.

He started with the stretches, folding one of her legs over the other and pressing down, down, leaning right into her, till her bottom was off the floor and she was folded up into a tight parcel like a contortionist, her glutes stretching till she bit her lip with it, strands of his hair coming loose from the ponytail and falling over his face.

'Hurts?' he said, those slanting grey eyes watching her, serious, making sure he didn't go too far.

'Hurts so good,' she gasped.

'Another inch?'

'Just one.'

'OK.'

He put slightly more weight on her, leaning into it, his eyes even more intent now, his hands feeling out exactly how far he could push to give her maximum stretch without ripping or tearing. Lawrence would never go too far, never over-work her. You could see that from his own body, which wasn't pumped-up like that of most muscle-crazed trainers going for the burn, but long and lean and endlessly flexible from three hours of yoga a day, from five to eight every morning. Lawrence treated his body as though it was his most precious possession, and when he told you that was his philosophy you found yourself wondering why everyone else didn't do that too.

And after the stretches, he turned her over, and she reached up and pulled off her sports bra, and he sat on her buttocks and worked on her shoulders and back and upper arms, smoothing in a cream that smelt of mint and geraniums, his clever fingers seeking out and undoing every tangle of muscle and cramp, digging all the way around her shoulderblades, finding areas of tension she hadn't even realised existed, and rolling them away with his fingertips and his knuckles and even, sometimes, his elbows. Pain burned through her and was gone as if it had never existed. Her eyes were closed, her breath was slow and, honestly, she was drooling a little, though she'd have died before she let him know.

By the time he moved lower and worked on her buttocks and all the way down her strong, tight hamstrings, she was in a trance, even though it always hurt so bad when he massaged her calves. They were so pulled up from all the dancing in heels that he had to hurt her to get into them and do any good. And by the time he turned her over again and straddled her and started smoothing the cream into her upper body – long, slow strokes to get to the hard pectoral muscles under her soft little breasts – she felt, as she always did at this stage, as if she were in another dimension, where time had slowed down with Lawrence's firm palms moving in small circles around her chest, easing out the muscles under her arms, which worked so hard to pull her up the pole and hold her there that they had always been tight till Lawrence started work on them.

She was in water. She was floating on the sea, buoyed up by gentle waves, totally safe. The water was blood-warm, and it would taste like her own salt skin, or Lawrence's, the moisture she could see collecting between his pecs as he bent over her, so close that all she could smell was him, his warm strong scent, the faint trace of shampoo on his hair from his morning shower. He rubbed cream into her stomach, and now she smelled geraniums again, soft and faintly peppery, and he was running his fingers round the waistband of her shorts, and she lifted her hips to help him slip them off, and he pulled them down and sat back and took hold of his T-shirt and pulled that off too in one smooth movement, and reached down for his sweats and, half-sitting, half kneeling, dragged them off, so he was naked.

The kitbag was close by; he had a condom out and on in a few seconds, and then he was back, pulling her up so she was sitting, pulling her up and down onto him and rocking them back and forth, knowing that Evie was in such a trance right now he couldn't expect much muscular effort from her. Sometimes the massages took her like that, and they would sit there, her on his lap, her legs wrapped round him, and he would rock them both, slowly, with huge care and control, for what felt like hours and hours, Evie clinging on to him, damp face against his damp shoulder, his cock hitting the exact spot inside her that made her shudder in spasms again and again, Lawrence holding on, moving her where he wanted, where he could sense she wanted it, his face the most serious she ever saw it, utterly concentrated so that his eyes and his cheekbones seemed to be slanting even more than usual with the effort.

Finally she roused herself, coming back a few stages towards full consciousness, reached round to sit so she was completely facing him, and took his face in her hand and kissed him: long slow druggy kisses. She was sitting harder on his lap now, pushing down more, feeling him higher and higher inside her, making him take more of her weight, rubbing her whole body against him, using those whip-strong thighs of hers to raise and lower herself till he started moaning.

'Evie, no—'

'Come on,' Evie whispered in his ear. 'I want you to, I want to feel you come—'

'No, Evie, wait, I'm holding on for it, it'll come when it's ready—'

Evie circled his ear with her tongue till he moaned even harder.

'Fuck that Tantric shit, Lawrence,' she whispered. 'I'm going to make you come so hard you'll feel your head's going to blow off.'

And she lifted herself slightly off him, reached down and slid her hand into the space she'd made, and, looking straight into his eyes, she made herself come as hard as she'd promised Lawrence he would, and as she screamed he did too, tightening his grasp on her hips and pulling her down on him so hard she screamed even louder and he shot himself up into her like a bullet, so that Evie felt it even through the condom, and they collapsed against each other, staying upright only because of the balance of their two bodies propped together.

'*God*,' Evie said eventually.

Lawrence sighed into her hair.

'I have to come out of you . . . I so don't want to . . .'

He lifted her as if she weighed nothing, and Evie made a small protesting noise as he slid out of her. They fell to the ground together, still touching at most points, and lay back down on the mat, breathing hard, facing each other. Lawrence pulled off the condom and wiped himself with Evie's sweat towel, hardly taking his eyes off her face through the whole process.

'You look like the cat that's got the cream,' he said, smiling at her.

'I am. I did,' Evie said smugly.

His smile faded.

'Don't do that again, Evie.'

'What, make you come like a train?' Evie ran her tongue around her lips, remembering him exploding inside her.

'Evie, I've *told* you.' Lawrence's brow furrowed, which it only did when the subject was of vital importance to him. 'When you have a Tantric orgasm, it's *transcendent*. It's worth the wait. And it's not like you didn't have tons of orgasms along the way. I'm not making you wait with me. I can't believe we have to go through this every single time.'

Evie rolled her eyes. How ironic was it that of the two men in her life, one was really tough to make come (God, the *things* she had to do for Benny sometimes!) and one was really easy, but bitched and moaned about it afterwards?

Men. The thing she was best at. Her specialist subject: men, and what men wanted. And still, they could be so fucking perverse that sometimes they made her want to slap them round the head till they rang like a bell.

Evie was showering, one of her favourite ways to pass the time ever since Benny had moved her into this penthouse apartment. The shower was about as big as her mom's living room, and had probably cost ten times as much to do up. It had a rainforest shower head, plus surround jets, and was lined in travertine marble; the dark blue ceiling was set with a series of tiny glittering lights that dimmed and dipped in endless permutations. Stars in the night sky, Benny had called them. It was one of the reasons he'd chosen this place: that, and the fact that the shower was big enough for Benny and Evie to fit in it together, which was no small achievement, considering Benny's bulk.

Benny only took showers. He was scared one day he'd take a bath and not be able to get himself out of the tub again.

Being in the shower with Benny wasn't so bad, because the stars-in-the-night-sky lighting meant that she couldn't see Benny all that clearly, which was always a blessing. But being in the shower by herself was bliss. Lawrence had taken a quick one, but he'd had another training appointment across town and had to run. So now Evie was

Rebecca Chance

all alone, turning slowly to get every single jet on every single part of herself, slicking herself at intervals with honey shower gel from Diptyque. In the main bathroom she had honey Diptyque candles burning in the built-in niches, and when she eventually came out of the shower she was going to slather herself in more of their honey body lotion. Scent layering, the guy at Barneys had called it. It was amazing to have so much money that you could just walk into a store and pretty much buy whatever you wanted. In addition to her credit cards, Benny had given her charge accounts at Henri Bendel and Barneys and Bloomingdale's, which pretty much covered everything. She was shopping in places she hadn't even known existed till she met Benny. Shit, she'd have thought she was lucky to get a *Macy's* charge card till she met him.

And she didn't even have to look at the bills. They went straight to one of Benny's many secretaries. Which, of course, meant she spent even more, because she had no idea how much she was racking up.

Though, considering all she had to do was shop, work out and maybe pop to an afternoon movie if she was sure Benny wouldn't be coming by, at least he'd given her plenty of resources. One thing she wasn't short of was time. These twenty-minute showers, if she was honest, were partly a way to kill the time before she turned on the TV and flicked through some gossip magazines.

But just then, Evie's ears pricked up. Even through the pounding jets of water, she thought she'd heard something. Growing up in the projects made you alert even when you were sleeping, always on the lookout for something that might be a threat to you. The urban jungle trained its kids well. Benny might have taken her away from the slums, but you couldn't take the slums out of the girl. So Evie stuck one hand out to whip off the water jets, and with the other she pushed open the heavy glass shower door and stepped out onto the plush bath mat, reaching for a bath sheet.

She stood, listening, her feet toasty on the bath mat, warmed by the constant underfloor heating. Yes, there was definitely someone in the apartment. Benny? But he always called first, always. Not that he suspected about Lawrence – Jesus, she damn well hoped he didn't! But Benny liked her to look a certain way. Dressed up, made up, hair done, and, of course, in some form of sexy legwear and high high heels. Often he'd specify exactly what he wanted her to wear when he called. He had a freaky memory: he'd say stuff like: 'Those knee-highs I bought you in that SoHo boutique, the white ones with the dots, and the mules with the Lucite heels and the red trim on the third shelf up, OK, baby?' And he was always right: the shoes were just where he'd said they'd be. She couldn't give him points for good taste when he thought up her outfits, but then, good taste wasn't exactly what most men wanted in a mistress.

Wrapping the bath sheet tightly around her, Evie looked around for her slippers. Benny would freak if she wasn't wearing something on her feet. Shit, they were nowhere to be seen. When he wasn't around, she didn't wear them: she loved the feel of heated marble, or luxury pile carpet, under her bare toes. It was a reminder of how rich she was living. She'd have to distract him by a complaint about his scaring her shitless just using his key and coming in like that when she was in the shower. Working up a rant about how much he'd freaked her out, she crossed the bathroom, biting her lip to get some tears starting. Benny hated it when she cried.

And after all, who could it be but Benny?

Evie flung the bathroom door wide, but the scene before her dried up both her tears and her shrieking reproaches to Benny about thinking he was a serial killer come to slaughter her in the shower. Her mouth dropped open, and all that came out was a gulp.

Standing in the middle of the huge, open-plan living room was a woman, a woman who was taller than most men, with white-blonde hair in a short cut that emphasised her knife-sharp bone structure and the eerie pale blue of her eyes. She was wearing a white cashmere coat, belted tightly at the waist, pearl earrings so huge it was hard to believe they were real, and knee-high brown leather boots. She looked like the villain from a designer sci-fi movie.

'What are you doing in my apartment?' Evie managed to

exclaim, praying to God that the woman was some interior designer Benny had sent round to surprise her.

But she had a horrible feeling that she knew *exactly* who this woman was. She'd seen photos of Benny with her in the society pages.

'Mrs Fitzgerald? Just pile all this stuff into trash bags?' came a man's voice, deep and rasping, and a Hispanic guy, dressed all in black, emerged from Evie's bedroom, a rack of her dresses hooked over one brawny arm. He must have been at least six-foot three, and with his shaved head, bodybuilder's walk and shoulders too big for his suit jacket, he was a type Evie had seen all too often: body-guard/bouncer/hired muscle. Benny had a bodyguard, sometimes, but Evie had never seen this guy before.

This guy was from the streets. She could tell by his eyes, which were hard dark shiny stones, and from the backs of his hands, which were marked with faded blue prison tattoos. Probably gang stuff. And it looked as though he was getting them lasered off, because they were blurry in places. But still, to have a bodyguard with visi-ble prison tats? Benny would never have gone for that. That was gangster stuff. Hardcore.

'That's right,' the woman said, staring straight at Evie. 'Everything into the trash.'

'You're kidding me!' Evie said. 'That's mine! That's my stuff!'

'Not any more,' the woman – Benny's wife – said. She smiled. It was terrifying.

'Benny *bought* all that for me!' Evie protested. 'It's mine! Look, it's shitty you found out about us this way, but that's all mine, you can't just *take* it—'

'Keep at it, Rico. You know what you're supposed to do,' the woman said to the hired muscle, who nodded and disappeared back into Evie's bedroom.

'You can't just *trash* it!' Evie stalked across the room to grab her cellphone. 'I'm calling Benny right now,' she said furiously. 'He won't let you do this!'

My *shoes!* she thought. All my porno sex shoes! Benny's *obsessed* with them – no *way* is he going to let this bitch dump them in the street!

'Call away,' Benny's wife said. It was like watching a skull smile.

Evie stabbed at her speed dial key, ringing Benny's private line, her brain racing frantically. She was used to crises, used to threats of trouble and violence – she had grown up in one of the worst projects in Spanish Harlem, a pretty girl with no one to protect her. Her father wasn't even a distant memory – he'd walked out on her mother when Evie's sister was still five months off being born. Evie's mother Mariluz was too busy complaining about her own troubles to spare a thought for Evie, and while Mariluz cosseted Evie's little sister Ria, Evie was out on her own, dealing with the gangs, the dealers, the guys trying to get with her, or pimp her out, or both.

Evie had had to fight for everything she'd ever got in life. Every single thing. She'd seen the worst things that could happen, and the people who'd done them and then laughed about it afterwards. And now, appraising Benny's wife, she knew instinctively that she was in the presence of an enemy worse than any she had ever encountered in her short hard life. Not just because she had that look in her cold blue eyes, the killer look. Because she had more power to execute her wishes than anyone Evie had ever met before.

Apart from Benny. And Benny wasn't answering his phone. Evie tried again, going for his cellphone number. It started to ring and, a second later, she heard Benny's ringtone in her ear, a classical music piece that he'd told her was his favourite. But how come she was hearing it? Was she so freaked out by this woman's invasion of her home that she was hallucinating Benny's cellphone ring?

Then she realised that she wasn't. Because Benny's wife was reaching in her coat pocket. The woman's smile deepened still further, like a slash, as her hand came out holding a ringing phone.

'Benny's not answering his phone any more,' she said. 'Benny will never be answering his phone again.'

Evie's phone dropped onto the wooden floor with an ominous cracking sound.

'Benny's *dead*?' Evie gasped.

'He might as well be. He's in a coma,' Benny's wife informed her with as much emotion as if she were reading out stock prices. 'Which means you're out of here. You've got twenty minutes to pack up as much as you can and get out.'

'But I *live* here! You can't just—'

The ice-blue eyes gleamed. 'You should have got Benny to put the apartment in your name, shouldn't you? Stupid girl. You won't make that mistake with the next man you whore for.' She lifted her wrist so the coat cuff could slide down her arm, revealing a watch so thickly studded with diamonds Evie was surprised it didn't blind her. 'Twenty minutes and counting,' she observed.

Evie knew she wasn't bluffing. She grabbed the towel tighter around her and sprinted for her bedroom door. The Hispanic guy – Rico – had already pulled out so many of her lovely things that she could have cried to see them so contemptuously tossed aside, her shoes knocked off the shelves to the floor as if he'd just swiped along them with his arm, her lingerie lying in piles on the bed and floor as if he'd lifted them out from their drawers and thrown them over his shoulder. But that wasn't what she was focusing on. She was staring at him as he pulled out a leather box from the built-in, cedar-lined cupboard and shouted:

'Mrs Fitzgerald? I think I found it.'

Evie's blood turned to ice water.

'No!' she screamed. 'No! You can't take that! It's *mine!*'

She leaped at him, fingers hooked into claws, pretty face distorted into a mask of fury, grabbing for it. Rico knocked her away with one elbow to her jaw, still holding the box. Evie landed on the bed face down, limbs sprawling, dazed from the blow, and then Rico did take one hand from the box. He leaned down and pulled the towel right out from under her, flipping her over like a pancake as he did so.

'Nice tits,' he said, staring at her naked body and nodding appraisingly. 'I don't like them too big.'

Fury gave Evie the strength to jump off the bed, drag on some sweatpants and a T-shirt and dash out of the room after Rico, despite the pounding in her jaw that was still making her dizzy.

In the living-room, he was standing holding the box open, presenting it to his boss, who was extracting from it exactly the items that Evie was desperate for. She held them up, one in each hand, tilting them back and forth, watching them shine. Twin circles, each the diameter of a small teacup, silver fabric richly encrusted with sewn-on diamonds, glittering as if they were worth a small fortune. Which, to Evie, they were.

'What do you call these again?' she inquired.

'Pasties, Mrs Fitzgerald,' Rico said, winking unpleasantly at Evie. 'Strippers wear 'em to cover their, uh –'

'Nipples,' Mrs Fitzgerald finished. She looked at Evie. 'And I suppose you generally tear them off for the grand finale and throw them into the audience, do you?' She was smiling still. 'Not these ones, though. Benny paid a hundred thousand for them. That makes them strictly for private performances only.'

And she tilted her hand still more so that the diamond-covered pasties dangled temptingly from her fingers, as if she were taunting Evie, daring her to come and take them.

'*Give them back!*' Evie yelled, running towards her.

Rico moved fast. He caught her upper arms, stopping her in her tracks. Evie wriggled and fought and kicked at him with her bare feet, but Rico's grip just tightened till she yelped in pain.

'I don't think so,' said Mrs Fitzgerald, laughing. 'Out of the question! This was how I found out about you – doing checks on Benny's credit cards. Custom-made diamond pasties. Very funny. I don't think I'll have them broken up – I think I'll keep them. They'll make me smile every time I look at them.'

Snapping open the crocodile-skin purse that hung from her wrist, she dropped in the pasties.

'You can't take those!' Evie screamed. 'OK, so the apartment's not in my name, but the pasties are *mine!* Benny *gave* them to me! They were a *gift!*'

'Sue me,' said Benny's wife. 'Really. Go ahead and sue me.'

And she smiled again.

Evie stopped kicking. She hung in Rico's grip like a rag doll, momentarily paralysed with the shock.

'Now, I'm being nice to you,' Mrs Fitzgerald said. She consulted her watch again. 'You have fifteen minutes left. I'd make good use of them if I were you. Or do you want me to tell Rico to throw you out now, just as you are?'

Evie had been right about Benny's wife. This was a woman who loved to exercise every ounce of power that she could, in the worst possible way. She was enjoying throwing Evie out of what she thought was her home, stealing Evie's property before her eyes, and mocking her with it. She was enjoying humiliating Evie by making her tear free of Rico, run back into the bedroom, drag down her suitcases and grab great handfuls of her clothes, stuffing them in as fast as she could, snatching as much of value as she could possibly manage, tearing into the bathroom to get her expensive toiletries, emptying out her secret stash of cash in the cistern, where she kept it in a plastic bag. She was enjoying watching Evie run around like a mad thing, those icy eyes gleaming with pleasure at having reduced her to the mortification of doing a supermarket sweep on her own possessions.

And when Evie pulled her suitcases out into the living room, sweating because she was wearing three coats, one over the other, since she couldn't fit them in the suitcases, that bitch was standing there, arms folded, swinging her shiny crocodile bag slowly back and forth from its gilt chain hung over one white cashmere-clad elbow, so as to emphasise that she had Evie's precious diamond pasties inside. Those diamonds were Evie's talisman, her security. They were everything she had in the world of solid value. Her fingers were itching to snatch that bag off the bitch's arm.

But Rico was standing right beside her, arms similarly folded, and Evie knew there was no way she could grab her jewels and run before Rico got to her. Besides, the bitch would just have her arrested.

So Evie stuck her chin in the air and crossed the room, pulling her suitcases behind her. She wouldn't look back for one last glance at her beautiful apartment, at its suede sofas and hardwood floors and recessed lighting, at the floor-to-ceiling windows with their view over downtown skyscrapers and the Hudson River beyond, because if she did, she might start crying. And she never cried.

She dragged open the door and pulled her cases through, swallowing hard as it shut behind her. Evie's perfect life was over, as if it had never been. She pressed the button for the lift. The only thing she knew for sure was that she was going down.

Behind her, her old front door swung open.

'Mrs Fitzgerald thought you might want this,' Rico rasped. 'She says she don't need it.'

And Evie heard the familiar clatter of a dismantled pole being dropped to the floor.

Evie wanted desperately to walk into the lift and not look back. But all she had in the world was the cash she had on her. She didn't have a bank account, only credit cards, and she was sure that the bitch would have had those all stopped by now. She couldn't afford to turn down anything she could take with her. And a good pole cost $250.

'I need the carrying case for it,' she said to Rico, trying to sound as if it didn't matter to her one way or the other.

'Oh yeah?' He wasn't fooled. Those hard black eyes looked her up and down, and slowly, he smiled. 'You want me to get it for you?'

She nodded.

'I can't hear you, babe.'

'Yes,' she said.

His tongue flicked out, and he licked his lips.

'How much d'ya want it?'

She shrugged, staring back at him. This wasn't the first time she'd dealt with men like Rico, and the most important thing was to show no emotion at all.

'Shit, you're a hard case,' Rico said, staring at her hard. 'I like that.'

He turned and went inside, coming out a short time later with the plastic carrying case for the pole. But he didn't go back into the apartment again straight away: he stood there, watching her, as she knelt down and slid the sections of the pole into each other, and then into the case, moving awkwardly in the bulky coats. Eventually she got it done and stood up again, pressing the button for the lift. Rico watched as she dragged in her cases and then came back for the pole, smirking at her efforts.

Just as the doors were about to close, Rico made his move. He stuck one meaty arm into the cabin, blocking the doors, and with the other he reached forwards and grabbed Evie's crotch through her sweatpants.

'Just so you remember me, babe,' he said, leering at her.

His fingers dug in so tight that when he finally let go, she could still feel their grip. She'd have bruises tomorrow.

Evie's eyes were dry as old bone. Her lips were set in a thin, hard line. She watched herself in the shiny brass doors as the lift sank towards ground level, towards everything she'd fought all her life to get away from, and she made a promise to herself: one day she'd be back in the sky again, up in a penthouse, with her name on it this time. And if it was the last thing she ever did in this life, she'd see that bitch crawling at her feet.

Chapter 3

*L*ola was dragged back into consciousness by a screaming headache. She fought it as long as she could, but eventually the sensation that someone had driven a metal curtain rod into one of her ears and out of the other was so painful that she opened her eyes and tried to sit up. She didn't recognise the room she had been sleeping in, but she didn't expect to. As soon as she'd woken up, she had remembered exactly what had happened just before she passed out. All of it. The universe had no mercy for Lola today. Her memory wasn't giving her a gradual release of information: it was all flooding back in one fell swoop.

She *had* to have a painkiller. Climbing out of the bed someone had put her in, she headed for the en-suite bathroom. In Lola's world, all bedrooms had en suites, and sure enough, this one did too . . . but its gleaming mirrored cabinets were completely empty. Damn. Guest bathroom. Raisin-Face had a lot more space in her small mews house than it seemed, because these rooms were huge.

Confused now, Lola pushed open the bedroom door, and got the kind of shock a first-time passenger on the Tardis must have. Instead of the narrow little hallway she'd been expecting, she was faced with the generous curve of a wide staircase, bathed in light streaming gently through a domed skylight set into the high ceiling, two floors up. Walls papered in pale-yellow stripes, hung with black-and-white 18th-century prints of birds and flowers . . . this house was definitely familiar, and equally definitely not Raisin-Face's. It had to be about ten times the size.

Lola racked what was left of her brain cells – i.e. the ones she hadn't burned out with cocktails and coke the night before – and came up with nothing. She started down the stairs, which ran all the way around the well of the atrium in a very dramatic fashion, and halfway down, seeing the black-and-white chequered marble of the entrance hall, she had the memory flash she needed to realise where she was.

This was Devon's in-laws' Belgravia town house. Devon and Piers had stood just where Lola was now for the wedding photos: she could still see Devon's priceless Honiton lace train, a family heirloom, carefully arranged by Madison to spill all the way down the rest of the stairs and puddle beautifully at the bottom. Devon's diamond tiara and necklace had been family heirlooms too, heavy enough to give Devon a sore neck of which she had boasted for months afterwards. Piers might not be the brightest lightbulb in the chandelier, but there were definite advantages to marrying the heir to the Claverford dukedom.

Hearing the gabble of her friends' voices now, Lola ran down the rest of the stairs and into the big drawing-room. Pausing in the doorway for an instant, mostly to let her poor aching eyes accustom themselves to the bright sunlight pouring in through the bow windows that gave onto the garden, she took in the scene. This room, too, was done in pale yellows and golds, with hints of baby blue. Devon had insisted on having the house completely redecorated when she and Piers moved in: she wanted it to be a perfect frame for her. The result was a life-size jewellery box in which Devon sparkled, her big blue eyes bright as aquamarines, her wheat-blonde hair matching the gilded furniture. Piers, a big slab of British beef, fair-haired, blue-eyed and pink-cheeked, was too large for the delicate furniture, but at least he suited the décor.

Even now, despite Lola's current misery, she had a moment of

complete appreciation for the picture Devon made in a camel cash-
mere-blend T-shirt and slim beige jeans, lounging on one of the
twin primrose silk sofas, a cigarette dangling from her fingers, fine
gold bangles clinking on her wrist. Madison and Georgia, on the
other sofa, were also clad in versions of the same chic leisure wear:
Georgia in a green silk sweater, to set off her flaming red hair and
white skin, Madison in a white T-shirt, her famously endless legs
clad in jeans specially treated to be as soft as suede and just as
expensive.

On the coffee table between the sofas were a couple of copies of
the *Evening Standard*, but the main focus of attention was the
screen of Devon's white laptop, together with half-drunk glasses of
champagne, a plate of strawberries and another one of edamame
beans. A big silver ice bucket was strategically placed next to the
coffee table, within easy reach, and the room was fuggy with cigarette smoke, rising in fragile white curls above the sofas. The girls
were so absorbed in chatter they didn't notice Lola's entrance.

'What is she going to *do*? So *humiliating!*' Georgia exclaimed
eagerly, pushing back her heavy red curls with both hands.

'I know,' Madison drawled, leaning forward to click on the keyboard. She took a long drag on her Silk Cut Ultra, reading what had
come up on the screen. 'I'm *so* glad now I didn't fuck Jean-Marc,
think what I might have *caught* –'

'Oh God,' Devon gasped. 'She'll have to get every test there is!
That tranny looks *riddled with disease* in the photos!'

They all bent forward to peer at the computer screen. Lola felt
tears pricking her eyes.

'Is it all true?' she asked, taking a few steps into the room, onto
the priceless Aubusson rug.

Dead silence fell as they all swivelled to look at her.

'Jesus, Lola, you look like shit on a stick,' Madison said frankly.

'Do I?'

Lola crossed the room to examine herself in the gigantic gilt-
framed mirror hanging over the fireplace. Although it was
age-misted enough to give a flatteringly softened reflection, she still

screamed when she saw herself. Her make-up was halfway down her cheeks, her hair was a tangled mess and her eyes were redder than twin traffic lights. Even her skin looked sallow.

'Here,' Georgia said, holding out a glass of champagne. 'Medicine.'

'I need painkillers,' Lola said, collapsing on the sofa next to Georgia and taking the glass.

'Here you go,' Madison said, rootling in her Bottega Veneta bag. After the rattling noise that Madison always made going through the pill section, she produced an orange prescription vial with a white lid and handed it to Lola.

'Vicodin. Take two,' she said. '*Fantastic* with champagne. You'll be on Cloud Nine in no time.'

Lola downed them immediately.

'How did I get here?' she said feebly. 'I fainted at my neighbour's, didn't I?'

'Ugh.' Devon made a face. 'She got my number out of your phone and rang me. Horrible. Lots of "Your Grace's" this and "Your Ladyship's" that. *So* nouveau. We sent the car for you and apparently she was standing in the mews yelling, "Out of the way for the Marchioness of Claverford's chauffeur!" at the top of her lungs, so that everyone knew who was visiting. Foul woman. You really owe me, Lo.'

Lola's head was still hurting so badly she couldn't take everything in.

'Why was she having to yell "Out of the way?"' she asked, sensing she wasn't going to enjoy the answer.

Devon's big blue eyes had not been Botoxed recently, as was evident by the amount they were able to widen.

'Because of the paps, of course!' she exclaimed.

'They're surrounding the front of the house, didn't you know?' Madison drawled, shaking out her long golden mane. 'They followed the Bentley here.'

'They got a lot of photos of the driver carrying you into the car,' Georgia said.

Her blood running cold, Lola sculled the rest of her champagne and reached for the *Evening Standard*.

'Lo?' Devon said. 'You might want to wait till the Vicodin kicks in before you look at that . . .'

But Lola was already scanning the cover, barely able to breathe for shock. This was the later edition, and the photograph of Jean-Marc on the stretcher was now shrunk down to make space for the main one – the transsexual in whose apartment Jean-Marc had over-dosed.

There are some transsexuals in the world who look even more beautiful than the most stunning of women. Gay fashion designers and Donatella Versace dream of their creations being worn only by Thai ladyboys, with their exquisite features, their improbably full and high breasts, and their narrow, narrow hips. And if Jean-Marc's transsexual, Patricia, had looked like Donatella Versace's ideal fashion model, Lola thought that she might have been able to bear the humiliation slightly better.

This one, however, resembled a reader's wife photo from *Razzle* magazine.

Patricia's bosoms were the size of footballs and placed so high on the ribcage that she could barely see over them. The Adam's apple had been shaved, too. Her hair was dyed a harsh dark brown, clearly by herself out of a packet, and her pores were so big they'd proba-bly have been visible from the moon. Patricia had been caught by the photographer clutching together – not very successfully – the edges of a ratty velour dressing gown, coming down the steps of her housing estate, following the paramedics carrying Jean-Marc's stretcher. Concrete, stained, windswept, covered in graffiti, with a group of jeering hoodies making V-signs at the camera from one of the crumbling walkways, the estate looked, compared to the luxury of the Claverford mansion, like the seventh circle of hell.

'She looks like a total whore,' Georgia observed.

'A total whore crossed with a really rough cleaning lady,' Devon added.

'She doesn't even look like a *whore*,' Madison sighed. 'She looks like an Eastern European *madam* who pimps out her *daughters*. I mean, who'd pay to get with *that*?'

'*My fiancé!*' Lola sobbed, breaking down in tears.

Madison wordlessly shook out another white pill and handed it to Lola, who managed to control her tears enough to swallow it obediently. The doorbell rang, and was answered by Devon's housekeeper, Josefina. As the door opened, there was an uproar from outside, shouts from the gathered paparazzi of, 'Lola! Come out and talk to us!' 'Lola, have you heard from Jean-Marc?' 'Come on, Lola, at least give us a photo!'

India rushed into the room.

'I brought *London Nite!*' she cried, brandishing a copy of the freebie paper. 'Wait till you see the cover!' Then she spotted Lola, and her face fell. 'Lo! I didn't think you'd be up yet! Um—' She made a ridiculously clumsy attempt at hiding the paper behind her back.

Lola held out her hand, still crying.

'India, don't—' Devon started.

'Ah, come on,' Madison drawled. 'The Vicodin'll kick in any second now.'

Lola *was* beginning to feel light-headed. India crossed the room to give her the paper, saying dubiously:

'Maybe it's best just to, you know, see it all at once and get it over with . . .'

But, unfolding *London Nite*, Lola wasn't so sure. It was worse than she could possibly have imagined. Devon's driver hadn't, as she had thought, carried her out of Raisin-Face's house in his arms: he'd slung her over his shoulder in a fireman's lift. And the photographers had had a field day with that. The photo on the front of the paper was mainly of her bottom, the combination of her white jeans and the upwards angle making it look mortifyingly enormous. The sandal with the snapped heel dangled off her foot. She looked like a broken-down doll. With a big white bottom.

'What's the headline?' Devon asked.

'Um . . .' India looked as though she'd rather be anywhere than there. *'IT'S ALL GONE ARSE UP FOR LOLA!'* she mumbled eventually. 'I'm so sorry, Lola . . .'

'Oh, *Jesus,*' Madison said.

A trilling from one of the phones on the table made Lola jump: she recognised her ring.

'It's been going madly,' Georgia said. 'We haven't answered it . . .'

Lola grabbed the phone and checked the number. Her father's lawyer, George Goldman! Trusty George, who had worked for Daddy longer than Lola could remember, the very person Daddy had always told Lola to ring if she ran into any trouble. *Just* the person she needed to talk to! Eagerly, she pressed the key to answer and babbled:

'George! Hi, it's me!'

'Lola? Honey, how you doing?'

No matter how upmarket George's legal practice was, he'd never lost his New Jersey accent completely. Benny, Lola's father, had always respected him for that: Benny was a Jersey boy made good too.

'Oh *George!*' It was actually, Lola realised, very hard to answer the question of how she was doing. Her vicious headache was fading, but still present, overlaid and muddled up by the champagne and the Vicodin, which was definitely beginning to have an effect. The combination made her feel as if someone were driving nails into her head, but had been kind enough to replace her brains with cotton-wool first.

'I don't know where to *start!*' she said hopelessly. 'Daddy – Jean-Marc – I'm locked out of my house—'

'You're locked out of your house?' George sounded baffled. 'Jeez, Lola, call a locksmith!'

'No, you don't understand! I rang Daddy because the key didn't work and Carin answered his phone and she says she has power of attorney and my house is in Daddy's name, or the name of one of his companies, so she's not letting me in, *and* my credit cards are being declined—'

'Shit,' George said. 'This isn't good.'

In her entire time of running to George with problems, this was the only time that Lola had ever heard George say those words. From a long way away – wow, the Vicodin really had kicked in – she felt her heart sink to her stomach.

'You mean she can *do this?*' Lola gasped.

'Lola, baby, I don't know! Your dad – or I should say Carin – fired me six months ago! Didn't anyone tell you?'

Lola sagged back into the soft sofa cushions.

'No!'

The idea of George no longer working for her father was almost blasphemous, like hearing that God had told the Holy Ghost that its services would no longer be required.

'Uh-huh. Carin finally got to him. She had some fancy Park Avenue guy all lined up instead a me.'

Lola flashed for a second on George's offices, the whole floor of a nondescript Manhattan building on 36th Street between 6th and 7th Avenues. It was a shitty, ugly block, lined with delivery trucks, dumpsters and lost tourists wandering in circles, looking for Macy's. But George, and Benny, liked it that way. What was the point in spending big money on Park Avenue office space when you didn't need to?

'But Carin didn't just sack you because you weren't on Park Avenue,' Lola said weakly.

'Honey!' George sighed. 'I know you're in shock, but you gotta wake up! Carin's clearly got some shyster to draw her up a power of attorney, and now your dad's' – he paused – 'um, temporarily out of circulation, she's calling all the shots! That's why I'm on the phone with you now! You want me to act for you?'

Lola's face brightened.

'Oh George, would you?'

'Of course! You nuts! We gotta find out what's going on here!' His voice became even more serious. 'But Lola, baby, things could be pretty bad for a while. You know how your trust fund works?'

'Um, it gives me money?' Lola suggested hopefully.

'It's all administered by your dad,' George continued. 'He's the sole trustee. I did tell him he ought to give you more responsibility, but he wouldn't listen to me.'

'So how come Carin got him to give her power of attorney?' Lola said. 'That means she controls everything, right?'

'Exactly.' George sighed. 'And she must have got him to make her a co-trustee too, otherwise she couldn't control your trust fund. OK, here's what I'm going to do. I'm going to fax over to you a letter confirming you're hiring me to act for you. You sign it and send it right back to me. I'll get onto this new lawyer now and get a look at that power of attorney, check everything out, see if we can find any way to get your trust fund under your control, or at least give you access to it.'

'Oh God, that would be *great*.' Lola sagged with relief. 'But what about Daddy? I need to find out how he is!'

'You hafta come to New York as soon as you can,' George said.

'I know! But Jean-Marc – my fiancé – he's in hospital here, he just overdosed, I need to go and visit him as well—'

'Oh *Lola*. Honey. I don't know what to say. He going to be OK?'

'I don't know – I have to ring the hospital—'

'You got some good friends around you, honey?' George sounded really worried. 'Maybe you should call your mom—'

'*No!*' Lola looked at her four girlfriends, lounging on the sofas, listening avidly to her side of the conversation. India had already finished the edamame beans and had started on the strawberries. *God, that girl was such a pig.* 'I've got really good friends here, George. They're taking great care of me.'

Devon and Madison raised their champagne flutes to her. Georgia, who was sitting in the bay window, talking on her mobile, wiggled her fingers at Lola. And India gave her a lovely big smile, her teeth only slightly stained by the strawberries.

Going in search of Josefina, Lola tracked her down in the kitchen and handed her the phone so she could sort out the whole fax situation, something Lola couldn't remotely have coped with at the best of times. Then she returned to the living-room.

'*So*,' Madison said, her green eyes glinting. 'Tell us *all* about

Jean-Marc! Did you *know*? What kind of stuff did you guys do? I had no idea he was that filthy!'

'*What?*' Lola stared at her, uncomprehending.

'Well, you know, if he's into *trannies*—'

But Devon had already read Lola's expression.

'You didn't know *anything*, did you?' she exclaimed. 'Oh my God, you must be in total shock right now!'

'Oh Lola, poor you,' India whispered, her pretty round moon-face, framed by light-brown curls, genuinely sympathetic.

'So did he just have totally vanilla sex with you?' Madison continued, her perfectly shaped eyebrows raised.

'Under the covers with the lights off?' Georgia added.

'*Missionary?*' Devon capped it off, as the girls fell about in hysterics.

'We didn't actually have sex that much,' Lola said simply. She was halfway through her second glass of champagne, and, as Madison had said, the combination of fizz and Vicodin on an empty stomach was making her feel increasingly dissociated from reality.

The laughter stopped as if it had been turned off at the mains.

'What?' Devon said, baffled.

'We didn't actually have sex that much.' Lola took another swig of champagne. 'We sort of did at the beginning, but neither of us were that into it, so after a while, we didn't bother.'

They were staring at her, speechless.

'Frankly, I've always thought sex was really messy,' Lola continued. 'All that humping and fussing and getting sweaty, and then you're lying in a—'

'Sticky, oozy mess,' India contributed, pulling a face.

'Exactly,' Lola said gratefully. 'I never really liked it, even before Jean-Marc. I hate when men caress you and look into your eyes and do slow kisses all over you for hours, you know? Besides, sex messes up my hair. Actually, that's why we stopped. We did it once and I'd had my hair put up for a charity auction we were going to afterwards and my hair got pulled around, and honestly, I don't know who was crosser about it, me or Jean-Marc. So after that we'd sort of joke, "Oh, no, careful of my hair!" and not bother any more. We were really happy,' she added sadly. 'I mean, we'd cuddle together and hold hands, and that was perfect.'

The girls were gaping like groupers packed in ice on a fishmonger's slab.

'But what did you do to get off?' Georgia asked.

'Oh, I've got a vibrator,' Lola said cheerfully.

'And I think we all know what Jean-Marc did!' Devon said, tapping the cover of the *Evening Standard*. 'Miss Patricia from Kennington!'

'How *could* he?' Lola shuddered.

She jumped up.

'I'm going to the hospital,' she announced. 'I have to find out what's going on with Jean-Marc.'

'We'll all go with you!' Devon said, rising too, as all the girls snatched for their handbags. No one was going to be left behind: the opportunity to be right in the epicentre of the biggest scandal in years was far too good for them to miss.

'You can't go like that,' Madison said, surveying Lola from head to toe. 'You're a wreck. You'll be on the cover of every paper tomorrow morning looking like a soap star coming home from an all-night bender with some football players.'

Georgia sucked in her breath.

'Harsh but true,' she confirmed.

Devon grabbed Lola's hand.

'Come upstairs with me,' she commanded. 'I know *just* the right supportive-but-hurt fiancée outfit for you to wear. I'm thinking Elizabeth Hurley just after Hugh Grant got caught with that hooker on the Sunset Strip . . .'

'Lola! Over here!'

'Lola! It's Richie from the *Mail!* Did you know about Jean-Marc's drug addiction?'

'Lola, are you going to forgive him?'

'Lola! Devon! Can we get you both together, girls?'

Devon had decided that Elizabeth Hurley's Hugh-Grant-forgiving outfit – all white, with a large crucifix at the throat – might just be overkill, especially as the London sun was considerably fainter than the LA one. She had dressed Lola in black trousers and a poloneck, worn under a short white trenchcoat, cinched at the waist with a wide black leather belt. Since Lola's Jimmy Choos were ruined, Devon had lent her a pair of black patent Gina boots, which Lola had had to stuff at the toes with toilet paper, as Devon's feet were a size bigger (something Devon hadn't been very happy to discover).

Lola's golden hair was pinned back in a deliberately dishevelled chignon at the back of her head – 'Not *too* tidy,' Madison had cautioned. 'If she's too pulled together everyone will hate her' – and large black sunglasses completed the look. Devon had helped Lola do very discreet make-up, just enough to make her skin flawless for the photographs, but not so much that it seemed as though she cared what she looked like. Lola applied a final coat of pale pink lipstick just before they climbed out of the Claverfords' Bentley.

'Fab,' Georgia said approvingly. 'Very Grace Kelly.'

'If Grace Kelly were visiting her tranny-loving fiancé in hospital,' Devon muttered.

There were paparazzi ten-deep outside the main entrance to the hospital, and when they saw Devon climb out of the Bentley they turned as one, a huge pack of predators spotting their prey. Camera shutters clicked. A couple of security guards rushed forward, clearing a sort of path for Lola and her posse. Lola walked straight ahead, sunglasses on her head to allow the photographers a good view of her face – pale, resolute and slightly tragic. At the entrance, the girls paused for a second and swivelled to give the screaming paps a few snaps of them before letting the automatic doors swing open.

As they closed again, Madison was already at the reception desk, her long legs giving her an easy advantage.

'Fourth floor,' she announced after a quick interchange with the receptionist.

'Eew,' India said as she stepped into the lift, looking dubiously at the scratches on the floor, the bolted-on steel panelling, and the chipped control panel. 'This isn't as nice as I was expecting.'

'Private hospitals never bloody are,' said Devon dourly.

'Shocking, when you think how much it costs,' Georgia commented.

'I know!' Devon said. 'For that much money it should be like a *hotel.*'

The lift pinged, the doors slid open, and the girls stood back to let Lola exit first. She went up to the nurses' desk.

'I'm Lola Fitzgerald,' she said, giving the nurse her best you-knew-who-I-was-already-but-I'm-pretending-to-be-modest smile.

'Oh yes – I mean, of *course* you are—' the nurse babbled, the tip of her nose turning an unflattering pink. Plump and freckled, with her hair scraped back for work and not a stroke of make-up on, dressed in unflattering bright blue scrubs, she looked almost like a different species from the glossy It girls. And from the way she was ducking her head, she knew it all too well.

'I'm here to see Jean-Marc van der Veer,' Lola continued.

The nurse was positively writhing with embarrassment.

'Miss Fitzgerald, I'm *so* sorry,' she mumbled. 'I'd *so* let you in to see Mr van der Veer, but I'm not supposed to let anyone in.'

Lola's eyes dilated in shock.

'He's – they said he was out of danger!' she gasped.

'Oh *no*, Miss Fitzgerald, it's not that, you mustn't think—' The nurse's blush increased, a hectic red circle appearing on each cheek. 'It's just that he can't have any visitors at the moment – he's not in critical condition or anything, please don't worry, he's going to be fine—'

'Is that what the doctor said?' Lola asked, slowly recovering from her panic.

'The doctor says he's out of danger, but it's Mr van der Veer – I mean, *your* Mr van der Veer's brother – who said no visitors,' the nurse said.

Lola read the plastic name-tag pinned over the nurse's capacious right breast.

'Deirdre,' she said, 'I'm his *fiancée*. If anyone should be allowed to see him, it should be me.'

Deirdre looked overwhelmed.

'Oh, I don't know what to *do!*' she said, wringing her hands. 'Mr van der Veer *specifically* said – he was *so* firm about it – but I'm sure he couldn't have meant *you*, Miss Fitzgerald—'

'That's exactly who I meant!' came a man's voice from the end of the hall. Low and harsh, it cut through the hubbub like a rusty chainsaw.

Deirdre jerked towards the sound as if he'd just Tasered her.

'Mr van der Veer – I wasn't sure what to do – this is your brother's fiancée, Miss—'

'I know damn well who she is,' said the man, striding towards them. 'I've seen enough photographs of her by now.'

He halted a few feet away from the desk, in the middle of the corridor. But he was the kind of man who would automatically seem to be in the centre of anywhere he stood: power and authority radiated out from him in almost-visible rays. His barely controlled anger, however, was even more obvious. His arms were folded across his chest, and Lola instantly sensed that, though this stance was meant to intimidate, it was also because he didn't trust himself at this moment unless his hands were tucked safely under his well-formed biceps.

'You're Jean-Marc's *brother?*' she exclaimed.

'Niels van der Veer,' he said, fixing her with a terrifyingly piercing stare. 'Jean-Marc's older brother. Did Jean-Marc mention me at all? Or was he too busy shoving illegal substances up his nose to bother?'

India, standing by the lifts with Georgia and Madison, did the worst thing she could possibly have done under the circumstances: she let out a nervous giggle. Lola could have killed her. Niels van der Veer's cold grey gaze turned briefly to India, who wilted underneath it like a flower in a speeded-up nature film, blooming one second, dying the next.

His chilly grey eyes swivelled back to Lola, who gulped. She was trying to see any resemblance between Jean-Marc and his brother, and failing. Jean-Marc was golden and sleek, soft-featured and full-lipped, with a tumble of silky blond hair. And he was as slender as a wand.

Niels, on the other hand, was big and looming: much taller than Jean-Marc, with square shoulders, a broad chest, and an air of complete command. Jean-Marc smiled easily, while Niels's mouth was set in a straight line, and he looked like an attempt to smile would shatter him in pieces. His hair was dark dirty-blond, as Jean-Marc's would be if he didn't help it along with discreet gold highlights, but Niels's was cut shorter than his brother's, and pushed back from his brow.

Jean-Marc, with his melting blue eyes and soft skin, was the epitome of male beauty. But his brother, far from being beautiful, wasn't even handsome: his face was much too craggy, his jawline too pronounced, his grey eyes cold. The blondish hair didn't soften his masculinity at all. Lola doubted he'd look good in photographs; his strong bone structure, his big frame, wouldn't translate well to film. If he ever wanted a portrait of himself, he'd have to commission someone to chisel it out of a block of granite.

Lola supposed he was good-looking, if you liked men that big and butch. But she didn't. She never had. And she certainly didn't like men who looked this angry. Especially since his anger seemed, bizarrely, to be directed at her.

'You don't look anything like Jean-Marc,' she blurted out, and then could have bitten off her tongue for the irrelevance of the comment.

His eyebrows drew together in a scowl.

'Different mothers,' he said concisely, his voice harsh. 'Aren't you going to ask me how he is?'

'Of course!' Lola protested. 'Why do you think I'm here? I came to see him!'

'Did you? Or did you bring along your girl group all dressed up for the photo opportunity outside?' he sneered, casting a comprehensive glance of scorn over Lola's friends.

Madison glared back at him; India whimpered; and Georgia and Devon preened themselves a little, flattered at being compared to pop stars.

'How dare you!' Lola was furious. She took one step towards him, but came up against what she could only describe as a force field. His anger was like an invisible shield blocking her path.

'I'm not letting you near Jean-Marc,' he pronounced. 'You've done enough damage to him already.'

'*What?*' Lola's voice rose dangerously high. 'Are you *joking*? Did you not notice that Jean-Marc overdosed when he was hanging out with some tranny in a council block? Do you think I sent him off there to get off his face and totally humiliate me?'

Niels van der Veer unfolded his arms, and Lola, involuntarily, took a step back again, hating herself for having done it. But she couldn't have stood her ground. In all her spoilt, soft, featherbedded life, she had never met anyone half as intimidating as Jean-Marc's older brother.

'Humiliate *you?*' he said, and now he did smile, and it was even more frightening than his scowl, a smile with no humour in it at all. 'Humiliate *you*, Princess? How funny – that's exactly what you need. Maybe that would make you think about someone else for one damn second of your life. Look at you, all dressed up to the nines, like you're ready for one of those damn photoshoots you and my brother whored for every time someone asked. You worked out exactly what to wear for those paparazzi scum outside, didn't you?'

'Jean-Marc would have hated me to turn up not looking my best!' she flashed defiantly. Behind her, she could hear the other girls murmuring agreement.

'Oh for God's sake, what kind of spoiled bitches are you?' he demanded, rage gathering in his face. 'You!' He pointed at Lola, his hand coming close enough to touch her. 'Can you even tell me that you *love* my brother? Can you?'

'I—' Lola started, and then the words died on her lips.

Not because she didn't love Jean-Marc: she did. She always would. But she didn't love him the way his angry brother meant. He wasn't her one true love, the man she wanted to spend the rest of her life with.

She'd never admitted it to herself before – never realised it before now. But here it was, the truth, and if there was one thing she seemed to be completely unable to do, it was lie to Niels van der Veer.

'I *do* love him,' she stammered. 'But maybe . . . I mean . . . I do *love* him, but—'

She shifted nervously, and her foot slipped in the over-large boot. The toilet paper she'd stuffed in the toes had compressed since she'd put them on, and now her feet were sliding around in the too-wide space. Off-balance now, her heel turned under her and she tripped, catching at the top of the counter for support.

Awkwardly she regained her balance. But now Niels was staring at her with open contempt.

'Are you *drunk*?' he demanded.

'No!' she said defensively. 'Of course not! I just—'

And then she remembered the Vicodin and the champagne. Was she a bit woozy still?

'Oh, for God's sake!' Niels's hand clenched into a fist. Tightening his lips, he looked at it as if he were angry with it too, angry with the world. He thrust both hands in his pockets, shifting on his feet as if needing to burn off his restless energy.

'Get out,' he said to Lola between clenched teeth. He glanced over at the rest of her friends. 'All of you, out. And don't come back. Jean-Marc needs society trash like you like he needs a hole in the head.'

He turned on his heel and strode away down the corridor from the direction in which he had come. Lola stared after him, incredulous. Her brain was racing with stinging retorts: suddenly, she had hundreds of ways to tell him what she thought of him, that his opinion of her was all wrong, that he was the most hateful, horrible man she had ever met in her whole life. But he had tied her tongue into knots. That steely grey stare was paralysing. She was lucky she hadn't fallen over and twisted her ankle.

'How *dare* he?' Devon gasped. 'Does he have *any idea* who I am?'

'"*Society trash*"!' Madison hissed. 'Outrageous!'

'That,' India sighed, 'was the most gorgeous man I've ever seen in my *life*.'

'India, how can you!' Georgia rounded on her.

'He looks like Daniel Craig's meaner older brother,' India muttered.

'Look, he's not going to let you in to see Jean-Marc,' Devon said, belting her camel Loro Piana cashmere coat around her waist, 'so let's just go. I'm certainly not going to stay in this *dump*' – she cast a disparaging glance around the nurses' station that encompassed the faded industrial green walls, the vinyl floor, and the ugly blue uniform Deirdre and the other nurses were wearing – 'to be insulted any longer.'

Lola looked pleadingly at Deirdre, who was sucking in her lips, hunching up her shoulders, gestures that meant to indicate her helplessness in the face of Niels van der Veer's much greater power. And Lola couldn't blame her.

But, for some reason, it only increased her determination to get in to see Jean-Marc. He was her fiancé, and he had nearly died. She had a right to visit him in hospital, for God's sake! She needed to see how he was doing: she needed to ask him what on earth he'd been up to the night before, and whether their engagement could be salvaged at all. She had no idea what she wanted to happen, whether they should get married or not, but, with her father's sudden illness (that was what she was calling it; she couldn't deal with the idea of Daddy being in a *coma* right now), one of the two props she relied on had been pulled away, and Jean-Marc was even more important to her than ever before.

And besides wanting to visit Jean-Marc for his own sake, she desperately needed money. Carin had stopped all her cards and told her to go to Jean-Marc for help, and he was exactly the person to ask. Now he was on the mend (and frankly, they all knew people who'd gone a bit too far with the controlled substances, had their stomach pumped and were right as rain afterwards), she knew that Jean-Marc would throw his wallet at her and tell her to use anything she needed for as long as she wanted. He was the soul of generosity anyway, but after the embarrassment he'd caused her, she knew he'd do anything he could to help her. Her girlfriends had already done so much for her – throwing that amazing hen night, rallying round her in this awful crisis – that she was loath to ask them for anything else.

She would see Jean-Marc, and get the financing from him to fly to NYC to see her father. Beyond that, she couldn't even imagine her next step. It was all too frightening: the mere idea of life without her huge, protective, all-powerful, endlessly indulgent father, whom she adored beyond anything, was so terrifying that every time it tried to enter her consciousness, she jumped on it with both of Devon's Gina patent-leather boots till it subsided again.

One step at a time.

See Jean-Marc.

Get to New York.

Lola set her jaw. She was determined. And not even Jean-Marc's arrogant bastard of a brother was going to stop her.

Chapter 4

$\mathcal{E}$ vie lumbered out of the lift like a big awkward bear in the three coats she was wearing one over the other. It was complete humiliation. Especially as she was bent over, dragging first one, then the other suitcase, and finally the pole, out of the lift, as its doors repeatedly tried to close on her. At least she was so padded by the coats that she barely felt the thuds.

Catching her breath, she stood in the lobby for a moment, looking around her. Its granite floor, flecked with sparkling mica, glittered under the huge glass lighting feature. The sight of the lobby had never failed to make Evie's tiny hard heart sing with happiness. It always reminded her of how far she had come from those filthy projects. You were lucky if the graffitied lobby there didn't stink of piss and sweat, and the only receptionist was a crackhead or two slumped on the floor, vials crunching under your feet as you picked your way gingerly around them.

Normally, Henry, the day guy, would have jumped to help Evie with her cases. But clearly Benny's wife (that *bitch*) had informed him that Evie was being evicted, and Henry barely turned his head to look at her as she reached down for the pull-handles of the suitcases and started to drag them across the lobby, the wheels scraping on the granite floor because the suitcases were so weighted down with stuff.

Suddenly, she was nothing. Dirt on his shoes. This man – who'd *grovelled* to her for tips and his Christmas envelope – was treating her as he would a food delivery guy: like she was invisible.

Evie had never been invisible. Girls who looked like Evie were never invisible.

Till now.

It was another item to put on her hate-list against Carin Fitzgerald.

She was brainstorming where she could possibly crash, tonight at least. As soon as she'd left the Midnight Lounge, she'd dropped the girls she worked with there: she was determined to better herself, and she wouldn't do that hanging out with those wild party girls, who'd just have got high, spilt JD and coke over her suede sofas, and tried to steal her meal-ticket sugar daddy.

So, no friends from the Lounge would take her in. Her mom would, but Evie would starve in the street before she went back to Mariluz's. Because of the shame of it, crawling back home years after she'd defiantly declared that she didn't need anything from her mother, that she'd make it all on her own; and because it would be a huge step back, returning to that one-bedroom apartment fifteen stinking floors up in the sky, sleeping on her mom's couch, just like she had throughout her childhood.

No, not her mom's. No turning back. Move on or die, that was Evie's motto.

There was only one person who would take her in. Only one person she could bear to ask for a favour.

She knew she couldn't afford a car service. All she had was the cash in her wallet and the stash she'd been keeping in the cistern – the cops-are-coming, get-out-of-town money. She didn't want to dip into that unless she absolutely had to. So, dragging the suitcases half a block, then coming back for the pole, sweating under the heavy coats, Evie lumbered gradually along Harrison, heading for the West Side Highway. Tribeca, the best place in the world to live if you belonged here, gleaming loft buildings inhabited by black-clad multi-millionaire hipsters, film stars and Masters of the Universe like

Benny. Superb restaurants, hip boutiques, bars where a glass of champagne could set you back twenty-five bucks easy.

But it was the worst place in the world if you didn't have the money to live the lifestyle. The glances Evie got were horrified, then blank, eyes forward. No one wanted to know. She was a bag lady in one of the richest areas in the world. She might as well have had leprosy.

She tried her cards at a Chase Manhattan branch, but it not only denied access, it ate them up, one after the other. Evie watched the machine swallow her plastic and felt her blood pressure spike with fury. Those precious plastic rectangles, one black, one gold, had been her passport to Benny's world of luxury and ease. All gone now, all cleaned out.

She set her chin and reached down for her suitcase handles once more. Only one more block to go, manoeuvring round FedEx trucks and loading bays, black garbage bags, deliveries for warehouses close to the river. Traffic blared down the West Side Highway: Mack trucks, yellow cabs, limos, private cars, weaving in and out at high speed, chasing each other's tails down to Battery Park.

Streetwise in the ways of New York, Evie propped her suitcases on the sidewalk, her pole beside them, and waited. Various yellow cabs slowed down, but she shook her head at all of them; she was holding out for an illegal, unmetered, gypsy cab. Eventually, a battered Lincoln Town Car veered across two lanes of traffic, causing a riotous blare of horns from the trucks it had cut off, and squealed to a halt next to Evie.

'Where you going?' the driver, a sweaty middle-aged guy, called over the roar of traffic.

'Bushwick,' Evie said reluctantly.

He looked her up and down.

'You're kidding, right?'

'I wish. I really do.'

'Seventy bucks,' he said, looking at her handbag, her expensive suitcases.

Evie stepped closer so he would focus on her pretty face and not her Vuittons.

'Hey, don't go by those! They're all knock-offs, I bought them on Canal!' she lied. 'I got forty, that's all.'

'Forty to Bushwick in rush hour? You *are* kidding.'

She'd known he wouldn't take that. But always start low and bargain up was her rule. She sighed, pushing back her hair, letting the coats fall open so he got a good look at her body in the clinging T-shirt: she hadn't had time to put on a bra.

'I could maybe manage fifty, but that's it,' she said helplessly. 'Come on, buddy, help me out, won't you?'

He groaned and popped the trunk.

'Just cause you're cute, and it's change-over shift time,' he said. 'Fifty it is.'

Evie's legs were strong and flexible as steel, her abs taut and powerful. Lifting and hoisting the cases into the capacious trunk of the Lincoln and arranging her pole crosswise on top of them was no big deal for her. She slid into the back and the driver pulled into traffic, the horns blaring again because he hadn't bothered to indicate.

Evie didn't even notice: this was standard for New York. She was fully occupied rummaging in her big Tod's bag for her phone. There was still a dialling tone; she scrolled through the stored numbers, hit one, and heard, with great relief, that it was ringing. Thank God, Carin hadn't had her service cut off yet.

Disappointingly, though, it went straight to answerphone. Lawrence must be training someone, his phone turned off.

'Babe?' she said. 'It's me, Evie. I need to crash at yours for a little while, OK? I'm on my way there now in a cab. Are you coming back soon? Can you call me when you get this? I just don't want to be sitting out there for hours, you know? Call me, OK?'

Evie slumped back in the seat, the coats itchy and uncomfortable with the sweat she'd worked up prickling at her. The driver was swinging the car up the ramp for the Brooklyn Bridge. Evie practically never crossed the bridges that connected Manhattan to the rest of New York, or, God forbid, Jersey. Why would she need to? She was Manhattan born and bred. And now she was taking all her worldly possessions to Bushwick, of all godforsaken places. She had become bridge and tunnel, like the rest of the New Yorkers who dreamed of living in Manhattan but had been priced out decades ago. They had to catch the subway or the Jersey PATH or drive in over the glittering bridges – Brooklyn, Manhattan, Williamsburg – for the hip restaurants and bars and clubs that had the cachet of being on Manhattan, the tiny sliver of island packed in so tight with seething humanity you often wondered why it didn't sink under the sheer weight of people and traffic and fifty-storey steel skyscrapers.

Bridge and tunnel. It was so depressing Evie couldn't stand to think about it.

They turned onto the BQE – the Brooklyn-Queens Expressway – firing the Lincoln Town Car through tiny gaps between swaying trucks and coaches heading for the airport. It was such an ugly highway that Evie closed her eyes, but even when she opened them a few minutes later, as they raced down Metropolitan Avenue, with its burned-out lots and seedy storefronts, the view was no better. God, she couldn't believe what she was being reduced to.

All she knew about where Lawrence lived was that he rented a room, or a space – he hadn't been specific, and she hadn't cared enough to ask – in a warehouse building that wasn't zoned for domestic use. But when the Lincoln Town Car pulled up outside the building, even the driver looked dubious.

'You sure this is the right address?' he asked.

'Yeah,' she said, heaving a deep sigh. 'He's got some illegal warehouse let.'

Evie tried Lawrence's number again. Still nothing. Reluctantly, she climbed out of the car. The front of the building looked like a prison: steel bars, grey industrial paint. The number was scrawled on the steel door with what looked like Magic Marker, and the buzzers by its side were so chipped and scratched Evie wasn't even sure that they worked. She knew Lawrence was on the top floor, so she tried the top buzzer, but could hear nothing inside the building.

It was as grim and forbidding as if it were derelict, totally uninhabited. On either side were similar buildings, one set back behind a fence topped with barbed wire. Behind it, Evie could see a pair of Alsatians on thick chains, lying slumped by a corrugated-iron shed. She pressed the buzzer again, and, waiting for some reply, she made a 360-degree turn, surveying the street. Across the road was a steel-works, a pair of huge gates swung open, and, staring into the dark interior, she could see a group of men hooking a rusty-looking piece of metal onto a chain hoist. Whines of factory machines, big electric saws, scraped through the air. The street itself was filthy with litter and discarded drink cans.

Evie shuddered.

'Hey!' called a woman's voice from up above.

Evie tilted back her head to see who it was: one of the big windows had been pushed open on the top floor, and a girl was craning out of it.

'What do you want?' she called down.

'I'm a friend of Lawrence's,' Evie yelled back. 'I need to come in and dump my stuff.'

'You're a friend of *Lawrence's*?'

'Yeah!' Evie was growing irritated, standing out here looking like a fool on the sidewalk. 'Look, come down and let me in, OK?'

The girl's head disappeared. Evie went over to the back of the car and started pulling out her pole and her suitcases.

The driver got out to help. 'Hey, baby, I'd take you home with me in a heartbeat!' he said, throwing his arms wide, showing the sweat stains under his arms. 'But my wife, she might throw us both out, you know, and then we'd be right back here—'

There was a clanking sound from the door, and Evie's head jerked round eagerly.

'Who are *you*?' the girl from upstairs demanded.

She was average height and quite pale, her dark hair pulled up on top of her head in a messy ponytail, dressed in leggings and layers of T-shirts. Her skin had a light film of sweat, and her cheeks were bright pink: it looked as if she'd been working out. Despite the paleness of her skin, the shape of her dark almond eyes, her flat chest and long, squarish torso suggested to Evie that she had some

Korean blood in her. From her time working the Midnight Lounge, Evie was very used to assessing other women: her eyes zipped up and down the girl in the doorway, picking out her strong and weak points as if she were a horse in an auction, checking out the competition.

'I'm Evie,' she answered. 'A friend of Lawrence's. He's talked about me, right?'

From the narrowing of the girl's eyes, Evie saw that her gamble had paid off: Lawrence *had* mentioned her.

'He might have,' the girl said reluctantly. 'So what?'

'So I'm crashing here for a few days with Lawrence,' Evie snapped.

'He didn't say anything about it to me,' said the girl, starting to close the door.

Her heavy fringe was tipped in bright red, as were the ends of her ponytail, as if she'd dipped them both in scarlet dye. She had a silver hoop in her eyebrow, a stud in her nose, and on the arm pulling the door was a heavily patterned tattoo curling up from the wrist to the elbow. It gave her conventional prettiness the edge she'd doubtless wanted: she probably thought all this ornamentation made her look cool and hip. And tough.

Well, she was wrong there. Evie would put her money any day of the week on a hustler from the Midnight Lounge against a would-be urban hipster. She pushed back against the door with such a shove that the girl's eyes widened as she involuntarily took a step back.

'You really think that if Lawrence comes back and finds me sitting out here on the street, he's going to be happy about it?' Evie said from between clenched teeth.

The girl sighed.

'OK, I'll let you in,' she said, making it sound as if she were doing Evie a favour, rather than having been muscled into it. 'But you're not going to like it,' she added smugly, looking at Evie's expensive Vuittons.

'What's your name?' Evie asked the girl as she heaved her suitcases into the building.

'Autumn,' the girl said.

It figured. Hippie parents.

'Well, Autumn, can you take this for me?'

Evie handed her the pole in its plastic carrying case. Autumn staggered slightly under its weight.

'What *is* it?' she asked.

'It's my pole,' Evie said shortly, bending down to pick up one of her suitcases.

'Eew!' Autumn dropped it on the concrete floor, pulling a disgusted face. 'No way I'm carrying that! Pole-dancing's *so* anti-feminist!'

So Evie had to make three trips up the rickety old stairs to the fourth and final floor, where Autumn had left open the huge steel door for her and retreated to what Evie supposed they called the kitchen. It was a gigantic open room, flooded with light.

That was the good part. The only one. Because the kitchen was an ancient gas cooker and an equally ancient fridge, standing next to an industrial steel sink, which was piled so high with washing-up that Evie could barely see its outlines. Autumn was sitting at a huge Formica table which was so badly chipped and dented that it must have been salvaged from a skip. Looking around, that went for the rest of the furniture: the kitchen chairs, the sofas, the coffee tables, were all the kind of scrap that people had put out on the street like trash. Salvation Army charity shops would have split their sides at the suggestion that they take this crap. The coffee table was missing not one, but two legs, and was propped up on crates. The walls were bare brick, but not the lovingly tended kind that was fashionable right now because trendy interior designers considered it authentic: this was the real deal, crumbling, ugly, and damp.

It was the standard artists-and-performers deal. Priced out of anywhere decent, they took over the places no one else wanted to live in and landlords couldn't rent out to industry: the cold-water flats, the rat-infested warehouses with barely basic plumbing. The landlords turned a blind eye to the fact that their tenants were actually living in their alleged work studios, which of course meant that they could be evicted at any time.

'Lawrence and I want to do this place up and make a yoga studio here,' Autumn informed Evie. 'It's our dream.'

'Oh really?' Evie countered. 'That's news to me. Lawrence never mentioned you at all.'

Evie knew this girl wasn't Lawrence's girlfriend. No way was Lawrence the type of guy to cheat on a steady, someone he was committed to. Even if Lawrence and Autumn hooked up occasionally – and Evie figured that Lawrence was too sensible to do it with a roommate – Evie was sure he hadn't ever agreed to be exclusive with her. Lawrence, bless him, was honest to the core.

Autumn glared at her.

'You can throw your bags in his room,' she said, nodding down the corridor. 'It's the last one on the right. And the bathroom's next to it.'

She smiled maliciously.

'It won't be much by your standards,' she added, picking up a copy of a yoga magazine and starting to flick through it. 'Oh, and you might see the occasional rat. Lawrence and I don't believe in putting down poison for them. We're very strict vegans.'

Dragging her bags down the corridor, such as it was – the residents had put up cheap partition walls, open at the top, to divide the vast space into separate rooms – Evie reached Lawrence's room. It was at least exquisitely neat, and someone, probably Lawrence, had built a big platform for a loft bed at the rear, plus long wooden shelves and a hanging rail for clothes. Books were arranged on the shelves, and Lawrence's clothes, mostly in shades of khaki, taupe and beige (i.e. colours that could be achieved without bleaching, using natural dyes) were ranged in tidy piles further down. There was a desk and a chair, a sisal rug on the floor, and some Japanese scroll paintings hung on the walls.

That was it.

Not a single real creature comfort.

Slowly, she took off her coats, one after the other, and hung them over the chair. Then she sat down on one of the rungs of the wide ladder leading up to the sleeping platform, and stared ahead of her blindly, barely even seeing the particle-board wall. Everything had happened so fast. She was still barely able to process the wreck of her life – how far and fast she had fallen since she had woken up this morning in her beautiful penthouse, cosseted, beloved, wrapped in 400-count sheets, cashmere blankets and silk bedspreads, scented with expensive moisturiser.

She was busting for a pee, but she couldn't face investigating the bathroom. From the way Autumn had smirked at her, she could tell it would be very bad.

Footsteps came down the hall. Could it be Lawrence? Had he picked up her message and rushed back to see her? Evie's heart raced with anticipation. Lawrence was all she had left: she hadn't realised till this moment how eager she was to see him.

But it was Autumn who put her head round the door, Autumn who said, with the triumphant air of a woman who is just about to score a major point over her rival:

'Oh, by the way, I noticed that's a leather bag you were carrying. And those suitcases are leather too, aren't they?'

Her gaze went to the chair over which Evie had carefully draped her coats, and her eyes widened in horror.

'Oh my God, is that *real fur*?' she breathed.

She walked into the room and bent over the chair for a closer look at Evie's shaved mink, letting out a scream when she confirmed her suspicions. Turning to Evie, she put her hands on her hips.

'We're a cruelty-free household,' she declared. 'Every animal product you own will have to go by *tonight*. And that *includes* products tested on animals!'

Turning on her heel, she stormed out, her red-tipped ponytail swinging in an effect that Evie had to admit was dramatic.

Evie almost felt like laughing. Her situation was so comically appalling. Stuck in a building that wasn't fit for human habitation, probably with rats crawling over her in the night – she had the horrible feeling that Autumn had been serious about that – and now about to have 90 per cent of her worldly goods confiscated on moral grounds. She put her head in her hands.

And then, as her palms grew damp, she realised she was crying. Evie never cried.

But she climbed up the ladder and buried her face in Lawrence's pillows just the same, because the last thing she wanted to do was give that bitch Autumn the satisfaction of hearing her cry her heart out.

Chapter 5

'This is the last straw, Dev! The last straw!'

Someone was shouting so loudly that Lola, carefully plucking a hair that threatened to unbalance the perfect symmetry of her eyebrows, put down the tweezers and tilted her head in the direction of her bedroom door.

'Not one more night! It's gone beyond a joke!'

Worried now, Lola stood up and crossed the room, pushing open the door. Voices floated up from the marble hallway below, and, leaning slightly over the corridor balustrade, she could see the golden heads of Devon and her husband Piers, Marquis of Claverford.

'I simply won't stand for it!' Piers was bellowing. 'She'll have to leave! Today!'

Oh *no* . . . Lola's heart sank to the floor. She might not have any A levels, but you didn't need formal education to work out who Piers was referring to.

Devon's softer voice was barely audible, but she was clearly pleading for Lola, because Piers's response was a roar of anger.

'Dev! Have you *seen* the papers? She's all over the damn tabloids, shoving a straw up her nose!'

Leaning further over the balustrade now, Lola had a good view of the scene in the hallway. Piers, in the baby-blue sweater, stripy shirt and loose jeans of the Sloane at play, was pacing back and forth on the checkerboard marble tiles, waving a newspaper at Devon, who looked tiny next to his large, beefy frame.

'We can't have it, Dev,' Piers insisted. 'They're surrounding the bloody house. I caught one of the blighters trying to climb over the garden wall. Gave him a good spanking with a spade – he won't be sitting down for a week.' Piers chuckled. 'But look!' He waved the paper at Devon again, stabbing at the front page with a big pink finger. Painstakingly – Piers didn't have that many A levels either – he read out:

> *Troubled Lola is holed up at the Eaton Square mansion of her best friend, Devon, Marchioness of Claverford. Former It-girl Devon was present at the infamous hen night where these pics were snapped – and was apparently very appreciative of the bootylicious physique of Cris, the stripper who entertained the girls by letting them eat sushi off his naked body. And that was only the start of the evening! Turn to Page 11 for Cris's tell-all story and saucy pics! EXCLUSIVE to* The Herald!

'Oh *shit*,' Devon gasped.

'Exactly! The crumblies are going to hit the roof! I wouldn't be surprised if this gave the old man a coronary!'

From her awkward angle hanging over the banisters, Lola couldn't make out Devon's expression, but she was sure Dev had suddenly perked up at the thought of Piers's father, the duke, having a coronary, and Piers becoming the Duke of Claverford in his stead. Which would make Devon the Duchess.

'She has to go, Dev!' Piers was insisting. 'I know she's a friend of yours, fair enough, loyalty and all that, but it's gone too far now. God knows what the other papers are saying. We have our reputation to maintain!'

Lola seethed at the lofty tone Piers was taking. Everyone knew he was a horribly lecherous drunk – no woman, not even a friend of

Devon's, was safe after Piers's second bottle. He'd even cornered his sister Venetia once against the downstairs bar, too smashed on claret to realise who she was. She'd had to spray him with a soda siphon to get him to calm down.

Still, if Piers was taking this line, she had lost her cosy berth here. Dully, absorbing one shock after another, Lola went back into what was now no longer her bedroom, and dialled George, her father's old lawyer.

Just as she was finishing the call, Devon tapped on the door, then stuck her head round it, pulling an apologetic face.

'Come in,' Lola said, snapping her phone shut.

'Lo, I'm so sorry, but—' Devon started.

'It's OK,' Lola sighed. 'I heard him already.'

'His parents are such stuffy old things . . .' Devon said helplessly. 'They're bound to get wind of this, and if they hear you're still staying in the house, they really will hit the roof . . .'

She tossed back her silky blonde curtain of hair, sitting down on the bed next to Lola and taking her hand.

'We'll ring round and see if we can find you somewhere else to go,' she offered.

Lola grimaced.

'No one's going to take me in, Dev, not after this,' she said. 'The paps'll follow me wherever I go, and no one wants this kind of publicity.'

She reached for the newspaper Devon was holding. The cover photo was a grainy, blurred snap of her, leaning over a black surface on which a series of white lines could clearly be distinguished, angling the straw she was holding so she could hoover up one of the lines of coke. From the background, it had been taken in the Japanese restaurant: she could make out some details of the painted screen behind her.

'It must have been the stripper who took it,' Devon said, too quickly.

'It wasn't the stripper.' Lola pointed out where, just visible at one corner of the photo, the main table could be seen. Cris was still lying there: if she squinted, she could just make out some pieces of sashimi that remained on his leg.

'One of the waiters, then.'

'Oh, come on, Dev!'

Impatiently, Lola dropped the paper on the bed. Devon immediately snatched it up to stop the cheap ink staining the Porthault sheets.

'We both know it was one of us!' Lola said. 'No way a waiter managed to bring out a camera, let alone one with a flash, without any of us noticing! I don't care how blasted we were, one of us would have spotted that!'

Devon hung her pretty head, hair tumbling forward, a silent acknowledgement that Lola was right.

'One of the girls sold camera-phone photos and their story to the *Herald*,' Lola continued bitterly. 'I bet they made a ton of money off dragging me down.'

'Oh, Lo, you mustn't say that—' Devon mumbled.

'Why would anyone *do* this to me?' Lola said, jumping up and striding to the window. Opening the curtains a crack, she peered down at the waiting paparazzi outside, drinking coffee from take-away containers, talking on their mobiles, waiting for Lola to come out.

'Jealousy,' Devon said simply.

'Really?' Lola let the curtain fall and turned back towards Devon, who was pulling a pack of cigarettes out of the pocket of her slim-legged jeans.

'God yes!' Devon lit up and waved away the smoke. 'Lola, you're getting married to the guy everyone was after! Or you *were*, who knows now . . . And your father has more money than God! Everyone wanted your life! Well, everyone but me,' she added conscientiously, taking another drag. 'Because I have the title. But let's face it, Jean-Marc's a lot hotter than Piers. I mean, you can't have it all.'

'So you think—'

'Of course! Someone was out to get you! To be fair, they probably sold the pics before all the scandal broke. Otherwise, that would be *too* awful.' The hand that was holding the cigarette sagged dangerously close to the expensive sheets.

'I tell you, Dev, I don't know anything any more,' Lola said bitterly. 'I thought I was getting married to the catch of the century. It turns out he's a drug-addicted tranny-lover. I thought my friends were 100 per cent reliable, and it turns out one of them's sold me out to the tabloids. I thought I'd never have to worry about money, and look at me now!'

Devon's blue eyes went saucer-wide. 'I thought your New York lawyer was sorting that out,' she breathed, reaching for the ashtray on the bedside table.

Lola heaved a deep sigh.

'I just spoke to him,' she said, collapsing on the bed. 'He says we can challenge the power of attorney, and the fact that Carin's controlling my trust fund. But it could take ages, and in the meantime, all I have is what's in my bank accounts.'

'How much is that?' Devon asked.

'About fifteen grand in the UK one.'

'God.' Devon pulled a face. 'That won't go far especially with lawyers' fees to pay, and getting to the states – let alone staying there in a decent hotel . . .'

'I *know*! And the US bank account isn't much better. I barely use them. I mostly just live on the credit cards.'

Devon stubbed out the cigarette and slumped back on the pillows.

'I'm so sorry about kicking you out,' she said helplessly. 'But you know what Piers is like when he gets an idea in his head.'

She lit up another cigarette.

'You know,' Devon said, inhaling, 'what you were saying about sex . . . I feel like that with Piers. I don't mind just lying there, but when he wants me to *do* stuff to him – you know – ugh, I really could live without it. I wish he'd go and get that somewhere else, I really do. I keep telling him it's fine if he wants to.' She glanced at Lola as she puffed on her Silk Cut. 'I *have* enjoyed sex before. I'm not completely like you. But with Piers—' She drew the corners of her mouth down sharply. 'So I do understand. You can't have everything, right?'

Lola nodded. 'Though I *did* with Jean-Marc,' she said sadly. 'It was perfect. Even if we both got totalled and started messing around because we were off our heads, and it didn't work out, we'd just giggle and giggle and fall asleep. I mean, sex just never *mattered* that way.'

Just then, Lola's phone, sitting on the dressing table, started to buzz. She dashed to see who was calling, and when she saw the number in the display window, she ripped the phone open eagerly.

'Hi!' she said. 'Yes, it's me . . . Oh, thank you! That's great! I'll be there in twenty minutes . . . Thank you so much!'

She snapped the phone closed and turned to Devon, face shining with excitement.

'Jean-Marc's conscious and can have visitors – and his horrible brother won't be in till lunchtime, apparently! That nurse – Deirdre – rang me to let me know.'

'The nurse rang you?' Devon said, raising her eyebrows. 'How did she get your number?'

Lola smiled.

'I wrote it down and gave her twenty quid when you lot were all fussing round the lifts,' she said. 'I asked her to call me when it was safe to visit.'

'Gosh, Lola,' Devon said, gazing at her admiringly. 'I never knew you were so . . . *enterprising.*'

'Me neither!' Lola pulled open the wardrobe door and grabbed the trenchcoat, plus a scarf Devon had lent her which she could use to cover her head. 'Now,' she said, 'how are we going to smuggle me out of here so the paps don't follow me? Can I climb over that garden wall Piers was mentioning?'

Deirdre had instructed her to go round the back of the hospital, to the staff entrance. She was waiting there, pink-faced with excitement and she hurried Lola through a door and into a lift at the back of the building.

'This is so exciting!' the nurse gushed. 'It's like being in a film or something, smuggling you in. I *know* Jean-Marc is *dying* to see you, he keeps asking after you, and it's so romantic, isn't it! Bringing you two together in secret—'

Lola smiled and agreed, trying to give Deirdre the thrill she wanted, but honestly, she didn't know *what* she was feeling. She was worried about Jean-Marc, of course, hoping that he was recovering OK, but she was also furious with him at the scandal he'd dragged her into. Still, she needed money from him, which slightly weakened her righteous anger – God, she was a seething mass of emotions. Deirdre bustled her down some corridors, tapped on a door and cautiously put her head around it, to make sure that Niels van der Veer hadn't suddenly materialised.

The coast was clear. Beaming, she indicated for Lola to go in.

And as soon as Lola saw Jean-Marc, looking pale and wan and pathetically frail in his hospital gown, both arms hooked up to IV drips, all her anger and fear drained away instantly. All she could think of was how much she loved him, and how she never, ever wanted to see him in this condition again.

'Hello, darling,' he said, managing a smile for her.

'Jean-Marc!' Lola breathed in horror. 'Are you – are you OK?'

Deirdre had told her he was out of danger, but his skin was so grey, his blue eyes so dull. His golden hair seemed faded, limp. He was still handsome – with his bone structure, he could never fail to be handsome – but he was a shadow of the Jean-Marc Lola had seen on her hen night, so vital and lively that all the girls had been excited by his presence. It was more that he seemed to have been drained of some vital force, some essential fluid that he needed not just for survival, but to keep his spirits alive.

'I'm fine,' he interrupted. 'That is, I'm alive. They've probably changed all my blood by now!' He hacked a little laugh. 'So you'd think I wouldn't be addicted to anything any more, wouldn't you? But it doesn't work that way, apparently. They'd need to give me a brain transfusion.'

Lola pulled up the chair and sat down. She hadn't been able to see anything but Jean-Marc when she came in, but now she realised that the side tables were crowded with bouquets of flowers, huge, expensive ones, each showier than the next.

'I didn't bring you anything,' she said hopelessly. 'I'm so sorry . . .'

'Oh, don't be ridiculous!' His smile this time was a little more human. 'You came! You got a nurse to smuggle you in! Darling, that's more than enough!'

His fingers twitched as his hand tried to reach for hers. Swiftly, Lola covered his with her own.

'What *happened?*' she asked, curling her fingers around his as much as she could without imperiling the catheter in the top of his hand.

'Oh, God, Lola!' He heaved a deep sigh. 'I just wanted to make everyone happy, believe it not. And look how it's all ended up.'

Lola bit off a question. She sat there, holding his hand, sensing that he needed to keep talking without interruption from her.

'I treated you so badly,' Jean-Marc was saying, his fingers trembling under hers. 'I didn't tell you about Patricia and her . . . friends . . . because I knew you'd leave me if I did. And I didn't tell you about the drugs, because I knew you'd say I was crazy for trying all the bad stuff.' He shivered. 'Even Patricia told me I was going too far. But the closer it got to the wedding, the worse I got. And I *wanted* to marry you, darling! We were going to be so happy! I still want to marry you, have a couple of lovely little golden children, like we talked about. But I know I've ruined everything.'

He looked as if he were on the verge of tears: his voice was trembling, his eyes moist.

And Lola, squeezing his hand as best she could, realised that for some inexplicable reason, she hadn't, in these past two days, truly wondered whether she and Jean-Marc would get married after all, whether their engagement could be salvaged. And, as she explored her feelings now, she realised too that she didn't actually mind that much. She had loved the idea of marriage: the ceremony, the publicity, the security, the fiancé with whom she'd never exchanged a cross word, let alone fought, because somehow, nothing had ever been important enough to fight about.

Now it was all over. The wedding planner had left her several increasingly desperate messages, but Lola hadn't rung back: she hadn't had the faintest idea what to say. As soon as she left here, she would: she'd tell the planner to bill Jean-Marc, who would certainly pay for everything and throw in extra for her trouble, being generous to a fault.

And that would be that.

It was odd how free she suddenly felt.

'Can you even tell me that you love my brother?' that obnoxious, bullying Niels had demanded of her yesterday. And she hadn't been able to say 'Yes' – not in the way Niels had meant. Lola, who had no siblings, and had never wanted any – it was perfect, being the only apple of her father's eye – knew that she loved Jean-Marc like the brother she never had. He was a kind of twin, golden like her, beautiful like her, always wanting to cuddle, to stroke each other's hair, to tell each other how lovely they were, curled up in a nest of luxury.

No wonder she had never really wanted to have sex with him. Nor he with her.

'I don't mind about not getting married,' she said. 'Honestly, I don't.'

'Really?' Jean-Marc looked amazed. 'I thought you'd be devastated! I mean, *all* women want to get married!'

'Not if it's making you do drugs!' Lola exclaimed. She frowned. '*Why* did it make you want to do drugs? I thought we were so happy!'

'I did too . . . Oh, Lola, I did too. I thought I'd found the perfect woman.' He smiled painfully at her. 'You're so pretty and sweet and we get on so well. I love you *so* much, darling.'

'I love you too,' she said, feeling tears welling up in her eyes. With the hand not holding Jean-Marc's, she scrabbled in her coat pocket for a tissue.

'They're sending me off to rehab, Lola,' Jean-Marc said.

Lola nodded: she'd expected this. Tons of people she knew went to rehab, for all sorts of things. It was very fashionable nowadays.

'The Priory?' she asked hopefully, naming a famous one near London.

Jean-Marc shook his head.

'Niels says I have to go to Desert Springs, in Arizona. He's being so strict about this, Lola, you cannot believe.'

'But that's so far away!'

'I know! He wants me to be completely isolated. Ugh, I'm dreading it. I mean, London's full of bad influences, but where isn't?'

'Tell me about Patricia,' Lola said, looking him firmly in the eyes.

He closed his own. 'I hate to talk about her,' he said faintly. 'I know you deserve an answer, but I can't bear to talk about her. It's all so complicated. I hated her for what she did to me – I felt so degraded – but I kept on going back. I couldn't stop. She knew exactly what . . .' He shivered. 'Please don't make me talk about it. It's over. I'll never see her again.'

But his voice wavered on the last two sentences. With horror, Lola realised that Niels van der Veer was right, much as she hated to admit it. Jean-Marc was hooked on Patricia, and the drugs she provided. It would take more than an overdose and a near-death crisis to make Jean-Marc give her up. He needed to be sent far away for a long time.

'Jean-Marc,' she started, feeling that it would be OK now to broach the subject of money, 'I need to ask you something – a favour—'

'Anything!' he interrupted, his fingers tightening on hers. 'Anything! After what I've put you through, you only have to ask.'

'All this awful stuff has been happening to me, you won't *believe* it,' she began. 'Carin's cut off my trust fund and I need to get to New York, because—'

'She's *cut off your trust fund*?' Jean-Marc boggled at her. 'How can she do that?'

'Oh, it's all so awful, Jean-Marc!' The relief of having his sympathy and friendship was so huge Lola felt she might be about to burst into tears again. 'Apparently Daddy's—'

'*What the fuck is going on here?*' demanded a harsh voice from the doorway.

Horrified, Lola and Jean-Marc turned their heads towards the sound, and jumped like a pair of naughty children, cowering under the fury of Niels's stare. She was extra-glad, suddenly, that she'd never had a big brother. It would be *awful* to have someone like Niels, older than you, bigger than you, bossing you around like this all the time, always convinced that he knew best.

'Niels, Lola came to visit me!' Jean-Marc protested. 'I wanted her to come! She's my fiancée!'

'Not any more she isn't,' Niels said succinctly.

He stepped into the room, and Lola found herself short of breath, as if Niels's presence were sucking up all the oxygen. She remembered a nature documentary she'd seen once, flipping channels late-night, coked up, unable to sleep. There'd been a rabbit on it, trapped by a snake. The soft drone of the presenter's voice had explained how the rabbit was dazed by the raw power of the snake's eyes, unable to see its mouth opening, its jaw detaching, about to swallow the rabbit whole . . .

She'd switched channel at that point, unable to watch the poor bunny being eaten. Even then, she'd wondered why it didn't hop away, run for its life. But now she understood: it had been paralysed by fear, just as she was now under Niels van der Veer's piercing grey eyes.

'She was telling me something really important!' Jean-Marc continued. 'You're interrupting a private conversation!'

Behind Niels were two white-coated men, big and brawny, and in the background Lola could see Deirdre in her bright blue uniform, hovering nervously.

'How the hell did you get in here?' Niels demanded, standing over Lola and folding his arms.

'I sneaked in,' she said defiantly, raising her small round chin and staring back at him, doing her absolute best not to be intimidated. 'I wanted to see how Jean-Marc was doing. I *do* love him!' For some reason, it was very important that Niels be aware of this.

'And I love her!' Jean-Marc said.

They sounded like two teenagers, Lola thought, silly and puny against the might of a grown-up. And Niels must have thought it too, because he unfolded his arms (again, Lola couldn't help noticing the size of them under the superb tailoring) and clapped his hands slowly, one, two, three times, in mocking applause of their pathetic little declaration.

'Great,' he said sarcastically. 'Fantastic. Really, you two should both go on the stage. Now, if you've quite finished the amateur dramatics, I'll get on with my business here.'

He nodded at the two men, who came over to Jean-Marc's bedside. One started checking Jean-Marc's various drips; the other took his pulse, watching a monitor by the bed as he did so.

'What's going on?' Lola asked, hearing panic in her voice.

'We're taking your *fiancé* away, Princess,' Niels said, loading the word 'fiancé' with irony. 'You'll have to find someone else to marry.' He looked at her, a head-to-toe glance that acknowledged her beauty but was simultaneously insulting, like a man sizing up a prostitute in a brothel. 'You shouldn't have much trouble with that. Though it might be hard finding one as rich as Jean-Marc.'

Lola started to exclaim furiously that she had plenty of money of her own, that she didn't need Jean-Marc's, but she couldn't: her tongue was tied by her desperate financial situation. She stared helplessly, furiously, at him, as the male nurses began to unhook Jean-Marc from the monitor.

'What's happening, Niels?' Jean-Marc asked, looking frightened.

Niels switched his gaze from Lola to his brother, and Lola sagged back in her chair, feeling as if she had been released from a tractor beam. Niels's voice, when he addressed his brother, was completely different. The harshness was gone. This was as gentle, Lola sensed, as Niels van der Veer knew how to be.

'You're going to Desert Springs, Jean,' Niels said, and his expression softened as he looked at his brother lying fragile and grey-faced in the hospital bed.

'Now?' Jean-Marc looked at the nurses, busy checking that the IV drips would slide along the floor easily.

'Right now. This moment. I've had the jet fully equipped for medical transport. And the sooner we get you into a healthier atmosphere, with no bad influences around you' – he sneered at Lola – 'the better you'll be.'

'Lola isn't a bad influence, Niels! You've got this all wrong!' Jean-Marc pleaded. 'And I need to help her now, I've dragged her through the mud with this awful scandal—'

'Everyone you did drugs with is a bad influence, Jean,' Niels said coldly. 'Everyone you drank with. And I think the entire population of Great Britain knows, as of this morning, that your charming ex-fiancée isn't exactly a drug-free zone.'

Jean-Marc turned his head to Lola.

'What does he mean?' he said.

Lola hung her head. 'Someone sold pictures of me at the hen night to the tabloids,' she said.

'Oh, *Lola!* Darling, how terrible!'

Lola nodded, unable to speak. She felt covered with shame, humiliated in front of Niels van der Veer. No wonder he was looking at her as if she were dog mess on his beautiful Italian shoes.

'You're upsetting my brother,' Niels said icily. 'Up.'

'What?' Lola stared at him.

'Up! Get up! Leave this room now! You're making Jean-Marc worse!'

Lola's brown eyes flashed with anger.

'How dare you!' she said. 'Jean-Marc's upset because you're yelling at me!'

But she wasn't expecting the consequences. In two swift strides, Niels van der Veer was looming over her. Before she had time to realise what he was going to do, he reached down, grasped her upper arms and hauled her out of the chair. Her hand slipped out of Jean-Marc's grasp. She was pulled upright, shocked into absolute capitulation by his strong hands digging into her, the scent of his aftershave, the warmth of his grip. She found herself unable to do anything to resist him as he picked her off her feet and carried her bodily to the doorway.

Behind them, she heard Jean-Marc protesting, but her face was so close to Niels's neck everything else was drowned out by the rasping sound of his breath. When he put her down in the corridor she staggered slightly, tipping on the same high-heeled boots she'd been wearing before, the ones that were a little too big for her.

Niels was looking down at her, and it was an act of tremendous bravery for her to raise her head and meet his gaze. When she did, it was a physical shock. He looked like the snake she had pictured before, about to eat her up, consume her whole. It was too much. He was too close. She tried to pull away from his hard grip, and now she did struggle against him, because for some reason he didn't let her go immediately.

When he did, she reached up to rub where he had held her: the tops of her arms felt scorched, as if he had burned through the fabric of her coat.

'I'll have bruises,' she said furiously.

She was close enough to see that his pupils dilated. With what emotion, she couldn't tell. He opened his mouth, and she waited, still staring at him defiantly, to see what he would say. It seemed to take forever.

'Stay away from my brother,' he finally snapped.

And then he turned on his heel and strode back into Jean-Marc's room, slamming the door behind him.

Lola sagged back against the wall; her heart was racing. She hated having been torn away from Jean-Marc like that: she had wanted more time with him.

And, horrible though it sounded, she was also desperate for money. It had been so close – Jean-Marc would have given her anything she needed – and now it had been snatched away. She made some frantic financial calculations to work out how far the money in her bank accounts would go. She needed to get to New York, give George some money on account, maybe pay for a hotel . . .

The door of Jean-Marc's room was flung open. Niels van der Veer stood there, sneering at her.

'Here,' he said, folding something up and throwing it at her. It fluttered to the floor at her feet. 'My brother wouldn't calm down till I gave you this.'

Lola glanced down. It was unmistakeably a cheque. Still, she was damned if she'd stoop down and pick it up in front of Niels van der Veer, like a beggar picking up coins.

'I'll pay back every penny,' she said, meeting his eyes.

He shook his head.

'Consider it a gift. With one condition. Stay away from my brother.'

And he stepped back and closed the door.

Lola wished with all her heart that she could walk away and leave the cheque where it lay. But she couldn't. She needed everything she could get her hands on to reach her father and hire lawyers to fight her stepmother.

So, hating that she had to pick the cheque up from the floor where Niels van der Veer had thrown it, she bent down and did exactly that. She couldn't help unfolding it immediately and looking to see how much it was.

Twenty thousand pounds.

Lola had very little idea of the value of money; her father had kept her so sheltered and cosseted that she had never had to work, never had to pay a bill directly, never had to work out whether she could afford anything, because she always could.

But, added to what was in her bank account, this *had* to be enough. Enough to get her to New York, to find somewhere to stay, to pay for a retainer to challenge Carin's power of attorney and her control of Lola's trust fund.

Enough to get her to see her father, and to find out what had really happened to him.

Lola folded up the cheque again and slipped it into her pocket. And, walking now as if Devon's Gina boots were made for her, with not a single stumble, she stalked down the hospital corridor, heading for the exit.

Chapter 6

'Evie? Evie, wake up. It's morning. Time to get up.'

Defiantly, Evie squeezed her eyes shut, refusing to respond, as Lawrence shook her gently.

'Evie, I've left you alone like you wanted,' Lawrence said softly. 'But it's been three days now, and you haven't had a bite to eat in all that time. You have to get up.'

No I don't, Evie muttered in her head. *I don't have to do anything any more*.

'You need to eat something, Evie. I made you soup.'

She could smell it now that he'd mentioned it. Cooked vegetables, something a bit cabbagey. It turned her stomach.

'Come on, Evie,' Lawrence insisted, as gently as ever. 'I've respected your need to be left alone, but it's time to get up now. Autumn and I have to go out to run a yoga workshop. I want to see you up and on your feet before I go. The world's waiting.'

No it isn't, Evie told herself. *He can't make you do anything you don't want to do. Benny put you up in a fabulous penthouse and gave you credit cards and fed you sushi from Blue Ribbon and bought you anything you wanted, so you had to do stuff for Benny. But Lawrence lives in a shithole and he's trying to feed you cabbage. You don't have to do a damn thing he says.*

'OK,' Lawrence said, removing his hand. He had slept beside her in the huge loft bed these last nights – three nights, had it really been that long? – and at first had made an attempt to spoon her. She had shrugged him off. And, Lawrence being Lawrence, he had accepted that. So he had slept here too, but without touching her.

Odd: Lawrence had been her lover for six months now, but they'd never slept together. And now they had, but without even touching. Everything in her life was upside down and wrong way round.

Lawrence leaned over and dropped a light, delicate kiss on the back of her head.

'Eww.' His voice was full of laughter now. 'You might want to consider washing some time this year, by the way. You're beginning to stink out my bed.'

Evie rolled over, full of indignation. She was so fastidious about her personal hygiene, so concerned to be sweet-smelling, depilated, smooth to the touch, that this was almost the worst thing Lawrence could have said.

'I had a shower before I – before she—' Evie began.

It flooded back to her now in one go: her lovely shower, the sparkling starry lights on its ceiling, the honey scent of the Diptyque shower gel. And then, that long slow walk through Tribeca, dragging her cases and her pole, sweating heavily under the sunshine and the weight of the three coats . . .

'Oh God,' she said reluctantly. 'I must *reek*.'

'I wouldn't say *reek*, exactly.' Lawrence pretended to consider this, his eyes smiling. 'I'd give you a few more days before you actually start to reek. Right now, I'd say you were just smelly.'

Evie ducked her head to smell her armpit.

'OK, I need a shower,' she admitted.

'I'll go and turn on the water,' Lawrence said.

I guess I'm lucky this place has hot water plumbed in at all, Evie thought sourly.

Lawrence was back almost immediately, coming up the treads of the ladder to the loft bed so lightly that he hardly seemed to be putting any weight on them.

'The water heater's on,' he said, 'and I've told Autumn you're having a shower.'

'Is it OK for me to be here?' Evie asked bluntly, spurred into it by the mention of Autumn's name. 'She gave me a hard time about my stuff.'

Evie wriggled to the edge of the bed platform and peered over it. Her suitcases were nowhere in sight, but her clothes had been taken out and folded on the shelves, her coats hung neatly on the rail. On a small table – or rather, a stack of bricks topped with a piece of board – were arrayed all her creams, lotions and cosmetic bags. Her heart lifted. Suddenly she felt more buoyant. It was ridiculous how far she'd sunk – to be grateful that she had managed to keep the measly possessions she'd managed to claw from the bitch's clutches.

'Of course you can stay! It's an emergency,' Lawrence said. 'Normally, we do have a cruelty-free rule here, but you weren't to know that. I explained that to Autumn.'

'I bet she took that really well,' Evie said with great satisfaction. The thought of Autumn's discomfiture was so pleasing that it gave her the energy to sit up.

'The fur really is too much, though, Evie,' Lawrence said, fixing her with a pure, serious gaze, his eyes wide and limpid. 'We do need to get rid of that when you're feeling better. It's terrible karma.'

'Oh, don't worry about that. I'll sell it as soon as I can,' Evie said sadly.

Lawrence looked troubled.

'I think you should just hand it into PETA,' he said. 'They have a fur collection amnesty.'

Evie snorted with laughter.

'You're kidding, right? I'm totally broke, Lawrence. I need every cent I can get my hands on.'

She swung her legs out from the covers, over the edge of the platform, and started to climb down the ladder. But she was appalled to find her legs practically giving way under her. Lawrence grabbed onto her, steadying her.

'Easy, tiger,' he said. 'You've starved yourself for days now, and it wasn't like you had much weight to lose. I'll go first and help you down.'

Evie was too shocked at her feebleness even to protest. Lawrence helped her down the ladder and then swung her up and into his arms, carrying her effortlessly into the bathroom.

Evie had been hoping that it wasn't as bad as she remembered from her brief forays into it, when the pressure of her bladder had got so insistent that it had driven her to the toilet. But, if anything, the bathroom was worse in daylight. If the cheap industrial tiles had once been white, they'd lost that freshness decades ago. Now they looked like English people's teeth: yellowing, chipped, broken in places. Any grouting left was so mouldy and green that it looked like moss.

The toilet had no lid, and the seat was from a different model, too large, so you had to position yourself carefully not to leak pee onto the floor. And by the yellow streaks on the concrete below, many people had failed to do that . . . The floor slanted down in the centre towards a drain, which caught the water from the shower head jerry-rigged on the far side of the room. There was no shower stall, no tray, no curtain. The sink was industrial, an old ceramic one bleached and stained by various chemicals, and the only place to put any sort of beauty products was the windowsill, high up on a wall. The window itself was so thickly smeared with pigeon shit that it hardly let in any light at all.

'It's not much at the moment,' Lawrence apologised, lowering Evie to her feet. 'But I'm going to do it up once I've finished the kitchen.'

'Once you've finished the kitchen?' Evie echoed feebly. From the state of it, she hadn't imagined that anyone could have *started* on the kitchen yet.

'Oh yes! You should have seen it when we moved in!' Lawrence said blithely.

Evie closed her eyes in horror.

'I'll turn on the shower for you,' Lawrence said.

He had already brought through her beauty products. She could hear him turning the tap on the ramshackle water heater. Steam began to fill the room, steam and heat. It softened her mood. She opened her eyes and started to peel off her clothes, the stinky T-shirt and sweatpants she'd been sleeping in for three days and nights now.

'Shall I leave you alone?' Lawrence asked.

Naked now, Evie looked at him standing there in his cotton sweater and loose track pants, his hair, drawn back in its ponytail, his clear light eyes regarding her with the sweet, gentle calm that was the very centre of his nature. Most men would have been unable to stand still under a long stare from a very pretty naked woman, but not Lawrence: hands hanging by his sides, his back straight in perfect posture, his feet set just a little apart, he returned her gaze, his full lips quirking up at the sides in a little smile of reassurance. He looked like a yogi, or a martial artist, perfectly poised, perfectly comfortable in his own body.

'No,' Evie said finally. 'Stay with me.'

'Shall I shower with you?' Lawrence asked, careful to take nothing for granted.

She nodded, and stepped under the spray of water, bending to pick up her shampoo. As she soaped her hair, she watched Lawrence undress, pulling the sweater over his head, hiding his face for a moment but revealing his flat stomach, his smooth, almost hairless chest, his lean, muscled shoulders and arms, the erotic shock of light brown hair under each one. He pulled down his tracksuit pants and his boxers in one go (Lawrence only wore loose underwear, believing genitalia shouldn't be confined too tightly), kicking off his yoga slippers as he did so. In one swift, elegant move, it seemed, he was naked, walking towards her.

Evie watched him approach, his bare feet padding on the floor, his cock already rising, looking large and rosy when the rest of him was so pale.

'It's true what they say about thinner men,' she said as he joined her under the water.

'What do they say about thin men?' Lawrence asked. He bent over to pick up the shower gel, and Evie licked her lips at the sight of his ass, small and plump, dusted with golden hairs.

'Their dicks look bigger,' she said naughtily.

For an instant she thought of Benny, so huge – so *obese*, to be honest – that she had to lift layers of fat to even find his dick, and the memory was so unpleasant that she shoved it right back again where it came from, and told it to stay there. There was *one* upside to this whole shitty mess, and that was that she'd never have to play Find The Needle In The Haystack with Benny's dick ever again.

'Oh yeah?' Lawrence squeezed some shower gel onto his palms and started soaping her breasts. 'And do they feel bigger, too?'

'I'll tell you when it's inside me,' Evie said, pushing her hair back with both hands, suddenly wanting Lawrence's cock inside her so badly that she felt she couldn't wait another second for it.

Then she gasped, because Lawrence had gripped her hips and lifted her two feet into the air as easily as if she weighed nothing at all.

'Jesus, you're skin and bone, Evie,' he said, concerned. 'Look at your hipbones! They're poking out!'

Evie rolled her eyes.

'I'll eat afterwards, Lawrence, OK?' she moaned. 'Whatever vegan crap you want to feed me. Just fuck me now.'

Water was pouring down on her head. The room was filling with steam. Lawrence shifted her slightly, she looped her legs around him, and in one movement, he lowered her down on his cock. She moaned again, this time in utter satisfaction, locking her legs tighter around his back, leaning into him, wrapping her arms around his neck.

'At least your being skinny makes this really easy,' Lawrence gasped into her neck as he raised and lowered her, thrusting up into her with each movement, deeper each time, so deep that Evie could think of nothing else but his cock driving inside her. 'You don't weigh anything . . .'

'It *does* feel big,' she gasped back. 'Really, really big . . .'

Lawrence didn't answer. He just kept on fucking her, his skin slippery against hers, the water pouring down on both of them and Lawrence driving up inside her, and it was too much, too much, it was everything. Evie closed her eyes and gave herself over completely to what he was doing, trusting him to pull out in plenty of time, clinging to him, telling herself that the water and the sex would rinse off everything bad that had happened to her, be a new start that would wash her clean.

And as she started to come, she remembered that Autumn was in the apartment, and she started to scream, as loudly as she could, cries of encouragement and pleasure and triumph. Cries which she hoped to hell would rise over the noise of the water, penetrate the bathroom wall, and reach Autumn, making it impossible for her to concentrate on anything but listening to Evie and Lawrence fucking, Evie reaching climax over and over again, cries that would make it abundantly clear to Autumn that Lawrence was Evie's and always would be, for as long as Evie wanted him. That Evie would be staying in Lawrence's room, getting Lawrence off in an extremely wide variety of ways, as long as Evie felt like it, and there wasn't a damn thing Autumn could do about it—

And just then, Lawrence hit her G-spot so perfectly that she came so hard she thought her head would explode, and she let out a scream that Autumn would have to be deaf, or hiding her head under the mattress, not to have heard. Somehow, the thought of Autumn listening, a helpless auditor to Evie and Lawrence's pleasure, made the orgasm even stronger, the sex even more powerful.

Collapsing, boneless, on Lawrence's shoulder, Evie smiled to herself. At least Autumn was good for *something*.

Chapter 7

'Oh God, look at how much *stuff* I have!' Lola wailed plaintively. 'What am I going to *do* with it?'

She looked at her watch, an elegant slip of a thing by Breguet, platinum-strapped and diamond-faced.

'I've only got a couple of hours left,' she said hopelessly.

'Oh, they can't just kick you out like that!' exclaimed Madison, who had only arrived at Lola's mews house twenty minutes ago.

'Those men in the living-room are the lawyers for her step-mother,' Devon told Madison. 'They've given Lo till four to get her things out.'

'*Jesus*,' Madison breathed. Tall, with the wide shoulders of a swimmer, Madison always looked as though she could take on anyone or anything: she had the superb physical confidence some Americans possessed, nurtured on high-quality proteins and vita-mins, stronger and brighter than the decadent old-world Europeans with their bad diets and worse teeth.

But even Madison couldn't fight Carin's lawyers. Lola's hopes were all pinned on George Goldman, in New York, but George had said it might be a month at least before any decision was made on the trust-fund issue, and right now Carin controlled the purse strings. If she said Lola had to leave her house, then Lola had to leave.

Lola sank onto the pretty little mulberry velvet loveseat she'd had made for her bedroom window embrasure. She lifted the blind half an inch and peered out through the gap she'd made. As soon as one paparazzo below saw the blind moving, he started snapping, and the rest of them immediately followed suit, calling up to her like a whole group of East End Romeos after a single Juliet.

'Lola, is that you?'

'Lola, give us a last shot from your window, eh, babe?'

'Come on, Lola, let's have a look at you!'

Lola heaved a huge sigh, dropping the blind again.

'To think I used to *get cross* when they didn't want my photo,' she sighed.

'Like when Dev was getting married, and they only ever wanted to snap her,' Georgia agreed. She flicked back her long red hair and shot Devon the saucy, not-wholly-friendly glance of a girl who hasn't yet scored a rich or titled husband, looking at one who has. 'But now that's all changed, hasn't it, Dev? No one wants the boring marrieds. Sexy singles are *so* much more interesting.'

Lola stared hopelessly at the huge pile of suitcases in the middle of the room. It was like a modern art installation.

'Shoes take up so much room!' she said.

'God, *tell* me about it! I haven't got a spare inch of room myself!' Madison laughed, which Lola took to be a tactful way of saying that she couldn't help Lola out by storing any of her cases.

'I'd love to help, Lo, but I can't,' Devon chipped in, widening her baby-blue eyes and tipping her head on one side to demonstrate how sincerely apologetic she was. 'Piers will *kill* me if he finds out I've got any of your stuff in the attics.'

Lola turned to India, but the latter was already shaking her head.

'I'm so sorry, Lola, I really am. I've had Tiggy camped out in the spare room for *months*, and that's the only place I could possibly put all this.'

Damn, Lola thought meanly. She had really been hoping that India would offer. India, a size ten to twelve (*huge*, by the girls' anorexic standards), wouldn't fit into any of Lola's clothes, so she would have been safer leaving them with her than anyone else.

'I mean,' Georgia added with killing accuracy, 'you don't even know how long it'll be before you have somewhere to live, do you? It could be *ages.*'

'*Georgia,*' India said reproachfully.

'Well, it's true,' Georgia said, lighting up a cigarette. 'I'm sorry, but someone had to say it.'

Lola stared at Georgia, who was looking particularly striking today, her crimson lipstick setting off her white skin and red curly hair. Or maybe it was just that Georgia was flourishing in her enjoyment of Lola's misfortune? With a sharp stab of remembered betrayal, Lola wondered whether it was Georgia who had sold that video of her doing coke to the tabloids. *Someone* had, after all, and Georgia did unabashedly enjoy her friends' troubles . . .

'Do you know anyone who's got more space?' Devon asked, curling up on the loveseat next to Lola and lighting up too. She gestured with her cigarette, an idea having just hit her, her blue eyes sparkling. 'Maybe someone in the country!'

Yes, I do, Lola thought angrily. *You. Your in-laws have a stately home the size of Monaco. You could fit my entire house in one of your barns and not even notice it was there.*

But what was the point in saying it? Devon clearly wasn't going to offer the ample storage facilities of Claverford Hall.

'Doesn't your mom live in the country?' Madison asked, wandering over to the full-length mirror and examining her reflection critically.

'My *mother?*' Lola's eyebrows shot up so high they nearly hit her hairline. 'I haven't talked to her in *years!*'

'Well, maybe you should start, sweetie,' Madison said dryly.

Lola reached for one of Devon's cigarettes. She had been trying to cut down, but the mention of her mother immediately made her want to shove the entire pack in her mouth and start inhaling.

'She was really famous, wasn't she?' Georgia drawled. 'Like a supermodel before there were supermodels.'

'She was the Sunsilk girl!' Devon said. 'I've seen pictures – in that blue swimsuit with all that blonde hair down her back. She was *gorgeous*. And *super*-famous!'

'Weirdly, she wasn't interested in any of that,' Lola said. 'My mother's a hippie at heart. All she wanted to do was live in the countryside and have lots of pet goats.'

'Eww,' Devon said, wrinkling her expensively bobbed nose.

'Exactly what my dad thought. They should never have got married. Dad ended up spending more and more time in the States, and eventually he met Carin and she insisted he stay in New York and divorce Mummy.' She grimaced. 'And Carin gets what Carin wants.'

'We noticed,' Madison drawled.

'Daddy didn't want to get divorced,' Lola explained. 'And Mummy didn't want to get divorced either. I could never understand it, because by the end she and Daddy never really saw each other at all. But Carin got her way, and ever since then it's been miserable.' She grimaced again. 'I used to spend so much time with Daddy, but Carin hates me. She just elbowed me out of everything, and Daddy let her. It was horrible.'

'And where's your mother?' India asked.

Lola pulled a face.

'Living in a gigantic house in Whitstable, of all places, with tons of cats and dogs and goats and God knows what,' she said. 'It's like a hippie commune, only Mummy's the only one that lives there, thank God.'

'*Whitstable?* Where *is* that?' Devon asked.

'On the coast,' Georgia said. 'It's hugely trendy now with the alternative fashion types.'

'Mummy likes it because she says it's unspoilt,' Lola added.

'*Ewww!*' Devon said in a horror reflected in Madison and Georgia's faces. The word 'unspoilt' was on a level with 'natural look' or 'full-fat cream' in their vocabulary.

Mentioning her father made tears prick at Lola's eyes. She missed her father so badly. She'd been missing him for years, really, the three years that he had been with Carin. And now he might be gone forever. It was unimaginable.

Her cigarette was burning down. Lola looked around for an ashtray, but it was on her bedside table, hidden behind the huge pile of suitcases. Georgia picked up the one she'd been using, on the mantelpiece, but Lola waved her away, a sudden impulse striking her. Vindictively, she stubbed out her cigarette on the arm of the velvet loveseat, and then threw the butt to the floor.

India gasped.

'What?' Lola said, gritting her teeth. She reached for another of Devon's cigarettes and lit it up. 'It's Carin's house now! Why should I care?'

Georgia, giggling madly, emptied her ashtray on the exquisite silk carpet and ground in the ash with her heel.

'You are such a *psycho*, Georgia,' Devon said with grudging respect.

'Let's trash it all!' Georgia said, giggling even louder.

Lola's eyes widened. She had been completely shocked by her own action: that kind of wannabe-rock-star room-trashing was totally unlike her. Lola might do drugs and drink too many cocktails, but deep down, she was very well brought up and fastidious. She hated to get her hair tangled or her make-up smeared. If she chipped a nail, she had a meltdown. Her clothes were all dry-cleaned after use, hung up in their plastic bags till it was time to wear them again. Her cashmere sweaters were neatly folded and packed with cedar balls to ward off moths. Her shoes were polished and taken to the cobbler by her cleaning lady as soon as their high heels started to show signs of wear.

She didn't even like sex that much, because it was too messy.

So the thought of trashing a house, let alone her *own* house, was contrary to her entire nature.

Or at least, what her nature had been up to now.

'It isn't your place any more, Lola,' Georgia said, sensing that Lola was wavering.

'No, it isn't,' Lola said slowly. 'And it won't ever be again. I mean, even if – *when* – everything gets sorted out with my dad's money, I won't want to come back here, will I?'

'No! You'll buy something bigger and better!' Madison confirmed. 'With more than two bathrooms, for God's sake!'

Lola stood up. Everyone looked at her. She looked at herself, in the mirror over the fireplace. Her big brown eyes were huge and dark, her pretty little jaw set with determination. She looked – well, she looked like the girl who had stood up to Niels van der Veer yesterday, and lived to tell the tale.

'Right,' she said. 'We're going to trash the place. Then I'm going to call some cabs and load everything in and take all my cases to Mummy's, so she can look after them for me. And then I'm going to turn around and go to Heathrow and get on the first plane to New York and find out exactly what's happening with Daddy!'

'Wey-hey!' Georgia crowed, picking up a vase and throwing it to the floor, where it bounced harmlessly off the carpet.

'I'm going to write things in lipstick on the walls!' Devon jumped up excitedly.

'I'm going to cut "I HATE YOU CARIN" into the bathroom mirror with my engagement ring!' Lola capped that.

'Jeez,' Madison drawled. 'You girls are *wild*.'

'This it, Miss?' the cab driver asked, slowing down in front of a pair of stone gateposts, rather overgrown with ivy.

Behind them, two more black cabs, dutifully following in file, slowed down as well. Lola's entourage had drawn stares from every car passing on the motorway and what felt like the entire population of Whitstable: one black London cab down here in the country was unusual enough, but three of them was a once-in-a-lifetime sight. They'd probably be telling their children about it for years to come.

Particularly since the second and third cabs didn't have passengers, being stuffed to the gills with expensive suitcases.

'Yes, this is the one,' Lola said regretfully.

The cabs turned into the drive, climbing up it with much chugging and changing of gears. Suzanne Myers, the Sunsilk girl, had chosen a rambling stone house on the clifftops of Whitstable, overlooking Tankerton Bay. It was all very pretty and scenic, Lola was sure, but it was also totally typical of her mother not to pick a location that was slightly more *normal*. And by 'normal', Lola meant chic.

Beauty was most definitely in the eye of the beholder. Most observers would have considered Whitstable charming, with its narrow cobbled streets, its little painted shop fronts, its complete absence of the ubiquitous chain stores that had taken over almost every other small town centre, turning them into outdoor shopping malls. Whitstable, by contrast, offered oyster bars, local fishmongers, little galleries selling stained glass and ceramics, old-fashioned tea shops.

It was more than Lola could bear. The knowledge that she couldn't walk on those cobbles in her Manolos – and if she did snap a heel here, there wasn't a single shop in town selling something she could bear to put on her feet instead – made her close her eyes as they drove through what she considered no better than a village. How could Mummy, who had been famous for her beauty over at least three continents, bear to be cut off from civilisation like this?

'Lovely spread, isn't it?' said the driver, looking at her in the rear-view mirror.

Lola didn't even dignify this with an answer. Her mother had an absolute fortune from the divorce settlement with her father – he had been so generous her mother's lawyer might as well not have bothered to turn up at all – and she'd chosen to spend it on a glorified donkey sanctuary. Really, it would make Lola furious, if she didn't have more important things to worry about right now. She climbed out of the cab onto the gravel drive.

'Shall we start unloading the cases, miss?' called the driver of the second cab.

'Hold on,' Lola said, walking towards the house. 'I want to get the front door open and then you can take them straight in – *aaaah!*'

The scream had been provoked by the appearance of a very large white bird, waddling round the corner of the house on its big orange feet. Planting them on the drive, it squawked threateningly at Lola.

'Oh my *God!*' she exclaimed. 'Is that a *swan?*'

'I think it's a goose, miss,' the second driver said.

Suzanne lived in a traditional country style. The front door was practically never used: the main access to the house was the kitchen door, round the back of the property, accessed by a wide stone path.

But right now the goose was standing on the path. And there was no other way round the house.

'Shoo!' Lola said hopefully. She advanced a pace closer to the goose, waving at it impatiently.

But the goose didn't shoo. Instead, it picked up its rubbery feet and took a couple of steps towards Lola. And it opened its bright orange beak and made the same awful squawking sound, even louder and more threatening now.

'I'd be careful, miss!' yelled the first driver.

'Those things can break a man's arm with their wings!' added the second driver. 'Nasty, they are!'

'Nah, that's swans, you pillock,' called the third driver, not wanting to be left out of the fun. 'Geese can't break your arm.'

'They could bite, though,' the second driver retorted. 'Look at the beak on that!'

'*Shoo!*'

Lola windmilled her arms at the goose, trying to scare it off. It paused for a moment, and she thought she'd won. Then it lifted its wings menacingly, hunched its back, and went into a tirade of squealing and hooting as another goose appeared from round the side of the house. And this one was hissing.

Lola stared at them in horror. The first goose had now started hissing too, and that was even worse than the squawks. Their nasty beady eyes were fixed on her, and what she could read in them chilled her blood.

For a moment, there was a standoff. And then the geese started advancing on Lola, both hissing worse than the snake in *The Jungle Book*, and Lola let out a terrified scream and started to run.

'Come on, miss!' yelled the first cab driver, reaching out his arm to unlatch the door for her.

At least Lola hadn't worn stilettos to visit her mother. She was in her version of casual wear, which meant that her stack-heeled boots were only two inches high, and her jeans weren't so tight they cut off circulation to her crotch every time she sat down. She managed a sort of sprint, her boots crunching on the gravel, the geese hissing like demons after her. As she fell into the open cab and the driver heroically slammed the door behind her, the lead goose went for the driver's arm. It just missed, but its fury was such that it slammed its beak against the paintwork of the taxi.

'Little *bastards!*' the driver said in amazement. 'Little fucking *bastards!*'

Then he had to jam his finger on the button to close his window, as the goose was trying to stick its beak into the cab, squawking furiously.

'Fucker!' he yelled. 'You little fucker!'

Scrabbling up to the seat, Lola looked behind her and saw that the second cab driver was doubled up with laughter, his face bright pink. And the third cab driver – oh *God*, the third cab driver, damn him, was holding out his mobile phone, recording the entire thing. Lola muttered a heartfelt 'Fuck!' under her breath.

Lola practically never swore. But she knew exactly what was happening: the driver had recognised her and was going to sell the mobile phone clip to the tabloids. Her inglorious scramble across the gravel was going to be front-page news tomorrow, posted on all the internet gossip sites. She was so angry she wanted to get out and punch that bloody goose right in its mouth. *Beak*.

'Honk your horn, OK?' she instructed the driver. 'My mother never answers her bloody phone, I've been trying all the way here.'

The driver leaned on the horn. The loud parp-parp drove the geese into a frenzy of hissing. Somewhere in the distance, dogs started barking. Lola thought she could hear the donkeys, in a field below the house, braying in response. And into the middle of all this noise, from the walled orchard on the opposite side of the house, strode Lola's mother Suzanne, in faded jeans, Wellington boots and an ancient T-shirt, her famous blonde hair now streaked with grey and pulled back from her face in a frayed hairband, her equally famous face lined and worn by years of working outside in the wind and the sun.

But her legs were as long as ever, her waist as slim, her breasts as high and small as they had been in the glory days of her early twenties, when every man and quite a few women all over the world had looked at the gigantic billboards of her in a royal-blue swimsuit, holding a bottle of Sunsilk shampoo, her golden hair tumbling down her back, and fallen in lust with her on the spot. And her face was still so beautiful that the cabbie jerked his hand from the horn and said: 'Fucking *hell*, that's your *mum*?' in reverent tones.

'What is this racket?' Suzanne said furiously. She walked up to the first cab. '*Lola*? Is that you? What on *earth* do you think you're doing? The animals aren't going to settle down for *days* now!' She looked over at the geese, who were both waving their wings and hissing like banshees. 'Hamlet and Ophelia are both *very* sensitive!'

Lola watched the three cabs disappear down the steep hill, taking a substantial amount of her money with them. She couldn't believe how much it had cost.

But right now, she had a more immediate problem to sort out: her suitcases, which were piled in a heap in the middle of the drive, looking like the lost luggage for an entire business-class-only airline.

'You can't leave these here!' Suzanne was insisting, her hands on her waist. 'I should never have let you get those cabbies to unload them.'

'Mummy! What was I going to do, turn round and drive round England in a procession of black cabs, looking for someone with a big house and a lot of room?'

'There are such things as storage units, you know, Lola,' her mother protested.

Lola's face went completely blank.

'*Are* there?' she said. 'How do they work?'

Suzanne threw up her hands in desperation.

'We've ruined you!' she cried. 'Your father and I have ruined you!'

'Oh Mummy, not that again—'

'We've spoiled you so much you don't know how to do the slightest thing for yourself!'

'I do!' Lola said crossly. 'I worked out how to get all my stuff packed, and how to bring it here—'

'In *black cabs*! How much did that cost you? Did it never occur to you to rent a van?'

'Eeeww!' Lola was visibly taken aback. 'No! How would I even *do* that?'

'I need a cup of tea,' Suzanne moaned, and turned away, walking round the side of the house.

Lola followed her nervously.

'But what about my cases?' she asked.

'I'll give Neville a ring. He's the gardener, a total godsend. He'll find somewhere to put them,' her mother said over her shoulder.

'Oh, thank you, Mummy! Um, are you sure the geese are—'

'They're safely in their pen, don't worry,' Suzanne said. 'But I don't know what you can have done to upset Hamlet and Ophelia. They're the *gentlest* creatures.'

'Mummy, one of them attacked the cabbie when he was slamming the cab door for me! It tried to take a bite out of his arm!'

'Oh, for goodness' sake, Lola,' Suzanne said, sighing. 'You've always been jealous of my animals. I can't understand why. You know I loved you best.'

They paused for a moment to look over Tankerton Bay, which was laid out below the cliffs, shingle beach stretching away as far as the eye could see. It was an overcast day, and the tide was out, which meant that the grey shingle sloped down to sloppy-brown mudflats, studded with old pieces of shell that would cut your bare feet. The sea, which would have made the scene much prettier, had withdrawn far in the distance, as if wondering whether it could really be bothered to come back in and cover all that dirty mud up again. Round the edge of the shingle beach was a line of brightly painted beach huts, little shacks without running water or electricity, which Lola had heard sold for a relative fortune.

Standing on the cliff, looking down at the bay below, Lola shuddered. Having to spend her summer holidays here would be the worst torture she could possibly imagine. She looked over at Suzanne, whose beautiful face had momentarily been washed clean of annoyance by the sight of her beloved sea view. Lola shrugged. *Well, each to her own*, she reflected. *If everyone wanted to stay in lovely hotels on the most exclusive Thai beaches, they'd get awfully crowded, wouldn't they?*

Suzanne took a deep breath of sea air, and reluctantly turned away from the prospect of Tankerton Bay.

'I'll put the kettle on and ring Neville,' she said, pushing open the kitchen door.

The house was accessed through a mud room, crowded with old Wellington boots, frighteningly sharp-looking racks of gardening paraphernalia, and dirty old raincoats. Lola shuddered again. She wished her mother wouldn't live like this. Even the kitchen, which, with its huge picture windows, could have been very nice if done up with the latest granite worktops and brushed-steel fittings, was resolutely rustic: an old cream Aga, acres of faded wood cupboards, and a huge old oak dining table. For Lola's tastes, it was horribly rustic. There was even a smelly old spaniel curled up in a basket next to the Aga, which whopped its tail on the floor at the sight of Suzanne.

'That dog really pongs, Mummy,' Lola said disapprovingly, pulling out a chair and inspecting it for cats before dusting off the animal hair and gingerly sitting down.

'He's old, Lola. We all get old, and then we die,' her mother said, as if this were somehow news to Lola.

Lola grimaced. Her mother would never change. She eyed the stinky spaniel, which responded by raising its upper lip to show her its teeth and growling faintly. Very friendly.

'So your father's ill?' Suzanne asked, sipping at her tea. 'I don't even quite understand what's going on yet – you were babbling away outside hysterically, and I had to calm poor Hamlet down—'

'Daddy's in a coma,' Lola blurted out. 'And Carin's in charge of everything and she's kicked me out of my house. Apparently it's not mine technically, it's all in trust—'

'Oh my God!' Suzanne's hand shook as she lowered the mug to the table. 'In a *coma*?'

'A diabetic one,' Lola explained, taking off her Gucci sunglasses, which were propped on top of her head, and putting them on the table.

'I *told* him!' Suzanne wailed. 'I *warned* him! He was getting more and more unhealthy! But he just wouldn't stop eating. It was compulsive. I couldn't bear to see him like that.'

'He was getting pretty big,' Lola admitted, fiddling with the arms of the sunglasses.

'Well, why didn't you say something, Lola? He's your father! Couldn't you see his weight was out of control?'

Lola looked blank again. The idea of acting like a responsible adult around her father was completely alien to her.

'I did tease him about it,' she offered. 'You know what he was like, he didn't like me to put on a pound, and sometimes I'd say, "Well, Daddy, *you* try living on edamame beans and sashimi and see how you like it!" He wouldn't have lasted an hour! But he was *Daddy*. I mean, what could I have said to him? Why would he have listened to *me*?'

Lola knew perfectly well what her role in her father's life had been: to look pretty, to be frivolous, to lead a sparkling social life and be photographed in fabulous dresses at fabulous parties, to be a glittering butterfly, demonstrating by her appearance how successful Ben Fitzgerald was. It certainly hadn't been to tell him the truth about his lifestyle.

'I despair, Lola. Really I do,' Suzanne said, sighing. 'That woman was feeding him up like a pig to market, and you didn't say a word. Lola, do you know what a diabetic coma is?'

God, how Lola hated it when people asked her questions like that in a patronising tone of voice, indicating that she was too stupid to know the answer. George, Daddy's old lawyer, had done it too.

'It's a coma!' she said crossly. 'Like—' Her only references were people in comas on TV, so she tailed off at this point.

'He'll be lucky to come out of it at all,' Suzanne informed her. 'And if he does, he may well be brain-damaged. I don't think you've quite realised how serious this could be, Lola. Your father could die.'

'Oh *no*, Mummy.' Lola shook her head so vigorously that her blonde ponytail danced and her yellow diamond earrings sparkled in the pale light trickling through the window. 'I'm sure you're wrong. Anyway, I'm shooting off to New York, and I'm going to go and see Daddy and talk to the doctors and hopefully get my trust fund unblocked and get everything sorted out, *so* . . .' She looked hopefully at her mother. 'I sort of need to borrow some money for all of that.'

Suzanne, who had been reaching for her now-cooling cup of tea, paused, turning to stare at her daughter.

'Lola,' she said, 'I really don't understand this. Why on earth do you need money?'

'Because Carin's cut off my trust fund, Mummy!' Lola's voice raised to something like a wail. Her parents always had this effect on her: she ended up sounding like a small child in their presence. 'I don't have any money! My credit cards don't work – all I've got is what's in my bank accounts, and that's practically nothing! And she's kicked me out of my house! I don't have anywhere to live!'

Lola wasn't surprised that her mother had absolutely no idea of the dramatic events that had recently engulfed her daughter's life. Suzanne had a basic internet connection, but she only used it for email.

Lola knew her mother would much rather she was working as a volunteer for a refugee organisation in some war-ravaged area of the world. Or saving baby crocodiles from extinction. Well, then Suzanne shouldn't have married a multi-millionaire! She should have picked some Green Party worker instead, and brought their daughter up in some crunchy-granola Stoke Newington commune!

Thank God, at least, *that* hadn't happened.

'What about Jean-Marc?' Suzanne asked, her beautiful face baffled.

'He's in rehab in Arizona,' Lola said impatiently.

'Oh my God! Poor Jean-Marc! What happened?'

'He overdosed in the flat of some sordid tranny,' Lola explained. 'He's fine now. I mean, they've pumped him out and now his horrible brother's packed him off to rehab and said I can't see him any more, which means—'

'*Lola*! You must be so upset!'

'Actually, we decided we were better off as friends,' Lola said blithely, 'so that part's all OK—'

'How much is in your bank account?' her mother asked, frowning.

'Barely fifteen grand!' Lola said, throwing her hands wide to show how desperate the situation was. She decided not to mention Niels van der Veer's cheque. That would just make the waters even muddier than they were already.

'That would be a lot of money for most people,' her mother observed.

Lola rolled her eyes.

'I'm not most people, Mummy. And neither are you,' she snapped.

'Oh, *Lola*—' her mother started.

'Mummy! You were the Sunsilk girl! People recognise you on the street thirty years later! You married a multi-millionaire and you live in a ginormous house! And I can barely move without a ton of paparazzi chasing me. We're *not* most people!'

'Well, we should be,' Suzanne said, standing up and walking across the kitchen to the big sink, under the picture window. Leaning on it, she stared outside at the sea view, refusing to look at Lola as she said:

'I'm not going to give you any money, Lola. You're going to have to do this on your own.'

'*What?*'

'Maybe Carin's right. I've always disliked her, but maybe this time she's right. You do need to stand on your own two feet, and perhaps now's as good a time as any. God knows, I told your father not to give you your own credit cards when you were barely fourteen, but he never listened to a word I said about you. You were his little princess, and nothing was ever good enough for you. And it's turned you into an extravagant, spoiled . . .' Suzanne sighed. 'Go and see your father. Find out how he is, and let me know. But I'm not going to throw money at you like he did, Lola.'

Lola was finding it hard to get the words out, because she was gasping at her mother's hypocrisy.

'How dare you!' she said finally. 'You're living in a huge house and you don't have to lift a finger if you don't want to – you haven't worked since you met Daddy—'

'And I regret that.' Suzanne turned round to look at her daughter, bracing her hands behind her on the rim of the sink. The faint English sunlight lit up her hair, turning it into a halo around her head. 'But I'm doing something good now. Saving animals, taking in the ones that no one else can look after. And if you find yourself running short of money, you could always get a job. This could be the making of you, Lola.'

'Oh, for God's sake!' Lola grabbed her bag, threw it over her shoulder and stormed towards the kitchen door. On the fridge were stuck a series of magnets holding notes, cards, scribbled lists on torn pieces of paper. Lola reached out and grabbed one, a card from a local minicab firm. 'I'm calling a car,' she announced. 'I'll wait outside.'

'Lola!' her mother called, her tone suddenly urgent.

Lola spun on her heel eagerly, sensing that her mother was about to add something important – perhaps, seeing how upset Lola was, Suzanne was going to offer her some money after all . . .

'If it doesn't work out in New York,' Suzanne said, 'as far as the money side of things goes – of course you're going to want to see your father and check how he is, but what I mean is, if you can't get any more money from your trust fund—'

'Yes?' Lola prompted impatiently.

'You can always come back here to stay!' Suzanne finished. 'You're my daughter. I'll always make a home for you. You could help me with the animals. They always need someone else to love them.'

Right, Lola thought as she marched back down the garden path. She pulled her phone from her bag and dialled the number from the card, ignoring the gasp of breath and then the sheer incredulity of the dispatcher that one lucky driver was about to make a fortune on a Heathrow run. That was all her mother had to offer? Living in rustic solitude while grooming geese and letting her nails chip and break?

All that goose needs is a good punch in the mouth, she thought furiously. *With a baseball bat.*

Chapter 8

*L*ola had forgotten how much she loved New York: it was as buzzy as a hive of bees lit up with a firework display. London seemed very slow by comparison. Well, so did everywhere, apart from maybe Hong Kong. In New York, everyone was on the make, pushing and shoving for advantage, sharpening their elbows, desperate to be seen at the latest trendy place first, to know the gossip before anyone else, to snatch that coveted job or magazine cover out of someone else's grasp. New York never slept, not because some bodegas were open 24/7 (New York wasn't as much of an open-all-hours city as the myth had it: you just had to visit the Upper West Side at four a.m. to find *that* out) but because someone's brain was always whirring, figuring out a way to gain a toehold in society, work their way up the ladder, be a bold-faced somebody on Page Six of the *New York Post*.

It was Old World versus New World. In London, you knew who you were. In New York, you knew who you wanted to be.

"Miss Fitzgerald! Welcome back!" said the black-clad doorman as Lola stepped out of her limo.

New York boutique hotels: you just couldn't beat them. There was so much competition that if you rested on your laurels, some other bright spark would nip in to steal your A-list customers with an even sexier, trendier, hip venue. And though Lola always stayed here, at 60 Thompson, she expected a great deal for her loyalty. Immediate recognition by every one of the good-looking black-clad doormen with their throat mikes and sexy Secret Service vibe; her favourite luxury suite, with champagne perfectly chilled in a designer ice bucket; a maid on standby to unpack her suitcases and press anything that needed it; and, of course, in every member of the chic, black-wearing, hyper-attractive staff members, the perfect attitude of friendly but appropriate deference to her social status and her unlimited credit.

Oh well, at least she had *one* of those left, Lola thought as the elevator whisked her up to her exquisite suite, all white upholstery and sexy dark polished wood, with a raised mezzanine bedroom with the sweetest little balcony, so romantic. She had never realised how much Virgin first class one-way across the Atlantic actually *cost*. The woman at the Heathrow ticket office did explain that it wouldn't be quite so expensive if you booked it in advance, but Lola had just stared at her blankly. She practically never booked anything in advance if she could help it. That would be stressful, because it would mean you were rushing around on someone else's timetable rather than your own. Lola didn't think she'd ever advance-booked a plane ticket in her life: there was always a seat in first class available when she needed one. And she'd never bothered about the cost before, as her credit-card bills went directly to her father's secretary.

And often she would travel by private plane anyway, which was *so* much nicer. She sighed, remembering the luxury of the Van der Veer jet, on which she and Jean-Marc had often hopped down to St Barts.

Anyway, Lola thought regretfully, she had better try to be a little careful with money: that ticket had eaten a larger-than-expected hole in her £35,000. And 60 Thompson wasn't cheap . . .

She poured herself a glass of champagne, pulled out her phone and hit some buttons. It was nine p.m., which meant that downtown would be jumping. One of the reasons Lola always chose 60 Thompson to stay at was that it was the epicentre of the small area of SoHo and Tribeca otherwise known as Eurotrash Central, where all her set hung out. To the west, its boundary was 6th Avenue and the restaurants Bar Pitti and Da Silvano; then it ran down across Broome Street, where a friend of Lola's lived in an enormous loft and threw parties that were always crammed with supermodels playing pool with rap stars, over Canal to Odeon and the Bubble Lounge on Broadway, where they would slice a champagne bottle open with a sabre if you ordered one expensive enough.

Lola hit lucky with the second call: there was a posse hanging out at Cip's Downtown, aka Eurotrash Headquarters. On the next block over, Cipriani's was so close to 60 Thompson that it practically backed onto it. Fabulous. She'd washed a sleeping pill down with a glass of champagne and crashed out on the lovely flat bed for most of the flight. Right now she was fresh and ready to go – the bubbles were already helping to pick her up – and the maid, bustling away in the bedroom, had mostly unpacked her cases. Lola slipped on a black Hervé Léger that wrapped her slim body like a series of incredibly expensive surgical bandages and a pair of wittily clumpy silver Miu Miu slingbacks, and pinned up her hair. Grabbing a tiny clutch made from baby alligator stomach, she tossed a twenty on the bedroom chest of drawers for the maid, who picked it up gratefully.

Throwing a dyed sable stole round her shoulders – the sweetest thing, it was the palest buttercup-yellow, silky soft, and quite safe to wear in New York, where the anti-fur protesters were much less vehement than in London – Lola tip-tapped out of the suite and into the lift once again. As the doorman threw open the big glass entrance door for her, she briefly considered taking one of the waiting limos, and then rejected the thought with a rush of virtue. Cipriani Downtown *was* literally round the corner, after all. She would economise by not being driven. And walking in these shoes wasn't absolutely *impossible* . . .

'Lola! *Chérie!*' someone called as soon as she entered Cipriani's.

'Ciao, Lola!'

'Hey, sweetie!'

The large table, their favourite, was packed with downtown society: international bankers, heirs to hotel empires, *Vogue* stylists cruising for a rich husband, and the inevitable gossip columnist.

'Welcome back to Eurotrash Central!' said Thom, a bond trader from Strasbourg, pulling her out a chair.

Everyone laughed: the joke was on the Americans who, disliking the confidence of the already-rich Europeans who dropped into New York for a few years to make even more money, before heading back to their home countries to crack superior jokes about the lack of sophistication of the American race, had dubbed this circle 'Eurotrash'. The men were unashamed of looking what Americans would consider homosexual: they sported tight cashmere sweaters, designer stubble, lavish watches and plenty of aftershave, all of which, blended with their sexual confidence, made American straight men extremely insecure and hostile.

The table was laden with plates: carpaccio with rocket and truffle shavings, artichoke salad, grilled tiger prawn risotto. Light food, which barely anyone had touched.

'Are we all still drinkorexics?' Lola asked, sitting down and taking the glass of champagne proffered by Thom who, off-duty, was in his usual black polo neck and wire-framed glasses. He wore suits and contact lenses to work, but preferred, away from his desk, to look like a fashionably minimalist architect.

'Just sticking with what works,' smiled Mandana, an Iranian-English girl who preferred to be described as Persian, and had superb dark flashing eyes and a magnificently hawkish profile.

'I'm actually hungry,' Lola admitted shamefacedly, forking up a piece of rich scarlet carpaccio and allowing herself just a sliver of Parmesan with it, because she was jet-lagged.

'*Lola*,' breathed a gossip columnist, his beady eyes gleaming. 'Honey, tell us *everything!* We've all seen the British papers online! Has Carin really cut you off? How's Big Daddy doing? Is he *really* in a coma?'

Lola looked around the table. Not only their circle, but most of the people at adjoining tables were leaning forward avidly, desperate for the latest gossip from the horse's mouth. She took a long sip of champagne, and Thom eagerly leaned forward to refill her glass.

At least as long as everyone wants to hear all about my scandals, she suddenly realised, *I won't be picking up a single tab! Wonderful! As well as not taking limos round the corner, this is going to be another* great *way to economise . . .*

Lola was dreaming, a hectic, upsetting dream in which she was having to climb a huge stack of suitcases, which were wobbling dangerously underfoot. She was in her silver Miu Miu slingbacks, but they weren't that easy to walk in, let alone climb, and she asked Jean-Marc to help her, but he was too frail, and besides, some awful woman with huge fake melon breasts and cheap dyed hair was pulling him down somewhere she couldn't see. She tripped on the edge of a suitcase and nearly went flying, but someone caught her. It was Niels van der Veer, glowering down at her, and she tried to shake him off, but he was very strong and they were all tangled up and they rolled around, Lola finding it harder and harder to move. For some reason he kept calling her 'Miss Fitzgerald, Miss Fitzgerald', shouting in her ear, tapping on her head, which was all echoey, and then the noise got louder and louder till she gasped and woke up to realise she was tangled in the bedsheets, actually a little sweaty from the nightmare, and someone was knocking on the door of the suite, calling, 'Miss Fitzgerald? Miss Fitzgerald?' in a gently persistent tone of voice.

'What is it?' she called, unpeeling the silk sleep mask from her eyes. Eew, that was sweaty too. She'd have to get the maid to hand-wash it.

'Miss Fitzgerald? It's Tai, the day manager. May I come in?'

'Give me twenty minutes,' Lola called back, irritated at being woken like this at the crack of dawn. 'No, half an hour. And could you bring me a skim-milk cappuccino when you come back?'

Wincing from a hangover, she climbed out of the deliciously soft bed and padded down from the mezzanine level to draw the floor-to-ceiling curtains. The living-room was two storeys high, and the spring sunshine flooding in was blinding. You forgot how much sun there was in New York when you were used to grey old London. She pinned up her hair carefully, to avoid messing up her blow-out, and took a long shower. By the time the rainforest shower head had done its business, Lola was feeling so revived that she was actually humming to herself as she massaged her BeauBronz tan extender into her smooth skin, wrapped herself cosily in a big white robe and slipped her feet into her cashmere slippers.

The clock in the living-room said it was past noon. Lola's eyes widened. And then she looked around the room, beginning to notice the number of empty glasses and overflowing ashtrays stacked on every surface. Memories from the night before started to drip back into her consciousness, one drop at a time, like Chinese water torture. A whole group of them hanging out in the garden at Barolo, which was just below 60 Thompson, wanting to move on, looking up at the roof terrace bar, deciding to go up there. On the terrace, everyone laughing and smoking up a storm, ordering more cocktails, cocooned in a cosy nest of brick walls and lush plants, the New York skyline glittering in the dark velvet sky. Then, being kicked off the terrace, because some stupid neighbours had complained about the noise and made them close the bar at midnight or something ridiculously early. Going down to the hotel bar, but not being able to smoke there, and everyone pretty drunk by this time, not wanting to move too far, so a smaller group of people heading up to her room, where they *could* smoke . . .

'Miss Fitzgerald?' The knocking on the door started up again. 'It's Tai again, with your cappuccino? Skim milk?'

Lola crossed the room to open the door, wondering whether the coffee would be enough to cure the slight headache she was suffering, or whether she should go for some codeine.

'Hi!' Tai said, smiling brightly. She had a very American mixed-race beauty, with pale creamy-gold skin, dark almond eyes and a sprinkling of freckles over the bridge of her tip-tilted nose. Her black outfit, a cheong-sam-inspired shirt over slim black trousers, hung loosely off her slender bones, and her dark chestnut hair was pulled back into a tight ponytail. The archetypal New York career woman, she was extremely slim, dressed all in black, her make-up blending in so perfectly you could hardly tell she was wearing it, every hair smooth and in place.

'I brought you coffee and some fruit,' she said, indicating the dark wood tray she was carrying. 'And we're just going to clear up a little bit for you.'

Behind her was a bus boy who slipped into the room, produced a large tray he had been holding discreetly under one arm, and loaded it up with most of the debris from last night, leaving the coffee table free for Tai to deposit Lola's breakfast upon. Lola sat down on the sofa, sipping her cappuccino, and waited until the bus boy had left, closing the door quietly behind him. Grateful as she was for the coffee, she was beginning to have a bad feeling about this visit.

'So,' Tai began, 'I hope you don't mind, Miss Fitzgerald, but we were wondering how long you were planning to stay with us.' She flashed Lola another smile, her teeth dazzlingly white. 'Of course, we're always very happy to have you with us – you're welcome to stay as long as you want! We've had guests who settle in for months on end!'

'I don't understand,' Lola said, reaching for a blueberry. 'Can't I just stay on and let you know when I'm leaving? I mean, I'm not sure now how long I'll be here.'

'Of course you can!' Tai's teeth flashed again. 'That's exactly why *I'm* here! We just need to talk it over and decide how often you're going to settle your running expenses. Once a week is usual for our longer-stay guests.'

'Running expenses?' Lola had clearly not had enough coffee yet.

'Your bill,' Tai clarified.

There was a long pause.

'You said a week,' Lola said, feeling her way, 'and I've only been here four days—'

'Five days, actually,' Tai corrected her with a little smile.

'Really? It's been five days?' Lola said, shocked.

Lola still hadn't been to visit her father. Or George, the lawyer.

Every morning (or noon) she'd woken up and told herself that today was the day: she wasn't going to put things off any more. She was going to ring Carin, arrange a time to go and see her father. But after making that brave resolution, her nerve dwindled. She was intimidated by Carin, to be honest. She always had been. And since Carin had cut her off from her trust fund, she had become even more scary, because someone who had the nerve to do something that unpleasant to her stepdaughter was a person who clearly didn't care what anyone thought of her, and those people were very difficult to fight.

She didn't want to see George, not really, because she knew that if he'd had good news he would have rung her with it immediately, and so when she went into his office he would tell her a lot of things she didn't want to hear. And she didn't want to see her father, because the mere idea of seeing Daddy lying helpless in a bed, unconscious, hooked up to a lot of tubes, was so awful that it brought tears to her eyes just thinking about it.

Lola had been living in a bubble for the past four – *five* – days, partying and shopping and clubbing and resolutely pushing aside any thoughts of the crisis she was in, all the trouble that was brewing overhead for her. But now, as she looked at Tai the day manager, and the envelope that Tai had propped up on the tray, which Lola had vaguely thought before might contain messages for her taken by the front desk, she realised that her bubble was about to burst.

'It wouldn't normally be hotel policy to have this conversation with a valued guest after only a few days,' Tai was saying, 'so I do apologise for that. But there have been, ahem, mentions in the papers about some difficulties you may be having with, ahem, funding issues. . . and then there was that party last night, which did run up quite a substantial tab to your room account . . .'

Oh my God, Lola thought in horror, *all of that got billed to me? I thought Thom was covering it! Shit! Drinks at the upstairs bar, all those little nibbles people had ordered to pick at . . . the cocktails downstairs, the bottles of vodka they'd had brought into the room, even sending out for cigarettes . . .*

'So we just thought, why not give you a statement of your account now,' Tai said, 'and you can settle that at your convenience. Then we can just roll over to a weekly bill? Does that work for you?'

Tai was as smiling and friendly as ever. But the last sentence was only there for politeness' sake, as were the question marks. Lola might not have had enough coffee – and not nearly enough codeine, as her headache was now raging – but she could tell that much.

'I'll drop off a cheque at the front desk when I come down,' she said bravely.

And then Lola could tell, by the slight widening of Tai's eyes, that she had made a huge, and possibly fatal, mistake. Nobody paid with a cheque any more. Lola had had to get temporary cheques from her bank, because none of her cards worked any more; but someone who could afford to stay for an indefinite time at 60 Thompson was the kind of person who had cards with a pretty much unlimited line of credit. If Lola couldn't manage that, if she had to pay by cheque either because she had cards with a low limit, or, even worse, no cards at all, she was *not* the kind of person whom an expensive boutique hotel wanted as a long-term guest.

'That would be great,' Tai said, professionalism enabling her to keep her composure. She pushed back her chair and stood up. 'I'm so sorry to have bothered you like this, Miss Fitzgerald.'

'Oh, not at all,' Lola said brightly. 'Could you get them to send me up another cup of coffee, by the way?'

'Of course,' Tai said, smiling automatically. 'Skim milk again?'

Lola nodded.

'I'll see myself out,' Tai said.

As the door closed behind her, Lola grabbed for the envelope and ripped it open. The three pages of closely printed items on the bill were an ominous detailing of charges that horrified her, with a final sum that was so enormous it would take a huge chunk out of the bank balance that had looked relatively healthy when she arrived in New York and deposited horrible Niels' cheque. *How* much was dry-cleaning nowadays? How could they charge that much for *laundry?* Had she really spent that much on *water?* And, oh God oh God oh God, *how* had they possibly managed to run up a steep four-figure bar bill last night?

She did a quick calculation. Cocktails at eighteen dollars apiece, 20 per cent service, bottles of vodka for so much money it sent a shiver down her spine. . . God, it was all too possible. Then her eye fell on the charges for her regular morning coffee, and she couldn't believe it. She was paying that much for *coffee?* Surely you could get a cappuccino for much less than that from Starbucks. Couldn't you? Was it too late to ring down to room service and cancel that second cappuccino, save some money that way?

And as the horrible realisation slapped her in the face, that she had to get out of this hotel as soon as possible, that she was going to have to *economise on cappuccinos* from now on, Lola stuffed one hand into her mouth to suppress a little scream of fear.

She had absolutely no idea how to economise. None at all. What was going to become of her?

Chapter 9

'*I* want her out, Lawrence! She was never supposed to move in here!'

'Autumn—'

'She's a whore! She was screwing a rich guy for money!'

The sound of the argument hit Evie as soon as she stepped out of the bathroom, hair newly washed, skin freshly scrubbed, wearing round-the-house sweats. Autumn's screeching didn't surprise Evie. She'd known that bitch was gunning for a fight ever since Autumn had heard Evie was trying to sell her fur coats.

Evie checked her appearance. Fresh-faced, not a scrap of make-up, her big brown eyes doe-like and her blonde hair pulled back and shiny, she looked as if she were still in her teens, her skin peachy-smooth. As she appeared in the kitchen doorway, both faces turned to her. Even though the gigantic windows were filthy with decades of grime and pigeon shit, sunlight was pouring into the huge corner room through the dirty glass, and after the darkness of the unlit corridor, it was as if Evie were walking onto a stage.

Lawrence was leaning against the wall, holding a steaming cup of herbal tea, smiling at her fondly, while Autumn was striding up and down the living-room, her red-tipped hair flashing in the sunlight. She was wearing her usual hipster workout clothes – faded black vintage T-shirt, low-waisted black leggings rolled up to mid-calf, accessorised with a big silver-link belt hanging low on her waist – and her eyes were heavily rimmed with black liner. She stopped dead on sight of Evie.

'You've had it really easy, Autumn,' Evie said, taking one more step into the kitchen. 'I don't think you've got any idea how easy you've had it. What are you, a nice suburban girl? Grew up in some nice little town in upstate New York?'

Autumn's eyes narrowed, and Evie knew she was right.

'Know how I figured that out?' Evie asked. 'Because it's nice suburban girls like you who get all that crap done to themselves. Piercings. Tattoos where people can see them.' She gestured at Autumn's nose stud, her eyebrow ring, the sleeve tattoo on her arm. 'Showing off how hip and radical you are. Because for you, it doesn't really matter. You're middle class. You got a good education, maybe even at some private school. You can stop living in a Bushwick slum anytime you want – Mommy and Daddy will bust their ass to throw money at you the moment you tell them you're ready to quit being a vegan yoga-teaching alternative nut-job.'

Autumn, bubbling with fury, started to say something but Evie continued:

'Me? I got no Mommy and Daddy to back me up. I was raised in a skanky project in Spanish Harlem and believe me, if you thought growing up in New Paltz or wherever safe little white-bread town you come from was bad, you've got no idea what I've been through, OK? The school I went to, we didn't have nothing. All the money went on the metal detectors at the doors and security guards. Let me tell you, you wouldn't have lasted two minutes in the life I grew up in.'

Autumn was looking good and guilty by now, exactly as Evie wanted her.

'So yeah, I did what I needed to do to get out of the projects. I danced, and then I met Benny. I'm not going to apologise for it. I'll kick you guys in some money for rent while I'm staying here, till I can figure out somewhere better. You still got a problem with that?'

Lawrence said very gently, 'Autumn, you know we always talk about forgiveness and tolerance in our meditation practice? This would be a really good opportunity for you to work on that goal.'

He took a sip of grassy-scented tea, his calm gaze fixed on Autumn. For a moment, it looked as if Autumn was softening. She returned Lawrence's stare, tilting her head to one side, her red-dipped fringe tilting too, thinking over what he had just said.

Then Evie stretched her arms above her head, cricking out her back, and Lawrence's eyes went to her involuntarily. Seeing the way Lawrence was looking at Evie, Autumn snapped.

'That's all very well for you to say!' she said angrily. 'She's screwing your brains out! No wonder *you're* OK with her being here!'

Evie couldn't help giggling.

'She does sort of have a point there, Lawrence,' Evie said wickedly. 'I mean, I *am* screwing your brains out.'

'That's it! You're a total whore!' Autumn, flailing her arms at Lawrence, completely lost it. 'She's out, Lawrence! It's her or me! We *agreed* we'd keep this loft a special place, we *agreed* no long-term visitors without each other being OK, we *agreed* no meat or fur or cruelty-made products . . .'

Fuck this, Evie thought. *I don't need to hear this neurotic banging on about my coats again.* She swivelled on her heel and slipped down the corridor to Lawrence's room, where she rifled through her clothes and pulled out the Chanel suit she had bought with Benny's credit card. She'd never really worn it: Benny hated it, thought it was too uptown for his downtown girl, and it wasn't like she had many opportunities to wear Chanel.

But today, she was making one. Hair up in a twist, pale pink tweed suit, white silk tie-neck blouse, grey suede heels. Discreet make-up, Manhattan-style – which meant lots, but so carefully applied that she just looked magically perfect. Her Metrocard went in a little grey clutch bag. When she appeared in the kitchen again, Lawrence and Autumn were still at it: Lawrence was talking about inner balance and prana-yama-rama-something, Autumn was lecturing him on vegan values. They both turned and gawped at her as she clicked through the room. Hey, no one had ever accused Evie of not knowing how to make an entrance. Or an exit.

'I'll see you later, sweetheart,' she said, blowing a kiss at Lawrence, and exited the flat, a stunned silence at her transformation hanging in the room behind her.

God, she was jonesing for a cigarette. By the next landing down she'd already fished a pack of menthols out of her clutch bag. Pausing to light one up, she was nearly knocked over by someone stampeding out of the second-floor apartment.

'Impossssible! Impossssible! I cannot vork like zisss!' shouted the stampeder, gesturing furiously in a way that made Autumn's armflailings look like amateur hour. 'Ve are not compatible! Not!'

She was tall and strapping, dressed in a grey tank top and black denim button-top dungarees, with shoulders like a linebacker. Her hair was straggly, in that layered cut that was very fashionable with sexually androgynous skinny hipsters.

'Waltraud—' yelled someone else from deep inside the apartment.

'No! No more! I go back to Berlin! Today!'

Waltraud, hair falling over her face, eyes glaring, put her hands on her hips, and took in Evie's presence on the landing.

'Nice costume,' she said approvingly.

'Um, thank you,' Evie said, taking a drag of her cigarette.

'Oh my God! You are a woman! You are zo – zo' – Waltraud gestured comprehensively at Evie's Chanel suit and uptwisted hair – 'zo *kitsch*, I zought you were in drag! Give me a cigarette.'

Evie handed her the packet. Waltraud took one.

'Ugh, menzol! I hate menzol!' she announced ungratefully. 'It is like smoking toozpaste! I go now.'

She adjusted the strap of the big leather bag slung crosswise over her body and pounded away down the stairs. Evie followed her. Out in the street, she heard more cries of 'Waltraud!' and looked up to see someone leaning from one of the huge second-floor windows and yelling. Waltraud, legs wide, fists planted on hips, stood on the sidewalk, shouting back. Black binliners, filled with God knew what, began to rain down, thrown by the person on the second floor. Waltraud kicked them away contemptuously, insisting at the top of her voice that she vos going back to Berlin today, now, zis moment. The guys from across the street piled out of their engine room to watch appreciatively.

'Fuckin' artist shitbags,' said one. 'Ruining the fuckin' area.'

'Oh man, they're good TV!' protested another.

'Yeah! Like, is that a *chick?* Look at the shoulders on her! You think she wants a job here?'

'She'd kick your ass, Mickey!'

In the commotion, Evie sneaked past without drawing any attention. She was nervous about getting beaten up on the way to the subway, dressed up as she was, but the worst that happened were a few incredulous stares and some boys cutting school on the opposite platform of the L train, who threw a cup of slushy across the tracks at her, yelling, 'Rich bitch!'

Evie ducked aside, and the cup splattered over the edge of the platform. The boys hollered in amusement at having made her jump, but then their train mercifully pulled in and they slouched on, tugging listlessly at the baggy jeans hanging halfway down their butts, pulling faces at her through the window.

Never a dull moment in New York, Evie thought, as the L train to Manhattan chugged into the station. *And this is the calm before the storm.* She shivered at the thought of her destination. All dressed up, going to put her head in the lion's mouth.

Chapter 10

*N*o one would take Lola in. No one. As soon as they found out that she'd need to stay, not for a few days before she jetted off to the Bahamas with some fab new boyfriend, but indefinitely while she tried to claw some money out of her stepmother in Surrogates' Court, they didn't want to know. And word must have got around that she was desperate, because as she went down the list of people with New York apartments, her calls started going to voicemail, or, if they were answered, her so-called friends would launch into long and vivid explanations of how busy they were and how many people they had staying.

She kept working down the list grimly, but well before the end she knew how things stood. As a rich socialite, no matter how scandalous her life was, how many gossip magazines and tabloids snapped her falling out of limousines and into the latest clubs, everyone wanted to be friends with her. Even more so, frankly, now that she was notorious.

But as a poor girl, or at least one with no access to any of her money – well, they couldn't brush her off fast enough. The friends she'd thought she had in New York were turning out to be barely social acquaintances. And the girls in London weren't much better: one of them had sold those camera-phone photos of her to the

Herald. Devon had had to chuck her out and, somehow, no one else had been able to put her up.

Lola was going to have to rely on her wits.

God, that was a joke, wasn't it? Not a single person she knew thought she had any wits at all.

She stared at herself in the mirror. Wearing a featherweight black cashmere T-shirt and designer jeans, her hair pulled back in a high ponytail, Jean-Marc's yellow diamonds in her ears, sprayed from head to toe with Stella perfume, she looked and smelled as expensively beautiful as ever. If she'd been born poor, her face would have been her fortune. So she had better muster up all the wits she had, and use whatever beauty she possessed, to get herself out of this hole.

Taking a deep breath, Lola picked up the phone in the room and buzzed for a bellboy to come and carry her suitcases downstairs. Then she threw her pale-yellow fur stole round her shoulders and left the suite without looking back.

She'd settled her bill that morning with a cheque, and, thank God, they hadn't humiliated her by making her hang around until it cleared. Her impression was that Tai and the management were just grateful to have her out of the hotel. Downstairs, she got the bellboy to load her cases into a regular yellow cab, much to his shock. But he was even more shocked at the measly tip she gave him. Sliding into the beaten-up old cab, its seats partially slashed, its floor carpet stained, Lola blushed with shame at having practically stiffed the bellboy. He would tell them all how cheap she'd been. She could never go back there again.

'Where to, lady?'

'Seventy-second and Riverside,' Lola said, crossing her fingers and praying that this plan would work out.

If it didn't, she literally had no idea of what to do.

The cab swerved, honked and ducked into Broome Street and over to 11th Avenue. As it bumped and jerked up 11th in fits and starts, heading uptown, Lola stared out of the window at the highrises and ugly garages of Chelsea, the big new clubs, the shiny signs for strip joints. Maybe she'd have to get a job in one of those if everything else failed. Would they even hire her? It was the only job she could think of that paid well and might hire her just because she had a pretty face and a slim body. She had no qualifications at all, not a single one. All that money her father had spent on her English boarding school, and then the finishing school in Switzerland, and she'd come out of them both with rafts of beautiful friends, a smattering of languages, and the ability to ski.

Well, the friends were falling like flies, the languages weren't enough to get anyone to hire her, and how on earth did you make money out of being able to ski? She might end up in a strip club after all.

Her destination was a large pale stone Beaux-Arts building on the Upper West Side, built in the 1920s and called the Anhedonia, after the then-current fashion that gave ocean liners and big apartment buildings equally imposing names. The buildings looked like an ocean liner, too: white, massive, and festooned with ornamentation in the form of hundreds of small balconies. The cab pulled up outside, neatly enough so that Lola could step out directly onto the dark-green carpet that ran up the sidewalk right to the front doors, sheltered by a wide green awning, in case it were raining.

The doorman at the Anhedonia could move fast, despite the weight of his heavy red uniform, frogged and epauletted with gold braid. He was bending down to open the cab door almost before the vehicle had come to a halt. By the time she'd settled up, he had Lola's cases already stacked inside the red-and-gold lobby and was back outside, accepting a generous tip from her as he went.

'Miss Lola!' exclaimed Mirko, rising from behind his desk. 'Miss Madison didn't say you were coming to stay!'

'Didn't she?' Lola asked, smiling at Madison's doorman sweetly. 'How silly of her! Can you help me upstairs with these, Mirko?'

'Sure!' he said enthusiastically.

'Oh, and Madison forgot to give me her keys as well,' Lola said. 'If you wouldn't mind letting me in . . .'

'Sure, Miss Lola,' Mirko said, with just a shade less enthusiasm.

Lola kept up a friendly flow of chat as they went up in the elevator. The weather, Miss Madison's time in London, and Mirko's wife Rosalka, kept them busy until they were inside Madison's adorable corner apartment. Mirko lugged in her cases and stood waiting for Lola's tip.

She cleared her throat.

'Mirko,' she started. 'I need to ask you a little favour . . .'

Mirko's stolid Slovakian face immediately settled into a mask of impassivity, his eyes darting down to avoid meeting Lola's.

'It's about Miss Madison not giving me the keys,' Lola said. 'It's, um, a little bit more than that. Miss Madison doesn't actually know I'm here.'

Mirko's fingers flexed as if he were about to pick up Lola's cases and take them back down to the lobby.

'I just haven't been able to get hold of her,' Lola lied. 'She's travelling and her phone keeps cutting out. But she's always said if I needed to crash here for a little while, that'd be fine.'

Mirko didn't say anything. He just raised his head and looked directly at her, his eyes flat and expressionless.

'So are we cool?' Lola babbled. 'I mean, I wouldn't want Madison to know I stayed here without, you know, actually asking her first . . . so . . . I mean, you won't mention this to Madison?'

Madison was still in London, of course. Lola had rung her a few hours ago, saying that she had to leave 60 Thompson because she needed to draw in her horns a bit financially, and waited for Madison to offer her place in New York, sure that she would.

But she hadn't.

Mirko was still not saying a word, but his stare was making her distinctly nervous. She fidgeted until, eventually, she realised what was going on.

'I'm really short of cash at the moment, Mirko,' she said, tilting her head and giving him her best smile. 'That's why I need to crash here. You've probably seen stuff in the papers . . .'

Mirko nodded slowly.

'Yeah, I read some stuff.' He paused, thinking it over. 'We'll make a deal, you and me. You got no money?' he said. 'Then you gotta give me something else.'

And he nodded towards her, winking.

Oh my God! Lola thought. *No! I won't! I can't! . . . I mean, he's not the worst-looking man in the world, but still, no! And then I'd have to walk past him every day . . . or would he want to do it every day? How do these things work? God, no! I can't! I just can't! I can't believe I'm even thinking about this!*

Mirko must have taken her silence as assent. He walked towards her. Lola couldn't move a muscle, paralysed by shock at what was happening, what her life had suddenly become. She had sunk so low so suddenly she simply couldn't believe it. She had made herself so vulnerable that a doorman thought that he could blackmail her into having sex with him – put his *hands* on her—

Because Mirko's hands were on her shoulders, caressing them. Lola squeezed her eyes shut. Could she actually let this happen? He was pulling at her fur wrap, taking it off – *Oh God no, she couldn't bear it, she just couldn't!*

'Mirko—' she said, her eyes snapping open, her voice high and panicky. 'I don't think – I *can't*—'

He was stepping back, beaming at her.

'For my wife,' he said, stroking the beautiful pale-yellow fur as gently as if it were still the live animal from which it had come. 'For Rosalka. It's her birthday next month. She always wanted a fur. A good one.'

Lola had been holding her breath. Now, full of relief, she let it all out in one go and then choked trying to inhale again, coughing so hard that Mirko had to pound her on the back.

'You OK, Miss Lola?' he asked, looking concerned.

'Yes, fine, thank you!' Lola said, overwhelmed with relief that she didn't have to sleep with him.

'I still need two hundred bucks,' Mirko said, looking apologetic. 'For the guys on the door. A hundred a pop so they don't say nothing to Miss Madison when she gets back. Oh, and fifty to get you a set of keys cut.'

Lola fished in her purse. This was almost going to clean her out of cash completely.

'Miss Madison, she always calls me when she's coming back, so I can get Rosalka in to clean and do fresh flowers,' Mirko informed Lola. 'So you'll get a day's notice, OK? But then you clear out and it's gotta be like you were never here.'

Lola nodded, putting the $250 in Mirko's hand.

'Thanks, Mirko,' she said gratefully – more gratefully than Mirko would ever realise.

'You kidding me?' He looked at the fur wrap again. 'Rosalka's gonna cry for days when she sees this! How much did it cost?'

Lola blushed. 'I don't know,' she admitted.

'Five grand at least,' Mirko said confidently. 'Wow. This is going to be the best birthday of her life.' He nodded at Lola. 'I'll send Luis out to get you a set of keys. They'll be at the desk when you wanna go out.'

As he went out, folding up the fur wrap reverently, Lola walked across the room and stared out of the window. She wasn't seeing the stunning view, the spectacular buildings, the traffic far below, the sliver of the Hudson River with the Pacific Palisades on the far bank. She might as well have had her eyes closed. All she could see was a truth about life that her father had always known, and had done his best to protect her from finding out.

But here it was, staring her in the face, blinding her to anything but how powerful it was.

It all came down to money in the end.

Chapter 11

$\mathcal{E}$vie came out of the subway and stepped back, getting her bearings, figuring out which way traffic on the avenue ran – up or downtown. It was just a couple of blocks to her destination. She patted her hair down, checking it out in the window of the French restaurant next to the subway exit. A guy laying tables inside saw the movement and looked up, catching her eye, giving her a big smile once he saw how young and pretty she was.

Jesus, Evie thought, starting to walk the two blocks uptown to her destination. *Men. They'll do anything for a little attention.*

And then she told herself: *So work it while you've got it! You won't be young forever – what have you got, five good years left? Six?* She sighed. *Benny always said he'd put you in his will, but that was a load of bullshit. No way he'd have done that, not with a wife like that bitch. He'd never have wanted her to find out.*

Uff. Her heart sank to the soles of her grey suede shoes. This train of thought was a big, big mistake. She should never have let herself think of Benny's wife.

Lola hadn't considered the ramifications of visiting her father at all. She'd just walked up the stairs to the front door of his town house and rung the bell. She'd left this long enough; now she was determined to make seeing her father her top priority.

The door was opened by a young, extremely handsome man in a black two-piece uniform. Lola's eyes widened at the sight of him, so young and sleek and groomed, so designer-looking in her father's much more traditional house. And then she peered round his black-clad shoulder, and saw that the house wasn't traditional any more. The gilded French furniture, the tapestry hanging, the two huge, priceless chinoiserie vases on pedestals, flanking the red-carpeted staircase, had all vanished.

Instead it looked as if some minimalist, Scandinavian-Japanese interior designer had waved a magic wand and stripped the place bare of anything it didn't strictly need. A huge Japanese screen hung where the tapestry had been, two big white panels decorated merely with three huge swooping black brush-strokes. A glass vase on a dark-wood table held a single white lily. The black-and-white tiled floor was bare and highly polished, the staircase carpet white and new-looking.

It was very beautiful: but it wasn't her father's taste. Lola knew exactly whose eye was behind this makeover.

And it would never have been possible if her father wasn't in a coma.

'Lola Fitzgerald,' she said, rather curtly, to the man in the black outfit, stepping past him and into the hall. 'I'm here to see my father.'

'Panio? Who is it?' called a woman's voice impatiently.

Footsteps came quickly along the upstairs hallway and began to descend the stairs. Carin's feet appeared first, naturally, strapped into bronze gladiator-style stilettos whose complicated buckles reached halfway up her calves. Only someone over five foot ten could wear those shoes and not look ridiculous. On Carin, nearly six foot in stockinged feet, they looked perfectly proportioned. But the height of the heels was another red flag for Lola. *She'd never have worn those if Daddy were well*, Lola thought. Ben Fitzgerald hadn't liked Carin towering over him.

The rest of Carin's legs, topped by a white miniskirt, eventually came into view; it took some time, as they were so long. Then her torso, sheathed in a black polo-neck top, long and slim. And finally, her head, the pale blue eyes like two triangular pieces of platinum, the white-blonde hair cut short and slicked back. She looked like a pop singer from the 1980s, fierce and monochromatic.

She's done over the entire house to match her style, Lola realised. *Now it's nothing but a frame for her. Like Devon did with their London place.* But Devon had made a pretty bower of golds and blues, soft and welcoming. Carin's hostile takeover of Lola's father's town house was as sharp and angular as her own cheekbones. She had probably installed a torture room in the basement.

'What the *hell* are you doing here?' Carin demanded on sight of Lola. She stormed across the hall, her eyes flashing with rage. 'Get out! Get out this *moment!*' She flung one arm out, pointing at the door. 'Get the *fuck* out of my house!'

'It's not your house yet!' Lola retorted furiously. 'But you didn't lose any time redecorating, did you?'

'Get out!' Carin yelled. '*Rico!* Get up here right now!'

There was no way Lola was going to see her father, that was clear: but now her blood was up. Even after everything that had happened, she couldn't believe how aggressively Carin was behaving. Heavy feet came running up the kitchen staircase, and a man emerged, big, dark, intimidating and much too brutish to ever have been permitted in this house before Ben Fitzgerald fell into a coma.

'Rico!' Carin screamed, pointing at Lola. 'That's my husband's daughter, and she's *banned* from this house, do you understand? *Banned!*'

The man called Rico started towards Lola.

'Shall I throw her out, Mrs Fitzgerald?' he asked, and the look in his black beady eyes was so nakedly menacing that Lola narrowed her eyes and hissed back at Carin:

'You tell your thug that if he lays a *finger* on me he'll be sorry!'

She met Carin's eyes full-on. There was such anger in her stare that it was probably the first time Carin had ever taken her stepdaughter seriously. Carin paused for a moment and then said,

'Don't touch her, Rico. Just make sure she leaves.'

'Awww . . .' Rico whined, grinning at Lola. He stood, folding his arms across his big chest, staring at her as if he could see through her clothes, not just to her skin but to her bones. Terrified, but determined not to show it, Lola turned her back on him and grabbed the door handle. And as she was pulling it open, the doorbell rang.

Standing on the doorstep, Lola found herself looking into a mirror. It was as if a twin sister she'd never known about had suddenly appeared in front of her.

Carin burst out laughing.

And staring at the girl, Lola exclaimed, 'Who on earth are *you?*'

Chapter 12

'*Me*?' the girl said right back at Lola. 'Who the hell are *you*? Don't tell me he had another one!'

Lola's forehead crinkled as best it could.

'*Another* one?' she said. 'What are you talking about? I'm the only one!'

This was so weird it felt as if she'd been suddenly plunged into a parallel dimension, like those films where you opened a door and found yourself in another world where there was already a you in existence. This girl was the same height as Lola, more or less. Her blonde hair was delicately streaked – not quite as well as Lola's, now she looked more closely, but Lola's hairdresser was the best in London, so what could you expect? The girl's eyes were brown, and almond-shaped, like Lola's, and her features were small and pretty, her nose exquisitely straight. The blonde hair was swept back in a style Lola sometimes wore when she wanted to look classic, and Lola had the disconcerting feeling that she had actually tried on that pale-pink Chanel suit last season. She couldn't remember, actually, why she hadn't bought it.

The girl was gaping at her.

'You thought you were the only one too? Jeez, Benny really had us both going!' She clicked her tongue. 'Well, I guess that makes us both morons.' She paused. 'Look, I just came to see if I could visit him,' she said quietly. 'I know he isn't sitting up and talking or anything, but I'd really like to see him, just once, say my goodbyes. Did you just see him? Was that OK with his wife?'

Lola realised she had put a hand to her head, like an actress in a bad 1950s film feigning confusion.

'There's no *way* he had another daughter,' she said, grasping at the most basic truth of the situation. 'Everyone would know. Wouldn't they?'

She almost turned to Carin, to see if she knew anything about her husband having an illegitimate daughter of Lola's age.

'Another *daughter*?' The girl stared at her in horror. 'You're kidding, right?'

She looked Lola up and down, her eyes widening.

'Of course I'm not kidding!' Lola retorted, getting angry now. 'I'm his daughter! Who the hell are you?'

The girl was genuinely appalled. She put one hand to her mouth. The nails, Lola noticed, though French-manicured, were longer and tartier than anyone in Lola's circle would have chosen, their tips aggressively square.

Carin started to clap, the kind of long slow hand-claps an audience makes when the act onstage is so terrible it deserves to be rewarded with sarcasm.

'What a *fantastic* scene,' she said. 'Do keep going, Lola. I'm really going to enjoy the part where Daddy's little princess realises that Daddy had another princess on the side.' She looked at the girl. 'Though you're not a princess any more, are you? You never really were. Just another cheap whore pretending to be better than she was.'

'Hey, join the club!' the girl spat back. 'You screwed him for money just as much as I did! Where I come from, lady, that makes you a whore too!'

In a small, shadowy back of her mind, Lola was very impressed at the way the girl was standing up to Carin. But the front part of her brain was fully occupied with the horrific revelation that, according to what the girl and Carin had just said, this twin sister standing in front of her was in fact—

'You were Daddy's *mistress*?' she said, utterly horrified.

The girl actually ducked her head for a second, refusing to meet Lola's gaze. So it was true.

Colours spun before Lola's eyes. The girl's face, so like her own, split into a thousand little pieces. Lola felt suddenly weightless, dizzy, her vision blurring. Then everything went dark, and she had the sensation of being pulled down a long, twisting tunnel—

Even though she was standing still, she somehow lost her balance. She stumbled, and someone caught her by the forearms, helping her right herself. When she could open her eyes again, she saw that face, eerily close to her own, and she realised it was the girl who had saved her from falling.

Outraged, Lola pushed the girl away so violently that she stumbled in her turn.

'How dare you *touch* me!' Lola screamed.

'Catfight!' Rico said appreciatively, so close that Lola could feel his hot, eager breath on her neck. 'My money's on the little ho. The trashy ones always fight dirty. What d'you say, Panio? You wanna put some money on the princess? Hey, as long as they both strip off, I'll be more 'an happy—'

The girl had got her balance now. She advanced on Lola furiously.

'Hey, I was trying to *help* you,' she hissed at her. 'Don't you shove me away like I'm not good enough to touch you!'

'You aren't!' Lola retorted furiously. 'You're *disgusting!*'

The girl's cheeks were pink with fury, her eyes sparkling with rage.

'This has made my day,' Carin announced, her voice ripe with amusement, 'but I can't have a scene for too long on the doorstep. So you'll both have to take this somewhere else.' She stared at them. 'And don't come back. Either of you. Panio, get the door.'

'It isn't much fun for me either!' the girl said to Lola, almost defiantly, as the door slammed shut in their faces. 'You think someone likes you because you're pretty, and you dance really well, and then you find out it was just because you looked like—'

'*Stop!*' Lola screamed, clapping her hands to her ears so she couldn't hear another word. She scrambled down the steps to the sidewalk and ran along it, not even sure which direction she was taking, until, mercifully, she saw a cab dropping someone off down the street and she sprinted towards it, arms flailing in a wild semaphore to catch the driver's attention. Even by New York standards, it was a frenzied way to hail a cab. The cabbie didn't even have the time to switch his light on and then off again: Lola was already collapsed in the back seat.

'Where to, lady?'

Lola managed to give the address of Madison's building. And then she wrapped her arms around herself, making as tight a little ball of her body as she could, and rocked herself, keening, trying vainly to console herself for the worst shock that had ever happened to her in her life.

Evie watched Benny's daughter dash off down the sidewalk and fall into a cab. She couldn't blame the girl – Lola, that was her name – for being so upset. Fuck, if she'd just found out her daddy had a mistress on the side who looked exactly like her, she wouldn't exactly deal with it any better.

There weren't many times Evie was glad she didn't know who her father was. But this was definitely one of them.

She turned and looked up at the mansion where Benny had lived. Still lived, if she was being accurate. Jesus, it was some house. She hadn't even known you could *have* a house like this in Manhattan, a private one, all to yourself. Massive, imposing, everything perfectly kept, with what looked like a private garden round the back. Benny had more money than God.

Though now the Ice Queen held the purse strings. Fuck, she was a piece of work, that one. Watching Evie and the daughter go at it, standing back and laughing like it was the best bit of entertainment she'd ever had in her life. It wasn't as if that bitch had cared for

Benny at all: Evie could tell that loud and clear. Like Evie said, that bitch had fucked him for money, which is just what she'd done in her turn, but the Ice Queen'd managed to get a ring on her finger and all his multi-millions in her bank account. Well, good for her: but she didn't need to pretend she was so superior. Evie had actually cared about Benny, in her way. He'd been a gentleman. He'd looked after her, seen that she'd wanted for nothing, promised that she'd be OK, that he would always take care of her, she'd never have to go back to the Midnight Lounge again . . .

And Evie had believed him. What a sucker she was.

But she still believed that he'd meant it. Benny hadn't realised how sick he was: Evie had seen him, checking his blood sugar levels, making sure he was OK. He hadn't acted like someone who thought he might actually die if he fucked up his readings; he was always relaxed about it, joking with her about his insulin injections.

Still, an older guy with a 23-year old mistress didn't exactly want to go on about how sick he was, did he? That was why he was screwing the 23-year-old in the first place, to make himself feel young again. He wouldn't want to go and fuck that all up by telling her he was an old fat diabetic one step away from going into a coma and dying.

Sighing, Evie started to walk back to the subway. She was angry with Benny for failing to take care of her like he'd promised, of course she was. But she missed him, too. He'd been good to her. Much, much better than any sugar daddy any girl from the Midnight Lounge had ever had. She'd owed him something for that. That was why she'd made the effort to come and visit him, even though she'd known it was very unlikely that they'd let her in, even though she'd risked humiliation at the hands of the Ice Queen for even asking.

Sorry, Benny, she thought. *Bet your daughter finding out about me was the last thing you'd ever have wanted to happen. I really fucked up there, didn't I?*

Evie wasn't looking forward to getting back to the loft. God knew what Autumn had been saying to Lawrence in her absence. She let herself into the building, taking a deep breath as she started up the stairs, hoping that both of them would be out training some client. Lawrence had been so good to her, taking her in, looking after her: she didn't like the thought that the only reward she had for him was to bring perpetual conflict to where he lived.

Plus, she didn't exactly like it on her own account. Fun as it was to tease Autumn by fucking Lawrence's brains out noisily whenever she got the chance, it was beginning to get her down.

'Hey,' said someone as Evie came up the rickety stairs to the second floor.

'Hi,' Evie said, taking in the person, who was lighting up.

'You OK with me smoking on the landing?' the woman asked. 'It's just, everyone freaks if I do it in the apartment.'

Evie shrugged.

'Fuck it, I'll join you,' she said, pulling her pack of menthols out of her bag.

'I shouldn't,' the woman said.

'Me neither.'

They grinned at each other companionably as they drew in smoke.

'You living upstairs now?' the woman asked.

She was tiny. Really tiny, like a miniature of a person, tiny even to Evie, who wasn't that tall herself. She had a cute ugly little face, like a monkey, full of character, and she was dressed in layers of clothes like a refugee wearing everything she had one on top of the other, because she had no safe place to store anything she took off. Even the layers of clothing couldn't camouflage how skinny she was, though, like a 12-year-old girl. On her feet were huge furry slippers, beaten about and faded so you couldn't tell what colour they had been when new. They were much too big for her: they made her look like a hobbit, as if her feet were huge compared with the rest of her tiny frame.

'I'm not really living up there,' Evie answered. 'Just sort of camping out for a while.'

'They friends of yours?'

'I'm sort of seeing Lawrence,' Evie said. 'Autumn's definitely not a friend of mine.'

The woman pulled an expressive face.

'Autumn isn't that friendly to anyone,' she commented. 'She's always on at me about leaving our stuff in the hallway. Like it's that big of a deal to walk round it.'

Evie remembered tripping over an enormous circle of metal in the hallway just yesterday, nearly smacking herself in the face with it, and privately she thought that Autumn had a point there. But the last thing she was going to do was take the side of the person who was trying to kick her out of the only place she had to live right now. Especially as this little hobbit was being nicer to her in the space of a few minutes than Autumn had been for the last week.

So she nodded sympathetically as the woman continued:

'Plus, I sort of get the feeling she looks down on us, you know? Because we're performers? I mean, what kind of dipshit attitude is that?'

'You're performers?' Evie's interest was immediately kindled. 'No kidding. Me too.'

'Oh yeah?' The hobbit swept her with an up-and-down glance. 'That your costume? What do you do, performance art?'

'No, this is—' Evie decided she wasn't up to explaining why she was dressed up like a preppie uptown girl. She made a dismissive gesture with her cigarette, indicating that the way she was dressed had nothing to do with her life. 'I used to be an exotic dancer. Pole work. But I'm sort of between jobs right now. I need to make a change. I'm just not quite sure how.'

She knew that gyrating on a pole in a G-string wasn't quite what most people would mean when they said they were performers. But Evie took her work, and her technique, very seriously. To her, it was an art form like any other. It was just that you earned a lot more for pole dancing. Even if it was mostly in greasy bills.

'You know, that's really interesting,' the hobbit said, as friendly as ever. She stubbed out her cigarette in an old aluminium takeout tray wedged precariously into a space in the wall where a couple of bricks were missing. 'I've always thought pole dancing's pretty similar to the kind of stuff we do. Same sort of discipline, anyway.'

'So what's that?' Evie asked, following suit with her own cigarette.

'Trapeze, mostly. Some hoop work.' She kicked the metal circle with her foot.

'No shit! I've always loved watching trapeze!' Evie exclaimed.

'Yeah?' The hobbit smiled at her. 'You wanna come on in and see our setup?'

She turned and pushed open the big heavy door to her apartment. Evie followed her in, and the next second was gaping in astonishment. What was the kitchen, upstairs in Lawrence and Autumn's apartment, was here an enormous studio. Two trapezes were suspended from the ceiling, one higher than the other. Against the wall, now with ropes attached to welded-on rings at its sides, was the hoop Evie had tripped against. The floor was covered in mats – bashed-around, fraying old blue gym mats, lightly padded. A stereo played sad, slow music, a Portuguese woman singing fado, and, hanging from one of the trapezes, balancing somehow on the tops of his feet, was a man.

Evie had seen trapeze before, but only from a distance, at the circus, or watching Cirque du Soleil on the TV. From far away, it all seemed magical, impossible, unreal: you oohed and aahed at the feats of the performers, but they moved so fast, you didn't have time to take in every manoeuvre they made, how difficult it truly was. Seeing this man suspended like that, feet at right-angles to his legs just as if he were standing upright, the only difference being that his hair was hanging down below him, pulled by gravity, made Evie's mouth sag open with disbelief.

He turned his head slightly, seeing Evie and the hobbit come in. Then he curled his whole body up, rising slowly, still hanging from his feet, till he was folded in two and his arms were reaching high enough up to grab the bar. And then he bent his knees, curled his legs into his chest, and let himself fall down to the mat.

'That foot hang's getting better,' the hobbit commented.

'You think?' he asked.

She nodded.

'That must hurt like hell,' Evie said respectfully.

She looked down at his bare feet. Sure enough, there were two big red stripes where the bar had cut into him.

'You get used to it,' he said.

'She's crashing upstairs,' the hobbit informed him. 'Guess what? She's a pole dancer.'

'Cool,' he said, reaching out his hand so he could shake Evie's. 'I'm Jeremy.'

'Evie,' she said, thinking that never in her life had she told people what she did for a living and had such easy acceptance from them.

'So Evie, how's life upstairs?' Jeremy asked.

'Not so good,' she answered, grimacing.

'Autumn's driving her crazy,' added the hobbit.

Jeremy turned to look at the hobbit, who raised her eyebrows and nodded.

'You need to rent a room?' he asked. 'We just lost one of our merry little band. She went back to Germany today.'

'Oh yeah, Waltraud,' Evie remembered. 'I saw the scene outside.'

'She was dating someone in the group, and they had a bust-up,' Jeremy said, reaching for a dented old stove-top kettle. 'Tea?'

'Um, sure,' Evie said. 'Tea would be great . . . You're sure she's not coming back?'

'She texted Laura from the airport,' the hobbit said. 'Definitely got on that plane to Berlin.'

'Laura's her girlfriend?' Evie asked, as Jeremy filled the kettle from a big plastic jerrycan of water.

'Yup,' the hobbit said.

'But didn't they live together? I mean, in the same room?'

Jeremy twisted one finger in circles at the side of his head to indicate lunacy.

'Waltraud had to have her own space,' the hobbit said, putting the whole sentence into invisible inverted commas.

'It's a nice room,' Jeremy said, lighting the gas hob. 'Go look at it if you want.'

'I'll show you,' the hobbit said, leading Evie down the corridor.

It *was* a nice room, by the standards of the building. There was a big window, with curtains. The walls were of brick, not partition like Lawrence and Autumn's upstairs. Plus, it had a proper bed, and some basic furniture: a cupboard, a chest of drawers, a table and chairs. The hobbit rather apologetically mentioned how much it would cost a month, and Evie's eyes widened. A sum that tiny, she could totally afford. She would be free of Autumn and her grievances, living with a group of people who didn't give a shit how she'd earned her living. Plus, she could still go up a flight of stairs and fuck Lawrence whenever she wanted – drive Autumn crazy without having to deal with her on a daily basis.

This was so much a comedown from her penthouse in the sky that it would have driven her crazy if she'd let herself think about it.

So she wouldn't. Ever again.

'I'll take it,' Evie said decisively.

She smiled at the hobbit.

'I should know your name,' she said. 'Since we're rooming together. I'm Evie.'

'Hi, Evie,' said the hobbit, reaching out a tiny little hand for Evie to shake. They were sweetly formal here, Evie thought. 'I'm Natalie. Welcome to your new home.'

Chapter 13

*L*ola was still in pieces when the cab reached Madison's apartment. The revelation that her father had had a mistress wasn't what had upset her: if she'd thought about it, she wouldn't have been surprised that her loving, affectionate father, having felt the lack of warmth in his emotional life, would have found someone to provide it. How he had ever chosen to live with, let alone marry, Carin, whose blood was ice water and whose idea of affection was a sharp slap round the face, was something Lola had never understood.

Lola could have comprehended a nice forty-something mistress, pretty, domestic, sympathetic, cosy, everything Carin was not. But *this* girl? Not only Lola's age, but pretty much a dead ringer for her? It was horrible, shocking, unbearable. It made Lola sick to her stomach to think of it. Wanting nothing more than to curl up in a ball on Madison's soft-as-silk Signoria sheets from Italy, pop a sleeping pill, and pass out for a few hours of blissful release, Lola went into the Anhedonia building, nodding briefly at the doorman, who gave her a swift conspiratorial smile to indicate that he'd received the $100 and that her secret was safe with him.

Mirko wasn't on the desk. Grateful at being spared having to exchange a couple of friendly words with him, Lola crossed the lobby and pressed the button for the lift. She was looking up, count-ing down the floors on the old-fashioned marker above the doors as the lift descended, when she felt a tug on her arm.

Alarmed, she swung around to see Mirko standing just behind her, a panicked expression on his usually imperturbable face.

'Miss Lola – I'm so sorry – Miss Madison just called,' he muttered under his breath. 'She's coming into town late this evening. Flying in from London with a friend.' He actually wrung his hands. 'I'm really sorry.'

Which meant, of course, Lola realised, that he wasn't going to give her fur wrap back.

'I have to ask you to be out in a few hours,' Mirko continued, glancing over his shoulder as someone came into the lobby. But it was only a dog-walker, with five dogs in a tangled skein of leads: not a resident, nobody Mirko needed to smile at while making a friendly comment about the weather.

'But what am I supposed to do? Where am I supposed to go?' Lola's voice rose dangerously high, and Mirko flapped his hands to tell her to keep it down.

Thinking fast, Lola waited until the dog-walker had managed to persuade her entire group of charges to enter the lift, and the doors were closing. Then she said quickly:

'Isn't there anyone else who's away? Couldn't you let me camp out in another apartment? I'll be so quiet, you'll hardly know I'm here . . .'

But Mirko shook his head.

'I'm so sorry, Miss Lola – you see, most people don't let me know when they're getting back from their trips. Miss Madison, she's very precise. Always calls first, so Rosalka can come in and do the clean and I can organise the florist. But there aren't many residents who do that. I just can't run the risk of someone coming back and find-ing you in their place. I'd get the sack for sure.'

'But my wrap . . .' Lola said faintly. 'The $250 I gave you just this morning . . .'

Mirko avoided her gaze.

'Hey, what can I say? A deal's a deal,' he said. 'We said I'd let you stay till Miss Madison came back, and you told me it'd be a few weeks yet. It's not my fault she changed her plans.' He cleared his throat. 'Luis on the door, he's already had his hundred bucks. I could give you back the other hundred for the night guy.'

It had cost Lola a sable wrap and $150 just to rent out Madison's apartment for a couple of hours. She couldn't believe her bad luck.

Lola's whole body sagged in disappointment. She had been through so much in the past week that this was genuinely the straw that broke the camel's back. Realising that girl had been her father's mistress had completely overwhelmed her. She was completely out of ideas, completely out of any sense of hope.

'You need to be out by four at the latest,' Mirko was saying anxiously. 'You can give Rosalka the keys when she lets herself in.'

Lola stepped into a lift that was being vacated by a smart elderly couple, hearing Mirko's apologies following her as the doors slid closed. Pressing the button, her head sank against the mirrored wall. What could she do? Where could she go? She still had about $25,000 left, but that would vanish in no time if she had to pay for a hotel, her meals, her drinks . . . Vaguely, she realised that to most people, $25,000 would have been a whole lot of money, more than enough to survive on for a few months. But Lola, as she had said to her mother, wasn't most people.

Pulling her phone out of her bag, she dialled George Goldman's number. When George's secretary answered, Lola blurted out that she needed to speak to him urgently, immediately, and as soon as George came on the line Lola, fumbling for the keys to Madison's apartment, said:

'George! I need money, I'm really short of funds! And I need to see Daddy – I went there today, but that cow threw me out, if you can believe that, and I want to be able to visit him again! But right now, I really, *really* need some money—'

'Whoah! Calm down!' George said, as Lola managed to unlock Madison's door and fall inside. 'Look, Lola, honey, you have a strong case. But I don't think you've quite realised what a slow process this can be.'

'But if I have a strong case—'

'You'd better sit down, Lola,' George said firmly.

Lola sank reluctantly into an armchair in the bay window. It had a wonderful view over the Hudson, but it might as well have been of a string of tenements in the Bronx for all the aesthetic value it had for Lola.

'I've filed papers in Surrogate's Court on your behalf,' George was saying, 'to have Carin replaced as your trustee. We got plenty of grounds for that, believe me. Undue influence – that's her inducing him to do something he normally wouldn't have done. Conflicts of interest – well, that's obvious. And we're also arguing that he was incompetent to make the decision to change the trustee in the first place, because of his illness and the medication he was taking. Basically, we throw a ton of stuff at the wall and see what sticks.'

'So Surrogate's Court will decide if Carin can stay on as my trustee or not?' Lola asked.

'Hopefully, yeah,' George corrected her. 'Legally, we have to start by filing papers there, because that's the procedure when distributions from a trust are in question. But the actual outcome – what we want, a declaratory judgement saying that the power of attorney is invalid – that goes to the Supreme Court.'

'The *Supreme Court*?' Lola's head span. Seven old people in black robes. 'But that could take *years!*'

'Oh, not that long.' How could George sound so cheerful when he was giving her this horrendous news? 'It's the New York Supreme Court, honey, not the big one you've heard of.'

'And what am I supposed to do for money in the meantime?'

'Oh,' George said easily, 'we're applying for a temporary injunction to release payments to you from the trust fund, based on the fact that your father placed no limits on disbursements to you when he was, uh, in full enjoyment of his mental facilities.'

'*Really?*' Her heart lifted.

'Yeah. Of course, Carin's lawyers are fighting that too.' He sighed.

'They're lining up people to testify that your dad said you were spending too much. Plus, they have some emails he sent Carin saying much the same thing.'

'But Daddy *never*—'

'Look, even if they don't give you unlimited access to the trust fund, or appoint a new trustee,' George said reassuringly, 'we should be able to get fifty grand out of Surrogates' Court for you in a couple a weeks.'

'Fifty grand?'

It sounded like a lot, but Lola had the awful feeling that it wasn't at all. Not when she thought about paying for somewhere to live, all her usual expenses, eating out – and God, George's billable hours would probably swallow that fifty grand up completely by now—

'Will they give me that every month?' she asked hopefully.

'Oh, no. No, we need to keep making applications to the court, and that can take a while. No way we can guarantee how much they'll decide to cut you on a regular basis, I'm afraid.'

In the turmoil of misery swirling around her, there was one thing that Lola could cling onto. And she did.

'I need to be able to see Daddy, George,' she begged. 'Can you sort things out so she has to let me in to see him?'

'Now there we're on ground I'm not sure of,' George admitted. 'This isn't my area. But sure, I know someone we can consult.' He cleared his throat. 'The only thing is, Lola . . . and I didn't want to mention this to you before – after all, you've got a lot on your plate right now . . . but how much money do you have? I mean, this other attorney will want paying, and I'm racking up the hours myself . . . and, you know, I can wait awhile, I was very close to your dad, but eventually . . . well, I can make applications to Surrogates' Court for my fees, and the other attorney's too, and though the applications should go through OK – well, you know courts, nothing's set in stone.' He cleared his throat again. 'So what I'm asking, honey, is, worst-case scenario, have you got the money to pay us? Or at least guarantee our fees?'

*

So that was the $25,000 gone. Legal fees would eat up all the money she had left faster than her all-too-brief stay in Madison's apartment. Curled up in the armchair, staring bleakly ahead of her, Lola faced her options. She had two choices: go back to England and stay at her mother's – where at least she could live for free – until the battle for her trust fund was resolved. Or stay here, where she could – hopefully – visit her father every so often. That had to be the choice. There was no way she could leave New York, not while she had the chance of actually getting in to see her father.

But how could she afford to stay here?

Just then, her phone rang. She watched it vibrate and jerk on the arm of the chair, unable for a moment to find the strength to pick it up and answer the call. But at last, gingerly, she pressed the answer button.

'Lola! Darling, is that you?'

She couldn't believe what she was hearing. The soft voice; the accent that was a mix of his French mother, his Danish father, his English education and now the faintest overlay of time spent in America; the way he always called her 'Darling' so caressingly—

'*Jean-Marc?*' she exclaimed.

'Yes! It's me!' he carolled happily. 'Blast from the past!'

'The *past*? It's only been a week!'

'So *much* has happened to me, Lola darling,' Jean-Marc said joyously, 'it feels like months and months! Oh, I can't wait to tell you everything! Where are you?'

'In New York,' Lola said, still very confused. 'Are you ringing from rehab?'

'In *New York?* Oh my God, how fabulous! So am I! Come round immediately! I'm in the family suite at the Plaza. *Too* old-fashioned, but in a fantastic way.'

'You're—' So much was happening to Lola that she felt quite dizzy again: she took a deep breath and collected her thoughts. 'But what about Arizona? I thought you were supposed to stay in rehab for at least a month?'

Jean-Marc made a noise she couldn't identify over a mobile

phone: but it sounded as if he'd put his lips together and blown a raspberry.

'Darling, come round *now*,' he insisted, 'and I'll tell you *everything*. There's much too much to tell you over the phone, and I want to see you! My little golden Lola! Jump in a cab, I'll see you in twenty minutes.'

He hung up. Lola stared at the phone in disbelief. And then she jumped up and ran into the bedroom to start pulling her clothes out of Madison's wardrobe and into her suitcases. She had never been in the Van der Veer suite at the Plaza before; when she and Jean-Marc were together in New York they had always stayed at a downtown boutique hotel. But considering how rich the Van der Veers were, there had to be at least four bedrooms in a family suite.

Besides, Jean-Marc owed it to her to take her in. He had, after all, humiliated her in all the British, American and European tabloids. A bedroom at the Plaza was the least he could give her in return . . .

Oh, the bliss of getting out of a cab at the Plaza and having the doorman instantly whisk all her cases out of the trunk and onto one of those gold metal trolleys as she trod up the carpet into the beautiful foyer, another doorman holding the door open for her obsequiously, the concierge coming forward to say that Mr van der Veer had rung down to say that she was on her way and to go straight up, her luggage would follow by the service elevator . . . She felt like Lola Fitzgerald again, rich, privileged, spoilt, and it was simply wonderful.

When Jean-Marc, waiting for her at the door of the suite, dragged her inside, she could see instantly that there would be more than enough space for her here. Through the door of the living-room she could see rooms upon rooms stretching away, like a kaleidoscope when you twist it and it shows you endless variations of the same object: bedrooms, sitting-rooms, as far as the eye could see, all done up in luxurious shades of beige and gold and dull reds, muted and tasteful.

'It isn't really *us*,' Jean-Marc admitted, taking her hand and leading her to an enormous, over-stuffed sofa, 'it's a bit *classic* and *old-school,* but darling, it's *insanely* comfortable.'

They sank into the sofa, still holding hands.

'Now have some champagne,' Jean-Marc continued, 'we've got so much to toast!'

He reached for a bottle of champagne, which was nestling in a big silver ice bucket, along, Lola noticed, with two others still unopened.

'Are you supposed to be drinking?' she couldn't help asking.

Jean-Marc giggled. He looked great, she had to admit. His skin was lightly tanned and smooth, the whites of his eyes were as clear as ever, and his pupils weren't dilated, the telltale sign of drug use. His golden hair was pushed back from his face in a careless series of curls, and his blue eyes danced with happiness. She thought, too, that he had put on a few pounds, which definitely suited him: in the last days in London he had been too thin, which in retrospect had clearly been the drugs devouring him, taking away his appetite.

'I'm drug-free,' he announced, pouring her a glass and topping up his own. There was a third flute of champagne, half-drunk, which Jean-Marc refilled too. Lola parted her lips to ask whose it was, but Jean-Marc overrode her; he was in full flow. 'I can't give up *everything,* my God, that would be so boring! And besides, Lola, I had the biggest breakthrough. The *biggest.* I have to thank Niels so much, I should get down on my knees and thank him every day for sending me to that horrible place—'

'You should certainly get down on your knees, darling,' said a new voice with a light American accent. 'Whether it should be to your brother, though, is a whole different story.'

'David!' Jean-Marc jumped up, picking up the third glass. 'Darling! Here, we're toasting!'

The man had emerged from a door in the foyer which, from its placement, must be a bathroom. From Lola's vantage point on the sofa she had a good view of him: slim, hyper-elegant, with slicked-back black hair, dark as paint, and eyes even bluer than Jean-Marc's.

He was wearing a tight long-sleeved navy T-shirt with faint embroidery over one shoulder, jeans snug enough to leave it in no doubt on which side he hung, and a belt with a diamanté buckle. He took the proffered glass and wrapped his arm around Jean-Marc's waist, so that they both faced Lola, a matched pair, one blond, one dark, blue-eyed and smiling with elation.

'Lola, darling, this is David!' Jean-Marc announced delightedly. 'My *boyfriend!* Oh Lola, I've come out! I'm gay! Isn't it *wonderful?*'

And the boys turned to each other in unison, as if choreographed, and kissed, a long passionate kiss, their champagne glasses meeting simultaneously with a clink that rang like a pair of tiny bells.

Chapter 14

*L*ola got up, of course, glass in hand, to embrace the happy couple, and there was much hugging and toasting and clinking of glasses and general rejoicing before they all sat down again, David and Jean-Marc curled together on the big sofa, Lola in a very generously sized armchair.

'I ordered some food,' Jean-Marc said. 'Sushi, and edamame beans and strawberries for you, darling.'

David looked baffled.

'No, not you!' Jean-Marc giggled. 'My *other* darling. Lola exists on edamame beans and strawberries.'

'And sashimi,' Lola added.

'God, you must be hungry *all the time*,' David exclaimed.

'I am, really,' Lola admitted.

'So! I'll tell you everything, and then you tell me everything!' Jean-Marc said happily. He cuddled up against David, who started stroking his blond curls. Lola felt a sudden wave of jealousy: this was exactly how she and Jean-Marc used to sit, curled up together, caressing each other like puppies or kittens who lick and groom each other continually.

'Are you OK with all this, Lola?' David asked. 'I mean, it must be quite a shock for you.'

Lola noted he was acute enough to have picked up on her change of mood, and gave him points for that.

'Actually, I am,' she said, knowing it was true, despite her wash of envy at seeing Jean-Marc in someone else's arms. 'Honestly, as soon as Jean-Marc said he was gay, I thought: *Well, of course you are! Why didn't any of us realise it before?*'

'Oh my God, that's *exactly* how I felt. *Exactly*,' Jean-Marc said, drinking some champagne. 'I mean, all that stuff with Patricia—' he looked guiltily at Lola. 'I'm so sorry again for dragging you through all of that, Lo. I mean, coming out's one thing, but all that scandal, the overdose, the tranny stuff—'

'And not even a pretty tranny!' David chimed in. 'A pig-ugly one! I mean, *honestly*, Jean, what were you *thinking*?'

Jean-Marc sighed deeply.

'Darling, we've been through this,' he said, reaching up a hand to stroke David's, which was resting on his shoulder. 'You heard me say it in group. I wasn't thinking. It was all just blind panic and running away from my problems. Running away from my sexuality. I hated myself, and I hated the fact that I was about to get married – sorry, darling—'

He glanced apologetically at Lola, who flipped a hand to indicate that he shouldn't worry on her behalf. She noticed, as she did so, that her manicure was badly chipped. Well, that wouldn't be a problem any more. She could afford any beauty treatment she needed. Lola wriggled in her chair with pure pleasure at the thought.

'I mean, if I had to marry anyone, any woman, I mean,' Jean-Marc continued, 'it would be my darling Lo.'

'Oh God yes!' David agreed. 'I mean, look at her! She's so beautiful! And you could have so much fun dressing her up – she's like a gorgeous little doll, and her boobs and ass aren't big, she could wear *anything*—'

'I *know*,' Jean-Marc said. 'I used to dress her up all the time, it was so much fun . . .'

They both tilted their heads to the side and stared approvingly at

Lola, David's dark head resting on Jean-Marc's blond one, two pairs of blue eyes beaming at her.

'You can still buy me clothes and dress me up,' she assured them. 'I've only got three cases with me.'

'Oooh, shopping for girls' shoes!' David sang, clapping his hands. 'My *fave* thing in the world!'

A few doors down, someone was moving around the suite; it was the bellhop, leaving Lola's cases.

'Would you give him a twenty from my wallet, darling?' Jean-Marc said to David. 'And tell him to send up housekeeping to unpack for Lola? Thank you, darling.'

As David jumped up to carry out these instructions, Jean-Marc readjusted himself, sitting up straighter. He was in his usual outfit of fitted silk shirt over slim jeans and suede loafers; Eurotrash style converted so well to gay-about-town that he hadn't needed to change his look at all when he came out.

'David's a godsend,' he said fervently. 'He saved me. Really, he saved my life.'

'So how did you meet?' Lola asked, finishing her champagne and reaching for a cigarette. 'I still don't understand why you're not in rehab—' *and, frankly, why it's OK for you to be drinking*, she wanted to add. But she thought it best to take one step at a time. As it were.

'We met in rehab! That's the amazing thing! I was such a wreck when I arrived – well, you *saw* me. Was it only last week?' he reflected. 'My God, I can't believe it. It feels like an eternity, so much has *happened* . . . Anyway, I arrived quite late at night and they put me in a room by myself, but the next day they woke me up for group at some frighteningly early hour—'

'Nine in the morning, godawful,' David said, re-entering the room.

'*So*,' Jean-Marc continued, 'I walked into the room where group was – God, I *tottered*, I was barely walking – and there he was. A blue-eyed angel in tight jeans. I looked at him and he looked back at me and I just *knew*. I mean, all pretence was gone by this time. And also, to be totally frank, as soon as I laid eyes on David I got the most enormous hard-on.'

David, on the hotel phone ordering food, collapsed with a fit of giggles and had to apologise to the person he was talking to.

'So I mean, I knew I was gay at *that* point,' Jean-Marc said so seriously that Lola got the giggles too.

'I should say so,' she commented. 'Did you get a hard-on too, David?'

'*Gigantic*,' David mouthed, still on the phone, holding his hands a foot apart to indicate its size.

'So there we were!' Jean-Marc said. 'Just in mad, total lust! And it was perfect, because it was literally the first thing I said in group – not that I was totally in lust with David, of course, but that I was gay. And it was the first time I'd ever said it, naturally, and everyone clapped. I was terrified, but it was the proudest moment of my life.'

'I was so proud of you!' David said, his call finished, plopping down on the sofa behind his lover. '*So* proud! I just wanted to run over and kiss you then and there.'

'It didn't take us long, did it?' Jean-Marc said smugly.

'After lunch I cornered him in the smoking area,' David added happily.

'He said if I needed any practical help he was there for me,' Jean-Marc smiled.

'Ooh, I was smooth, wasn't I?' David said.

'I didn't know you could have sex in rehab,' Lola said.

The boys rolled their eyes in unison.

'You're not supposed to,' Jean-Marc said, 'but I just couldn't keep my hands off him. It was amazing. David's my drug of choice now,' Jean-Marc said happily. 'I'm addicted to David. And I realised, once I'd come out, everything was all right!'

'I'm so happy for you both,' Lola assured them. 'And I'm really fine with Jean-Marc coming out, and us not getting married, because honestly, I look back and I wonder, what was I *thinking*? No offence, Jean-Marc—'

He shook his head fervently, his golden curls dancing, to show that none was taken.

'But I knew,' she continued, 'I *knew* deep down it wasn't what it was supposed to be. No matter how happy we were.'

'Oh darling, we were *so* happy!'

Jean-Marc stretched out a hand to her, and she came out of her seat to take it. He pulled her towards him, till she was sitting on the sofa too, and the two boys adjusted to make room for her, so they were all curled up together. Jean-Marc's hand came up to stroke her hair, and David smiled sweetly down at her, and it was all so lovely, so welcoming, so safe, after all her struggles, that she burst into floods of tears.

Jean-Marc, who cried at the drop of a hat, at the sight of a cute puppy in the street or even the mention of a sad film, started sobbing too, and though David didn't actually cry (which Lola was grateful for, as she would have considered it a bit hypocritical, considering that her and Jean-Marc's tears were mourning their dreams of a life together as the perfect heterosexual golden couple) he hugged them both, and mumbled nice things, and got up to get them both tissues, and opened the door to the room service person who was bringing their food.

'Oh dear,' Jean-Marc said eventually, wiping his eyes. 'We could still have our lovely golden children, Lola, if you want.'

'Oh, that would be fantastic!' David cried, tipping the room service person from Jean-Marc's wallet. 'They'd be the prettiest kids in the whole world!'

'I'll think about it,' Lola promised, smiling as she dried her face. 'God, I must look like a wreck.'

'You *are* a little puffy,' David said honestly.

'We'll get someone in to give her a facial,' Jean-Marc said. 'And anything else you want, Lo. What do you want? Just say the word. I owe you so much. I'll never be able to repay you for letting you down like that. The wedding being cancelled. And all that awful, awful stuff in the press.'

'I need a lot of money,' Lola said simply. 'For lawyers. And somewhere to stay.'

'*Mi casa es su casa*,' David said, laying out the food on the coffee table in front of the sofa, so no one had to get up. 'Well, it's Jean-Marc's *casa*, technically, but I don't know how to say "his" in Spanish.'

'Not "his", "ours". It's *nuestra*,' Jean-Marc said fondly. '*Nuestra casa*, darling. Our house. Stay as long as you want, Lo. You've got a whole suite down at the end, you never need to see us if you don't want to. And I'll get a card made for you on my account. I'm getting one for David, too.' He rolled his eyes. 'At least *I* haven't had my trust fund cut off by my awful stepmother!'

'Is that what happened to you?' David asked Lola, eyes wide.

'Yes, tell us everything,' Jean-Marc said, picking up his chopsticks and selecting a salmon-skin roll from the sushi platter in front of him.

So Lola began.

By tea-time the next day, Lola was almost perfectly back to her usual state of exquisite, groomed glossiness. Her hair and nails were done, her legs and bikini line waxed; she had had a long lovely facial, a detoxifying wrap, a full-body massage, and she was BeauBronzed from head to toe, a flawless spray tan. She even had an appointment with the best eyebrow specialist in town, in two days' time, and being able to get one at such short notice was a minor miracle that told her God truly was looking out for her now. Her luck had turned. She had rung George, told him there would be no problem about any bills at all, no matter how large, and instructed him to hurry up the lawyer who was filing some sort of motion for her to get access to her father.

In short, every pressing need had been met. She hadn't even bothered to get dressed so far today, as a procession of beauticians had come to her, filing in and out of her large, luxurious set of rooms – bedroom, bathroom, living-room – at the far end of the Van der Veer suite. She was lounging on her sofa in a silk negligee, watching her plasma TV, or, rather, flicking idly through the channels, one trashy and addictive reality show after another, when she heard someone let themselves in through the main door of the suite, far away down the long series of rooms.

'Jean-Marc?' she called. 'David?'

David was at work, Jean-Marc gone out for lunch and shopping, and they had all arranged to meet up in the early evening and have dinner somewhere unspecified, maybe catch a movie. Jean-Marc and David had banned themselves from going near clubs of any description, because those places were so rife with drugs, and Lola was more than fine with that: after the drama and upsets of the past week, a series of simple evenings spent on dinner-and-a-movie dates with the two boys was all the social life she felt she would need for weeks to come.

It did seem a little early for them to be back, though.

She got up, slipping on the silk robe that matched her negligee, and padded on bare feet out of her living-room and down the internal corridor. Maybe some delivery had come in, or someone had come to change the flowers – Jean-Marc was obsessed with lovely arrangements and insisted they always be as fresh as possible – but it seemed odd that they wouldn't have rung up first, to alert her that someone was coming in . . .

In the main sitting-room, a man was standing with his back to her, looking at something on the desk. She knew instantly that it wasn't either of the boys: firstly, because his back was much too wide and muscular. Both Jean-Marc and David were delicately built, slim and elegant. This man had the shoulders of a bruiser by comparison. And secondly, he was wearing a grey suit, which neither of them would ever, ever have done.

Suddenly she had a very bad feeling indeed. She was actually about to turn and flee when he spun round. He must have had the hearing of a cat to pick up the almost-inaudible sound of her feet on the thick carpeting.

Lola's entire body froze. She literally could not move a muscle. The way he was looking at her was so frightening she was paralysed to the spot. She was the rabbit once more, staring at the snake.

'*You!*' Niels van der Veer's silver eyes narrowed in fury and contempt. 'Little Miss Spoilt Princess! What the hell are *you* doing here? I told you never to come near my brother again!'

And he started towards her menacingly, his shoulders bunching under the expensive suit.

Chapter 15

*L*awrence was sulking. Evie had never seen him in this mood before, and she didn't much like it. Lawrence was always so balanced, so calm; even when they were having sex he maintained a Zen-like state of poise and equilibrium. But as soon as Evie had announced that she was moving – not miles away, not to Bay Ridge or Hoboken or somewhere an hour and a half away on the subway or PATH train, but just one floor down – his self-control had slipped, and he had become, by his own high standards, quite impossible.

'I thought you'd be *pleased!*' Evie protested, for the tenth time that day. 'You and Autumn were fighting all the time because I was staying here! Now I'm just on the next floor down, I've got my own room, you can come visit me whenever you want – I thought this was perfect!'

Lawrence shrugged and mumbled something under his breath. His full lips were pushed out into what, on anyone else, Evie would have called a pout, and his shoulders were hunched in what, on anyone else, he himself would have called terrible posture.

'I just don't understand why you've done this,' he said finally, pacing the length of the kitchen. He'd been working on some stretches when Evie came in to tell him her news, and he was wearing a singlet and an old pair of running shorts. Even now, annoyed as Evie was by his attitude, she couldn't help watching the flex of the long muscles in his thighs, the round firm bulge of his buttocks in the tight shorts, and feel herself getting more than a little turned on.

'I thought it was a great idea,' she repeated impatiently. 'I mean, it's the best solution. You know, it isn't so cool for me to have Autumn always sneering at me because of Benny and my fur coats and everything—'

'Oh, Autumn's coming round,' Lawrence said. 'Don't you think? I think she's warming to you.'

He stopped in his tracks and fixed Evie with a pleading grey gaze.

'No, Lawrence, I *don't* think,' Evie said firmly. 'She hates my guts.'

Because she's in love with you, she added beneath her breath. She wouldn't say that out loud, though, because she was much too wise for that. Evie had a lot of experience with men, and one thing she knew was that if you told them a woman was in love with them, it made them more interested in her. And Evie didn't want Lawrence getting interested in Autumn. There was no mileage for Evie in living out some sort of bohemian love triangle.

Lawrence had kept Evie satisfied sexually for longer than any man before him, and she had no intention, if she could help it, of letting that go; it had been nearly eight months now, and she still got hot looking at him the way he was now, his bare shoulders with those gorgeous caps of muscle, the slight dent in the centre showing how defined they were. She loved to run her tongue along that dent, taste the delicate salt of his sweat, lick down to his armpit, which always smelt and tasted delicious.

She shifted on her chair, wanting to stop talking and start making out.

'Look, come here,' she coaxed him. 'Let's not fight. There's so many more fun things we could be doing.'

And she gave him that look from beneath her eyelashes, ducking her chin down and looking up at him with her big brown eyes, the look that never failed to get a rise out of him.

She saw it immediately, his cock beginning to stir in his shorts, and her lips curled into a little smile of triumph.

'No, Evie!' he said crossly, turning away. 'This is important! I'm not going to let you distract me. I thought we were – I thought we had – I thought you *liked* us living together.'

'I don't even see that much of you, Lawrence,' Evie pointed out. 'You're up at the crack of dawn, doing your yoga, and then you're out training and taking classes all day—'

'Which makes it *more* important that we're sharing a room, because at least we sleep together!' He turned to face her again, his light brown hair falling over his face, and impatiently he tilted his head back, pulling his hair into a ponytail, twisting it into its elastic band. 'I wake up and you're there, lying next to me, sleeping so soundly . . . I creep out of the room in the mornings so as not to wake you up . . .'

'Isn't that a big nuisance?' Evie asked, not understanding his point.

'No! I *like* it! God, you're just not getting this – it's like talking to a wall!'

He paced back again, to the table where she was sitting, and pulled up a chair to face her, twisting it so he was straddling the seat, his arms propped on its back.

'I want us to be a couple, Evie,' he said quietly. 'I've really enjoyed having you here.' He gazed at her, his handsome features very serious, his high cheekbones elegantly carved. 'I believe in sexual freedom, you know that. I don't think anyone should ever tie any other human being's sexuality down, or try to control it. But I want us to be a couple. I think I realised that the first day you were here, when I came in and found you curled up in my bed.'

'Oh, Lawrence . . .'

Evie's face knotted up with embarrassment. She thought she was so clever with men, did she? Thought she knew them inside out, how to manoeuvre them, get them to do exactly what she wanted? Well, she sure as hell hadn't seen this one coming.

And now she was fucked.

Because if she agreed to what Lawrence wanted, it would weaken her. Maybe fatally. If she were living with Lawrence, coming home to him every night, how could she still be focused as hard as she needed to be on looking for the rich man who would take her away from this crappy place and install her back in another Tribeca penthouse?

Evie faced the truth about herself. She hadn't taken the room downstairs because she couldn't stand Autumn, and the tension in the loft, any more. She'd taken it because she needed to be free. Not softened up by Lawrence's sweetness, the way he mumbled her name in his sleep when she crawled into bed beside him, and pulled her close, spooning her, his breath warm on the back of her neck.

Her feelings for him would ruin her dreams. She'd end up living here with him in even worse squalor than she'd grown up in.

'I can't,' she said simply. 'I'm sorry, Lawrence.'

Lawrence nodded slowly.

'You just can't settle down with a poor yoga teacher,' he said softly.

She couldn't answer him. But his clear grey eyes looked directly into hers and read the truth there.

'Then you're right,' he said, swinging one leg easily over the chair seat, standing up, pushing it away from him. 'You should move out.'

Evie jumped up.

'I still want us to—' she started. 'This doesn't need to change anything—'

But Lawrence dodged her as she came towards him, shaking his head.

'Yes, it does,' he said sadly. 'I'm sorry, Evie. I thought I was OK with this. I thought I could handle it. But I guess I can't handle it after all, and I have to be honest with myself and you.'

He reached his arms up behind his head, cracking out his shoulders in a long stretch. The sight of his biceps flexing and swelling with the movement, jutting forwards, the light brown hair in his pale armpits, slightly damp and salty, made Evie's thighs twitch together with desire.

'Lawrence—' she tried again.

But he shook his head, almost angrily, and plunged away from her, towards the door.

'I'll go out for an hour,' he said over his shoulder. 'That should give you time to move your stuff downstairs.' He darted a quick look at her. 'I'll see you around, Evie.'

And then he was gone. She heard him taking the stairs two at a time.

It was the right thing to do. Evie was absolutely sure of it.

It was just shitty that seeing him go made her feel like bursting into tears. Totally shitty.

She turned and walked slowly down the corridor, to the room she'd shared with him, the room she was leaving. The first thing she saw as she pushed open the door was her pole, still in its moulded plastic carrying case, leaning against the wall, and for some reason the sight of it lifted her miserable spirits just a fraction. She picked it up, slung the strap over her shoulder, and carried it back through the apartment and downstairs.

Everyone was out in her new place. The trapezes were pulled back up to the ceiling, as they always were when not in use, cords slung round them and wrapped around figure-of-eight hooks on the wall, holding them out of the way. So there was plenty of room for Evie to take out her pole, open it up, and extend it till it touched the ceiling. She was relieved: these old industrial lofts had such high ceilings, she hadn't been sure if the pole would be long enough.

She pulled out the little screwdriver she kept in the pole case, and heaved the pole into position at the centre of the room, screwing the base tight till she was sure it wouldn't budge a fraction of an inch. A quarter of an hour later, she had forgotten everything but the reality of the pole between her ankles, digging in, as she climbed it yet again. At the top, close enough to reach up and touch the ceiling, she gripped it hard instead, making sure she had a good wrap, working it under one arm so it was tightly clamped into her armpit.

She squeezed it in, getting secure. Then she took her legs off the pole and stretched them out, away from each other, into near-perfect splits. It was one of her signature moves, this ability to make and hold the splits in mid-air, and she was very proud of it.

For a moment, Evie was static, holding the pose, in perfect balance. Then she loosened her grip on the pole with hands and arm, just fractionally, but enough to start her moving, sliding down it, keeping her legs in the splits all the way down, till she landed on the floor, legs sliding along it, and let go of the pole, reaching back with both hands to grasp the foot of the leg stretched out behind her.

The sound of clapping came from the open door, and she twisted round in surprise.

Natalie and Jeremy were standing there, smiling at her. But the applause wasn't coming from one of them. They fell to either side of the doorway as a woman walked through, a woman one definitely needed to make space for: she was of medium height, with bleached-blonde hair, milky-white skin that should never see the sun, and weighing a good two hundred pounds – every pound of which, as far as Evie could tell, looked to be in exactly the right place.

She was wearing a 1950s-style dress, a red-and-white print cinched in at the waist with a big patent-leather belt, and red shiny pumps. The dress must have been made for her, it wrapped so well around her opulent curves. Her make-up was 1950s too: heavy black eyeliner, flicking up at the outer corners to make cat's-eyes, light powder to keep her pale skin matte, and bright red lipstick. Over her shoulders was draped a black cardigan, and the plumpness of her bare white arms, the roundness of her equally white calves, was so rich and satisfying that Evie suddenly felt skinny, scrawny even, by comparison with her.

'Evie, this is Laura,' Natalie said. 'She has the room next to yours—'

'*Honey,*' Laura said in a little piping Minnie-Mouse voice, 'you should *totally* work up a burlesque act with that!'

Chapter 16

*N*iels van der Veer was almost upon her before Lola managed to summon up any control over her muscles. She was remembering, all too vividly, their last encounter, when he had picked her up and carried her bodily from Jean-Marc's hospital room.

'Don't you dare touch me!' she said, and to her great annoyance it came out as a breathy little gasp. 'Look what you did to me last time, you *bully!*'

And she gripped the edge of her white silk dressing gown and jerked it angrily off her shoulder, down to just above her elbow, so that he could see her bare arm, revealed by the strappy negligee, and the clear mark of bruises on her skin. Four pale amethyst stripes, fading to green at the edges, the marks of his fingers where he had gripped her so tightly he had lifted her off her feet, just a few days ago.

'There's exactly the same ones on the other arm,' she said furiously, staring back at him, suddenly able to meet his bright silver stare without flinching, now that she was challenging him back. 'Do you want to see them too? Or is this enough for you?'

And even then, she couldn't read his expression. It changed, certainly. His craggy features froze; his strong jaw, the straight hard line of his mouth, looked even more sculptural than before. His shoulders were as wide as a wall; she couldn't see beyond him, he towered over her. The sheer weight and mass of him was so imposing that it was hard for her to stand her ground, but she planted her bare feet and wouldn't give an inch.

How dare he be so angry with her? she thought furiously. As if she had had anything to do with Jean-Marc's problems and his overdose – anything, of course, beyond being the fiancée with whom an imminent marriage had sent Jean-Marc into drug overdrive? And she had ended up just as damaged as Jean-Marc, despite the fact that she was completely innocent of anything but not being able to spot that her fiancé was gay. Even Jean-Marc himself had only just realised he was gay, so you could scarcely blame Lola for *that* . . .

Niels van der Veer reached towards Lola, and she flinched back, unable to stop herself. But his grip, when it closed around her elbow, was gentle, though irresistibly firm. His hand was as big as she remembered, and looking down at it, as it held her in place, she noticed the sprinkling of gold hairs on his knuckles. Their presence was so masculine that it made her shiver.

And then he lowered his head.

She stood there in absolute shock as he pulled her closer, and that strong, imposing head bent over her arm, and Niels van der Veer's mouth, warm and moist, kissed the bruises he had made on her skin.

Her eyes closed. She thought she ought to push him away, because she was still furious with him, and he shouldn't just think that by kissing her bruises he could somehow redeem himself, and after all, he hadn't actually apologised: but the touch of his warm mouth had put her into some kind of trance, and as he kissed up her arm, and sank his lips into her neck, biting at the skin gently, gently, but just enough to let her feel his teeth against her flesh, she actually thought she was going to faint, and she realised that her arms had raised and she was clinging on to him so she didn't fall over.

That was when it really began to spiral out of their control. Because when Lola grabbed onto his forearms, just to keep her steady, her fingers closed around such solid muscle that she could-n't help moaning in appreciation. His tailor, she observed with the one small sane part of her mind she had left, must be very good indeed, because Niels's biceps really were very well-developed, and it would take a great deal of skill not to make his upper body look ridiculously huge in a suit. And then she couldn't help thinking about what the rest of his upper body must look like, and the one small sane part of her mind went up in flames, like the rest of her, and she realised she was moaning still, and tilting back her head, so he would kiss her on the mouth.

And he did.

Fireworks went off inside her head. Chrysanthemums and rock-ets and spinning Catherine wheels, great explosions of colour and light. Niels's mouth was hard and insistent; his teeth sank into her lips, his tongue invaded her mouth. His hands gripped her tightly, moving her exactly where he wanted. She sensed that by opening her mouth to him, letting him in, she had given him consent to everything he wanted. Somehow she knew that he wouldn't ask from now on, he would just take, forceful as a battering ram. It would be up to her to say no, to push him away, and how could she do that, when she was longing for him to touch her everywhere, all over her body, every single part of her, from the soles of her feet to the crown of her head . . .

He was consuming her. He kissed her as if he wanted to eat her up, as if she were a banquet and he had been hungry for so long he couldn't remember what it was like to be satiated. She tried to kiss him back, so he didn't have it all his own way, to nip at his lips with little bites and kisses, and when she did, it made him grind her against him even harder, so she felt the length of his body all the way down hers, the swell of his pectorals, his flat stomach, his cock pressing into her stomach, his muscled thighs, and she moaned again, despite herself, into his mouth.

That moan seemed to trigger something in him, because the next thing she knew his hands slid down her to grasp her bottom, cupping her, pulling her into him, lifting her so she was suddenly not supporting her own weight: her hands were twined in his dirty-blond hair, which was just long enough for her to twist it a little round her fingers. His hands were so powerful on her, moving her where he wanted as if she were a doll, and she wanted to make him feel her power just a little in return: she pulled at his hair, making him gasp, and he dragged his head back just enough so she couldn't get a grip any longer, and looked down at her with such a scorching stare that she literally felt as if she were melting. Her core was liquefying, so hot and insistent she had less and less control over it, flowing out, reaching for him—

He was carrying her now, as easily as if she weighed nothing at all, carrying her across the room, and she closed her eyes again and hid her face in his shoulder, overwhelmed by what was happening. Then she felt a hard cool surface under her bottom, and realised that she had wrapped her legs around him, twined her arms around his neck.

God, this was awful. She had given in to him completely without even realising what he was doing. One touch of his hot arrogant mouth and she had parted her legs for him and let him pick her up and carry her around, a man she had absolutely loathed and despised till this very moment; actually, someone she *still* loathed and despised, it was just that he was kissing her so hard he wasn't giving her any opportunity to tell him so. And he had put her down on the desk, and was standing between her legs, pressed up against her, so that she could feel his entire cock, rubbing exactly where she wanted it, and how was she supposed to tell him what she thought of him when he was getting her so damp between her legs, without even having touched her there with any part of his body – unclothed, that was – so that she could barely breathe with desire for him—

He pulled away, and Lola's eyes snapped fully open in horror, scared that he was going to shake his head and run a hand through his disordered hair and walk away from her, spreadeagled on the desk, making her look like an utter fool. But then she saw that he was tugging at his belt buckle, and the relief was like a surge of hot liquid through her veins. She wanted to help him, but it was all she could do, gripping the edges of the desk, not to fall over, she was so dazed and wet with lust. It seemed to take forever. But finally he had his belt unbuckled and his trousers unzipped and he'd shoved his boxers down, and Lola's eyes had never gone quite so wide, because it was one thing feeling it against you and quite another seeing how large it was when it sprang free, and even another thing altogether – oh God, *oh God* – feeling it drive up inside you, as Niels's big powerful hands closed around her buttocks again and pulled her relentlessly onto it until she couldn't think in words any more.

Just sensation. Just Niels, sweating against her – she could feel his heat through his shirt and his jacket, and she could smell his hot strong scent, so good that she buried her face in his armpit, wanting it all around her, to have him in her nostrils as much as she had him between her legs, driving into her, hurting her, because she wasn't used to sex like this, not at all. But it was so relentlessly good that all she could do was cling to him and moan and listen to him swearing above her head as he fucked her so hard she thought she would die and go to heaven from it.

Her dressing gown seemed to have come off completely. Her negligee was bunched around her waist, and Niels was ripping down the straps so he could kiss her breasts. His teeth closed around one nipple, and she screamed in pleasure and pulled him even closer, which made him buck inside her still harder, still further, so much that he actually pulled back and stared down at her with what looked like sheer amazement on his face.

By now Lola was transported, gone. No man had ever fucked her like this: they had always been hugely respectful, treated her like the porcelain doll she resembled, clothes exquisite, make-up perfect, not a flaw on her smooth pale golden skin. No one had ever bruised her and ripped her clothes and shoved himself up inside her so hard and fast that he hadn't given her time to catch her breath. And if anyone else had tried, she would have slapped their face and made them apologise profusely. She caught sight of their straining bodies in the mirror behind Niels – his back bunching with muscle under his shirt and jacket, his strong thighs bare and pounding, almost comically naked, and her equally bare legs wrapped round him, her head thrown back. Lola didn't remotely recognise herself in this girl so overwhelmed with passion that she would let an almost-complete stranger, who had manhandled her appallingly the last time they had met, basically pick her up and fuck her senseless on the closest level surface they had to hand.

Niels van der Veer was crying out something in a language Lola didn't know. His hands tightened still further on her buttocks. She could feel his pubic hair scratching against her newly waxed skin. It hurt, but deliciously. She would be so sore after this she would be barely able to walk. And the thought, so scandalously filthy, so alien to her, was so exciting that she rammed herself down on his cock and, to her enormous surprise, had the first-ever orgasm she had ever had with a man.

She screamed in pleasure and amazement, a long, exquisite scream that was caught by Niels as he took one hand off her buttocks and twisted it instead into her hair, pulling her head towards him so he could grind his mouth down on hers. Lola saw stars. Her entire body was overloading with sensation. Niels gasped, reared, and pulled out just in time to shower her upper thigh with a hot stream of come.

Lola had thought she never wanted it to end; but now, as Niels's cock pumped over her leg, she realised she was in a state of utter, perfect bliss. There was something so sexy, so powerful, at having made this bossy, bullying, autocratic man so overcome with lust for her that he had ripped her clothes, fucked her, and then come over her in absolute surrender. Her entire body fizzed with release and triumph.

Besides, she had come herself. She had ground herself down on him and made herself come. She was in awe of what she had achieved. Lola had always thought she needed to be the perfect girl-friend, beautiful and elegant at all times: which meant absolutely not letting out, in the company of a man, that raw sexual energy that made you groan and pant and look needy, let alone mess up your hair, in front of a man.

Well, that idea had disappeared forever. And she certainly didn't miss it.

Niels's eyes were closed. She watched him for a few moments, as the aftershock of his orgasm still flooded through him. Then, slowly, his eyelids lifted, and he looked at her.

He was the sexiest man she'd ever seen in her life. He was pure, raw sex in a big, muscular package. It was quite extraordinary that she hadn't realised that before.

He looked down at their bodies, Lola's pale thighs still wrapped around his waist, his cock, dwindling now, but still very impressive, rosy and swollen from its exertions. And he blushed.

Lola did her absolute best to keep a straight face.

He reached down for his cock and wrestled it impatiently back into place, ducking to pull up his boxers and his suit trousers, swearing again in what she assumed was Danish when the zip and the belt resisted his clumsy fingers. Lola closed her legs together, not wanting to look too whorish, and flicked the skirt of her negligee down to cover her to the knee, though avoiding the part of her thigh that was covered with come, because she didn't want to stain the nightdress if she could manage not to; but she still sat there, on the edge of the desk, her bottom pulled forward where Niels had dragged her, to get her at the best angle for him to fuck her hard. Partly, she didn't move because she was in such a state of absolute physical satisfaction that moving was near impossible; partly because she knew, somehow, without quite sensing why, that to look at her still sitting there like that would embarrass Niels almost beyond measure.

He was all tucked in now, all put away. Only the burning light in his eyes, the flush on his cheeks, indicated what had just happened between them.

'I—' he started. 'I – I'm . . .'

He looked at her helplessly. It was how, Lola imagined with great satisfaction, a hugely powerful wounded boar would stare at the person who, though much more fragile than itself, had somehow managed to make a dent in its hide.

One of his hands rose up, and grabbed a hunk of his dirty-blond hair, pulling at it, as if he wanted to punish himself by causing himself pain.

'I—' he tried again.

And then he turned – his powerful back, his strong shoulders, bunched with strain – as he strode to the door of the suite, pulled it open and dashed through it, slamming it shut behind him.

Lola looked down at herself. In the old days – which was, suddenly, how she seemed to be referring to her sex life, pre-Niels – she would have been revolted by a man doing anything so vulgar as come over her. And now, the sight of his come on her slender thigh, a white, thick pool of liquid, was the most erotic thing she'd ever seen in her life. If, of course, you excepted the sight of Niels's erect penis. She ran a finger through the residue on her thigh and tasted it, savouring the sweet-sour flavour of almonds and lemon. Then, holding up the skirt of her negligee to her waist, she slipped, wincing, off the desk, and crossed the room to the toilet in the foyer, where she washed down her leg and dried it with a hand towel.

Catching sight of herself in the mirror, she barely recognised the girl who was looking back at her. Golden and glowing, eyes dark and starry, a gorgeous flush of colour on her cheeks, her hair tumbled on her shoulders. She couldn't help giggling: it was the perfect bedroom hair, the style girls had in Victoria's Secret catalogues, carefully arranged and teased out to look as if they'd just been fucked. It was very rare that Lola looked at herself without vanity, but now she did, and she knew that she had never looked so beautiful in her life.

She got herself cleaned up just in time. She was just picking up and slipping on her dressing gown when a key turned in the door and Jean-Marc and David tumbled through it, babbling excitedly about the encounter they had just had in the corridor with Niels.

'Did you *see* him, Lo? Did you tell him anything?' asked Jean-Marc, who had sent his brother a cryptic email, saying that he had left rehab and hinting that he had also come out of the closet, without quite being brave enough to tell him directly. He had hoped that Niels would understand.

'And by the way he looked at me, I'm *sure* he knew,' David added rather nervously. 'I thought he was going to *hit* me – he had this look in his eyes, so scary—'

'He just *growled* at us and kept walking!' Jean-Marc said. 'I haven't seen Niels that angry *ever*!'

'He's so butch, isn't he?' David murmured. 'I mean, terrifying, but *thrilling* too. I bet he's *fabulous* in bed.'

'David! Stop that!' Jean-Marc elbowed his boyfriend. 'You are so naughty – that's my *brother*—'

'Well, but I bet he is, though,' David muttered rebelliously. 'Those shoulders! God!'

He closed his eyes and shivered theatrically.

'Did you have a fight with him, Lo?' Jean-Marc insisted.

'Um, he was cross that I was here,' Lola said cautiously, having no wish to reveal to two excitable gays that she had just had wild sex on the desk with her ex-fiancé's brother. She was barely able to process what had just happened, and she knew instinctively that if she talked about it to anyone, it would spiral away from her and turn into something different, a piece of fantastic gossip rather than the intensely personal encounter between her, Niels and their respective private parts.

Besides, she was also aware that Niels would absolutely loathe it if anyone else knew what had taken place between them. She hardly knew him, but she sensed very strongly that having lost control of himself like that was probably the worst thing that could have happened to a man so used to being in charge of everything around him, including his own emotions. It was ridiculous, after the way he had just manhandled her, but she felt an inexplicable urge to protect him.

'Ugh, I *hate* that he's so horrible to you,' Jean-Marc complained, flopping onto the sofa. 'I'm going to talk to him about it. As if *you* had *anything* to do with me having that breakdown! It's ludicrous!'

David was staring at Lola so intently that she found herself blushing under his scrutiny.

'*Well*,' he commented, and for a moment Lola held her breath, terrified he'd realised what had just happened, almost where they were standing. 'I must say, that hairdresser has done the most *fabulous* job! And the facialist! You're glowing! But the hair is just amazing.' He reached out and played with a strand that was curling round her face. 'Before, I saw you as really china-doll, you know? Pretty-pretty. But *now* – darling, you look so *womanly!*'

'Really?' Lola managed.

'Oh God yes. Positively *sensual*. Promise me you'll only use this hairdresser from now on, OK? You're just *transformed*.'

Lola had a stabbing memory of Niels's hands buried in her hair, pulling her head up, and it was so powerful that the throb between her legs was like a mini-orgasm.

'I'll try,' she assured David. ' I really will try.'

Chapter 17

*T*he infusion of Jean-Marc's unlimited funds into Lola's legal war chest had had near-instant results. In a visit to George Goldman's office just the next day, Lola received fantastic news: George had taken a second opinion on the matter of Carin's usurpation of control of Lola's trust fund, and was now convinced that Lola's case was very strong indeed. Chubby, cheerful George smiled broadly as he told her how good her situation was.

'Plus,' George added, 'Carin's prejudiced the case by doing everything so abruptly. It looks very bad for her. Throwing you out of your house, changing the locks, while giving you the news of Ben's illness—' He sucked in his breath and shook his head. 'You know, every case is judged on individual circumstance. That's how the law works. It's very subjective. And this – well, it sure as hell gives the appearance of vindictiveness, and that won't look good for her. I'm actually hoping we might get this matter settled in a few days. We're applying for an order to show cause why a temporary restraining order shouldn't be applied to enjoin her from acting as trustee, and I'd say we're almost definitely going to get it.'

'That means she wouldn't control my trust fund any longer?' Lola was amazed. '*Fantastic!*'

'We'll certainly be successful in applying for a healthy sum for you for temporary maintenance,' George assured her, nodding happily. 'We'll ask for $200,000 and maybe get $100,000. And I don't think there'll be any problem getting the court to agree to pay all the attorneys' fees directly from your trust fund.'

'Wonderful! And Jean-Marc's guaranteeing all that till the trust fund kicks in,' Lola said with huge relief.

George steepled his pudgy fingers together and rested his chin on the top of them.

'But that's not even the best news!' he said, a huge smile creasing his face. 'You know I passed your visitation rights case over to the absolute best lawyer in this field? Well, he's applied for a temporary access order, and informed Carin's lawyers, and they just rang an hour ago to say you can go see Ben this afternoon!'

Lola felt a warm surge of happiness flooding through her. She was going to see her father! Today!

'I can't *believe* it,' she breathed.

George looked at her closely.

'So you'll be at the Plaza now for a while?' he asked. 'With your fiancé?'

'He's not my fiancé any more, George,' Lola informed him. 'He's gay. He came out in rehab.'

'Oh Lola, honey. You poor thing.'

George's smile faded, his face a pantomime of embarrassment and confusion. Lola did her best to put him out of his misery.

'I'm completely fine with it,' she said. 'We've realised we're much better off as friends. Actually, we're all sharing this big suite at the Plaza together – Jean-Marc, me and his new boyfriend David. And we're so cosy and happy together it's not true.'

George didn't look wholly convinced, but he made the best of it.

'Well, that's great,' he said, rubbing his hands together. 'Great. And, honestly, honey, I wasn't so enthused at the idea of you getting back together with a junkie. So maybe it's all for the best. I saw in the business section today that the brother was in town,' George added, getting up from behind his desk and pulling down his jacket over his plump tummy. 'That's a tough nut. Niels, isn't it? He's the business brains of the new generation. Your young man was always more the playboy type.'

Lola felt a blush enveloping her entire body. She hoped it was not visible to George: a tremendous sensation of burning heat, its centre firmly situated between her legs. Every time Jean-Marc or David mentioned Niels, this happened. She would get a flash of memory, like a flare gun going off inside her: this time, it was Niels dragging down her negligee to bare her breast, his mouth closing over her nipple . . . She couldn't believe she didn't go bright red every time this happened, but George wasn't mentioning anything, so hopefully she was getting away with it.

'Um, what time can I visit my father this afternoon?' she asked George, swiftly changing the subject. She couldn't talk about Niels with anyone; she was too frightened of the physical consequences if his name were mentioned repeatedly.

'Three-thirty!' George beamed. 'And we're talking to them about setting up regular visits for you. At least once a week.'

He ushered her out of his office, patting her shoulder.

'It's all going to be OK now, Lola,' he said happily. 'Don't you worry your pretty head any more. Benny would have hated that. We got it all under control from this point on.'

Lola rang the doorbell of number twenty-four 53rd Street precisely at three-thirty by her Breguet watch. The door was thrown open by Panio. He was as groomed as before, and showed no sign at all in his demeanour that he had any memory at all of the last time Lola had been here.

'I'll just take you upstairs, Miss Fitzgerald,' he said as deferentially as if that awful scene had never happened.

Panio led her up the stairs and through her father's sitting-room, which, Lola was surprised to see, had been left untouched by Carin's redecorations. The huge leather Chesterfield sofas, the thick Persian rugs, the Tuscan carved bookcases with all his first editions of classic spy novels, the marble fireplace, the gigantic purring cherry-wood humidor in the corner, the faint smell of cigar smoke . . . it was so familiar, like the essence of her father, all his favourite things collected here. And the enormous bedroom that lay beyond it was equally unaltered.

But her father had changed almost beyond recognition.

Lola had tried her best not to imagine the scene that was before her now because she had been so afraid of what she might see. She had put off her first attempt at visiting for precisely that reason. Her enormous, strong, powerful father, who could deal with any problem by making a quick phone call, pulling just one of the thousands of strings that were at his disposition, was lying in his gigantic canopied bed. Helpless. Unconscious. At the mercy of anyone who might walk into the room.

The only sounds were his faint, laboured breathing, and a small regular beeping from a machine standing where his bedside table had been. He was hooked up to a drip, but there were other tubes running into his arm as well. Lola walked slowly towards the bed, feeling her resistance, her fear, with every step she took. When she was close enough to see his face, she stopped.

She didn't even realise she was crying until she put a hand up, feeling an odd sensation on her cheek, and her fingers came back wet.

He looked so shrunken, so small. Being on nothing but a drip had caused him to lose weight, and the folds of skin that had once been plump with flesh now sagged, greyish, exposed in the bright morning light that flooded through the windows. The shape of his body under the richly quilted and embroidered bedcover would still have seemed large to anyone who hadn't known Ben Fitzgerald, but to Lola it was frighteningly reduced in size. She had grown so used to her father's bulk: there had been something comforting about it, his sheer size, the way it reflected the hefty power he could wield, the safety she felt knowing that she was always protected by his shadow.

His eyes were closed, of course. He looked almost dead.

Then she jumped. A nurse in a white coat over white trousers was standing by the bed, checking her father's UV drip. He had been half-concealed by the lavish swags of brocade curtains that hung from the huge carver tester above.

'Miss Fitzgerald?' he said. 'I'm Giuseppe Scutellaro, the day nurse.' He grinned. 'That's a bit of a mouthful, though. You can call me Joe. Everyone here does.'

He was very handsome, Lola couldn't help noticing; on the small side, with huge liquid dark eyes and a mass of thick curly hair, those amazing ringlets some Italians had, almost African in thickness and texture. His eyelashes were ridiculously long and curly, too.

'I was just about to give your father his injection,' he continued, his Italian accent light but noticeable. 'You'll be used to this. I understand his diabetes was of long standing. And then I can leave you alone with him. It won't take a moment.'

He picked up a syringe from a tray placed on top of the bedside table, which was actually a small carved oak cupboard converted into a miniature fridge to hold Ben's supplies of insulin: neat little phials, their liquid pale and cloudy, looking much too small and insignificant to save his life. The drawer was full of new needles, each in plastic wrapping. In Ben's private bathroom, under the sink, was a yellow sharps container, where Ben or his nurses disposed of the used syringes. The thought of this routine still continuing, even with Ben unconscious, unable to participate in it, made Lola's eyes prick and water with tears that she blinked back, determined not to cry in front of the nurse.

He was unwrapping the syringe.

'Oh, the pulse – I must record it, I'm sorry—'

He handed Lola the empty syringe and took Ben's pulse, recording the result in a little notebook he pulled from the pocket of his white coat.

'Do you want to take out the insulin?' he asked. 'We'll make this as quick as possible, to give you time alone with him.'

'Thank you,' Lola said gratefully, bending down to retrieve a phial of insulin from the fridge, sitting all by itself on the shelf.

'How's he doing?' she asked, handing it to Joe as he slid the notebook away.

'Not bad,' Joe answered. 'We just have to be careful for bedsores. You know, he lies there all day without moving. We must turn him over, make sure he is comfortable, keep him nice and clean.'

'He'll never—' Lola swallowed. 'He'll never wake up, will he?'

Joe shook his head, not meeting her eyes.

'Not from an insulin coma. If he had been in an accident . . . a different kind of medical coma, then, perhaps. But he's in a permanently vegetative state – there's no coming back from that.'

He turned the phial upside down, drawing out its dose of insulin with the expert swiftness of someone who had done this thousands of times before. Despite her best intentions, Lola looked away as he bent over her father. It wasn't seeing the needle slide in that she wanted to avoid: it was the sight of her father's sagging, mottled flesh, his arm so limp, seeming so lifeless, that saddened her inexpressibly.

He would have hated this, she thought suddenly. *He would rather have died than be this helpless, this vulnerable.*

'All done!' Joe said, stepping back. He put the insulin back in the fridge and capped the syringe again, carrying it into the big central bathroom, the one Ben Fitzgerald had shared with Carin, to dispose of it. There was a rustle, and the familiar sound of the sharps container snapping shut, and then Joe emerged again, saying:

'I'll leave you alone now.' He cleared his throat, a sign that something awkward was coming. 'Mrs Fitzgerald says she will be back at five.'

'That's fine, thanks,' Lola said, understanding exactly what he was saying: that she was to be gone by then. 'I'll go at four-thirty.'

'*Bene.* Well, I'll leave you alone now.'

'Thank you, Joe.'

He crossed the room and left through the main door that led to her father's sitting room, closing it discreetly behind him. It was very silent in here, just the sound of her father's guttural breathing. His head was propped up on two big pillows, his mouth slightly open, his jowls sagging onto his chest.

It was hard to look at him directly. Lola climbed onto the bed and lay down next to him, working her fingers through his limp ones to hold his hand. She closed her eyes and concentrated on bringing back memories of him. Playing with her when she was little, on the wide beach in Montauk, swinging her up through the air, pretending to drop her and then catching her at the last moment, her white-blonde hair blowing over her face as she squealed with excitement. The first time he took her to Venice, when she must have been about eight: on the private launch taking them to the Cipriani he snapped so many photographs of her with the breeze from the canals blowing her plaits over her face, sitting on the big white leather seat, holding onto the rail beside her with both chubby hands, looking around her with such excitement, that he finished a whole roll just on that boat ride. His expression when she slowly descended the stairs in this very house, all dressed up for a premiere at the Met, wearing an Alaia dress that had cost him an absolute fortune: the sheer pride on his face, the incredulous way he had said so fondly:

'God knows how an ugly mug like me ever managed to make such a beautiful daughter . . .'

Memories of her father filled her mind and heart, washing away everything but the happiness they had shared together.

Oh Daddy, she told him. *I love you so much. More than anything and anyone. I hope you can hear me, wherever you are. You loved me with all your heart, you took such good care of me. I promise you, whenever I think of you, whenever someone mentions your name, the first thing I'll always remember is how much you loved me.*

He hadn't wanted her to grow up. He had, in a way, done everything he could to stop her from growing up, because he loved her so much that was his ultimate gift to her, to keep her forever his beautiful, spoilt, sheltered princess. Now the fairy tale was over. The princess had been thrown out of the castle by the evil stepmother. What happened next was up to Lola: but for any kind of happy ending, she needed to dry her tears and do whatever she had to do to claim her throne back.

Her head resting against her father's bed, Lola made a promise to him.

I'll do it for you, Daddy. I'll be the daughter you really deserve, not the one you thought you wanted. I'll grow up. I'll stop being a little girl and I'll grow up into a woman. I'll fight Carin so I can come and visit you. I'll be strong, and I'll stand on my own two feet, and I'll be a daughter you can be proud of.

I know you're in there, somewhere, and maybe you can hear me. Maybe you know what I'm telling you. And if you do, don't be cross, Daddy. Don't be worried. It's time for me to grow up.

More than time.

Chapter 18

ola was on top of the world as she waltzed in through the main door of the Plaza, which was held open for her by the uniformed doorman. She rewarded him with a lovely smile, and he nodded at her admiringly. Both her hands were full: one had a Starbucks cardboard tray, containing a chai tea latte with skim milk for herself, and a grande cappuccino with extra foam for Jean-Marc. The other carried a bakery bag with chocolate croissants for both of them. The calorie content was insane, but she had just done a yogilates class, it was only eleven in the morning, and if she didn't eat a single carb for the rest of the day, she could allow herself that sort of crazy blowout every now and then . . .

She was in the rich-girl New York keep-fit outfit of black capri leggings, black fitted singlet top, hi-top trainers and a supersoft hoodie knotted round her waist. Her blonde hair was in the requisite straight ponytail, her sunglasses were propped on top of her head. At any moment, there were hundreds of women dressed just like Lola on the streets of Manhattan, jogging round the reservoir in Central Park, power-walking to their spinning or Ashtanga yoga class, showing off their slim bodies and the fact that they didn't have jobs and could work out while the rest of the world just worked.

And Lola Fitzgerald might just be the prettiest one of all.

She examined herself in the elevator mirror. Pink cheeks, flushed from the exercise. Bright eyes – she and Jean-Marc had spent a quiet and early night in watching movies and drinking tea, and an alcohol-free evening certainly meant that the whites of your eyes were nice and clear the next day. Flat stomach: fennel tea was lightly diuretic, which meant that she wasn't retaining any extra water. Good definition in her arms: the teachers of yogilates, which combined yoga poses and Pilates moves, knew very well that Manhattan women were as concerned about saggy upper arms as their abs and their hips, and they threw in a lot of plank position poses, which meant taking most of your body weight on your hands. It didn't pump you up like doing weights, but when you were as slim as Lola, you didn't need much to get your muscles showing.

And George was due to ring her at noon to confirm the date her trust fund case would be heard in Surrogate's Court.

Everything was going as well as it possibly could.

Ping! The elevator doors slid smoothly open and Lola walked down the long corridor, hitting the doorbell to the Van der Veer suite with her elbow. She'd brought breakfast: Jean-Marc could at least get up and open the door so she didn't have to put everything down and start fishing for her key.

To her surprise, the door swung open immediately. But it wasn't Jean-Marc standing there. It was a grim-faced man in a suit.

'Is Jean-Marc all right?' she demanded, instantly jumping to the conclusion that something was wrong with him.

The man frowned.

'Miss Fitzgerald? Lola Fitzgerald?' he asked gruffly.

'Yes,' Lola said impatiently. 'What is it? What's wrong with Jean-Marc?'

She hurried into the suite foyer, only to find herself surrounded by more grim-faced men and women.

Oh my God, she thought. *Jean-Marc has gone out and tried to score drugs on the street and he's got arrested, like that actress getting caught up in a drugs sweep, buying crack on the Lower East Side . . .*

But why have they sent all these people to tell me about it?

'*Lola!*' called Jean-Marc from the living-room. He ran towards her, and was blocked out of the way by a woman with shoulders like a linebacker and a face like a hatchet. 'I tried to call you, but they wouldn't let me use the phones – which I'm *sure* they're not allowed to do,' he added furiously.

'What is it? What's going on?' Lola said faintly, a sensation of utter and complete impending doom rising through her. She was so scared she could barely move her lips. And although she was asking, it was only in the weakest of voices.

Because something deep down was telling her she didn't want to know the answer.

'It's your—' Jean-Marc started, but a louder voice drowned him out.

'Lola Fitzgerald, you're under arrest for the murder of Benjamin Fitzgerald,' said the man who had opened the door. 'You have the right to remain silent. Anything you say can and will be used against you in a court of law. You have the right to have an attorney present during questioning. If you cannot afford an attorney, one will be appointed for you.' He stared her right in the face. 'Do you under-stand these rights?'

Lola's mouth opened, but no words would come out.

'It's your father!' Jean-Marc finally managed. 'He died last night! Oh, darling, I'm *so sorry*—'

Lola's muscles went weak. The Starbucks tray and the pastry bag dropped from her hands, and the police officers jumped back, cursing and pulling at their trouser legs, as hot chai latte and cappuccino splattered all over the marble floor. Jean-Marc, pushing past the woman to get to Lola, hugged her tightly, uncaring that his pale beige suede loafers were being irreparably stained by the spreading pool of brown liquid.

'I'm so sorry,' he said, kissing her cheek, 'so very sorry—'

But someone was pulling him off her and wrestling Lola's arms behind her back. She felt cold metal close around her wrists, bind-ing them to each other. It was like something out of a bad film; she couldn't believe any of this was happening.

'Get your hands off me! What are you *doing* to her?' Jean-Marc protested, struggling as the woman police officer hauled him back. 'I had no idea you were going to arrest her! She's not a *criminal!* How dare you?'

'She's under arrest for murder, sir,' the woman police officer snapped at him, manoeuvring round the chai and cappuccino lake. 'And *you'd* better not be hindering the execution of our duties.'

'This is ridiculous!' he insisted. 'Lola, don't worry, this is *ridiculous*, some idiotic mistake—'

'Do you understand your rights?' the grim-faced male cop bellowed in Lola's face.

Lola stared right through him, which infuriated him still more. But she could barely see him: she was picturing her father, the last time she'd seen him. His still, comatose body, the grey tinge to his skin, the stuttering breathing. Had he really been on the verge of death? But the nurse had said he was doing well . . .

They were turning her round roughly, opening the suite door again, pushing her down the corridor.

'I'm calling your lawyer now!' Jean-Marc, galvanised to action by having been dragged off Lola and seeing her in handcuffs, shouted after her. 'I'm calling George, he'll know who to get hold of! We'll have you out in no time! And *then*,' he added malevolently, 'we'll be pressing charges against all of you for wrongful arrest! And the city! I'm going to call my family lawyer as well! You have no idea who you're dealing with here!'

The cops were snapping instructions to each other over Lola's head as Jean-Marc's furious threats followed them down the long corridor. Another suite door opened, an elegant woman of a certain age in pearls and a silk Tory Burch dress emerging, frowning, to see what all the screaming was about: her eyes widened in amazement as she took in the scene, and she actually called back into her apartment to summon someone else to witness it too.

'In the *Plaza!*' Tory Burch Woman breathed incredulously. 'Chappy, darling, *do* hurry up – this is by far the most exciting thing to happen in the Plaza *ever*—'

Lola was manhandled into the elevator, the detectives pressing in around her, still talking to each other over her head. It was all a blur. Her head was swimming. Her father was dead. She would never see him again. She had sat next to him only yesterday, held his hand, talked to him, listened to him breathing . . .

And less than twenty-four hours later, he had died.

Not only that, but she was under arrest for his murder.

The elevator came to a halt, and they bustled her out, turning into the main hotel lobby. Lola was hustled towards the main doors as Plaza residents and staff universally stopped in their tracks to stare avidly at the extraordinary spectacle before them, a phalanx of New York City detectives tightly packed around a small, slender young woman in workout clothes, her blonde ponytail bobbing from side to side as they hurried her across the lavish expanse of tiled floor. Utter silence fell for thirty seconds, as the spectators realised what they were seeing, the latest twist in a saga that had already been splashed across every newspaper and tabloid magazine in New York.

And then there was a mad scramble for activity, as people grabbed for their cellphones and tried desperately to snap a photo of the dramatic event happening right in front of them.

A blaze of light greeted their emergence from the Plaza. A mass of paparazzi was already gathered there, supplemented by a rapidly growing group of spectators, shoppers from Fifth Avenue, people emerging from Central Park, who had been drawn, out of curiosity, to see why there were so many photographers gathered outside the Plaza. They had expected a quick celebrity sighting, the latest young starlet-behaving-badly, carrying a water bottle filled with vodka, flashing her knickerless crotch at the paps as she slid into a limousine.

Instead they were rewarded with a real one-off – an honest-to-goodness celebrity arrest.

Disoriented, blinking in the constant flashes and the screams to her to *look over here, Lola! Here!* it didn't even occur to Lola to duck her head. She stared around her, utterly confused, hypnotised by the red spinning lights on the three police cars – *three*, just for her? How could she possibly merit three police cars?

'Omigod, it's just like *Law and Order*!' one gawker cried as they pushed her towards the middle patrol car.

'For real? Are they filming?' someone else exclaimed, looking around for TV cameras but seeing only the ones from the daily news shows.

'Who's the actress?'

'She looks like Sarah Michelle Gellar, only prettier—'

Someone opened the car door and someone else put a big hand on the top of Lola's head and squashed her down bodily. She slid across the seat, sandwiched in by cops on either side. The driver was talking excitedly into her radio as the cars pulled away: dimly, she could feel the detectives' excitement, barely controlled. They were all sweating lightly, pumped up, psyched at having made such a high-profile arrest.

Leaning forward, unable to sit back because her arms were handcuffed behind her, Lola stared ahead at the wire screen that separated the front and back seats. The car was tearing through the streets, sirens whooping – sirens! For her! It was all so absurd that she could barely believe it was real, even despite the hard physical reality of the steel handcuffs cutting into her, and the way she was bouncing on the seat because she couldn't get any purchase with her feet on the wheel base.

The car slammed to a halt so abruptly that Lola jerked forward, unable to catch herself. As she crashed forward, the last thing she remembered was one of the officers beside her yelling:

'Shit! Grab her before she—'

Then her forehead smashed against the panel, and everything went mercifully dark.

Chapter 19

'*Look* at her!' yelled Simon Poluck, pointing dramatically at Lola.

All heads turned in her direction. Joshua Greene, the Assistant District Attorney, grimaced in embarrassment and annoyance all over again, even though he'd seen her bruised face and filthy condition already.

'My client was brought in wearing handcuffs behind her back, like a common criminal,' Simon Poluck continued. 'She was perp-walked out of the front of her residence, where photographers and news cameras were already waiting. Plus, she had absolutely no history of prior arrests, so why wasn't she handcuffed in front, which would have avoided her concussing herself on the divider of the police car?'

Lola had already seen the bruise on her forehead. It wasn't pretty: the metal screen had cut into her, grazing her skin in a layer of criss-cross bruising even deeper than the purplish background. She wasn't surprised that everyone was now averting their gaze from her.

'But then it really gets bad,' Simon Poluck continued heavily. 'Did they take her to the medical office at the Tombs to have her treated? No, they didn't even bother to have her concussion diagnosed. They took her prints, they took her photo – in which, let me point out, you can clearly see that bruise forming – and they put her in plastic flex cuffs, which have also left marks on her wrists, because they were too tight. Lola?'

Dutifully, Lola held up her arms, the sleeves of her cashmere hoodie falling back to show narrow twin purple lines running all round her wrists.

They were sitting in the DA's office, a lavishly appointed room in the downtown building at One Hogan Place. Though it was large, lined with custom-built bookcases holding arrays of legal reference books, and dominated by an impressive leather-covered mahogany desk, Simon Poluck's personality filled it easily: he seemed to loom over the other people present. The DA was in Albany, and Joshua Greene, one of his chief ADAs, sitting behind the imposing desk, seemed somewhat dwarfed by it. To one side was a woman from the DA's office, and a lieutenant from One Police Plaza in dress uniform.

The lieutenant looked at Lola's wrists and winced. Not because he felt guilty that she'd been marked in police custody: because he could sense lawsuits arriving.

'Then they dumped her in a holding cell with a bunch of hookers and arsonists—' continued Poluck.

'There was only one arsonist,' said the woman from the DA's office unhappily.

'—and moved her four times between cells, in the space of three hours, believe it or not, in what I am sure was a deliberate attempt to slow down my ability to locate my client and speed up her arraignment—'

'I can assure you that nothing of the kind was intended,' protested the police lieutenant. 'We may have been over-zealous in not wishing to seem to give Miss Fitzgerald privileged treatment because of her, um, social status—'

'*Social status?*' Simon Poluck demanded, reaching in his briefcase and extracting a copy of that day's edition of the *Ledger*, which he slapped down on the table. 'What kind of social status do you think she has left after *this?*'

On the cover of the tabloid newspaper was a blurred picture of Lola, hanging limply between two police officers, being half-carried into Central Booking, colloquially known as the Tombs. The headline blared:

'*DID DRUG-CRAZED LOLA KILL BILLIONAIRE POP?*' and the text below read:

'*Too drunk or drugged to walk on her own, former socialite Lola Fitzgerald hits an all-time low as she's arrested for the murder of her own father!*'

Lola, seeing it for the first time, drew in her breath in horror and turned away.

'Believe me,' said the lieutenant unhappily, 'the officers responsible for not securing Miss Fitzgerald's safety in the patrol car have already been disciplined—'

'She could have broken her neck!' Simon Poluck declared. 'It's *outrageous* to me that your office' – he glared at Joshua Greene – 'had the balls to ask for bail at all under the circumstances! She should have been released under her own recognisance! I can't believe she's being forced to surrender her passport – what an insult!'

'Miss Fitzgerald is without question a flight risk.' Joshua Greene defended himself. A small, white, balding man with glasses and a clear tenor voice, he gained confidence by knowing himself to be on stronger ground with this part of the latter's complaint. 'Through her ex-fiancé, who posted her bail, she has access to unlimited funds and the Van der Veer family's private jet. I frankly feel she should be under house arrest.'

'Even the judge didn't fall for that one, after seeing what your goons did to her when they had her in custody,' Poluck said contemptuously.

The judge had been a large, phlegmatic man, Lola remembered, but even he had come to life when he heard Lola's surname and identified her as her father's daughter. It had all been so unreal, like one of those nightmares where you're suddenly thrust onstage in your dirty, stained day clothes, and, blinking in the spotlights, forced to give a performance in a play you've never even heard of before. She remembered the dark shiny wooden rows of seats, the high ceilings, the panelled walls hung with bad oil paintings, the high windows behind the judge, who was hunching forward curiously to get a good look at the notorious Lola Fitzgerald, It girl and coke whore, whose fiancé had overdosed with a tranny on her hen night, and who was now accused of the worst crime in the world: patricide.

High drama. The spectators greedily took in every detail of Lola's appearance: bruised and wincing, her grey cashmere hoodie filthy, her shoes stinking of urine from the holding pen. If you loved to watch celebrities brought low, dragged down to the lowest depths of humiliation, Lola's appearance would be the high point of your year. Everyone was staring: the court officers, the court reporter, lifting her head from her transcription machine to look at Lola as her fingers flew across the keys.

Simon Poluck, who she'd never met before, turned out to be a tall, skinny black man in a superbly cut suit and a dashing mauve and yellow silk tie. And after her plea of 'Not Guilty', full of righteous anger at how bruised and dirty she was, Simon Poluck had demanded that a meeting be convened immediately following the bail hearing. So here they were in the DA's office, as Poluck hauled the New York police department over the coals for their treatment of her.

'Excuse me, Josh. Mr Poluck, if I could cut in here?' said the woman sitting to one side of the desk. She had pale skin and masses of dark red hair, pulled back into a thick plait. 'Serena Mackesy, ADA,' she said, swiftly introducing herself.

'Now that you've given us a hard time, Mr Poluck, could we get to the bit where you tell us what you want?'

'I'm glad that someone in your office can talk straight,' Simon Poluck said dryly to Josh Greene. 'Sure, Ms Mackesy. I want an apology to Miss Fitzgerald from One Police Plaza. All the tabloids today have been blaring headlines about Miss Fitzgerald being drunk or on drugs when she was arrested. Tomorrow, I want them to be screaming about how she was abused by the police who should have been securing her safety from the moment they took her into custody.' He glanced at his very expensive watch. 'That means a press conference in an hour. And I want someone from the top brass in full uniform doing it.'

The lieutenant winced as if he were in physical pain.

'And if we do that, you'll agree not to file any lawsuits?' he said hopefully.

'Believe me,' Simon Poluck said, waving one manicured hand, 'Miss Fitzgerald doesn't need the money.'

'*Now* she doesn't,' Joshua Greene said sharply. 'Because her father's death gives her fifty per cent of his entire fortune.'

Lola's eyes widened.

'I thought Carin would have got him to change the will,' she said naively. 'When she got him to give her power of attorney, and took over my trust fund.'

'Well, she didn't, Miss Fitzgerald!' Self-assured now, Joshua Greene steepled his fingers together on the desk into a little pyramid. 'And that's your motive in a nutshell! You faced a long, arduous court battle to wrest control of your trust fund back from your stepmother, and it was easier simply to murder your father, knowing you would inherit half his estate!'

'But he was alive when I left him!' Lola protested.

'You injected him with insulin when you were alone with him, knowing that an overdose would cause his death,' accused Serena Mackesy.

'*Knowing* – how would I even know that?'

'According to the nurse who was present during the first part of your visit with your father, you asked him a considerable number of questions,' Joshua Greene informed her. 'And he then discovered a used hypodermic needle and an empty vial of insulin in the sharps container, doubtless where you had hoped to conceal them. They have your fingerprints on them,' he added triumphantly. 'Oh yes, we expedited the process. We have a twelve-point match.'

'But he—' Lola began, desperately anxious to explain the truth of what had happened in her father's bedroom yesterday.

Simon Poluck raised a hand quickly.

'Not another word, Miss Fitzgerald,' he insisted. 'Not. Another. Word.' He smiled at her reassuringly and leaned forward, fixing Joshua Greene with a hard stare. 'Drop the case now, Mr Greene.'

'Not a chance in hell,' Joshua Greene retorted defiantly. 'We have a very strong case. No plea offers on the table. She's going to do twenty-five to life.'

'Hah!' Simon Poluck snorted. 'This fragile little creature? Who, after this evening, is going to be the latest pretty little white poster girl for the horrors of police brutality? *This* is what's going to face you on the stand,' he said, gesturing at Lola. 'There isn't a jury in the world who'd convict her of the terrible crime of which you've accused her.' He stood up. 'Drop the case now, Mr Greene,' he said. 'It's your last chance to save your career.'

And on that perfect exit line, he shepherded his client from the room.

Outside the DA's office, a blaze of camera flashes greeted them immediately. The bright flare of news cameras, collected in a group on the steps, made Lola blink and duck her head, but Poluck bustled her down the stairs and into a waiting stretch limo with darkened windows.

'*Darling*!' Jean-Marc and David screamed in unison from the facing seat.

They had champagne glasses in their hands, and they pressed one on her. Lola took it automatically, still dazed by everything that was happening. She took a sip. It went straight to her head as if it had been cognac.

'We've been waiting for *hours*!' Jean-Marc exclaimed. 'How *are* you!'

'Oh my God, *look* at her,' David said with horror as the limo pulled away from the curb. 'What did they *do* to you?'

'Did you get the charges dropped?' Jean-Marc begged Simon Poluck. 'Tell me you made it all go away! It's *so* ridiculous!'

They all looked at Simon Poluck, who was waving away the glass of champagne David was proffering to him.

'The good news,' he said, 'is that we're winning the PR war. By the time we get the police department's statement on the TV news tonight, everyone will be on Miss Fitzgerald's side.'

'And the bad news?' Lola asked.

'There isn't a chance in hell Greene will dismiss this indictment,' he told them grimly. 'The case against you is very strong indeed. I was just grandstanding in there to try to rattle his cage. But with that nurse's testimony—' he shook his head. 'We have an uphill battle ahead of us.'

'But he's *lying!*' Lola said furiously. 'Carin's paying him to lie!' She caught her breath. 'Oh my God, it's worse than that – Carin set me up!'

She played that scene back in her head, the time she spent with the nurse by her father's bedside. Various details that had struck her as odd at the time now had a totally plausible explanation. Joe, the nurse, had handed her the syringe, and asked her to take the insulin out of the fridge, because they wanted to get her fingerprints on both of them.

Plus, the sharps container had always been kept in her father's private bathroom: why had Joe gone to the main bathroom to dispose of the needle? Carin wouldn't have wanted an ugly yellow sharps container in her bathroom when there was a much better, and customary, place to keep it.

Lola had heard a rustle in the bathroom as Joe went in, a small noise that hadn't struck her at the time as noteworthy. But now she realised that it hadn't been made by Joe: she had heard the sound of his white coat over his trousers, and it hadn't rustled at all. Which meant that someone else had been in there.

Carin. Watching through the door, which had been ajar. Checking on how the plan was going, seeing Lola duly handle both the syringe and the insulin, approving Joe's actions in carrying out her scheme . . .

Which meant, inevitably, that Carin had killed her father. Whether he had died of the injection Joe had given him before Lola's eyes, or whether another, lethal injection had been administered after she left, Carin had murdered him and planned to pin the blame on Lola.

Gasping for breath, she was speaking so fast, Lola poured her theory of the case out to the three occupants of the limo. Jean-Marc and David gawped at her, dumbstruck by the idea that Carin could have orchestrated something so Machiavellian.

'Because I was challenging her for control of my trust fund!' Lola gabbled finally. 'She knew I was going to win – George said we had a really strong case! So she thought if she killed Daddy, and pinned it on me, she'd get everything!'

'I thought you inherited half,' Jean-Marc pointed out.

'No!' Lola said triumphantly. 'You can't profit by the proceeds of a crime! So if I'm convicted, then I can't inherit, and it would all go to Carin! I saw that on a Lifetime TV movie,' she explained, as Jean-Marc looked baffled by her unexpected command of the laws of inheritance. 'That's right, isn't it?'

She looked eagerly at Simon Poluck.

'Absolutely,' he said. 'But you do see how difficult this is all going to be to prove? It's going to come down to a he-said, she-said, and Mrs Fitzgerald and the nurse will deny everything. And as it stands, you have a much more plausible motive for killing your father than she does.'

Lola leaned forward in her seat, pounding her fist on her thigh.

'I don't care!' she said furiously. 'I didn't do it! I didn't kill my father! I loved him more than anyone else in the world!'

This was a new Lola, truly her father's daughter, determined and fearless. Not a victim any more.

'And I know that nurse is lying,' she concluded. 'So I'm going to find a way to prove it!'

Chapter 20

'*D*avid, this looks . . .'

   Lola was lost for words as she stared at herself in the mirror.

'I *know!* Hideous!' David said excitedly. 'But *just* the kind of hideous I was going for – not *actively* hideous, so nasty you can't take your eyes off it.' He picked up a fake silk scarf and started knotting it around her neck. 'I wanted *dull* hideous. Where if you kept looking at it, you'd pass out with boredom and crack your head on the way down.'

'Well, you've certainly managed that.' Lola fingered the scarf. 'What's this *made* of?'

'Eww! Polyester!' David giggled happily. 'It's probably *completely* flammable! Don't light up a cigarette when you're wearing it, for God's sake, or you'll go up like a firework!'

Lola had to admit that the scarf was an excellent touch. She did a full 360-degree turn, examining her grey wool trouser suit, with its pleated trousers that pulled at the crotch and bagged at the knees. The jacket had narrow sewn-in shoulderpads, unnecessary pockets on the chest, and loose threads already straggling from the button-holes. The buttons themselves were cheap plastic made to look like bone. Under the jacket, David had chosen a thin cotton-mix sweater in a putrid shade of pale green, and he had even insisted, for total verisimilitude, that she wear her tightest bra on the tightest set of hooks, so it cut into her and made her look a little lumpy. The flammable scarf was patterned in white, orange and a similar-but-different green to the colour of the sweater.

David had also done her make-up. He'd trowelled on much heavier base than she usually wore, which made her usually glowing skin look dull and greyish; a hard line of brown pencil completely circling each eye; no mascara; and cheap pink blusher.

'I look like a temporary secretary in an accounting firm,' Lola summed up.

'*Exactly!*' David clapped his hands with pride. 'That's *exactly* what I was going for! But wait for it . . . final touches coming up . . .'

With the excitement of a conjuror about to pull off a major trick for the first time, he reached into his large shopping bag and produced what looked like the cut-off toe of a pair of beige support tights.

'It's a wig cap,' he explained, seeing Lola's bafflement.

He smoothed down her hair and pulled the wig cap over it, carefully tucking in each blonde strand till it was perfectly smooth. Then he produced a pale brown wig, and, his expression as serious as if he were performing a heart transplant, hooked it over his thumbs, positioned it on her forehead, and flipped it over her skull, patting it down with his palms until it was just right. He secured it with a couple of bobby pins and stepped back, his expression quietly triumphant.

The wig was the ugliest thing Lola had ever seen. It made the cheap trouser suit look like Balenciaga by comparison. David's bobby pins had taken the shoulder-length hair back on either side, pinning it up above her ears, which succeeded, eerily, in making the wig look all too authentic.

Carefully, she put up a hand to touch it.

'It's real hair,' David said proudly. 'Cost a fortune, believe it or not.'

'Eww . . .' Lola said in repulsion. 'I'm wearing someone else's hair on my head?'

'Darling, it *has* to be real! That acrylic stuff looks so fake! We've got to get you past the paparazzi and, believe me, your disguise has to be perfect!' David's eyes were gleaming with excitement. 'Let's show Jean-Marc!'

Jean-Marc, who had been forbidden from watching Lola's transformation from beautiful princess into Cinderella secretary, so that he could comment on the post-makeover effect, was where he was usually to be found these days: lying on the sofa watching daytime TV on the gigantic built-in plasma screen. Right now, it was Judge Judy, who was telling a woman severely never to lend a jailbird boyfriend her credit card. Jean-Marc, tucked up in a pale blue cashmere throw which exactly matched the colour of his eyes, sipping vitamin water, looked enthralled by Judge Judy and her no-nonsense attitude: he looked up briefly as David and Lola came into the sitting-room, his eyes flicking over Lola and ignoring her as being too dull to notice. He actually turned back to the screen for a second before snapping his head back again.

'*No* . . .' he breathed incredulously, his handsome face the picture of surprise. '*Lola?*'

David jumped up and down in glee.

'She's our secretary,' he pronounced. 'What shall we call her?'

'Gloria McUgly,' Jean-Marc said instantly.

'Patty McHideous,' David chorused.

'Jennifer Smith,' Lola said firmly.

'Perfect,' David agreed. 'That's so boring you can't even remember it while you're saying it. Jean, ring down and tell security she'll be going in and out. Tell them she came in through the garage by mistake, but she'll be using the front exit now.'

'Should I really use the main door?' Lola started. 'There's so many photographers and news crews out there—'

'And believe me, sweetie, there are plenty of them staking out the garage and the staff exits as well,' David said wisely. 'They'll be *much* less suspicious of someone just walking in and out of the front and not looking like they have anything to hide. I've got you a nasty cheap tote too, so you look even more secretary-ish. There's your Citizens

For All Humanity jeans and your Missoni cashmere sweater tucked inside, so you can change when you get there. It's over by the door.'

'You think of everything, David,' Lola said, impressed.

'Stay for dinner,' Jean-Marc begged him. 'I just ordered in your favourite!'

'Kobe beef burger with truffle fries and arugula?' David said excitedly. 'No!'

'Yes!'

'OK, but darling, I can't sleep over,' David said, pulling a face. 'I'm going to have to get up at the crack of dawn tomorrow, so I'll eat with you but then I have to go home and hit the sack.'

'Oh, *darling . . .*' Jean-Marc pouted. 'I get so lonely without you!'

'Jean, we've been over this,' David sighed. 'I have a job. I need to go to it. Being a motion graphics designer, I work on ads and TV promos and corporate stuff, and sometimes I have to start really early or work till really late. Plus, I have daily Narcotics Anonymous meetings to go to. I can't be with you every moment of the day, darling.'

Jean-Marc dragged the corners of his mouth down.

'Can't you just quit your job?' he said pettishly.

'No, I can't!' David said rather crossly. 'You need to respect that I'm earning my own living!'

'And Jean-Marc, isn't that a good thing?' Lola chimed in. 'I mean, you wouldn't want him to live off you completely, would you?'

'Of course I would!' Jean-Marc wailed, grabbing a pillow and clutching it to his stomach for comfort. 'I have so much money, I might as well share it with him! We could travel everywhere, have such a lovely time – how am I going to *cope* with him going to an office every day and being tired in the evening, when I'm just waking up? What am I going to *do* with myself?'

'Jean—' David began, an edge to his voice.

'Honestly, Jean-Marc,' Lola jumped in quickly, 'I think you should be grateful that David doesn't want to take advantage of you. I mean, most people who'd bagged someone as rich as you would give up work immediately, and that would be all wrong. You should—'

Jean-Marc currled up in the corner of the sofa, still clutching the pillow.

'If there's one thing I learned in rehab,' he said with great dignity, 'it's that one should never tell other people what they should and shouldn't do. It doesn't help *at all.*'

Lola forebore to point out that he had just done exactly that himself.

'I have my pride, Jean,' David said quietly.

'I know!' Jean-Marc moaned. 'And it's killing me!' His face crumpled. His periwinkle eyes were awash with tears, like overflowing fountains, water pouring over bright blue tiles. 'The trouble is when I'm with you, I couldn't be happier. I never want to do anything naughty, apart from drink a little champagne. But when you go, I feel so awful! So lonely! And *that* makes me want to go out and get high.'

'Oh *no* . . .' Lola began.

'That's when you go to a meeting,' David said to him. 'Or call your sponsor. I can't be with you every second of the day, darling. You're the one that has to keep yourself safe.'

'I know,' Jean-Marrc said sadly, still hugging the cushion. 'I just wish you could.'

'I won't be late,' Lola promised. 'It's just a girls' night in. I'll be back by midnight.' She looked at him, now wiping his tears away, and had second thoughts. 'Or should I cancel and stay with you?'

'No,' David said firmly. 'You can't run your life around Jean-Marc, and neither can I. He's an adult, he has to look after himself.'

'You're so mean,' Jean-Marc said, kissing him. 'I *hate* it when you tell me I'm an adult.' He managed a watery smile for Lola. 'Off you go, sweetie. Are you going to be all right? I mean, are you sure about what you're doing tonight?'

Lola nodded determinedly.

'I need to feel I'm *doing* something. There's nothing I can do about Daddy and the trial – we haven't even got a date for that yet, and Simon Poluck's got a whole team of private investigators tracking down that nurse and seeing if they can trace the money Carin must have paid him to lie to the grand jury. I'm going mad shut up in here, waiting.' She gestured towards the windows. 'This at *least* gets me out of the apartment for a little while. Plus, I get to do some sleuthing of my own.'

'Make sure you keep all those lies straight,' David recommended.

'Do it just like we worked it out. And be careful, Lo,' Jean-Marc emphasised.

'Believe me,' Lola said, setting her jaw martially, 'I know what I'm doing.'

As Lola stepped out of the lift, her heart was beating faster than usual with nerves. It was the oddest experience crossing the lobby of the Plaza: even before her arrest, everyone had turned to look at her, or at the very least been unable to resist a swift glance in her direction, checking out in the flesh the beautiful blonde socialite who was a staple of the glossy magazines.

And now she might as well have been invisible. She was a ghost of her former self, a girl with ugly hair and dowdy cheap clothes, completely out of place in this smartest of New York addresses. Head ducked, her leather-effect tote under her arm, she looked exactly like the part for which David had so expertly costumed her – a low-level secretary, not worthy of any notice.

It was the strangest feeling for a girl who couldn't remember a time when she hadn't been the cynosure of all eyes. It should have been intensely frustrating for Lola to find herself suddenly vanishing from the radar that had picked her up every time she stepped outside her house; but to her great surprise, she found herself enjoying it tremendously.

Everything in her life was upside down. It had taken her fiancé's overdose and coming out to make her realise that she hadn't wanted to marry him after all. It had taken his horrible older brother, who she still passionately disliked, to give her a taste of the kind of sex she had been craving her whole life, without ever being aware of it.

And it had taken her being arrested for the murder of her own father to give her the kind of anonymity she had never had, and show her how much she liked it.

Lola passed the paparazzi as if she were wearing a cloak of invisibility. As always, there was a line of yellow cabs waiting outside the Plaza, and she paused a moment for the doorman, who always in the past would have scrambled to open the door of the first one for her. It took her a little while to realise that he wasn't going to bother; she obviously wasn't going to tip him, nor was she pretty enough to make it a pleasure to do her a service.

God, she thought as she opened the door and climbed in. *Pretty girls really do have an easier time of it. I must be* much *nicer to plain girls in future.*

'*Lola!*' everyone screamed as she entered Madison's apartment.

If Madison's neighbours were on the ball, Lola thought dryly, they would be ringing the tabloids right now to let them know that Lola Fitzgerald was partying with her girlfriends: the screams were certainly loud enough to have been heard all down the corridor.

'Oh my God, *Lola?*' Devon exclaimed, sitting up straighter in the chair in which she'd been lounging, and goggling at the dowdy secretary who had just walked into the room.

In a dramatic gesture, which she enjoyed tremendously, Lola reached up and pulled off her wig and wig-cap in one smooth movement, revealing her pinned-back blonde hair.

'I would never have known it was you!' Georgia marvelled. 'I would have walked straight past you in the street!'

'*Darling!*' Madison rushed towards Lola, arms out wide in an embrace.

Right, Lola thought with that small cold part of her brain that she had learned to access ever since the first time one of her friends had betrayed her. *You're all over me now that I don't need a place to stay. But when I needed something, you couldn't get me off the phone fast enough.*

Tall, Amazonian Madison, enfolding Lola in a hug, made her disappear momentarily into a Gucci-scented whirl of cream silk and pale suede. Re-emerging, Lola looked wryly at her four friends, all dressed exquisitely, and pulled a face.

'I'm going to get changed straight away,' she said. 'Mad, come and talk to me while I do?'

'Of course!'

Madison looked mightily relieved that Lola didn't seem to have any resentment towards her because of her refusal to let Lola stay in her apartment. Snatching up two glasses of kir-laced champagne, she strode quickly after Lola down the hall to her bedroom.

'You've lost weight, honey,' she said, handing Lola one of the glasses. 'All the stress, right?'

'You can't imagine,' Lola said, sitting down on the bed and slipping off her heels so that she could take off her nasty scratchy-wool trousers.

'Where did you *get* that outfit?' Madison asked, distracted by its horror.

'David bought it for me at Macy's,' Lola said.

'Ewww!'

'David's a real sweetie,' Lola said. 'I'm so happy Jean-Marc met him. They're getting married, you know. In London. Next month.'

Standing up, peeling off her sweater, wearing just her silk La Perla bra and French knickers, Lola reached for her glass of Kir Royale and sipped some, her big brown eyes watching Madison limpidly. Madison's green eyes widened as she digested the news.

'Oh, whoops!' Lola clapped a hand over her mouth. 'Mad, I can't believe I told you that, it's such a secret! Please, *please* don't tell anyone! You know what the press is like – David and Jean-Marc just want to sneak off and have a really quiet ceremony, and if *anyone* knows it'll leak out. Please, you have to promise you won't tell!'

'Oh, I won't, I promise I won't,' Madison assured her.

'No, really!' Lola insisted. 'Jean-Marc's been so good to me – you know he's paying for everything, right? And he took me in and says I can stay as long as I want.'

She stared hard at Madison, who did have the good grace to look uncomfortable at this.

'So I mustn't, *mustn't* let him down – you promise you won't tell, Mad?'

'Cross my heart and hope to die,' Madison swore.

Lola pulled on her jeans and silk Missoni sweater, a knit so light but so elaborately patterned in a peacock design that only the slimmest of women could have carried it off, and went back to the living-room to be greeted ecstatically by the rest of the girls.

'*Such* a good disguise,' Devon said admiringly. '*So* clever.'

'You're not all staying here, are you?' Lola asked, taking prime position, in the centre of the white leather sofa, where everyone could see her. She sipped more Kir Royale and fixed Madison with another big brown innocent gaze. 'I didn't know you had room for this many guests, Mad!'

Madison laughed brightly.

'Oh no, just Georgia,' she said.

'Devon and I are staying at Soho House,' India said, smiling at Lola. 'The pool gets a bit crowded at the weekends, though.'

'The Meatpacking District's over already,' Devon sighed. 'I mean, Soho House is supposed to be a private club, but it's like they let in every single hedge fund manager in New York! And God, they bring in some trashy girls.'

'We were there last night,' Madison said, pulling a face. '*Not* as exclusive as it used to be.'

'But how are *you*, Lo?'

Georgia leaned forward, pushing back her red curls with both perfectly manicured hands, as if to bare both her ears to hear Lola's answer better. She was wearing sprayed-on jeans and a strappy green jersey top, large diamond studs glittering in her earlobes: even by Georgia's hi-glam standards, she looked very dressed up for a quiet girls' night in, Lola couldn't help thinking.

'I'm still in shock, I think,' Lola admitted, reaching for a pack of cigarettes on the coffee table and lighting one up.

Lola had cried solidly for the past three days, ever since she was given bail. Getting back to the Plaza, being able, finally, to let go after all the drama of her arrest and the time in the Tombs, had been as if she were a puppet and someone had cut her strings. She had collapsed. It had taken her two days just to get out of bed. And she probably would still be there, if the girls, come to New York en masse to 'see how she was doing', aka get all the latest juicy gossip from her imploding disaster of a life, hadn't kept ringing and ringing.

'Is there anything to eat?' she asked. 'I'm starving.'

'We got some negimaki rolls,' India said, jumping up. 'I'll find you a plate.'

'Oh, I'll come too,' Lola said quickly, rising to her feet and following India to the kitchen.

On the granite counter top was a big plate of negimaki – grilled strips of beef dressed with teriyaki sauce and rolled up with finely sliced spring onions. It was perfect food for watching your weight: rich-tasting and nicely chewy, so it felt satisfying, while the lean protein gave you energy without too many accompanying calories.

'I got some plain boiled rice, too,' India confessed. 'Madison was so cross. I had to promise to eat it all myself or throw it out with washing-up liquid poured over so she couldn't snack on it if she got a carb craving.'

'Give me a spoonful,' Lola said. 'I'm so hungry I could eat my own arm.'

India flashed her a quick smile. She was looking very pretty, Lola thought. India would always be the plain one of the group, comparatively speaking. But if you looked at her on her own, she had a lovely, gentle face, with wide-set hazel eyes, framed by soft tumbling light-brown curls. And OK, she might not be a size four, but she had a very nice figure, slim, with a naturally flat stomach. It was just the rest of the girls' competitive starvation stakes that made India look larger than life by comparison.

'Here you go,' India said, producing a takeout container of rice from the oven, which of course was only used as an extra cupboard: it was never actually turned on. India pulled out two spoons and shot Lola a comical, naughty glance, like a little girl sneaking ice cream from the freezer behind her parents' back.

'Just a couple of spoonfuls . . .' Lola said, loading hers up with rice and topping it with a negimaki roll. 'Mmm, *lovely*,' she said through a mouthful.

'We can finish it off,' India said happily, scraping out some more rice. 'Madison'll be much happier if there isn't any left. She really doesn't like complex carbs in the house.'

'I've barely eaten for the last couple of days,' Lola said, taking another piece of beef. 'It's been so difficult at Jean-Marc's.'

'Really?' India's eyes widened. 'I thought he was being amazing! We were all saying how lucky you were to have him still around!'

I am, Lola thought dryly. *Considering he was the only person to offer to help me, I'm pretty bloody lucky to have Jean-Marc in my life.*

'It's his brother,' Lola sighed. 'He keeps coming round and telling Jean-Marc to throw me out. There've been the *worst* scenes. I hear them screaming and shouting. Niels even told Jean-Marc he thought it was me that turned Jean-Marc gay.'

India's eye sockets were so enlarged by now her eyeballs were popping out dangerously.

'*No!*' she breathed. 'That's mad!'

'I know!' Lola shrugged helplessly. 'He completely hates me!' She pulled a face. 'Don't tell anyone, will you, India? Jean-Marc would be so cross if he knew I was talking about it – his brother embarrasses him so much.'

'Oh, I won't,' India promised eagerly. 'Lola, I'm so sorry – that must be so difficult for you—'

'What's up? Talking secrets? Ugh, are you two pigging out?' Devon said in disapproval, entering the kitchen. 'Is that *rice?*'

'I ordered some,' India stammered guiltily. 'Madison says I have to finish it or throw it out—'

'Oh God, give me a spoon,' Devon said greedily. 'Just a little bit. I get so terrible when I'm drinking.'

'India, would you get my cigarettes?' Lola asked. 'They're in my bag. If I don't have one I'll just keep eating . . .' She pulled a self-deprecating face.

India scurried out of the kitchen, always willing to help. Lola exchanged a glance of complete affection with Devon.

'I can't believe she got in *rice*,' Devon said, grinning. She allowed herself one heaped teaspoon of rice, chewing it slowly and making little noises of appreciation. 'Not even *brown* rice. India is such a little piglet.' She looked Lola up and down. 'You're thin as a rake,' she commented.

'I think it's the medication,' Lola said lightly. 'Jean-Marc got this doctor in to see me when I came back from the bail hearing. She put me on some sort of antidepressant. I haven't wanted a bite to eat ever since.'

'*Really?* Do find out what they are, won't you?' Devon exclaimed.

Lola looked panicked. 'Don't tell anyone about the pills, Dev. The lawyer says it might look bad if it gets out I'm on anything at all, what with the coke photos and everything.'

'Of course not! Oh God, will you listen to me?' Devon tossed the spoon in the sink and threw her arms around Lola, hugging her tightly. 'I'm going on about diets and how thin you are, as if all that stuff was important, with what you're going through! My God, they're *stalking* you through the streets!'

Devon put up a hand to stroke Lola's hair.

'Poor Lo,' she said, her voice soft. 'What you've been through! We came over as soon as we could.'

'Dev! Stop hogging Lola!' Georgia draped herself decoratively against the lintel of the door. She never merely stood when she could fall into an artistic pose. 'Come through, we've got a great idea for something to do tonight! Madison just thought of it!'

'Aren't we staying in?' Lola asked, following Georgia down the corridor as Devon threw the empty rice container guiltily into the dustbin and swept some loose grains off the counter top.

'We *were*—' Georgia said, 'but Mad's got *such* a good idea—'

'I really shouldn't go out at all,' Lola said doubtfully.

'Oh God, don't worry! Just put on that awful wig again! *No one*'ll recognise you in that!' Georgia assured her blithely.

'Georgia, can I ask you something? In confidence?' Lola paused momentarily in the corridor.

'Of course!' Georgia turned to look at her, the thick red curls sweeping over her face. Gold earrings dangled to her shoulders, swishing against the white skin amply revealed by Georgia's emerald silk top.

'I'm thinking of getting some work done . . .' Lola confessed. 'I saw myself in all those press photos, and it made me feel really bad about my—'

'Oh my God! Your tits! You're getting a boob job!' Georgia pronounced instantly, her gaze dropping to Lola's admittedly small (30B) breasts.

'No!' Lola said, insulted.

'Bigger's *always* better,' Georgia said smugly, regarding her own magnificent 32Ds.

'I like being able to get into any clothes I want,' Lola contradicted, still offended. 'Anyway, I was thinking of getting my chin shaved down a little bit. It looked really pointy in the photos, especially when I'm in profile.'

'Oh, I wouldn't bother,' Georgia said instantly. 'Remember when Dev got hers done and she was so cross because no one could tell the difference?'

'Don't tell anyone,' Lola begged. 'I don't want people to know I'm thinking about it – it would look so bad, with just being arrested and everything—'

'God no! Don't worry, I won't say a word!' Georgia assured her.

'*So!*' Madison announced triumphantly, tossing Lola her wig. 'Put that on, and plaster on some more of that horrible make-up!' She jumped up. 'Georgia, call a limo! I know *exactly* where we're going to have a good time and distract poor Lola from all her troubles!'

'I shouldn't go out,' Lola protested. 'I shouldn't even be *here*. My lawyer said I mustn't go anywhere at all, just lie low for a couple of weeks.'

'Don't be silly!' Madison overrode her. 'No one will know it's you! And you'll go mad if you stay cooped up inside for weeks and weeks!'

'It'd do you good, Lo,' Georgia coaxed. 'Take your mind off your troubles.'

'Where are we going?' Devon asked, reaching for her bag.

'Maud's!' Madison said. 'It's this new, hot vaudeville club on the Lower East Side. Tables cost $2,000, but we're getting one for free, because I did some PR for the guy who owns it, and he said to bring as many sexy girls as I could. Oh, and we're drinking for free all night too.' She winked at Devon. 'Nothing like saying you're bringing a marchioness!'

'I never have to spend a *penny* in New York,' Devon said complacently.

'I really don't know if I should go,' Lola said weakly. 'It sounds like there'll be photographers everywhere—'

'Not inside, darling,' Devon assured her, carefully patting Dior lip gloss onto the bow of her bottom lip to make it look fuller. 'Never inside. Or no celebs would ever go.'

'Maybe it's not such a good idea,' India said doubtfully.

'Oh, don't be a party-pooper, India!' Madison waved a hand at her dismissively.

'Here, Lo, have some of this,' Georgia said, dumping a gram of coke out of its tidy little wrap onto Madison's glass coffee table. 'This'll get you in the party spirit.'

'Can't we just stay here?' Lola pleaded.

'What, with the hottest vaudeville club in New York reserving us a table?' Georgia laughed, expertly hoovering up a fat line of coke with a cut-off straw. 'Are you joking?'

'I should really just go home,' Lola said, looking around for her bag.

'And curl up on the sofa with Jean-Marc and his boyfriend being all lovey-dovey?' Madison snorted. 'Don't be crazy! Come out with us instead!'

Lola was rummaging through the nasty plastic tote bag, pulling out her disguise clothes, but as Madison's words sank in, she stopped, staring down at the sickly lime-green sweater in her hands. She *didn't* want to put this cheap acrylic thing on, slip back into those scratchy trousers, and trudge back to the apartment to spend yet another night on the sofa with Jean-Marc watching the Lifetime TV movies to which, post-rehab, he was currently addicted.

Lola hadn't realised till that moment how much she was longing for a girls' night out, the first one since her hen night. The realisation of how much had changed since then couldn't help but horrify her. She no longer had a fiancé. Her father was dead and she was accused of killing him. And she was living on charity – handed out very willingly by her ex- fiancé, but still, charity.

She had never before been so aware of how precarious existence could be.

India was still looking concerned. But when Devon refilled Lola's glass of champagne, and Georgia handed her the straw, winking at her to take her turn at the cocaine, and Madison grinned at her encouragingly, all Lola's demons flooded in to tempt her; even though she knew she shouldn't, she couldn't seem to help choosing drink-and-drug-fuelled distraction from her woes over the sensible option of going home and having an early night and perhaps a bed-time cup of camomile tea . . .

'You're all so naughty,' Lola sighed, taking a healthy gulp of her champagne and then bending down over the coffee table, straw at the ready. 'I *know* I'm going to regret this somehow . . .'

But her demurral was drowned out by the cheers and whoops from almost all of the girls.

Chapter 21

'*T*ake it off! Take it *off!*' Georgia was howling.

'Um, Georgia, it's not a strip clu—'

'Take it *off!*' Georgia whooped, deaf to anything but the charms of the six-foot-six, oiled, and frighteningly flexible contortionist onstage, who was busy twisting himself like a pretzel between his own legs and up his own back.

'You can't take her anywhere,' Devon sighed, as the contortionist, mercifully, squished and packed his long, glistening limbs up into the tightest of balls and somehow managed to roll himself offstage.

Tumultuous applause rewarded him. Above the stage, a big metal hoop lowered with a girl draped inside it, covered in what looked like nothing but gold body paint and glitter. It revolved slowly, glitter trickling down over her, distracting the audience, as it was supposed to, from the black-clad stagehands setting up the stage for the next act.

'Pretty!' Georgia exclaimed. Her eyes were shining feverishly and her focus was blurred: by now she had half of Colombia's annual coke harvest up her nose and about the same percentage of France's vintage champagne swilling around in her stomach.

'She's always like this when people start taking their clothes off,' India reminded them. 'Remember Lola's hen night? Her and that stripper guy in the club? I think they actually did it behind the banquette. Oh – sorry, Lola—'

Lola waved a hand airily.

'Honestly, you can talk about my hen night all you want!' she said happily. 'It wash – *was* – a lovely evening, we all had a very good time—'

'And now you can spend all Jean-Marc's money without being married to him, which is the ideal arrangement!' Devon said, raising her own champagne glass.

Everyone toasted to Lola's perfect arrangement as the next act took the stage.

'Ugh, fire-eaters,' Georgia said loudly. 'Who cares?' She waved her glass of champagne around wildly. 'I want people to be *naked*. Don't you, Lola? Don't you want people to be naked?'

'*Please* stop saying my name!' Lola hissed.

Lola had barely drunk a drop of alcohol for the past few days, and the combination of not much food, a lot of champagne and a few helpings of Georgia's Colombian marching powder was making her feel dizzy, fizzy, and divine. She was off her head in the nicest possible way, all her worries and cares, the death of her father, her own arrest, washed temporarily away on a sea of bubbles and nose candy.

Still, the one thing she was clinging to was that no one must realise that, underneath this dowdy wig, spackled-on make-up, Missoni sweater and narrow jeans was one of the most notorious women in New York: Lola Fitzgerald. Paparazzi were doubtless camped outside the Plaza still, waiting to see if she was going to try to sneak out under cover of darkness. The doorman had told David that they didn't go home till at least two a.m. At the rate they were going, she wouldn't get home till way past that. But if anyone here heard Lola's name being bandied around, and rang the tabloids, she'd really be in trouble.

Lola looked around her. They were sitting at a table in what had once been the stalls section of this little theatre, which had been decorated to resemble a miniature version of the Royal Opera

House, if it had been left to decay for a century or so and then been taken over by artistically dishevelled squatters. The upholstery was red plush, the carved woodwork around the balconies and proscenium arch painted gold, but everything was faded and distressed and ripped to look in a state of decadent decay. Tattered silk canopies hung from the ceiling; the chandeliers were sculptures, wax stalactites dangling from their gilt curlicues, the candelabra on the walls draped with strings of tarnished pearls. The wait staff wore 19th-century-styled outfits, corset tops laced too tight, black chokers round their necks, hair piled up loosely on top of their heads or dyed and curled into weird shapes, their faces decorated with beauty spots and smudged red lipstick.

And the patrons, the people rich enough to pay thousands of dollars for a table and hundreds more for drinks, were all decadent enough themselves to fit into the theme perfectly. Their eyes were glittering, their mouths open, pumped up for the next sexy or dangerous act that would appear onstage. At the next table, Lola saw a girl with a vial hung around her neck unscrew the cap, lift it to her nose and sniff, taking a hit openly. A plump boy in a silk jacket was snorting vodka up his nose with a straw. A girl still in her teens, as long and thin as a toothpick, wearing only a miniskirt and a ripped T-shirt, lounged on the lap of a man twice her age; as he slid one hand up her skirt and the other into the rips in her top, her expression was as bored as if she were in school listening to a teacher explain calculus.

'Put your hands together for Diamond, boys and girls, making her debut here in an act created specially for us!' piped the MC, a dwarf wearing a shiny Lurex jumpsuit and a top hat. 'Ever lusted after the Little Mermaid? Well, get ready to go crazy for this one!'

And, suddenly, a series of spotlights picked out a glimmering silver pole in the centre of the stage.

Drums rattled, bubbles burst, and 'This must be underwater love . . .' sang a girl with a deep alto voice and a faint Spanish accent. 'This is eet – underwater love . . .' There was movement high above, a flash of silver and green and the audience in the stalls tipped their heads back as one, curious to see what was up there.

They saw her hair first, a tumble of gold glinting with silver dust, and then her silvery arms, half-hidden by the hair. She was sliding down the pole as smoothly as if she were swimming down it into the depths of the ocean, her torso slender and silvered too. And then they saw her tail, and everyone gasped. It was green and sewn with a million tiny sequins that caught and refracted the light, dazzlingly beautiful. She twisted round the pole as she descended, the music swirling around her, dreamy and slow, and when she reached the ground she paused for a while in a handstand, her tail flapping in long graceful movements. Then she sank to the floor and arched back, and the audience, seeing her upper body for the first time, naked apart from two silver shells over her nipples, whooped their applause.

It was a kind of dancing, bending into a full arch, leaning into the pole, body-rocking against it, wrapping herself around it, flicking her tail up it, twisting up and down its length, so sexy and elegant and athletic that the audience was soon moaning with appreciation.

'Christ, I wanna fuck that little mermaid *so bad!*' groaned the plump boy at the next table.

And then, like a snake shedding its skin, the mermaid began to slither out of her tail, teasing the audience, letting them see every pump and grind of her slender hips as she worked herself free. It was a strip act, but the novelty of the reveal was so effective that it kept a jaded set of spectators on the edge of their seats, mouths open, screaming with excitement when her bottom worked free and they could see her whole, slim, near-naked, silvered body slipping from the green tail, which she turned to kick deftly into the wings.

'You know something weird, L – um, sorry?' Devon said, turning to look at Lola. 'She looks almost exactly like you!'

'Oh my God! She does!' Georgia exclaimed, staring at the mermaid's face.

The mermaid was fully lit now by the spotlights at the front of the stage, her long golden hair falling over one slim bare shoulder, her brown eyes made huge with fake eyelashes and green and silver glitter. Despite the heavy theatrical make-up, her resemblance to Lola was suddenly, dizzyingly obvious.

'She could be your sister!' Georgia giggled. 'You don't have a secret twin, do you?'

The transformed mermaid was twined around the pole again, gripping it between her legs in a way she couldn't have done in her tail, flipping herself upside down as she tossed her hair from side to side and played with the shells covering her nipples in a way that was making the plump boy at the next table grunt like a pig in heat.

'Ah, just take them off, baby!' yelled a man from the mezzanine, and the theatre went mad with applause and cheers seconding his suggestion.

But Lola could hear nothing but the blood pumping in her head. She saw the mermaid on the pole through a red filter, as if the blood were filling her eyes, working her up to a level of anger so extreme she had no control over it. The champagne, of course, didn't help; nor did the coke or the nicotine, making her heart beat faster, fuelling her fury at the girl on stage.

Because she recognised her now. Of course she did. As soon as Devon had pointed out the resemblance, it had all flashed back. The girl in the pale-pink Chanel suit, blonde hair twisted demurely at the crown of her head, looking like butter wouldn't melt in her mouth, standing on the steps of her father's house. The girl who had actually dared to think that Lola was like her – another one of Ben Fitzgerald's mistresses.

Well, so much for the Chanel suit and the elegant hairstyle! This was who that little slut really was, a stripper! Was this how the girl had met Lola's father – whoring herself on a pole in front of a crowd of people whooping and yelling at her? The thought of Lola's father, staring at this girl hanging from a pole, getting turned on by her, this girl who looked so like his own daughter, made Lola's stomach churn. She could feel the bile rising, bitter and acid at the back of her throat.

Every shout from the audience, every cheer of applause as the girl wrapped herself around the pole and tossed her golden flag of hair, was like another knife in Lola's stomach. She pushed back her chair and stood up. No one noticed, not even her friends.

And then the girl flicked one silver shell off her breasts, throwing it towards the front row of tables. Men jumped up and scrambled for it excitedly. The girl toyed with the second shell, building up the excitement in the auditorium, making them wait for a long, breath-suspended moment, before she flicked that off, too. It spun in the air, a small flashing twist of silver, travelling further than the first shell, and there was a rush of movement towards the front of the stage as people vied to catch it, grown men jumping in the air like single women at a wedding desperate to catch the bride's bouquet.

Lola found herself caught up in the rush towards the stage, pushed forward by someone behind her. Set in motion. And once she was moving, she couldn't stop.

It was all a blur after that, as she ducked and dodged round the men and women grabbing for the shells, as she found the steps at the side of the stage, as she scrambled up them and launched herself at the girl on the pole, the girl who had been her father's mistress, the girl who had dared to turn up at her father's house and ask to see him, as if she had any rights at all . . . Lola had thought that the silver stuff on her body would make the girl slippery, like a fish, but of course it couldn't, because she would have slid right off the pole if it were. So when she caught hold of the girl's foot, and yanked it down, she had a good firm grip, and she jerked the girl half off the pole.

The girl was strong, of course, though Lola hadn't anticipated just how strong she was. She clung on tightly to the pole and tried to kick at Lola, to make her let go. But as she twisted round and aimed her other leg at Lola, she lost her grip and tumbled down, her hands slipping off the pole. Grabbing at Lola in an effort to break her fall, she caught Lola's head with one flailing hand.

Lola felt her wig slip, and frantically she tried to pull it back into place. But it was too late. She was tumbling, knocked off-balance by the girl's body falling towards her, and she couldn't get her hands up in time. The girl's grip dragged Lola's wig off – not just the wig, but the wig cap too.

The audience, which was already screaming in shock and excitement at seeing Lola's stage invasion, started yelling now. Through the kicks and struggle with the girl, Lola heard:

'Oh my God! It's a setup!'

'Fuck, she's part of the *act!*'

'No way!'

'Yo! Catfight! Awesome!'

As the wig cap came off, it dragged painfully down the back of Lola's scalp, pulling at her hair, catching on the grips and pulling them out too. Her hair came loose, the wig falling away, to gasps from the audience.

'It *is* a setup! Look, she's wearing a wig!'

'Get naked! Come on baby, tear her clothes off!'

Despite it being strictly forbidden, hundreds of tiny flashes were going off in the audience as they held up their phones and frantically tried to snap or video the dramatic scene in front of them. Lola and the girl tumbled to the floor of the stage, the wind knocked out of them with the fall. Close up, the girl looked unreal, like a heightened version of herself, an illustration come to life, with her huge, heavily pencilled eyes, the inch-long lashes, the stage make-up, the thick silver and green glitter on her eyelids and the diamond shine of her pink glossed lips.

And she was almost naked, wearing only a tiny G-string. Lola could smell the girl's sweat, fresh, from the hard work of her act, and hear her panting for breath, and the thought that she was so close to a body that had been intimate with Lola's own father made Lola suddenly so revolted that she pushed the girl away with a shove as violent as she could make it from her prone position.

Catching her breath, the girl scrabbled away, getting up on her knees.

'What the fuck are you *doing?*' she yelled at Lola. 'Who the hell *are* you? Some fucking morality police?'

'Don't you know who I am?' Lola yelled back, getting up on all fours, shouting right back in the girl's face. 'Can't you *see* who I am?'

The girl stared hard at Lola, and her eyes widened, huge and dark, the ridiculous stage eyelashes framing them, making them look so big they took over half of her face.

'Oh my *God*,' she breathed. 'You're Benny's—'

'*Don't say his name!*' Lola yelled.

She reached out to slap the girl, who caught her wrist. The girl's grip was like iron. They wrestled awkwardly, twisting and turning on their knees. Lola managed to catch the girl with her other hand, but she wrested it away. The audience were whooping and screaming so loudly now they were drowning out the music: all Lola could hear was the constant cries of encouragement, feet stamping on the ground. It was like being in an arena, the spectators scenting blood, wanting someone to get hurt.

'Cat*FIGHT*! Cat*FIGHT*!' a group of men were shouting, stamping their feet on the ground, a throbbing, pounding rhythm that drummed around the walls of the small theatre as if amplified through speakers.

The MC was running out onto the stage now, his top hat bouncing awkwardly on his head, calling in his high voice:

'Break it up now, that's enough fun! *Break it up!*'

But nothing anyone said could stop Lola from going after the girl. All her anger, all her frustration at the terrible things that had happened to her in the past fortnight, was directed squarely at the little whore in front of her, the girl who had seduced Lola's beloved father, who had done things with him that it made Lola sick to think about, this girl who looked *almost exactly like his own daughter*—

Oof! Something hit Lola squarely in the face, knocking her sideways. For a split second, she had absolutely no idea what had happened to her. She was slipping, falling over – momentarily blinded, she blinked again and again, trying to open her eyes, realising that she had just taken a bucketful of water full in the face.

Spluttering, spitting out water, she wiped her face with the wool of her sweater. The girl was drenched too, but the contortionist had come on stage now and was helping her get up. He pulled her to her feet, and someone else was grabbing Lola now, strong hands closing round her arms and clamping them to her sides.

'Stay away from me!' the girl screamed from the other side of the stage. The contortionist had hold of her shoulders and was holding her back. Hair damp, water streaming down the glitter on her face, the girl – Diamond – looked more naked than ever as the silver body paint dripped off her, baring the pale skin beneath.

'Then you stay away from me, you *slut!*' Lola screamed back. 'You dirty little *slut!*'

'You bitch!' the girl yelled furiously. 'You killed your own *father!*'

'I did *not!*' Lola shrieked back. 'I would *never!* It was that bitch he married!'

Lola wouldn't have thought it was possible for the audience, already stoked up to absolute hysteria by seeing both her and Diamond dripping wet, to reach any further heights of frenzy. But this revelation did it. They went wild. Literally.

'Omi*god!* It's *her!*' screeched a woman at the top of her lungs. 'It's *Lola Fitzgerald!*'

The screams of excitement were deafening. Two huge bouncers thudded past the group around Lola, their tread so heavy it shook the boards of the stage. One threw himself against the wave of people trying to get up the stairs, yelling at everyone to get back. The other lifted up a guy who was trying to climb onstage, dumping him back in the crowd. Phone cameras were everywhere now, people jostling and pushing against each other to get a good view. Someone screamed in pain as a scuffle broke out right at the front of the stage, glass breaking as a table went over.

'Ooh! This is the best thing ever to happen to Maud's! You can't *buy* this kind of publicity!' giggled the little MC gleefully relishing the mayhem. 'And Diamond – your career is *made* now! We're going to be packed every night from now to Labour Day – fuck slow summers in New York!' His top hat tilted crazily back as he craned to look up at Lola. 'The only person who's in trouble is this young lady right here. You gotta control your temper better, Miss Fitzgerald. Aren't you out on *bail?'*

'Don't worry. I'm getting her out of here right now,' said the man holding Lola, in the grimmest of tones.

Lola's heart skipped a beat as she twisted around madly, suddenly frantic to get a look at his face, sure that she recognised the voice – but how was that possible, how could he be *here*, of all places—

She should have recognised the feel of his hands on her, and the scent of his aftershave, dark and woody and musky, like apple brandy aged for years in oak barrels.

It was Niels van der Veer, glaring down at her, dirty-blond hair falling forward, silver-grey eyes glinting so angrily she thought he might burn right through her.

Chapter 22

'Come on,' Niels snapped, picking up Lola, turning her round, and frog-marching her off the stage. 'You've overstayed your welcome here, Princess.'

Three performers, all dressed in skintight leopard-skin catsuits, their hair dyed scarlet, piercings gleaming in their eyebrows, turned to stare at Lola as if she, not they, were the curiosity.

'What are you even *doing* here?' she asked angrily over her shoulder. 'This isn't your kind of place!'

'I'm an investor,' Niels said shortly. 'Did you think it was funded by a bunch of hip bohemians, Princess?'

'Stop *calling* me that!' Lola twisted in an effort to get away from him. 'You're such a patronising bastard!'

Holding her with one hand, Niels reached out with the other to the fire door in front of her, dragging it open.

'Out,' he said succinctly, pushing her through onto a metal fire escape one floor off the ground.

'How *dare* you push me around!'

Lola finally twisted free. Hands on hips, she stood glaring at him, the smoggy New York night breeze chilly on her wet hair. Niels folded his arms over his broad chest and glared right back at her. She gulped when she met his eyes; seeing him again was so confusing, because he stirred up so many feelings in her that she was almost paralysed with conflict. Of course she was furious at him for picking her up and hauling her round; but to be honest, she was also grateful that he'd whisked her away from that scene onstage before it got any worse. And then, as soon as she'd realised it was Niels holding her like that, she couldn't help but flash back all too vividly to that time last week where he'd put her down on the desk and dragged up the skirt of her nightdress and fucked her so thoroughly she'd seen stars.

Thinking of it now, even for the brief second that was all she allowed herself, she felt her entire lower body churn and start to melt with heat, liquefying deliciously, her legs going weak. She reached out and grabbed the rail of the fire escape for support.

'What the hell do you think you're playing at!' Niels barked at her. 'Your father's dead, you've been arrested for his *murder*, for God's sake – you're out on bail, and you can't find anything better to do than come out with your society-trash friends, get drunk and attack some burlesque dancer? What the hell is *wrong* with you?'

'I didn't mean to come,' Lola said weakly. 'They talked me into it – they said it would take my mind off things—'

'Your *mind?*' Niels yelled. 'You haven't got a mind! You're just a collection of primitive impulses! If you ever stopped to think for more than a second, you'd realise that your entire life is just a piti-ful, pathetic—'

'I don't have to listen to you insulting me!' Lola shouted furi-ously. 'I *know* I shouldn't be out, OK? I get it! And believe me, I know how terrible this looks! I don't need you to tell me how badly I fucked up!' She let go of the fire escape, her anger giving her enough strength to stand on her own two feet.

'I'm going back inside to find my friends,' she announced, trying to push past him. 'And then I'm going back to the Plaza and never leaving the damn apartment again—'

Niels caught her arm with one big hand.

'Oh no you don't,' he said, shaking his head. 'If you go back inside, there really will be a riot. I'm taking you back to the Plaza right now. You can call them from there if you want.'

'But I need to get my bag! And tell them I'm OK!' she insisted, bringing up both hands to shove against his chest.

She didn't move him an inch, of course. But as she pushed at him, she felt it happen, that spark of electricity between them, just as it had happened before, in the sitting-room at the Plaza.

And she realised that she had done it deliberately. She had pushed him, knowing that it would provoke him, hoping that he would grab her and kiss her just as he had kissed her before. For some inexplicable reason, as far as Niels van der Veer was concerned, Lola had no shame. He could have ripped off her clothes and shoved her up against the dirty, peeling wall of the building and had sex with her right here and all she would do would be cling to him and moan encouragement.

He was the only man she had ever met who had this effect on her. And she had absolutely no idea why.

His jaw tightened. He let go of her arm, and suddenly she was terrified, afraid that he would turn on his heel and go back inside, slamming the fire door behind him, and that would be the last she would ever see of him.

The night breeze felt as cold as an Arctic wind. He despised her. He thought she was just a spoilt, hysterical drama addict who made scenes wherever she went. He thought she had murdered her father and come out on the town to celebrate. He was washing his hands of her completely . . .

But then he stooped down, and the next thing Lola knew was his shoulder slamming into her stomach, his arms gripping her legs, and she was shooting up into the air, her upper body sliding down Niels's back so that she squealed in fear until her hips caught over his shoulder. She realised that he had picked her up in a fireman's lift and was striding down the stairs with her body inelegantly draped over him.

'What are you *doing?*' she screamed, pounding at his back. 'Put me *down!*'

Relieved as she was that he hadn't abandoned her, this was so humiliating that she couldn't bear it. She couldn't help but be grateful that he was carrying her as easily as if she weighed nothing at all; but it was so dismissive that it made her writhe with fury. Carrying her in his arms would at least have given her some dignity, rather than have her head bouncing around at the level of his jacket hem, as if she were a sack of potatoes he were hauling to a truck.

The next thing she knew, she heard a car door open and Niels was ducking down again. She was hauled around, swung through the air, and dumped onto a wide leather seat, which let out a soft whoosh of air as she landed on it. Niels dropped into the seat beside her and slammed the door.

Lola scrabbled back, getting as far away from him as possible. It was a large limousine, but not vulgarly so: Niels's taste was clearly for quality over showiness. The interior was gleaming, polished wood, and the facing seats were of a rich dark-grey leather, soft as butter. A smoked-glass panel separated them from the driver, and the windows were tinted too: it was as private in here as it was possible to be.

She was sealed off in a small enclosed space with Niels van der Veer, so close that she could smell not only his aftershave but the scent of him, and his physical proximity was making her heart beat so fast that she was surprised he didn't hear it and comment on it.

'You can't just *drive off* with me!' she said furiously. 'My friends are still in there!'

Niels laughed dryly.

'You mean those girls I saw you with at the hospital? I saw what state they're in – the redhead nearly fell over my table tonight. Believe me, Princess, they'll all be too drunk to even notice that you're gone.'

The limo was executing a tight three-point turn. Looking as best she could through the tinted windows, Lola saw that they were in a narrow alley at the back of the theatre. The limo crawled up it until she could see the main entrance and the queue of people lined up behind the velvet rope to get in. There were paparazzi outside, jostling each other as they shoved as close to the doors as they could get, clearly aware that a big drama was going on inside. The bouncers were yelling, trying to push them back, bright flashes from the cameras illuminating the scene in strobe vision.

'They'll be so worried!' Lola said, still thinking of the girls. She knew Niels was right about Georgia: but what about the rest of them? They'd still be there, having seen her hauled off stage, not knowing where she'd disappeared to, and they certainly wouldn't be allowed backstage to look for her. They'd be going out of their minds with worry.

Impulsively, she tugged at the door handle as they passed the front of the theatre. The limo was still in the alley, still going so slowly that she was sure she could jump out safely. She'd wait outside for the girls, across the street, somewhere the paps wouldn't spot her—

'What the *hell* do you think you're doing? Are you trying to get yourself killed?'

Niels grabbed her by the waist and pulled her away from the door so roughly that Lola flew back and landed ungraciously almost on top of him. She screamed, and she screamed even louder when he flipped her over so that she was face down, and, unbelievably, his open hand came down hard on her upraised bottom.

'Someone should have given you a damn good spanking when you were young enough for it to make a difference!' he said furiously. 'Are you *mad*? Trying to jump out of a moving car?'

He spanked her again and again, his left hand pressing hard between her shoulderblades, holding her down, as his right hand descended remorselessly, relentlessly, on her raised buttocks. Lola squirmed frantically, trying to get away, not wanting to give him the satisfaction of thinking that she was giving in to him; she managed to pull her hands out from where they had been trapped under her body, and flailed, trying to hit him. He caught them in his and clamped them together, forcing them down into the small of her back, making it much harder to resist him. And then he spanked her again, even harder, a stinging series of open-palmed slaps that, even through the fabric of her jeans, made her squeal with pain.

And then, wriggling helplessly on his lap, she felt how hard he was.

The length of his erection was rising up along his left thigh, a hard ridge beneath her lower stomach, so prominent that she couldn't help moaning as she felt its outline. As his hand came down again on her bottom, she rubbed herself against him, and she felt him swell in response, pressing up towards her through his trousers. She was so focused on his cock beneath her that she didn't realise immediately that Niels had stopped spanking her: it was only seconds later, with shock, that she felt his hand between her legs, parting them roughly, reaching under her, his palm coming up to rub against her exactly where she wanted it.

How he knew what to do so precisely, so perfectly, was something she didn't want to think about: how many women he been with, who had taught him so well how to touch her, even through her jeans, in just the right place. Her eyes closed, her eyeballs rolling back in her head with pleasure, and she drove her hips down onto his palm, moaning in excitement and anticipation. Niels's hand was up to her belly-button now, popping the button of her jeans open, forcing the zip down, his thumb finding her and drawing small clever circles on the silk of her knickers, the heel of his palm driving hard against her pubic bone, and before she could even draw breath she was coming so hard against him that, if he hadn't still been holding her down, her wrists still trapped behind her, she would have arched right off him as the spasms hit her.

He didn't even let her recover before he was working on her again, and this time it was almost instantaneous, as if once he'd lit the fire it had spread so far and so fast that just the lightest touch would send her up in flames once more. All her sensation was on what he was doing between her legs, his thumb sliding past the silk of her knickers now, sliding into her, finding her damp and more than ready for him, drawing circles inside her till she thought she would explode . . . and then she did, screaming against the wool of his trouser leg, words that she didn't even know she knew, helpless to do anything but come as long and as hard as he made her.

Niels drew his thumb back, just barely out of her, and flicked it once, twice, directly on her most sensitive spot, working the seam of her knickers against her skin. Her whole body convulsed against him, her hips pounding into him as she wailed in such pleasure she couldn't even remember her own name.

He let her go, and Lola actually slipped to the floor of the limo, unable to catch herself; her legs felt boneless, her mouth open, panting for breath. She looked up, dazed, her vision blurred, to see Niels above her, frantically working his belt buckle loose, his big hands, which had been so clever as they gave her one orgasm after another, fumbling now. He cursed it furiously in what she assumed was his native Danish, and the sight of him, so big and capable and strong, struggling with his own trouser belt, overwhelmed with passion for *her*, Lola Fitzgerald, was so exciting that she felt it like a rush to the head. Better than any drug she'd ever taken was this feeling of power: the power to make Niels van der Veer, international tycoon and by far the bossiest, most domineering man she had ever met, so overcome with lust for her that he couldn't get his own clothes to do what he wanted.

She knelt up and knocked his hands away, unbuckling his belt and pulling it open with slim, deft fingers. And then she had his trousers unbuttoned, unzipped, and she was reaching into his boxers, running her hand along his cock, pulling it out, and ducking her mouth over its head.

Above her, she heard Niels start to say something in protest, his hands under her arms, trying to pull her up. But she didn't want to come up. She wanted to stay right there. She held onto him and started licking up and down his cock, her knees bouncing as the limo pounded over New York's notoriously badly paved streets. Niels groaned, long and deep, a sound coming from the back of his throat, and his hands fell away as his cock drove itself up eagerly between her lips.

Lola hadn't planned this, hadn't meant to take him into her mouth. But when she saw his cock springing free, so big and juicy, the only thought in her head was how very badly she wanted to suck on it. Which was extraordinary, as she had never in her life wanted to put a penis anywhere near her mouth. Various boyfriends had asked, hopefully, if she would suck them off, but she had generally limited herself to dabbing a few kisses on the head of their cock and then maybe giving them a hand job, if she felt very well-intentioned and affectionate.

She hadn't dreamed of doing anything like this. It was too animalistic. There would be mess, and they would be offended when she spat it out. She simply hadn't wanted to, and, to be completely honest, she'd looked down on girls who did.

Well, she had fallen a long way since then, far and fast, all the way to her knees in a luxury limousine, wedged between Niels van der Veer's strong thighs, one hand braced on the rock-hard muscle of his quad to keep her balanced, the other wrapped tightly around the base of his cock, as she curved her lips over her teeth and sucked and licked up and down his straining thick length as if she could never, ever, get enough of giving head. Niels's groans were rising, and every appreciative sound he made was a huge relief, as she was worried she might not be doing it right. After all, it wasn't as if she'd had any experience with this.

But his hips were lifting, pumping his cock against the roof of her mouth, his hands were rising to twine through her hair, and she thought, as she licked the swollen head of his cock as if it were the most delicious lollipop she'd ever tasted, that she couldn't be doing it *that* wrong, because if she were, he'd scarcely be moaning:

'Oh yes, Lola, yes, like that, just like that – *God Jesus fucking God*—'

His hands were so tight in her hair now that she couldn't move her head. He was holding it where he wanted her, using her just as he needed to. The thought flooded her with happiness: Niels had made her come, played her like an instrument, and now what she was doing to him was working, because he was bucking now beneath her, his thighs thrusting up, the sheer size of his quad muscles amazing her as her hand slipped along his leg, and with one huge gasp he yelled: 'Oh *God yes! Fuck!*' and his cock started to pump inside her mouth.

She had never felt anything like this before. One moment she had thought she would choke on the size of him, and now he was pumping like a geyser. It was unbelievable, transcendent. Hot liquid flooded her mouth, foaming down her throat as she swallowed. It tasted of almonds and milk and lemon. She gulped for breath, pulling back a fraction so she could swallow it all, keeping Niels's cock still in her mouth, her lips wrapped round it, holding him, not wanting to let him go.

The limo swerved round something, and bounced over a pothole. Lola tipped back, and, to her great regret, Niels's cock slid out of her mouth. She sat back on the floor of the limo, licking her lips, feeling ridiculously, unbelievably, satisfied. Why had she ever thought she wouldn't like this? Why had she ever thought it might be demeaning? She'd had all the power there: she'd been the one to reduce big, strong Niels to – she almost giggled as she looked over at him, slumped in the corner of the limo – a drained, exhausted, shadow of himself. Talk about taming the beast. She suddenly understood why men were so nervous about sex. It made women feel stronger and men feel – well, drained. She had his essence now, swallowed down. He'd lost his strength. She had taken it from him.

The limo made a left turn and tilted downwards suddenly, sliding Lola across the floor towards Niels's seat. He reached down and hauled her up, one big hand in her armpit, lifting her and dropping her next to him on the leather upholstery before she'd even got her feet under her.

'Mr van der Veer?' said the chauffeur over the intercom as the limo slid to a halt. 'We're in the parking garage by the elevator bank. Shall I open the door?'

'Give us a minute,' Niels said, shifting to tuck himself back into his trousers and do them up. He nodded a command at Lola, who stared at him blankly before blushing furiously and reaching down to do up the zipper of her own jeans.

'I—' Niels started. He cleared his throat, and began again: 'You—'

He ducked his head into his hands. Lola stared at him in amazement: it was inconceivable to have big, powerful Niels van der Veer too embarrassed to meet her gaze.

'Look, this isn't a good situation,' he mumbled into his palms. 'You and Jean-Marc – you're drinking, obviously, and probably taking drugs too. Your friends were high as kites this evening. You shouldn't be around Jean-Marc. I know this isn't exactly' – he rubbed his face furiously – 'I mean, after what we just did, it seems very hypocritical of me – but your staying with him is just not a good situation. He shouldn't be drinking, and I know he is. He nearly died just a couple of weeks ago, for God's sake!'

Niels dropped his hands to look at Lola.

'The bottom line is, you're not a good influence on Jean-Marc, no matter what he says. I want you out of there. I'll pay you – however much you want – I know Jean-Marc's looking after you financially, and I'll match that – but you need to pack your things and leave.'

'How dare you!' Lola exclaimed furiously. 'If you think Jean-Marc would survive for a *day* without me staying there, you're mad. He can barely be alone at the moment, he's so vulnerable. David can't be around the whole time, and Jean-Marc gets so upset when David leaves to go to work that he crawls in with me and sleeps in my bed, just so he isn't by himself! And yes, we drink, but it's only champagne, and just a few glasses, and we're trying to get him to stop that too.'

She was frowning so hard her forehead hurt, her fists clenched with anger.

'You aren't around!' she added. 'You aren't there when he's curled up on the sofa crying because he misses David! You aren't trying to sort him out a sponsor and make sure he goes to Narcotics Anonymous meetings every day! You make me move out and Jean-Marc will be back on drugs in a week! He needs someone with him all the time, don't you get it? You haven't talked to him properly, spent any time with him – all you do is lecture him instead of working out how he's doing and what he really needs, you big arrogant bossy *bastard!*'

Panting for breath, she stared at him furiously, seeing that he was frowning too. He opened his mouth to say something, but at that moment the chauffeur, obviously having counted down a minute as per Niels's instructions, opened the back door of the limo, and Lola scrambled out as rapidly as if the upholstery had just burst into flames.

'Stay away from us!' she yelled over her shoulder. 'We don't need you! Just stay away from me and Jean-Marc!'

Her attempt to make a fully dramatic exit was frustrated by the fact that the strip-lighting of the Plaza's parking garage was so bright after the dark interior of the limo that it blinded her momentarily. She came to a halt after two steps, blinking frantically, scared that Niels was going to jump out of the limo and shout at her some more. But then she realised that there was a lift already waiting, its doors opening just at that moment: the chauffeur must have called it before unlocking the limo door. She muttered her thanks and dashed inside, holding her breath until the doors closed behind her and she was finally alone, in a different space from Niels.

There was a mirror in the lift. She stared at herself. Her hair was a messy tangle, her mascara smeared halfway down her cheeks. Her eyes were dilated; there was a hectic flush on her cheeks, and her skin was sweaty from exertion.

She was so confused by her own roiling emotions that she would have given anything to be able to ring a girlfriend right now and tell her everything. Talk it over, analyse what had happened, twice, between her and Niels – what seemed to happen every time they were alone together: fighting and sex. They didn't seem to be able to exchange two pleasant words with each other; everything they did triggered a fight, which triggered sex, and, as had just happened now, another fight after that.

Because Lola had no experience with this kind of insane, unbridled lust, she had no idea how to deal with it at all. Exciting though it was, sex with Niels was equally terrifying: it went from zero to 100 in the flash of an instant. Too fast, too out of control. Together, she and Niels were a Maserati with a hair-trigger accelerator. Was that normal? Lola really didn't think so. But Jean-Marc, who would be ideal to ask, was out of the question, because it would be much too embarrassing to tell him what she had just done with his brother.

And the girls – well, after the revelations about her that someone had sold to the British tabloids, she had no idea whether she could trust any of them. It would take a little while to check if any of the traps she had set last night would be sprung.

She stepped out of the lift and walked down the corridor. But as soon as she pushed the door of the apartment open, she heard sounds that sent all her senses on high alert.

Up till that moment, Lola had been exhausted, coming down from a high-grade combination of stimulants. She had been ready for nothing more than stripping her clothes off and crawling into her huge, soft bed.

That was, until she heard the thudding generic bassline of a pounding club soundtrack, laughter so high-pitched and raucous that it could only be drunken, and a provocative scream of excitement in a man's voice.

But I thought David wasn't staying the night? Lola thought. *He said he had to get a really early start tomorrow morning. And besides, that doesn't sound like David . . .*

All tiredness forgotten in her rising panic, Lola strode through the foyer, crossed the living-room and pushed open the door of Jean-Marc's bedroom. What she saw there was worse than anything she had imagined. Two half-naked young men – barely legal jailbait, by the looks of them – were curled up on the bed with Jean-Marc. The big mirror that usually hung over the bed-head had been taken down, and was now lying on the coverlet. Its surface reflected the glittering chandelier overhead, streaks of light glinting on the razor-blades propped next to the piles of white powder.

And there was a fourth person present, sitting in the big armchair next to the bed, observing the proceedings with the wide smile of a satisfied pagan idol. Lola recognised her immediately. The over-plucked eyebrows, the cheaply dyed hair, the pores so deep that foundation, rather than covering them up, had sunk into them and made them even more visible, the gigantic football-sized breasts resting just below her collarbones . . .

Lola stood and gaped at her, unable to believe anything about what she was seeing. She had seen pictures of Patricia in the tabloids, of course, but in the flesh she was infinitely more freakish, as if she'd taken everything associated with femininity – the breasts, the long hair, the make-up – and exaggerated them beyond the point of parody.

Patricia's head turned, sensing eyes on her. She didn't miss a beat when she saw Lola, standing in the doorway: she smiled instead, showing a set of teeth so bright and white that Lola shivered, thinking immediately of a crocodile rearing out of the water, its mouth open.

'Lola!' she said, in the rough, grating voice of someone who smokes two packs a day. 'Nice to meet you, darlin'! Johnny's told me all about you. Come in, join us!'

Jean-Marc raised his head from the mirror, catching sight of Lola. His blue eyes were glazed, his fair hair damp with sweat. He looked frenzied, his pupils tiny dark points, and white powder was caked round his nostrils.

'You like the white stuff too, don't you, Lola?' Patricia giggled. 'No point denying it, dear. We've all seen the papers! Come on, have a toot!' She winked at Lola. 'And feel free to play with the boys if you like. Believe me, dear, there's *nothing* they won't do . . .'

Chapter 23

*L*ola took a deep breath, grabbed the mirror with both hands, and up-ended it and its contents all over the coverlet and the carpet. Puffs of white powdery cocaine flew up into the air, momentarily blinding everyone on the bed. The boys screamed in fury and protest, ducking down as Lola sent the razorblades sliding across the mirror and onto the floor on the far side of the bed.

'You crazy bitch!' one of them yelled. 'Do you *know* what that's worth?'

Struggling under the weight of the mirror, Lola dragged it towards her and propped it against the wall behind her: it was still streaked with white residue.

'Naughty, naughty,' Patricia commented, her voice like gravel dragging against gravel. 'You've got quite a temper, don't you, dear? He's not coming back to you, you know. Our little Johnny's a confirmed homosexual.'

Patricia turned her head, the pencilled-in eyebrows raising in fake surprise as she failed to see Jean-Marc.

'Now, *where* can he have gone?' she asked. 'Lola dear, where *is* your fiancé? Have a look, why don't you?'

Tears came into Lola's eyes when she ducked down to see Jean-Marc crouched down beside the bed. His fingers were pinched together, desperately scrabbling white powder from the tufts of the thick pale carpet and stuffing it up his nose. Strands of carpet came up with the coke, and he didn't seem to care. His eyes were bloodshot, and he was moaning faintly.

As she straightened up and looked around the room Lola felt as cold as ice. She turned to stare at Patricia, who was still sitting in the chair, lighting another cigarette from the butt of the previous one, a small, amused, infinitely knowing smile on her face.

'Get up,' Lola said between her teeth. 'Get out. All of you. Get out and never come back.'

The sheer iciness of Lola's tone made the boys jump to obey, grabbing their clothes and hustling for the door.

'And you,' Lola said, staring at Patricia. 'You disgusting, horrible pimp. Get up out of that chair now, before I call security and make them throw you out on the street where you belong.'

'You *bitch*,' Patricia hissed, her eyes narrowing. 'How *dare* you call me a pimp? It's *madam* to you! Can't you see these?' She hoisted her breasts at Lola. 'Bigger than those little fried eggs on your skinny little chest!'

'You're a drug dealer!' Lola snapped. 'And a pimp! Now stand up and get the hell out of here!'

Patricia's aura of malevolence was now so strong that Lola was amazed when her enemy did in fact slowly stand up, easing herself out of the armchair.

'You'll regret this,' Patricia said quietly, and Lola found herself taking a step back.

'Oh yes you will,' Patricia continued, almost crooning the words. 'You'll regret this. No one crosses me and gets away with it. I know you, Lola Fitzgerald. I know all about you. You've got nothing of your own any more, and you're on trial for murdering your own father. You're in no position to be causing me any problems.'

She took another deep drag at her cigarette. 'You should have played nice, dear,' she said. 'I gave you the chance. You could have partied with us and had the little tarts, if you'd wanted, or just turned a blind eye and left Johnny to me and my boys.' She sighed. 'But no – you had to get up on your moral high horse.'

'Get out,' Lola repeated between gritted teeth. 'You're disgusting.'

Holding Lola's eyes with her own, Patricia took her cigarette out of her mouth and dropped it to the carpet beside her.

'Disgusting, am I, Miss Lola Fitzgerald?'

She leaned closer to Lola, so close that Lola could see every pore in Patricia's face, every sag of her skin, pulled down by the heavy make-up. Patricia's grey roots were beginning to show at the hairline, and her breath was so reeking that it was all Lola could do not to turn her face away: under the stink of menthol cigarettes was something decaying and corrupt, like rotten food or old vomit.

'You're everything I hate,' Patricia whispered into Lola's face. 'Rich, privileged, pretty as a picture. Everything's been given to you on a silver platter. Well, I'm going to take it all away from you, dear. I'll see you in the gutter by the time I've finished with you. I'll see you crawling at my feet. And then, maybe, I'll let you work for me.' She smiled maliciously. 'I've got some male clients who'd love to teach a girl like you a few facts of life.'

With all the strength she had from her yogilates and boxercise classes, Lola struck Patricia across the face, so hard that Patricia's head snapped back with the force of the blow. They stood there for a moment, staring at each other, neither able to believe what Lola had just done.

And then, without another word, Patricia turned on her heel and stalked out, snapping her fingers at the boys, who scurried after her. Lola slammed the door behind them, and then frowned, suddenly smelling smoke: looking down at the carpet, she was horrified to realise that Patricia's cigarette was still alight. It had started to smoulder, burning a hole in the carpet. She stamped it out furiously, with much more effort than she needed to use, grinding her heel into the fibres, panting with the effort.

Then, bracing herself, she went back into Jean-Marc's bedroom to begin the long task of cleaning him up and getting him to sleep.

Chapter 24

Summoned into the manager's office at Maud's, a short while after the onstage fight with Lola Fitzgerald, Evie hadn't had the slightest idea what to expect. She was taken aback to see not just Pete, the manager, present for the talk; off to the side of Pete's desk, standing with his arms folded across his chest, was that big, brutally handsome guy in the very expensive Brioni suit who had picked Lola Fitzgerald up and pretty much just walked off with her.

Wow, he really is a looker, Evie thought. *Like that guy who plays James Bond, the blond one, only even meaner-looking. In a good way. He could pick* me *up and carry me off any time he wanted.*

'Diamond!' Pete jumped up. 'How are you? We're so sorry about what happened!'

'Security's been hauled over the coals,' the James Bond guy assured her. His accent was foreign; she couldn't place it, but it was incredibly sexy, with more than a hint of gruffness. 'No one should ever have got onto the stage let alone attacked you.'

'I can't apologise enough,' Pete said, coming round the desk to take her hand and pump it between both of his. 'Really. We take care of our performers at Maud's. This was a total aberration. Sit, please!'

Evie sank into the chair he had indicated, while Pete lifted the tail of his jacket and perched his buttocks on his desk. The James Bond guy remained standing, though.

He's all wound up, Evie realised. *I wonder why?*

'Diamond, we realise you must be really shaken up by what happened tonight,' Pete started.

It was all Evie could do not to roll her eyes.

You guys, I was a stripper, *OK?* she wanted to say. *Other girls stole my stuff and tried to sabotage me. I gave freaking lap dances in the private room. Men groped my tits and put their fingers up me and worse. Playing Find The Needle Dick with my sugar daddy was all in a day's work for me. Trust me, getting dragged off a pole by his spoilt little daughter who can't fight for shit is so low down on my radar that it barely registers.*

'I did get bad pole burn,' she said demurely.

'That sounds painful!' Pete said, wincing. 'Diamond' – he leant forward – 'believe us: we're really sorry this happened. We want you to stay at Maud's. We want to compensate you. You have a great act. You're a star. And now – let's be honest – you and Maud's are going to get a ton of attention. Let's make the most of it together, OK? Let's really build your career.'

He reached behind him on the desk and grabbed a piece of paper, which he handed to Evie. As she took it, her eyes widened. Clipped to the top of it was a cheque for $10,000, made out in her name.

'That cheque's for you, whatever you decide,' Pete said. He gestured to the James Bond guy, who nodded. 'Diamond, this is Niels van der Veer, one of our investors. He took Miss Fitzgerald home, came right back here and wrote that cheque out to you by way of apology.'

'Wow!' Evie said, still hypnotised by the amount of zeros on the cheque. She dragged her eyes away from it to look up at the James Bond guy.

Does he have the hots for me? she wondered. *Is that what this is really about – a down payment on some private dancing? Jeez, as if a guy who looks like that ever had to pay for it!*

But then, meeting – she read his name on the cheque again – Niels van der Veer's grey eyes, she saw immediately that she had got it wrong. This guy wasn't after anything from her. In her short, eventful life, Evie had got very experienced at reading men, and she could tell that this one was a million miles away. Even though Evie was nearly naked under her thin robe, her skin still glittering with silver dust, her golden hair curling down her back – looking pretty damn sexy, though she said it herself – he wasn't registering any sexual interest in her.

If he wasn't into Evie, especially Evie all dressed up like Diamond, that could only mean one thing: some other woman had her hooks into him real good.

Lucky bitch, Evie thought ruefully. *He's gorgeous* and *loaded. Lucky, lucky bitch.*

Oh well, maybe he's got a needle dick too.

'We've drawn up a contract for you, Diamond,' Pete said. 'Just a rough one for now, but we can iron out the creases over the next couple days. We'd like to book you exclusively for Maud's for the next six months. That's huge, you know? We've never done this before. But we want to show you how much we value you as a performer.'

Niels van der Veer nodded.

'Take your time, look it over,' he said. 'Get a lawyer to check it out for you if you want. Meanwhile, I've got my limo waiting for you out back. It'll take you wherever you want to go.'

'Wow, thank you,' Evie said gratefully. 'I'll read this over' – she waved the contract – 'and get back to you.'

And I'll deposit the cheque first thing tomorrow morning, believe me.

'Do you think you'll be OK to go on tomorrow?' Pete asked anxiously.

Evie couldn't help grinning. Pete was so transparent; he was desperate for the publicity, the table sales, if she did her act tomorrow night. *I'd better not make it too easy for them*, she calculated. *That way, they'll value me more.*

'I'll rest up tomorrow and see how my bruises are doing. But I'll do my best to make it in,' she said, lowering her eyes. 'I'll call you in the morning to confirm, is that OK?'

'Sure, sure,' Pete said, jumping down from the desk and pressing her hands eagerly again. 'Anything you want, Diamond. Anything you want.'

Evie had been repressing it the whole time she was in Maud's, but she couldn't help the huge smile breaking out as soon as the chauffeur closed the door of Niels van der Veer's limo behind her. Ten grand! Ten grand just for a couple of bruises! And a contract with Maud's, the best burlesque joint in New York! Visions of even more success floated before her eyes. With this money, she could hire a publicist. She could start making appearances at parties, maybe get a residency in Vegas once Maud's had made her name, maybe even work up to the ultimate dream for a burlesque dancer who couldn't sing for shit and thus would never be asked to be in a pop group: endorsements.

She thought of Dita von Teese, the famous burlesque star who had come from some nowhere town in the Midwest and was savvy and ambitious enough to be the ambassador for Cointreau, a spokeswoman for M.A.C. Viva Glam lipstick, have her own lingerie line, a deal with Swarovski. Dita was a brunette: why shouldn't there be room for a blonde out there too, with her own special gymnastic skills?

Evie poured herself a glass of cognac from the limo's built-in bar and lounged back in the leather seat, savouring the rich golden taste. Boy, this was a great way to end the day. From the moment she'd woken up, she'd been on tenterhooks about how her debut act would be received: could a stripper really make the transition to burlesque artist? Or would she be booed off the stage?

Well, she knew the answer now. Her act had been a triumph, even without Lola Fitzgerald's intervention. They'd been cheering her on, yelling louder for her than any other act this evening. She was making good money without having to spread her legs for it, without having to whore herself for Benny.

But you're still being driven back to Bushwick, a voice inside her head reminded her. *You're still living in one room in an illegal warehouse with a shower you have to share with three other people and a boiler that cuts out every half an hour. And yesterday Laura saw a rat the size of a small cat running down the stairs. OK, ten grand sounds like a hell of a lot, but with rents in Manhattan the way they are – plus deposits and agent's fees and all that crap – it'd get swallowed up straight away if you use it to move out.*

Besides, you don't want to throw money away in rent, fuck it. Renting's a mug's game. You had a lovely apartment, your dream place, and Benny told you it'd be yours forever. You earned that apartment, goddammit.

I want my apartment back. And I want my pasties back.

I still want everything that bitch Carin took from me, just as badly as I ever did.

Plus, I want her to pay for killing Benny.

Ever since she'd started working up her burlesque act, Evie had been so focused on survival that she hadn't given herself time to think about anything but her new routine, on endless hours spent devising it, rehearsing it with feedback from her new housemates, pushing herself to exhaustion and crashing out every night with the hope that this could be her ticket to a new and better world. One where she didn't have to fuck anyone she didn't want to, because she made enough money on her own.

Evie had fucked Benny for money, and she hadn't been paid for it. Carin Fitzgerald owed her, big time.

And Evie owed Carin Fitzgerald, for having killed a guy who'd been nothing but good to Evie. Sure, he'd cheated on his wife. But he didn't deserve to be killed for that. And, after tonight, Evie was sure it was Carin who had killed him. Evie had looked into that soft little spoilt princess's eyes as she yelled that Carin had killed her father, and Evie had believed she was telling the truth.

Evie yawned, a slow, deep yawn that came right up from her toes. Today had been the biggest day of her life. She could have sacked out right here, in this incredibly comfortable leather back seat.

But tomorrow, she was going to strategise. Because it was time for Carin Fitzgerald to get her comeuppance. And Evie Lopez was just the girl to give it to her.

Chapter 25

S ipping her coffee, staring out over Central Park from her bedroom window, Lola caught her reflection in the glass and winced. She hadn't got to bed till five, when Jean-Marc had finally crashed out, helped along by a sleeping pill. This morning it had taken half a pint of Benefit's Ooh La Lift under her eyes to get rid of her circles, and she was doused in Stella McCartney's Peony scent: rose, amber and black pepper, floral and sweet, she'd hoped it would pick up her spirits. It wasn't helping as much as she had anticipated.

The bedside phone buzzed, and she jumped for it, not wanting the ring to wake up Jean-Marc.

'Miss Fitzgerald?' said a voice. 'It's the front desk. Um, there's a young lady down here asking for you. She won't give her name.' The concierge cleared his throat. 'Normally I would insist, but she says it won't mean anything to you, and these are kind of special circumstances. Um, I think you should probably come downstairs to see her. Meet her,' he corrected himself.

Lola had no idea what was going on, what was concealed behind the awkward, slightly embarrassed tone of voice the concierge was using. But she didn't care; she was feeling so claustrophobic that she would have grabbed at any excuse to leave the apartment for a little while.

'I'll be right down,' she told him, hanging up the phone.

It was only as she was crossing the lobby that it occurred to her that the woman waiting for her downstairs might be Patricia, and she froze in the middle of the huge marble floor. Then she noticed a small, slight woman standing beside the concierge's desk, wearing a baseball cap, and saw the concierge's nod, and Lola relaxed. Apart from anything else, the fleece workout top the woman was wearing was close-fitting: it would have been impossible for Patricia to disguise the two huge melons on her chest to that extent.

Spotting Lola, the woman started walking towards her, so quick and lithe that Lola instantly re-categorised her to girl. And then, as Lola got a glimpse under the cap, she stared at the girl for a second longer in utter disbelief, realising instantly why the concierge had sounded so uncharacteristically awkward on the phone.

It was that little whore. Diamond. The girl outside her father's house, all dressed up in pale-pink Chanel. The girl on the pole, wearing just a few strategically placed pasties.

Lola felt her fingers twitch with the impulse to stride up to the girl and slap her across her face. The paparazzi were just outside; she could see them massed beyond the glass doors. Lola couldn't take the risk. She just couldn't trust herself to control her actions around her father's mistress. Who looked so much like Lola that they could be sisters.

Lola spun on her heel and ran back for the lifts.

'Lola! Wait! I really need to talk to you! Wait for me!'

Evie sprinted after Lola, her fantastic physical condition making it effortless for her to hit a racing speed from a standing start. Still, Lola Fitzgerald was no slowcoach herself, Evie had to admit that. Probably put in a lot of gym time. All these rich girls were obsessed with being as skinny as possible.

Lola didn't seem to be listening to Evie. She shot across the lobby and disappeared round the far corner. Terrified that Lola would disappear, that she'd lose her one shot at saying what she'd come to say, Evie sped along so fast she was almost a blur of motion as she rounded the corner.

In a flash, she took in the scene in front of her: more lavish marble with, in the centre, a bank of elevators, gleaming with chrome and brass fittings. In front of them was Lola Fitzgerald, slender and elegant in a grey sweater and slim-cut jeans, her long legs making her look much taller than her five feet five inches. She was jabbing desperately at the call button with one slim finger. Just then an elevator pinged further down the line, and Lola turned and raced for it.

Evie wouldn't have thought that she could lengthen her stride even more. But after all, she was a superb athlete. She practically flew the last few feet, bounding across the marble as if it were the yielding sprung-floor of a gymnastics studio, and she threw herself at the closing elevator doors as if she wasn't in serious danger of hitting them headfirst.

She made it into the elevator by the skin of her teeth, slamming into the crack between the doors so fast that she shot right across the cabin, her hands coming up just in time to pound flat into the mirror on the far wall. The mirror, which was actually hung there as if it were a real room, not a steel-framed cage, rattled ominously under the impact, and Evie had to hold it there with all her light weight so it didn't come loose and fall to the ground.

'Fuck!' she said, breathing hard. 'Thank fuck that didn't break! The last thing I need right now is seven years *more* bad luck!'

Behind her, the elevator doors opened again, the sensors automatically pulling them back so that anyone trapped could jump clear. Which meant that Lola Fitzgerald had the chance to dash to the front desk and tell security to throw Evie out on her ass. Evie's one precious opportunity of talking to her could be over before it had even begun.

And then Evie heard something completely unexpected.

Laughter.

Lola Fitzgerald was laughing.

Sure, it was pretty dry, as laughs went; but still, she was laughing.

Then she said, in the snotty, upper-class English accent that Evie remembered all too well from last night:

'Believe me – the last thing *I* want is seven years extra bad luck either!'

And, taking a step towards Evie, she grabbed the edge of the mirror, steadying it: helping Evie to make sure that it wasn't going to fall and shatter on the elevator floor.

'I know you didn't kill your dad,' Evie said intently, her eyes fixed on Lola.

Standing on the apartment terrace struggling to light a cigarette, her hair whipped by the wind, Lola was unprepared for this statement. She finally managed, more through luck than skill, to get her cigarette drawing, and swung round to stare at Evie.

'Why would you say something like that?' Lola demanded.

Evie still couldn't get over how much this girl looked like her.

'Because you're not the type,' Evie said frankly.

She leaned back on the balustrade, the roar of Fifth Avenue traffic muted to a dull steady rumble thirty storeys below her. Lola had brought her up here, to the private terrace of the apartment she was staying in, and it took Evie's breath away. This was the way the rich saw New York, with Central Park spread out before them like a magical forest. They were so high up here that the huge spreading trees down below looked like a moss garden, the Great Lawn like a shiny piece of green velvet. Through the trees, the water in the lake by the south-east corner of the park glistened in the sunlight. Even the air was fresher up here, less humid. No stink from tyre recycling firms or meat processing plants on this part of the island.

And Lola lived like this. Lola took this kind of luxury for granted. It was hard for Evie not to feel just a little intimidated.

But she was damned if she'd show it. She took a cigarette of her own and lit it, ducking over the lighter, twisting her hand round to cover it and the cigarette, with the skill of a girl who'd grown up in the projects and was more than used to lighting up thirty storeys in the air. Though Evie's experience came from windswept concrete balconies covered with graffiti tags, not castles in the sky.

'Doing what you say they did,' Evie continued, 'sticking a needle into your dad – that's really cold. And with the nurse right there, or just outside the room – that's really ballsy. No offence, but no way did you pull that. She set you up, didn't she?'

Lola was taking all of this in, Evie could tell. She was pretty as a picture, the perfect princess who belonged high up here in the fairy-tale castle. Well, fairy tales were dark, weren't they? The real fairy tales? Evie had been brought up on all that Disney crap – play nice, look pretty, and you'll get a prince and a kingdom and a dress with a big skirt – but she'd read some of the real stuff in the library once. Stepsisters with their toes cut off, bleeding into the magic slipper. Crows coming down and pecking out their eyes. The guys who wrote those stories knew what life was really like.

Evie waited for Lola to think over what she'd just said, smoking her cigarette, watching the crests of the trees in Central Park wave gently in the wind, the crenellations and balconies and high towers that capped the huge grey buildings along Fifth Avenue, each one a palace. She sure as hell wouldn't see this view again in a hurry; she might as well make the most of it.

'That's not proof,' Lola Fitzgerald said eventually. 'You didn't see anything that could help me.'

Evie held up her left hand and ticked her points off one by one, bending down her fingers to count them off.

'One: that bitch killed him,' she started. 'We both know that. Two: she's managed to frame you for it, and she's done a good enough job of it to get you arrested. Three: I'm guessing that the reason she's gone to all this trouble is that there's a shitload of money involved, else why would she take the risk of doing this? I mean, why not just wait it out? Benny's in a coma, she's got control of everything, he's not going anywhere, right? So there must've been some major benefit to her in pulling something like this.'

Evie squinted under the peak of the cap, watching Lola's reactions intently. Despite Lola's clear intent not to give anything away,

Evie had seen her make a tiny, involuntary nod as Evie outlined point three.

So Evie had been right. This was all about money.

Emboldened, Evie continued, her voice gaining strength:

'Four: you gotta fight fire with fire. She's pulled a dirty trick on you, and you gotta pull one back on her to make sure you don't go down for this.'

'There's a five, isn't there?' Lola said, a faint smile on her lips.

'Sure,' Evie said. 'Can't have four without a five!' She thumbed down her little finger. 'Five: I can help you. Or at least, I got a plan that could help you. But you gotta do something for me in return.'

The fresh wind, sweeping across from Central Park, brought a hawk with it, drawing lazy circles high in the sky above them, its reddish-orange tail feathers unmistakable in the sunlight, even the predatory hook of its beak clearly visible for a few moments as it wheeled on the wind. Suddenly, it dived, swooping down close to the building, dislodging a couple of terrified pigeons from their roost below one of the cornices. They flapped desperately, squawking as they flew towards a nearby tree, and the hawk made a couple of passes at them, sizing them up. For whatever reason, it decided against them as prey. And in a couple of seconds more, it was gone, disappearing with a few heavy beats of its wings in the direction of Sixth Avenue.

Evie and Lola looked back at each other, the drama of seeing a beautiful wild creature chase its prey alive and vivid in their eyes.

But hey, the drama here on the terrace is just as big, Evie thought. *If things don't go well for Lola, she'll be doing twenty-five to life in fricking Bedford Hills.*

Evie shivered at the thought of Bedford Hills. Though it sounded like a country club, it was the only maximum-security prison for women in New York State, like Attica or Sing Sing for women. Pretty, fragile Lola Fitzgerald would be eaten alive in Bedford Hills. She'd be a pigeon for every single hawk in there, torn to pieces as soon as she landed.

'You really need to listen to me,' Evie blurted out. 'Trust me, you can't go to jail. You won't survive in there.'

'What do you want?' Lola Fitzgerald said finally, and Evie's heart leaped in excitement.

'Carin threw me out of my apartment,' she said. 'Benny'd always said he'd put it in my name' – she ducked her head, not wanting to see the anger in Lola's eyes – 'but I should have known better. He said he'd take care of me in his will, and who the hell knows what happened there? But she stole stuff that he'd given me. This diamond . . . um, *jewellery* . . .'

No point telling the girl that her dad bought me diamond pasties, for Christ's sake, Evie thought.

'He'd *given* it to me,' she said firmly. 'And she came into my apartment – which wasn't mine after all, go figure – and chucked me out on my ass, and stole my diamonds. I want them back. And also' – she took a breath – 'I'm not saying you need to set me up for life. But that was supposed to be my apartment, and I want the deeds to it.'

It seemed like years before Lola finally answered.

'So what's your plan?' Lola asked, lighting another cigarette. 'You've told me I'm in trouble, and you've told me what you want. And I'm still listening. So go ahead – what's your plan to save me from prison?'

Chapter 26

*F*or a moment, Evie thought that Lawrence and Autumn were having sex. Her reaction was instant and furious: her hands curled into claws, and she took two quick steps forward, her arms flexing, about to grab Lawrence and pull him bodily off Autumn. Then, as the red mist before her eyes faded enough for her to take in the situation, Evie saw that not only were they wearing workout clothes – just tank tops and shorts, but still, clothes – but as far as she could tell, their crucial parts were all covered.

What they were doing was definitely weird, though. Autumn was in Downward Dog, the classic yoga pose where you put your hands and feet on the ground, at enough of a distance so you're sticking your ass in the air, pushing it back, flattening your heels, like a dog doing a stretch after waking up. Only Autumn's hands were wrapped round Lawrence's ankles, and his hands were on her ass, pushing it away. The more Evie looked, the more she could see that this wasn't any sort of sex act, not even a preliminary: their bits were all in the wrong places for them to be getting it on.

But seeing Lawrence with his hands on Autumn, touching that dumb middle-class girl who thought she was cool and hip with her weird hair colour and her piercings and her sleeve tattoo – Evie's blood boiled. Lawrence was an idiot if he thought he could abolish jealousy just by saying that it shouldn't exist.

Autumn and Lawrence were oblivious to her presence. The front door had been ajar – they mostly left it open when they were in, since there was nothing worth stealing in the place, plus Lawrence had a touching faith in the goodness of human nature – and there was some rhythmic, Indian-sitar, hippie music playing on the stereo, so they hadn't heard Evie's footsteps.

She could have announced her entrance more discreetly – clearing her throat, maybe, saying something – but she was pissed now at the sight of the two of them with their hands on each other. So she banged the heavy steel door, and she must have used more force than she realised, because it slammed against the metal frame so loudly that both Lawrence and Autumn jumped and nearly toppled over.

'Evie!' Lawrence exclaimed, turning his head towards the doorway.

'*Evie?*' Autumn hissed.

'I need to talk to you, Lawrence,' Evie said, doing her best to ignore Autumn.

'What's this about, Evie?' he said, his voice as gentle as ever.

'What's it *matter* what's it about?' Autumn said angrily.

Autumn had re-dyed her hair, Evie noticed: it was all jet-black now, and her eyes were heavily lined in black pencil, emphasising the Asian upwards tilt to them, the almond shape. Her tank top was purple and her cycling shorts, which she'd rolled up to just below her crotch, were black. She looked less boho-radical now, more biker-chick Goth. It was a striking look, but, in Evie's possibly biased opinion, it made Autumn even less like a good match for Lawrence, who didn't wear black because it was negative. Nor did he believe in piercings and tattoos, because they were a mutilation of the human body.

It was undeniably true that Lawrence could be a bit of a buzz-kill on occasion.

'She walked out on you, Lawrence!' Autumn continued, glaring at Evie. 'You shouldn't listen to a word she says!'

'She didn't walk out on me, Autumn,' Lawrence corrected. 'We chose to take different paths.'

He looked gravely at Evie. Clad only in a white tank top and dark-blue running shorts, his feet bare, Lawrence somehow managed to have the dignity of a man wearing a three-piece Hugo Boss suit and handmade Lobb shoes.

'Is it important?' he asked. 'Autumn and I were in the middle of practice, as you could see. I'm sure you'd only interrupt us for something that you really thought was important, wouldn't you, Evie?'

She nodded.

'OK,' he said. 'We can talk in my room.'

'*Lawrence!*' Autumn protested, stamping the ground in frustration.

'I'm sorry to break up our practice, Autumn,' he said. 'I'll try not to take too long.'

As Lawrence turned towards his room, Evie shot Autumn a full-on malicious smile, bright and dazzling. Let her sweat it out, wondering what Evie wanted to talk to Lawrence about so urgently . . .

'Where are you going?' Autumn wailed, twenty minutes later, as Lawrence emerged from his room, hopping as he pulled on a pair of track pants. 'You said you wouldn't take long!'

'I have to go out for a while,' Lawrence said apologetically.

'With *her*?'

Autumn pointed accusingly at Evie, who noticed smugly that Autumn's fingers were stubby, her nails bitten down to the quick: she had tried to disguise the latter fact with deep purple nail polish, but the eagle eyes of a born-and-bred New Yorker like Evie swiftly picked out the flaw in Autumn's appearance.

'Autumn,' Lawrence said reprovingly, 'remember how damaging jealousy can be. I know you're feeling hurt, but you have no need to get this angry. We can't control other people, only ourselves—'

'For fuck's sake, Lawrence, enough with the Zen Master bullcrap!' Autumn yelled. 'Stop fucking telling me how to feel!'

Evie couldn't completely repress her smile. For a moment, she was in complete sync with Autumn – Lawrence's nuggets of Eastern philosophy could be incredibly annoying. Autumn's eyes met Evie's and the two women reluctantly shared a look of absolute agreement before Autumn narrowed her gaze, glaring at Evie.

'You'd better not be trying to get back with him!' she warned.

'Autumn . . .' Lawrence said rather helplessly, stooping to grab his sandals.

'Yes, Autumn, that sounds very *possessive*,' Evie said tauntingly. 'Better watch that, eh? Possessiveness is the enemy of the balanced soul—'

'You *bitch*!' Autumn made a lunge at Evie, her tattooed arm reaching out to grab in Evie's direction.

Ewww. Evie pulled a face. *She doesn't shave her armpits.* She easily ducked back from Autumn and her hairy pits, dancing around the door and out into the hallway.

'I'll wait for you on the landing, Lawrence,' she called blithely.

Yay! So far, Evie's day was going really well. Lola had heard her out, Lawrence was agreeing to the next step at least, and Autumn was royally pissed off. *Nice, Evie! Good going!*

Lawrence bounded downstairs, light as a cat, and followed Evie into the shared kitchen of her apartment.

'You brought her *here*?' he couldn't help saying.

'It's her first time in the scary suburbs,' Evie said, unable to repress a smile. 'Every time we stopped at a light, she freaked. She kept thinking someone was going to smash a window and pull off her earrings, or something. 'Bout time Little Miss Princess saw how the other half lives,' Evie added unapologetically.

'You should've come here on the subway if you wanted to give her the full Bushwick scenic tour.'

Evie snorted.

'Are you kidding? We got her super-upmarket car service here, and the only reason it isn't waiting outside is that the driver freaked about hanging out in this neighbourhood. Lawrence, you've got no idea how these people live. I'll bet you she's never been on the subway in her life. Seriously.'

Lola was sitting on Evie's futon, looking as if she was scared to move a muscle. The expensive, Upper East Side elegance of Lola's appearance – the cashmere sweater, the simple designer jeans, the golden highlighted hair, the watch whose face glittered with diamonds – was such a contrast to her surroundings that Lawrence blinked in surprise, and Evie was embarrassed by the shithole where she lived all over again.

'You must be Lawrence. Thanks so much for coming to meet me,' Lola said, standing up and holding out her hand for him to shake.

Nice manners, Evie thought sourly.

'I'm sorry for your loss,' Lawrence said to Lola. 'And the arrest and everything . . .' Lawrence looked grave. 'I can't imagine what you're going through right now.'

Lola looked up at Lawrence, her face very serious.

'Will you help me?' she asked, her voice soft and halting. 'This idea of Evie's . . . it's fairly extreme, but it's the only one we've got. Will you help us do it?'

Right, like any man could possibly refuse her when she asks them like that, Evie thought. *Those big brown eyes, the helpless air – I wonder if she knows what effect she has on men. Maybe she just takes it for granted. Jeez, there's something about these rich girls. This one doesn't act entitled – it's worse than that. She acts like she's already sure everyone will* want *to help her, 'cause she's so used to getting her way it doesn't occur to her that anyone might say no. And that 'Daddy's little girl' act she's doing – she doesn't even realise she's pulling it. I bet it worked on her daddy when she was just a baby, and she's been doing it ever since.*

Ugh. And with that thought, Evie couldn't help remembering her own relationship with Lola's father Benny. Duck head, look up coyly from under your lashes, ask in a little voice if you can please have that lovely Gucci bag you saw on West Broadway this afternoon, the one you just can't live without. Only Evie had had to do a lot more for Benny than Lola ever had . . .

Had Benny been consciously aware of how much the mistress

he'd picked looked like his daughter, Evie wondered? Or had he been blissfully unaware of how weird his desires might have seemed to anyone who put his daughter and his mistress side by side and made him look at how alike they were?

At least he never made me call him 'Daddy', Evie reflected with considerable gratitude. *I'd be throwing up in my mouth right now if I remembered him ever doing anything like that.*

'I loved my father very much,' Lola was saying to Lawrence. Pale, beautiful as an angel in a painting, her expression was utterly sincere. 'It's not just about making sure I don't go to jail for killing him. I want her to pay the price for what she did.'

'You mean his wife?' Lawrence prompted.

Lola nodded vigorously. 'I know she killed him. There's no other explanation for why they're trying to frame me like this, why she got the nurse to lie. That's why we need you.'

She reached out, and put one small hand, its ring glittering, on top of Lawrence's.

Lawrence looked from her to Evie.

'Aren't you putting the cart before the horse?' he asked. 'I mean, you don't even know if you can get me in.'

Lola shook her head.

'No, that's all taken care of,' she said, gesturing at her cellphone, which was lying on the futon. 'I rang a friend while I was waiting.' She smiled dryly. 'Maybe one of the very few friends I've got left. She's pulling some strings, but she's pretty sure she can manage it. She knows someone who'll give you the most amazing recommendation.'

'Are you serious?' Evie exclaimed.

'It's almost definite,' Lola confirmed. She had never taken her eyes off Lawrence. 'We can get you a job as Carin's personal trainer.'

Chapter 27

'Miss Carin?' Panio, Carin's handsome butler-cum-manservant, said nervously as he swung the front door open. Spotting the orange Hermès bags hanging from Carin's wrist, each one tied exquisitely with the signature brown *bolduc* Hermès ribbon, Panio reached for them deferentially. 'Let me take those for you! Um, and Miss Carin, your three o'clock is here.'

His tone suggested that it was considerably past three by now, but that Panio wasn't brave enough to point that out to Carin. That morning he had slipped and called her 'Mrs Fitzgerald' – a title she had banned from the house ever since her husband died – and her wrath had been so extreme that he was terrified now of rousing it again.

'My three o'clock?' Carin frowned, peeling off her coat – white cashmere, silk-lined, and so slim-cut that it could be worn only over the lightest of clothes. 'Panio, this coat needs to be overnight dry-cleaned every single time I wear it, you understand? I want it back in my coat cupboard by tomorrow morning.'

'Of course, Miss Carin,' Panio said, draping the coat over his arm with as much reverence as if he were a lowly deacon cradling an archbishop's gold-embroidered chasuble. 'I'll call them to pick it up right away.'

'No,' Carin snapped. 'Take it there yourself. Now. Those lazy bastards take forever to come over. It was *half an hour* last time.'

She was walking over to the huge mirror in the hall, which reflected the Japanese screen on the opposite wall: two panels of silvered paper on which a few delicate brush-strokes had created a mountain scene, hills covered in snow, a single traveller on an ox-cart just cresting one of the peaks. She stared at it for a moment. 'Time to rotate the art, Panio. Take this one down and hang the screen with the dragon instead.' She flashed herself a smile in the mirror, her pale blue eyes cold as ice. 'It fits in much better with my mood.'

'Of course, Miss Car—'

'And what was my three o'clock?'

She leaned into the mirror, fractionally adjusting a short strand of hair. Frédéric, her stylist, had, to his credit, been nothing but gleeful when she had walked into his studio a few weeks ago with her hair shorn: he had cropped the sides a little more and teased the front lightly into a short, dramatic sideways sweep of pure, natural white-blonde, fixing it with the lightest of products. It looked wonderful. She woke up every morning feeling free as a bird, not fettered down any longer by that wretched mane of hair her husband had insisted she keep.

Of course, she also felt free as a bird because she wasn't fettered any longer by her wretched husband.

Carin's smile of triumph at this thought was so frightening that Panio averted his gaze from her as he answered:

'The new trainer, Miss Carin. He's waiting in the gym.'

Carin clicked her tongue.

'I completely forgot about him!' She frowned. 'I was hoping it was the architect. I can't *wait* to gut this house and remodel it. Strip it all the way down and start again.'

Get rid of every last trace of my husband, she meant. *Of course, I could move in a second to anywhere in the world I wanted: but that wouldn't be half as much fun as erasing him from the house he made his own, would it?*

The surge of excitement this gave Carin made her feel restless suddenly, a wave of energy that her shopping rampage at Hermès must have failed to satisfy.

'I'll see the trainer,' she decided. 'Tell him I'll be down in ten minutes. Oh, and Panio?' She flicked the exquisite pale green-white trumpet lily in the vase by the mirror. 'I'm bored with lilies. Find me something else to go here. Something more unusual than this. And very expensive-looking. Something that no one else has.' She turned to look at Panio, who was visibly wilting under this stream of commands. 'And Panio? I want it here by the time I've finished with the trainer.'

Well! Carin thought as she entered the gym. *This one's certainly interesting!*

Because Carin was unable to keep herself from having sex with any man who worked for her, she went through personal trainers like a flu sufferer did tissues. A man had to be very good, and very accommodating, to keep Carin interested: Panio and Rico, in their very different ways, both had what it took. As had the little nurse, Joe. And God knew they were all paid well enough for the privilege of doing the boss.

Carin didn't have women friends. But then, most New York society women were the same: they had social acquaintances instead, who functioned on a complex barter system for invitations, parties, and tips on the best facialist or plastic surgeon. This latest piece of young male meat had been recommended to Carin by Lady Julia Listwood, someone she hadn't heard from in a while: but Lady Julia had been simply *dying*, she'd said, to tell a few friends about her new trainer.

From the look of Lady Julia, Carin was surprised she even used a trainer; dumpiness ran in the family, or on Lady Julia's side of it, at least. Both her daughters had inherited their mother's pear shape, and poor moon-faced India was no beauty – at least Sylvia, the older one, had her mother's aristocratic bone structure. But Lady Julia was impeccably well-connected, and though she could be an awful bore, she never bothered to ring people to let them know about something new and exciting unless she really thought it was worthwhile.

Carin stood in the doorway of the gym, surveying the man who was balancing in a perfect handstand in the centre of the stretching area. *Lovely tight ass*, she observed. *A little leaner than I usually like, but nice definition. And fairly hairless, apart from that ghastly ponytail. I wonder if he waxes?* Watching him, her tongue slid out and slowly traced the contours of her narrow lips. She felt her nipples tighten. Yes, she definitely owed Lady Julia for this one.

The trainer lowered both of his legs to the ground, slowly, under complete control. He straightened up and looked gravely at Carin. She couldn't tell whether he'd been aware of her presence or not, and that impressed her: Carin was so used to being in control of her surroundings, and of the impact she made on those around her, that the fact this man wasn't visibly fazed by her was a pleasant change.

She'd break him, of course. Make him jump to attention. But this was a nice little challenge.

'Mrs Fitzgerald—' the trainer started.

'Just Carin,' she interrupted. 'I never liked Fitzgerald.' She smiled. 'I'll be reverting to my maiden name soon.'

Just as soon as that idiot daughter is convicted, she thought. *It wouldn't look too good to do it during the trial, now, would it?*

'I'm Lawrence,' he said, crossing the room, reaching out his hand to shake hers.

'Well, Lawrence, what do you propose for me?' Carin said, holding his hand and looking into his eyes. Lawrence was about to withdraw his hand – she could feel it – but she held on for a few more seconds. He would have to learn that she ran things around here, not him. Goodness, he was handsome. He had the face of a classical sculpture; long straight nose, large clear grey eyes, full lips.

She imagined that calm, handsome face later on, working hard between her legs as she sat in the thigh adductor machine and spread them wide. The picture made her lower stomach twitch with anticipation. She'd ride him hard this first time, show him how things worked here, down in her private gym with its mirrors and its machines, so many of which could be adapted for other and more interesting purposes. And if he were any good, she'd give him the kind of bonus that would make him try even harder to please her the next time.

Lawrence was looking her up and down, not a shred of anything but professional interest in his eyes. Carin was all too used to being surveyed by men, and she knew that she had never been in better shape. Her Stella McCartney steel-grey capri leggings and white racerback sleeveless top showed her long slender body off perfectly. No bra, she barely needed one: and besides, she liked to see men's expressions as they watched her nipples, which were dispropor-tionately large for her small breasts, move and harden against the shiny Lycra-mix fabric. Her long waist meant that a good couple of inches of her dead-white skin were exposed below the hem of her top, and her stomach was as flat and smooth as a lacquered piece of ivory. It should be, after the money she'd spent on SmartLipo.

She posed, turning on her heel, giving him a view of her back, her small tight buttocks flowing into long, long legs.

'I have to be honest,' Lawrence commented as Carin finished her rotation. 'All you need is maintenance work, Mrs – *Carin*,' he cor-rected himself. 'Your waist is as narrow as you can make it, your shoulders haven't been over-worked. You don't have any over-aggre-gation of muscle that we need to stretch out. I can happily train you and work with you, but I can't promise any changes, because there aren't any to be made.'

Carin laughed, an almost-silent laugh that nevertheless opened her mouth wide, showing her sharp white teeth.

'Flattery,' she said, 'will get you everywhere with me.' Her ice-blue eyes gleaming, she slid her tongue over her lips. 'And I mean *everywhere*.'

She dipped her gaze down to the front of his track pants. No move-ment there that she could see, not even with that clear innuendo; but then, the pants were fairly loose. Carin liked her trainers to wear tighter leggings. She'd have to mention that to him for the future.

'Let's get you on the cross-trainer,' Lawrence suggested. 'We'll do a warm-up, then I'll measure your recovery rates. And after that, I'd like to do some Power Plate work. Check your posture in various positions. It's a great invention, the Power Plate, but you have to use them right. So let's make sure you are.'

Okay, I see how you want to handle this, Carin thought. *Workout first, play later. I can respect that. This guy is nothing but professional. And after all, it'll build the anticipation . . .*

'I'll finish by stretching you out,' Lawrence said. 'After that, I'll have a good sense of your body. We can do some massage too, if you want.'

'Oh, I'm sure I'll want,' Carin said, smiling to herself. 'Absolutely sure.'

He's amazing, Carin thought dazedly, an hour and a half later. *Unbelievable. No one's ever done anything like that to me before.* She stretched out her feet, pointing her toes, rotating her wrists slowly, gradually coming back to full consciousness.

'God,' she purred, looking up into Lawrence's eyes. 'You are *fantastic.*'

'Thank you!' he said, sitting back on his heels.

'I'm sure you get that a lot,' Carin said dreamily. She turned her head from side to side. 'Your hands are *magic.* God. When you did that thing to my breasts . . .'

Carin closed her eyes, remembering the sensation of his hands running over her breasts, her buttocks. She raised one of her hands, stroking where Lawrence had done, feeling how hard the nipple was, how swollen it had become when he touched her. He'd known exactly what she needed – she hadn't had to say a word, give one command or instruction. That was unbelievably rare in a man. He'd be walking away with a huge bonus today.

Lawrence cleared his throat.

'I massaged your back, your shoulders and your pectorals,' he corrected.

'You certainly did.' Carin writhed a little as she remembered it.

'I know it's rarely done, but in my opinion it's an essential part of sports massage,' Lawrence continued. 'Those chest muscles tighten up there just like any other ones, and we did a lot of push-ups today. It's good to work out the knots straight away.'

'And now it's my turn to work out your knots, don't you think?'

Carin sat up, swinging her legs underneath her. She reached down to the hem of her top and wriggled it off in one smooth motion. Her nipples, big and dark, were full and hard just thinking about Lawrence's hands on them. Smiling at him, she made pincers of her fingers, taking hold of her nipples, pinching them till it hurt, watching his face all the time.

'Don't worry,' she said. 'I like it rough, but I'll go easy on you this time. And no marks, not unless you want them.' Her smile deepened. 'Trust me, you're going to love it.'

Lawrence was still sitting back on his heels, the position he'd adopted after Carin's full-body massage. He gazed at her, his eyes calm and clear, no change in his expression even after Carin had bared her breasts to him.

He's very cool, this one, Carin thought. *Oh, I like this. I like this a lot. I can't wait to see him get hot and sweaty. I'm going to make him moan and pant for me . . .*

Going on her knees on the soft blue gym mat, she reached out towards him, one hand slipping up his thigh, over the fabric of his track pants, letting him feel her nails as they dragged lightly, pressing into the skin below. He barely moved; of course he didn't. He must be enjoying himself tremendously now he knew what was about to happen. This was the dream for most trainers, wasn't it – get to make a nice amount of extra money by having sex with a woman with a kick-ass body?

Carin's hand cupped into Lawrence's crotch. *He knows how to be passive*, she thought, very pleased: *he knows how to sit still and let me run the show.* Carin was all about switch-hitting, and she liked a man to be able to do that too, give her a good hard fucking when she wanted it, but lie there and take whatever she wanted to do when she felt like dominating.

Still, there was a reason Carin always preferred to fuck her employees. In the end, she had to be in charge. And she was more than happy to pay the men who worked for her extra so she could snap her fingers and get them to dance to her tune whenever the impulse took her that way.

Lawrence was shaping up to be a great addition to her stable.

And then she realised, in absolute shock, that he wasn't shaping up at all. Her hand closed around an unmistakeably soft, yielding package of male genitalia. She could feel his balls in the palm of her hand, could roll and separate them out like ripe, slightly squashy nectarines. She loved to feel men's balls, their weight, to stroke and cup them and then squeeze them, just a little too tightly, seeing if their owner would respond by a groan and an extra stiffening of the dick, to see if his dick wanted a sharp slap or flick of the fingernail. You couldn't teach that. Either a man's dick and balls liked a little pain, or they didn't.

But right now, all she was aware of – with rising indignation and amazement – was that Lawrence's goddamn dick, which she was now holding through his sweatpants between thumb and fingers, was as soft as fucking toffee.

'What the hell is *wrong* with you?' she demanded, her head snapping back, staring angrily into his face. 'Why the fuck aren't you getting it up?'

Lawrence's hand closed over hers, and gently, but firmly, lifted it and removed it from his crotch.

'I think there's been a misunderstanding somewhere,' he said, his expression apologetic. 'You're a very beautiful woman with a fantastic body, Carin, but I play for the other team.' His hands turned upwards, in a 'what-can-I-do?' gesture. 'I'm gay.'

'You're *gay*?' Carin sat back on her heels, facing him. 'You're *kidding*!' She stared at him, taking this in. 'Shit, Julia could have fucking warned me!'

And then she burst out laughing. 'So that's why you did that tit massage. There was me thinking it was the best come-on ever! But to you it was just a chest massage, yeah?'

He smiled at her, such a sweet, yet detached smile that any doubts she'd had about his homosexuality were swept away. Reaching up to pull his hair out of its elastic band, he said:

'It's always a pleasure to work on such an aesthetically pleasing body, Carin. But no, I'm sorry. It was purely business.'

Carin let out a long whoosh of air, shaking her head from side to side, trying to clear some of the built-up sexual tension.

'Do you want me to continue working with you as a trainer?' Lawrence asked, smoothing back his hair and re-tying it in the elastic. 'If the misunderstanding doesn't bother you, it certainly doesn't bother me. I'd be more than happy to keep you on as a client.'

'Oh hell, yeah!' Carin said, standing up. 'I'm not going to can someone who does massages like that. You'll be here three times a week, two hours at a time. Panio will book you in and pay you on the way out. Tell him if you need any extra equipment, and he'll order it in for you.'

'Great,' Lawrence said, jumping easily to his feet. 'Sorry about the misunderstanding, Carin.'

She shrugged.

'Just be careful you don't make your massages *too* good,' she warned, raising her eyebrows. 'You don't want me getting carried away and raping you, do you?'

Now he did look disconcerted. As he went upstairs, she smiled, watching him go. She'd thrown him off-balance, and the power had shifted back to her again.

Which was exactly the way she liked it.

Chapter 28

'*A*re you ready for this?' David asked.

Lola nodded grimly. They were sitting in the office of the suite at the Plaza, which was appropriately business-like with its dark striped wenge wood furniture, the latest in leather-upholstered swivel chairs, and a whole wall of conferencing screens and control panels. In front of David was a pile of gossip magazines, tabloid papers, and his own laptop.

'OK. Item One,' David started. 'Jean-Marc and I are getting married next month. In London.'

He slid two tabloid newspapers, one English, one US, across the desk, folded to the right section, the articles circled with a red marker pen. Lola scanned through them swiftly.

'Madison,' she said, her heart beginning to sink. 'That was what I told Madison, in confidence.'

'Item Two,' David continued. 'You think your chin is too pointy, and you want to have it shaved down.'

He opened several magazines to the right pages, which he had marked with those little stick-on coloured tabs. Close-ups of Lola's face from different angles, with big arrows indicating her chin, and headlines screaming: '*DOES LOLA NEED A CHIN JOB?*'

Lola grimaced.

'I thought we'd picked that one because I *didn't* need a bloody chin job,' she said fretfully. 'But when you see yourself all blown up like this . . .' She poked at the picture of herself in *Star* and *Heat* magazines. 'It *does* sort of look like my chin's too pointy.'

David rolled his eyes.

'Get over yourself,' he said. 'Your chin's fine. Who did you tell that story to?'

Lola sighed.

'Georgia. I didn't really expect her to keep her mouth shut, though. I mean, she promised, but Georgia'd tell anyone anything when she's drunk or high. Which she is, seven days a week. Georgia and Madison . . .' Lola said, sadly. 'I was hoping that none of the girls would have told anyone what I said to them in confidence. I made them all *promise* not to tell. They're supposed to be my friends. And it's not a normal gossip situation. I've been *arrested for killing my dad*, for God's sake!'

'I know, honey.' David reached a hand across the desk and patted Lola's sympathetically. 'That's why we set these girls up, right? You wanted to find out who you could trust.'

'After those photos . . .' Lola shuddered, thinking of the photos of her doing coke at her hen night that had been blazoned across the tabloids when Jean-Marc overdosed.

'Who do you think took them?' David asked.

'One of them,' Lola said sadly. 'And I know you've got more bad news to give me, don't you?'

He nodded.

'You ready?' he asked.

Lola lit a cigarette. She was trying to cut down, but the way her life was spinning out of control right now didn't exactly make it easy for her to stop grabbing at the cancer sticks. Not having any alcohol in the apartment was doing wonders for her liver, but her lungs were suffering instead. Still, she couldn't think about that right now: she had much bigger problems much closer to her than lung cancer somewhere down the line.

'There's only one more,' David said, clicking on his laptop keyboard.

'Really?' Lola's heart lifted. *It won't be Devon*, she thought. *Devon's the one who took me in. Devon confided in me about not liking sex with Piers. Devon's the one I'm always been closest to. Devon's got all the money in the world – Piers gives her everything she wants, so she's got no reason to sell me out to the tabs for a pay cheque. And Devon's got a title and a husband who's going to be one of the most important peers in England when his dad dies – she's got no reason to be jealous of me!*

Devon's my one true friend.

'It's the one we made up about you having lost a lot of weight because you're on antidepressants,' David said, swivelling the screen of his laptop round so that Lola could see it. 'It's on Perez Hilton, and the *Mail on Sunday* just picked it up too.'

Lola stared at the picture of her, snapped yesterday, when she was coming back from her meeting with Simon Poluck and George Goldman. It had been a grim couple of hours. They had had time to review the nurse Giovanni's testimony to the grand jury, and it was utterly damning. If he repeated that in court, they thought Lola would be convicted. There was a watertight case against her: Lola's fingerprints on the syringe and on the insulin bottle. And the motive was plausible – instead of a long, expensive, highly contested lawsuit, with a lot of money siphoning off to the lawyers, she would inherit half her father's money as soon as his will was probated. For a girl who was living off an ex-fiancé who had already overdosed, fled rehab, and come out of the closet, having her own millions as soon as possible was hugely tempting.

Carin's motive simply didn't look as strong as Lola's: she was in possession of everything already, and possession was nine-tenths of the law. All she had to do was instruct her lawyers to fight Lola's claim, as long as it took, and hope that Jean-Marc would overdose again, or simply get tired of funding a protracted, very costly lawsuit against his ex-fiancée's stepmother.

Of course, this wasn't taking into consideration what Carin had actually done: killed her husband and framed Lola for the murder. If Lola were found guilty of his murder, Carin would inherit everything. It was the ultimate two-for-one deal: get rid of husband and stepdaughter at the same time.

But it would be impossible to prove.

No wonder, even after the coup of getting Lawrence to agree to spy for her, that Lola had been deeply depressed by that meeting with her lawyers. The paparazzi shots showed her with head ducked, big Dior sunglasses covering a large part of her face, a beige Burberry trench belted tightly round her waist.

'You *do* look skinny,' David commented. 'Makes the antidepressant story very plausible.'

'It's the cut of the coat,' Lola said automatically, staring at the picture of her, the words over it blaring: '*LOLA TURNS TO MEDS FOR COMFORT!*'

'*Could a reaction to the prescription pills she's popping like candy these days be the reason for Lola's breakdown in Maud's, the hip 'n' happening burlesque joint du jour?*' asked the writer breathlessly. '*She caused a huge scene when she ran onstage and attacked a pole dancer – were her antidepressants to blame? Or was it the buckets of champagne she'd been drinking that evening? Got a guilty conscience you need to drown out, Lola?*'

'It's Devon,' Lola said in a very small voice. 'I *told* her not to tell anyone! I said it would look bad for me.'

'Well, it doesn't look like she cared much, does it?' David said gently. 'Anyone who knows what you're going through – who knows how many stories have been sold about you – would keep their mouth shut tighter than Mother Teresa's legs.'

Lola managed a tiny giggle, and realised that she must be on the verge of tears because she was sniffing at the same time.

'Do you want a tissue?' David asked, reaching into his trouser pocket.

'No, thanks.' Lola's voice grew stronger. 'After all I've been through, I'm not going to cry about a few rich bitches who don't know the meaning of friendship.'

'Attagirl!' David applauded her. 'And don't forget – there's still one left!'

Lola had been so cast down by Devon's betrayal that she had completely forgotten about the fourth. She looked at David over the laptop screen.

'That's right! You told – ' he consulted his list – 'India that Niels had been trying to get Jean to throw you out of here. And that Niels thought you had turned Jean gay!' He giggled. 'Ooh, we had fun coming up with *that* story. And it's a juicy one. I can just see the *Post* now!' David made a sweeping, theatrical gesture, sketching headlines in the air. '*YOU TURNED MY BRO INTO A GAY HO! HOT BILLIONAIRE ACCUSES GORGEOUS BLONDE!* Niels *is* hot,' David added lustfully. 'I don't go for the big butch ones usually, but that man is *smoking.*'

'India!' Lola exclaimed, snatching up the name to avoid having any sort of discussion about Niels's hotness. Niels, altogether, was like some sort of radioactive matter that she had to avoid at all costs: she couldn't talk about him without blushing, she couldn't think about him without having the kind of basic, primitive physical reaction that no man had ever given her. And that was just *thinking* about him, hearing his *name*. Niels was like her own personal Kryptonite, she realised. He made her go weak at the knees.

Stubbing out her cigarette, she met David's eyes.

'India didn't say anything?' she asked him.

'Zip. Zilch. Nada,' David said gleefully. 'I've looked everywhere. Believe me. The weekly magazines all hit the newsstands yesterday evening and I bought the lot. Plus the newspapers, all the online sites – I've done a *major* search. I even got my intern to spend the afternoon checking in case I'd missed something. He was in heaven.' He picked up the magazines and papers and stacked them on top of each other. '*Nothing.* She's a hundred per cent passed the test. The only one.'

Lola nodded slowly.

'So now I know,' she said. 'And I think I always knew that I could trust India. I mean, I got her to set up Lawrence as Carin's trainer.

I could never have done that if I didn't believe she'd keep it a secret.'

'Now you know, honey,' David confirmed. 'The truth will set you free. You'd better delete those three other bitches' numbers from your phone right now.'

'I just don't understand why they would *do* this,' Lola said sadly.

'Money, for starters,' David said, raising his eyebrows. 'You could get a few grand for juicy info like this, babe. You're a hot topic right now.'

'Yes, but none of them need the extra cash,' Lola protested.

David rolled his eyes.

'Honey, we *all* need extra cash. I don't care how rich you are, everyone likes a bit of extra moolah. Look at how rich people love a bargain! Rich people are the worst for trying to get free stuff!'

Lola couldn't help but acknowledge the truth of this.

'Plus, they're jealous,' David added.

'Jealous?' This elicited a bitter laugh from Lola. 'I've lost *everything!* I don't have a home, a fiancé, or a trust fund. I attacked my dad's mistress and now I look like a psycho in the press. My father's dead and next month I'm going to stand trial for his *murder*, for God's sake!'

'And before that you were a total celebrity, more than any of them,' David said accurately, 'because you and Jean-Marc were such a gorgeous couple. Girl, *I* used to read about you in magazines and go green with envy! Plus lust after Jean-Marc, of course,' he giggled. 'And now you're an even *bigger* celebrity. You're on every magazine cover, Lola, you know that? Those bitches don't see the downside, what you're really going through, because their hearts are tiny cold pieces of lead. All *they* see is how famous you are and how much everyone writes about "Can Beautiful Tragic Lola Really Be Guilty?"'

Lola looked at him doubtfully.

'Trust me on this,' David said with a little nod. 'You need info on jealousy issues, honey, you come to a gay man. I know what I'm talking about.'

The doorbell chimed.

'It's Jean!' David carolled happily. He checked his watch. 'Nearly half-past six – that's later than I thought he'd be! I hope that means he had a good first day at rehab.' He jumped up and ran out of the office, eager to see his boyfriend.

Lola followed more slowly. Partly to let David have the chance to greet his boyfriend alone, and partly because she needed to collect her thoughts. The news about Madison, Georgia and Devon had been devastating. The list of people she could trust had shrunk down now to such a small group of names that it was humiliating for her to picture how tiny it was.

Jean-Marc, who, after his collapse, was in full-time outpatient rehab: he could hardly look after himself, let alone anyone else.

David, who she'd barely known for a fortnight.

George Goldman.

Simon Poluck, because if she didn't trust her criminal lawyer, she was in the worst trouble imaginable.

And out of all the girls who'd been at her hen night, just one left: India.

She wasn't counting Niels; she couldn't trust him to do anything but jeer at her and make her come like a train. If she asked him for help, he'd probably laugh in her face.

And Evie and Lawrence weren't on that list yet: how could they be? She barely knew them. And yet they were her only hope of finding something – *anything* – to break a hole in the wall that Carin had so carefully built around Lola, the wall that was going to entomb her alive if she didn't find a way to save herself. Unless Lawrence's access to Carin, and her house, could somehow dig up some proof of Carin's guilt, Lola was going to be convicted of murdering her father.

It was a very slim chance on which to base her hopes of avoiding a life sentence.

Strapped to Lola's slender feet were a pair of dark purple Manolos with ribbon ties that fastened round her ankles and stiletto heels nearly five inches high. But such was her depression, thinking of how few friends she had, and how tiny were her chances of staying out of jail, that she felt as if she were making her way slowly and painfully through a muddy field in a pair of fishing waders.

And that was why it took her so long to realise that David was sobbing hysterically.

'What is it?' she exclaimed, emerging into the foyer.

David was in Jean-Marc's arms, his head buried in his boyfriend's shoulder. Jean-Marc's face was very pale, his arms wrapped tightly around David's slender, Armani-clad back. And in the background was a third man, a tall, white, bulky, balding man with an impassive expression on his face, wearing nondescript clothes.

'Jean-Marc has decided to go into residential rehab,' the third man informed Lola.

Her eyes widened.

'I really need to go, Lola,' Jean-Marc said quietly. 'I've been talking about it with my sponsor all day. He totally thinks I should be in residential care.'

The balding man nodded.

'This is Frank, my sober buddy,' Jean-Marc said. 'He's going to escort me to California.'

'Jean-Marc has booked himself into the Cascabel rehab facility,' Frank said in a low, rasping voice. 'They have a room already reserved and waiting for him.'

'It's so far away!' David sobbed, still clinging to Jean-Marc.

'I need to do this, sweetie,' Jean-Marc said, stroking David's shoulder. 'And there's nothing to be afraid of. I'm going to come back stronger.'

Wow, Lola thought. *Jean-Marc suddenly sounds like a grown-up.*

'I'm going to miss you so much!' David wailed.

And that's turned David, who was always the more mature one in the relationship, into a baby, Lola observed. *Is that how relationships work? You take it in turns to be the grown-up and the baby?*

She'd never really had a relationship, she realised. Not a real, true one. Her engagement to Jean-Marc had been a nonsense, nothing real about it at all. The closest she'd ever been to a man, weirdly enough, was her beloved father. So she didn't know much about how adult relationships worked.

'Oh baby, I don't know if I can bear to have you gone—' David was crying. 'Don't go! You can do rehab here as an outpatient! Don't go! Don't leave me!'

Jean-Marc burst into streaming tears.

'I have to!' he wailed. 'I have to, David! I don't think I can do it in New York! There are so many temptations – what if Patricia comes back? I'm so frightened of her! At least in rehab I'll be able to walk around – talk to people, have a swim in the pool, sit in the fresh air – I can't just stay trapped in here, terrified every time someone rings, in case it's Patricia—'

Lola's phone buzzed. She pulled it out of her pocket and looked at the screen. George Goldman was calling. Oh God, more bad news . . .

She clicked the phone open, walking into the hallway, as she said: 'Hi, George,' hearing how nervous her voice sounded.

'Lola, honey? I got news. It's about your dad's funeral. It's happening tomorrow afternoon.'

'Tomorrrow *afternoon?*' Lola's eyes widened. 'I didn't know they'd even released his body!'

'Yeah, well,' George said, 'that's why you're paying a fortune to Simon Poluck, honey. He's got serious connections in the DA's office. Carin's got no obligation to inform you, but she goddamn well can't keep you away from your dad's funeral!'

He paused.

'You got someone to go with? I could come with you. Tell you what, I'll pick you up at three, OK? And Lola?' George cleared his throat. 'You should really call your mom and let her know.'

Lola hadn't been expecting this at all. It took her completely by surprise. Ever since her mother had refused to help her financially, Lola had been so resentful that she hadn't taken any of Suzanne's phone calls. Her mother had rung many times, but Lola wouldn't respond. But now, as George made the suggestion, Lola could feel the resentment draining away. Jean-Marc was leaving. She was more alone than ever. And suddenly, she found herself wanting her mother.

'Don't you think?' George said. 'I mean, she was married to the guy for twenty years . . . '

Slowly, Lola nodded her head.

Chapter 29

*F*or late spring in Manhattan, it was an unexpectedly cool day. Clear blue New York skies, a bright sun that cast a gentle heat, and a fresh breeze blowing from the Hudson River, which glittered in the sun, beyond the roaring traffic on the wide cement ribbons of Riverside Drive and the West Side Highway. For someone who loved Manhattan as Ben Fitzgerald had done, it was the perfect burial spot: a stunning view across the river to the rich greenery of the Palisades beyond, illuminated at night by the stacks of light on the George Washington bridge. No one knew how many strings Ben had had to pull to secure a crypt here, in Trinity Cemetery, on an island so tightly packed that there was no room for any more live people, let alone dead ones.

The *New York Post* that morning had reported that Ben had contacts at the mayor's office, who knew someone who ran Trinity Church's real estate division, and that he had paid a hefty sum towards church repairs as well as $50,000 for the plot. But that could only be the tip of the iceberg. Major bribes must have been taken to ensure that Ben Fitzgerald snagged this ideal burial plot in the highest part of Washington Heights, on a smooth mound of grass sweeping down to Riverside Drive and the Hudson beyond it. Behind the grave were the imposing marble walls of the mausoleum, lined by a row of huge elm trees, their elegant dark-green leaves moving gently in the river breeze, whispering against each other.

The congregation who had attended Ben Fitzgerald's funeral service were filing out of the church, following the pallbearers carrying his coffin. Made of mahogany with gold clasps, it was huge, custom-made, like everything Ben had worn for the last ten years of his life, when he really started to pile the weight on. Instead of the customary six pallbearers, Ben Fitzgerald's enormous coffin needed ten, and even they were struggling a little under the combined bulk of the man they were carrying and the solid weight of fifty pounds of dense mahogany.

Lola stood at the side of the knoll and watched the procession approach. She had tried to go into the church for the service, but had been barred by Carin's bodyguard, and though she was pretty sure that no one could actually prevent you from going into a church, she hadn't wanted to make the kind of scene that would be eagerly snapped up by every single funeral-goer and repeated excitedly to everyone they knew the moment they were back in their waiting limos.

'It doesn't matter,' her mother had said, squeezing her hand. 'It doesn't matter about the service, darling. We'll see him laid to rest. That's the most important thing.'

So they had walked slowly to the empty grave, and stood beside it, waiting, for half an hour, shivering slightly in the breeze. There were enough of them so that they didn't look completely forlorn: Lola; Suzanne; Neville, Suzanne's companion; George; and India.

Still holding her mother's hand, Lola realised how glad she was that Suzanne had come. Barely off the plane from London, Suzanne had only had time to run a brush through her hair, pin it up into a loose bun and pull on an old black crepe trouser suit. Of course, because she was Suzanne Myers, an ex-supermodel, she still looked as if she were about to be shot for *Vogue*. The trouser suit was Donna Karan, cut to show off Suzanne's endless legs. Her pearl necklace glowed against her skin, making its tan look healthy, rather than weather-beaten. And because Suzanne never dressed as lamb instead of mutton – because her suit, and the simple black blouse underneath it, was perfectly appropriate for a glamorous 55-year-old – she looked at least fifteen years younger than her real age.

The skinny, goateed, ponytailed young man at her mother's side was wearing a shabby black suit and scruffy shirt and tie; he looked more like an undertaker's assistant than a mourner at a society funeral. This was Neville, who seemed to have been promoted from gardener to Suzanne's boyfriend, judging by the fond glances they kept giving each other and the affectionate way Suzanne had straightened his tie earlier.

I'm glad she's happy, Lola thought. *I mean, he's not who I'd have pictured as my mum's boyfriend, but I'm glad she's happy. And he's obviously madly in love with her . . .*

She exchanged glances with India, who smiled back gravely. Lola had told India about the other girls' treachery, and India had been so shocked she hadn't been able to get a word out for ages. Lola had texted the other three to say she knew they'd sold stories about her and to stay away in future, and ignored the flood of pleading calls, texts and emails that had inevitably poured in.

At least I know who my friends are, she thought, tightening her grip on her mother's hand as the coffin approached.

'Your father will love it here,' Suzanne said bravely, her voice beginning to crack with grief, staring down at the huge hole that had been cut to accommodate the plus-size coffin. 'I see just why he bought it. Astors and Audubons, a famous battlefield – it's got high society, history, river views. The whole package.'

'Oh, Mummy . . .'

Tears pricked at Lola's eyes as she and Suzanne hugged each other tightly.

'I know we didn't agree on anything by the end,' Suzanne cried against Lola. 'I know we wanted completely different things. I just didn't want him to leave me, like that, for *her*. I never thought he'd actually want a *divorce*, not after all the years we'd had together.'

'Daddy always loved you, I know he did,' Lola said, hugging her mother even closer. 'But you knew Daddy, he always needed to know where the next party was. And, Mummy, you never wanted that kind of life. You were complete opposites.'

'I know . . .' Suzanne sobbed. 'I just wanted to be in his life still . . . I loved him so much . . . God, I *swore* I wouldn't cry!'

She pulled back a little, because Neville was offering her a tissue.

'Thanks, darling,' Suzanne said, taking it and blowing her nose. 'At least I haven't got any make-up on but waterproof mascara . . . nothing to smudge.'

'You haven't got any make-up on?' India said incredulously.

'Those days are long behind me, sweetie,' Suzanne said, crumpling up the tissue, handing it to Neville and taking a second one for another blow. 'You should all go make-up free, you girls. It's so much better for your skin.'

Even India couldn't help gaping at this and mouthing: 'She's crazy!' at Lola. Lola twirled her finger by the side of her head in response, to indicate that her mother wasn't always to be taken 100 per cent seriously.

'You always look wonderful,' said Neville worshipfully.

'She sure does,' George agreed fondly, smiling at Suzanne.

'Oh, George,' Suzanne said, patting him on the arm. 'It's so nice to see you again. I just wish it was in happier circumstances.'

'Me too, babe. Me too,' George said in heartfelt tones.

Organ music floated out from the church as the pallbearers rounded a stand of trees and came fully into view, carrying their huge burden. Suzanne paled visibly.

'Oh my *God*,' she breathed, fresh tears pouring down her face.

Wordlessly, Neville handed her more tissues. She took them with her left hand, her right still clutching onto her daughter's.

Lola was mesmerised by the sight of the coffin. Had her father really been that large? He must have been, of course, behind all that clever Italian tailoring of his suits, always with faint vertical stripes to slim him down. And he'd been tall, which meant he had carried his heft well. But still, the sheer bulk of the coffin was shocking.

A Canada goose from the ornamental lake chose that moment to take off, its heavy wings beating as it flew overhead, honking loudly. Lola's eyes followed its flight as it swooped past the big elm tree, and as she did so she noticed a small figure standing half-hidden behind the tree. It was a woman, dressed in black from head to toe: tight jeans, a polo-neck sweater, and a baseball cap pulled down over her face.

Despite the attempt to conceal her features, Lola recognised her instantly.

Her whole body stiffened in shock.

It was Evie.

Evie had been drinking latte in a local coffee shop and reading the *Post* that morning when she saw the Page Six item.

'*Guess it always helps to be connected – even when you're about to be six feet under!* **Ben Fitzgerald**, *legendary property developer and plus-size social animal, made his last and best deal when he cinched himself a coveted burial plot at Trinity Cemetery. Last guy to manage that?* **Ed Koch**, *no less, ex-mayor of this fair town. Kudos to Fitzgerald, those are some favours he called in! The funeral's at three this afternoon and expect fireworks – will his wife* **Carin** *clash with his daughter* **Lola**, *ex-fiancée of troubled industrial heir Jean-Marc van der Veer, who's recently checked himself into the* **Cascabel** *rehab clinic? Don't forget, Lola's due to stand trial in just a couple of weeks for murdering dear departed Daddy! Plus there's the wild card –* **Evie Lopez**, *aka* **Diamond**. *Remember her? Once a stripper and Ben's mistress, now showgirl supreme with her sexy sold-out mermaid act at hot burlesque joint of the moment, Maud's! Will Evie dare to show her face at the funeral? Won't be a dull moment at* this *interment, that's for sure – just the way party-loving Ben would have wanted!*'

To Evie's eternal shame, her first reaction was one of heart-pumping triumph.

They printed my name again*! They put 'Remember her'? like I'm a character in a soap opera, that's so cool! They said my show was sold out! God, Maud's is going to be so pleased with this!*

And then, even more shamingly: *I should ask for a bonus.*

It was only after all those thoughts had shot through her mind, as brightly coloured and fast as the *Pow! Zam! Kaboom!* in comics when the super hero's punching out the supervillain, that Evie came down to earth and realised what the real point of the story was.

Benny was being buried today: she had to be there.

But that wasn't all it meant.

Choking down her coffee, grabbing the pastry and throwing a ten on the counter to more than cover the bill, Evie turned on her heel and raced out the door of the coffee shop. Down Varick, across Flushing Boulevard, dashing straight across traffic, hearing a cabbie behind her scream curses as he veered into the next lane to avoid her, nearly clipping a truck, hitting the sidewalk and tearing back towards the warehouse, sprinting, her heels barely touching the ground. Three flights up, past her own steel door and up to Lawrence and Autumn's, through the open door and, thank God, a piece of luck, Lawrence in the kitchen juicing some weird-looking fruit in quiet, Zen-master-y concentration, and looking so handsome that Evie momentarily, just momentarily, forgot what the hell she was there for and just stopped dead in the doorway, gawping at him and fighting the urge to rip that fruit out of his hand, throw it over her shoulder and jump his bones.

No question. She definitely wasn't over Lawrence yet.

'Benny's funeral's today!' she blurted out.

Lawrence put the fruit down and contemplated Evie, his grey eyes full of empathy.

'And you want me to come with you?' he asked.

'No! The *last* place you should be is the funeral!' Evie was flushed with excitement, tripping on the sheer brilliance of her idea. 'Don't you see? The house will be empty! Practically everyone will be at the funeral! You show up, saying you had an appointment with Carin, and if there's someone there, you talk your way in, and you'll have the *best* chance to snoop around!'

She realised she was incredibly hungry, and that there was a crushed croissant in her hand, flaking and squished by being gripped hard, but still most definitely eatable. She took a huge bite.

'You get it?' she said, through a mouthful of flaky, buttery pastry. 'We really, *really* need to find that nurse, Lawrence. The PI Simon Poluck hired's coming up with nothing. Carin's hiding the nurse out till the trial so no one can get to him. But we *have* to. We have to get to him and persuade him to tell the truth on the stand. Or Lola will be convicted for something she didn't do, and that bitch Carin won't get what's coming to her.'

'This is about justice, Evie,' Lawrence corrected her gravely. 'Not revenge.'

By now, after some experience with the shit Lawrence was prone to coming out with, Evie had pretty much perfected the ability to feel like she was rolling her eyes without actually doing it.

'Oh, yeah, sure,' she assured him. 'Justice. Absolutely.'

'OK,' Lawrence said, taking up the piece of fruit again and twisting it on his little plastic juicer. 'I'll do it.'

'Oh, Lawrence! Thank you!'

Evie ran across the kitchen and hugged him – from behind, because there was a table in front of him. As she pressed her body into his, feeling his shape all too easily through his tank top and linen drawstring pants, she closed her eyes involuntarily, inhaling his scent, her nose pressed against his lean, muscled back, the few light gold hairs tickling her nose.

She thought suddenly of that fairy tale she'd read years ago. Some guy who was super-strong, but needed to keep his feet on the earth. That was where his power came from. Some other guy had picked him up and then he was as weak as a kitten, couldn't fight at all. No, shit, it wasn't something she'd read: she'd seen it on TV. That show *The Adventures of Hercules*. It was one of the guys Hercules had fought. Not a fairy tale. What was it they called that Ancient Greek stuff?

Myths. That's right. Myths. What a stupid word. Really hard to say.

Evie wasn't weak without Lawrence: she was never weak, god-dammit. But touching Lawrence gave her strength. He grounded her, made her feel incredibly secure. As if this was where she belonged.

Shit, Benny's impending funeral had made her sloppy and sentimental. Evie jerked away from Lawrence's warm back as if it were burning her and headed for the door without looking back.

Chapter 30

*T*wo big catering vans, one with a refrigerated unit clattering noisily, were pulled up outside Carin's mansion on 53rd Street. Lawrence stood on the sidewalk for a moment, watching covered trays being pulled out from the tightly packed shelves along the sides of the van and whisked down the side steps of the town house by a cadre of Mexican employees in white uniforms, their faces concentrated, their movements efficient. It took Panio a long time to open the door, and when he eventually did, he was clearly distracted, his smooth dark hair slightly disarranged.

'Sorry for the delay,' he said automatically, 'I'm supervising every-thing in the kitchen—'

He double-took when he saw Lawrence, his smooth handsome face registering complete surprise.

'Lawrence! You're *so* not booked in today!' he exclaimed, his language, under stress, reverting to a normal 27-year-old's, rather than his usual English-butler routine.

Lawrence hated to lie, and did it as rarely as humanly possible. But the extreme composure which he had developed through years of daily meditation enabled him to meet Panio's eyes with a limpid gaze and say, in a lightly surprised voice,

'Really? I was sure I had three p.m. in the diary. Shall I check?'

His hand went to the pocket of his track pants.

'No, no,' Panio, said, looking harassed. 'I mean, even if you did have it down, everything's up in the air anyway. The city morgue released Mr Fitzgerald's body yesterday afternoon, so we booked in the funeral for – like, *now*,' he said, checking his watch. 'And then there's the wake afterwards, and the caterers have shown up *way* later than they said they would, so you see—'

He gestured beyond Lawrence to the two catering vans.

'*Not* exactly a good time,' he finished. 'Just bill us for a session, OK? No problem.'

He started to close the door. Lawrence took a step forward.

'I don't feel right about that,' he said. 'Why don't I make myself useful? I've been wanting to do some adjustments on the gym equipment. I could make sure the hand weights are calibrated—'

'Sure, sure, come on in, then,' Panio interrupted him, flinging the door wide. 'You know your way around, yeah? Just let yourself out when you're done—'

As Lawrence walked into the hall, Panio flicked his eyes up and down Lawrence's lean body with a distinctly appreciative gaze.

'Or, hey, I'm super-busy at the moment, so who knows,' Panio said coyly, 'but come find me when you're finished, OK?' He winked. 'We could have a glass of champagne, and there's some *fabulous* blue-fin tuna downstairs. Endangered, but I won't tell if you don't! We could, you know, hang out for a bit if I have time. And there's this one hot boy working up a sweat over the stove downstairs. Diego. *Yummy*. Kitchen staff are always fun to play with.'

He reached out and tweaked one of Lawrence's nipples through his T-shirt.

'Mmm! Taut! And FYI, Carin *loves* to watch the staff get it on,' Panio added. 'It's *big* bonus time. I'm surprised she hasn't mentioned it to you yet, but she's been very busy with one thing and another . . . so think it over, why don't you? We could, you know, *book in a session*.' He giggled knowingly.

Lawrence nodded in what he hoped was roughly the way a gay

personal trainer would do when propositioned by a client's butler for an exhibitionist sex display, though he wasn't quite sure what emotion should predominate. Should he look flattered? Thoughtful? Blasé?

To Lawrence's relief, Panio seemed to notice nothing glaringly inappropriate about his response.

'Well, no rest for the wicked! See ya later!' Panio said, flashing Lawrence a smile and flitting off in the direction of the kitchen stairs.

Lawrence crossed the hall, in the direction of the gym staircase, and then feinted back at the last moment, darting towards a door at the back of the hall. He had heard this described by Panio as Ben Fitzgerald's study, but Lawrence would have known anyway as soon as he opened the door whose room this was. It had the unmistakably old-fashioned, masculine odours of cigars and leather, with a redolent undertone of malt whisky. Lawrence wrinkled his nose in distaste. Still, there was something poignant about this room, once you got beyond the smell of toxins. Lawrence was sensitive to auras, and this room spoke to him of absence, of sadness.

There was a large, leather-covered desk by the window, which looked over the back garden, a small stone area planted with greenery which, Lawrence observed sadly, was manicured to within an inch of its life. Nature was firmly under control in that garden, taught its place, which seemed mainly to be inside pots. Swiftly Lawrence ran through the contents of the desk drawers, the filing cabinet, but found nothing with any kind of medical reference. He did come across a section in the filing cabinets labelled with the address of the penthouse where Ben had set up Evie, and the sight of the address on Hudson, scrawled onto a label, actually made Lawrence's heart turn over.

There were no title deeds inside, of course. Just bills: electricity, gas, cable. Evie's cellphone bills, and the statements from her credit and store cards. The totals were terrifyingly high. Lawrence closed his eyes for a moment. If he had ever doubted the fact that he and Evie weren't suited to each other, this was the proof in black and

white that he could never truly make her happy. After the depriva-
tion of her childhood, Evie wanted a life of extreme luxury. She had
been a rich man's mistress when Lawrence had met her, and he had
accepted her for who and what she was, because that was his central philosophy: people made their own choices, and only your own
life was yours to control.

He had never judged Evie for the decision she had made. But,
looking at the evidence of her spending habits, he knew that he
could never satisfy the desire she had for continual, lavish spending
on unnecessary frivolities. Better that they had broken up sooner
rather than later, he told himself.

But the thought of Evie finding another rich sugar daddy made
the bile rise in the back of his throat.

He shut the study door behind him and ran up the main staircase, pushing all thoughts of Evie from his mind, focusing on the
mission he had to accomplish. It wasn't hard to locate Carin's
bedroom, which was in such a perfect state of polished tidiness
that it might have been the most luxurious hotel room in the
world, lying like a white sheet of snow, pristine, waiting for its next
occupant. The sleek Scandinavian furniture yielded only clothes,
exquisitely folded in cedar lined drawers. It was like a shop display,
not a home.

Trying various doors, Lawrence found the largest and most lavish
bathroom he had ever seen in his life; a walk-in closet as large as the
bathroom, with lights that clicked on the moment he entered and a
wall of shoe racks at the far end like a museum installation; and
finally, thank God, a private office. Like the rest of Carin's suite, the
office had the same spotless white carpet and built-in, pale wood
Nordic furniture – even the swivel chair was pale pine, upholstered
in white leather.

On the desk was a day planner, bound in snakeskin bleached to
ivory. It contained detailed notations of all her appointments: hair-
dressers, manicurists, masseuses, spas, personal trainers, dieticians
crammed the daytime hours full. In the evenings were parties and
dinners, an equally endless social round. But, scanning back a couple

of weeks, Lawrence hit pay dirt, in a scrawled name and address in a notes section. Who else could *Joe in Italy* be but Joe Scutellaro, the nurse who had looked after Ben Fitzgerald ever since his diagnosis with Type II diabetes, and the man who had sworn falsely on oath, in front of the grand jury, that Lola Fitzgerald had injected her comatose father with enough insulin to kill him?

Quickly, Lawrence scrawled down Scutellaro's address, closed the day planner and slid it back into place on the desk. As he left the office, he stopped for a second, turning his head. Ever since he had entered Ben Fitzgerald's office, he had the strangest sensation of being watched. But there was no one around, he was sure of it . . .

He looked up into the corner of Carin's bedroom. There was a motion sensor screwed high up on the wall, glowing red, part of an elaborate and no doubt hugely expensive alarm system. *That must be it*, he thought. *And anyway, I've got to get going. They could be back from the funeral any time.*

Reaching the hallway, he stopped dead. The caterers were coming up from the kitchen. A whole stream of people was passing below him in the hall: the Mexican guys, carrying stacks of the small gilt-framed chairs common to all upmarket party planning companies. In addition, the actual wait staff were arriving, handsome young white boys, part-time actors and models, hired mainly for their looks. It was always the same setup: small dark Mexicans (or Guatemalans, or Salvadoreans) were hidden away behind the scenes, doing 90 per cent of the work, while the taller, whiter Americans tended bar, carried drinks trays, flirted with the older, richer clientele, and made small fortunes in tips.

Lawrence waited in the upstairs hallway, watching the scene below, waiting for the right moment, as still as a statue from years of yoga training, not making a single movement that might draw a glance upstairs. Panio nipped out of the drawing-room and into the hall, complaining loudly about the positioning of the bar, and then ducked down the kitchen stairs. Some glass broke in the reception room; people rushed in to clear it up; and with Panio downstairs, that was as good a cue to Lawrence as any.

He walked down the staircase quickly but confidently, as if he belonged there, not giving any indication by an over-hasty pace that he might not have had perfectly legitimate business on the upper floors of the town house. Weaving round some chair legs, he slipped past and out of the front door, checking instinctively in his pocket to make sure that he had his notebook. No one gave him a second glance; they were much too busy racing against the clock to get everything set up before Carin returned from the funeral.

Heading back down 53rd Street, Lawrence pulled his phone out and texted Evie with the news. *Mission accomplished*, he tapped out, grinning despite himself.

He wondered if she'd managed to make her way into the funeral. It would be tough, but he wouldn't put anything past Evie.

Evie felt the phone buzz in her pocket, two short buzzes that told her a message had come in. But she was too caught up in the drama before her to check it straight away.

Because the funeral party had arrived at the grave by now, and Carin Fitzgerald was throwing a huge scene. Towering over everyone else, her height accentuated by the black velvet fedora she was wearing, her fuchsia-painted lips had set into a thin hard line the moment she had caught sight of Lola and Suzanne standing by the grave, waiting to see Ben laid to rest.

'No!' she had snapped at the minister when he opened his prayer book and tried to start the service. 'Not while those – *people* – are still here! I want them gone!'

'Mrs Fitzgerald,' the minister protested, 'this is a public place! If other mourners have gathered here, we have no right to remove them—'

But Carin talked right over him, pointing a black-gloved finger across the bulk of her husband's coffin at his daughter and his ex-wife.

'They were not invited to the service,' she said icily, 'and they won't be present at his burial either.'

The minister looked appalled. He started to murmur something which mainly featured the words 'proper Christian attitude', 'turning the other cheek', and 'time of uniquely shared grief', but Carin rode roughshod over him.

'*That* one,' she said with contempt, indicating Suzanne, 'is nothing but his ex-wife, who he divorced years ago. His ex-wife and his ex-lawyer. Has-beens. And *she*' – Carin swivelled to point fully at Lola – '*killed* the man who's lying in that coffin. My husband. If anyone's not welcome here, it's her.'

Evie watched, eyes wide, as the small crowd of mourners drew in their breat. Everyone knew, of course, who Lola and Suzanne were; but no one had expected Carin to go this far. It was, after all, a funeral, and as the minister was desperately trying to observe to Carin, they were standing on consecrated ground.

'It is for God to judge, not us,' Evie heard him say, before Carin overrode him ruthlessly with:

'God? God won't find her guilty! A jury will!'

'How *dare* you!' Suzanne said furiously, taking a couple of paces forward.

And Carin, never one to turn down a challenge, strode towards Suzanne, till the two women stood facing each other across the oversized grave waiting for the man they both had married.

'How dare *I*? How dare *you* show your face here!' Carin retorted.

The minister hadn't been able to silence Carin, but, to Evie's great surprise, Suzanne managed what he could not.

'Look at that grave!' she cried, pointing down to the gaping hole at her feet. 'See how large it is? That's what *you* did to him! Ben wasn't a freak show when I was with him! I took care of him! He knew he had to watch his weight and take exercise, and God knows he wasn't happy about it, but as long as I was with him he never got *huge*. Now – my God, he must have been *obese*! Look at that coffin! Aren't you ashamed of what you've done?'

Suzanne's fists were clenched, her eyes flashing with fury.

'You turned him into a joke!' she accused Carin. 'Something you'd see at a county fair! Aren't you ashamed of letting your husband degenerate like that, before your eyes? No, of course you're not! Because you did it deliberately – you must have fed him up like a prize pig! You knew he was greedy, and you fed his disease. You fed him up so much he became diabetic, for God's sake! What kind of wife stands by and does nothing when her husband gets into that state?'

Carin was gaping, her lipsticked mouth hanging open: she looked as amazed as if an animal she'd had every reason to assume was tame – a sheep, maybe, or a rabbit – had suddenly reared up and gashed its claws into her face.

'*You* killed him!' Suzanne screamed at her. '*You!* You let him get so overweight that his heart couldn't take it – you made him diabetic – *you* killed him! You took him away from me, and then you killed him!'

She crumpled, suddenly, her whole body folding up on itself. Suzanne didn't even put out her hands to save herself. She was no longer in control of her own body. Grief had crumpled her completely.

Lola screamed. The lawyer jumped forward. But it was the skinny white boy with the goatee, who didn't look strong enough to Evie to carry his own minimal weight, let alone someone else's, who reached Suzanne in time. Just as she was toppling forward, the momentum of her fall carrying her over the gaping maw of her ex-husband's grave, the kid grabbed her from behind and dragged her back, her heels skidding over the grass.

Suzanne hung there in his arms, limp as a rag doll, but safe, at least. On solid ground. And the minister, not too cowed by Carin to avoid seizing this excellent opportunity, stepped up to the head of the grave, gesturing to the pallbearers to take up their work of lowering Ben Fitzgerald's outsize coffin, finally, into the Manhattan soil where he had wanted so badly to be buried that he had paid a small fortune for the privilege.

'Ashes to ashes,' intoned the minister, opening his prayer book. 'Dust to dust . . .'

Tears prickled at Evie's eyes as she watched Benny's body lowered to its final resting place.

Lola's mom was right, she thought, lifting her eyes to the immobile figure of Carin Fitzgerald. *You* did *kill him. And you picked the wrong girl to mess with, bitch. I'm going to make sure you pay for what you did.*

Chapter 31

Joe in Italy
Barbiano 45
San Vincenzo
51048 Roma

*L*ola folded up the piece of paper and pushed it into her jeans pocket. She knew the address off by heart by now, but, like a talisman, she pulled it out every now and then, reading the four lines over and over. To remind her that she was on a quest, and how much depended on her being successful.

The couple in front of her were being summoned up to the check-in desk, and now a smartly dressed woman behind another desk, her pillbox hat at a jaunty angle, was beckoning her over.

'Evie Lopez, Rome, business class,' the woman said efficiently, scanning the passport and tapping the name into the computer. She looked at the screen. 'We've assigned you a window seat, Ms Lopez, is that OK?'

'Fine, thanks.'

'Just carry-on luggage?'

Lola nodded, hefting up her Louis Vuitton shoulder bag so the check-in official could see it.

'Travelling very light!' the woman smiled. 'Are you planning to do a lot of shopping while you're there?'

'Not really. It's just a flying visit.'

'Flying visit, very good . . . Well, you have an open return. Just call in when you're ready to use it. Or simply turn up at the airport. The flight's on time, boarding starts in an hour twenty, Gate 35, I've marked it on your boarding pass.'

She smiled again.

'Enjoy your flight with us, Ms Lopez.'

There was no way Lola could leave the country. The DA's office had confiscated both her British and her American passports. And even if she had had access to a Van der Veer jet, you still needed a passport, no way round it. Things were a lot stricter nowadays, post 9–11, than they used to be. Everyone had been so caught up in the excitement of Lawrence's discovery that they hadn't factored in that crucial piece of information: it had taken George Goldman to remind them that Lola was officially under arrest, out on $5 million bail, and strictly forbidden from leaving the country.

And then Evie, looking at Lola, had said:

'*She* can't go. But I can.'

Evie had never left the States; like 75 per cent of her compatriots, she didn't have a passport. It had taken five agonising days, with George Goldman and Simon Poluck pulling every string they could, to secure her an emergency passport. Simon had high-placed connections in the office of one of the New York senators, who had finally made the all-important call to expedite the process. It had arrived by FedEx, brand new, shiny dark blue, covers stiff, and the photograph of Evie inside very serious, her hair pulled back, staring directly at the camera. Not exactly flattering.

But it looked enough like Lola for her to run the risk of using it to travel to Italy.

Sliding the passport and the boarding pass into the outside pocket of the Louis Vuitton shoulder bag, she turned away from the desk, towards the big Departures sign. There was a small queue for business class; she wondered whether it would be full or not, whether she'd have someone sitting beside her who wanted to talk. Business travellers with briefcases clipped to their carry-on suitcases, going to meetings in Italy. A couple in casual lounging clothes, smiling at each other, holding hands; their big suitcases and happy smiles indicating that they were going on holiday. And a woman at the back of the queue in a kaftan draped over her substantial bulk, bent forward over a trolley on which a single small piece of luggage was propped, wheezing, clearly only using the trolley to take some of the weight off her trainer-shod feet.

Probably travelling business class because she won't fit into an economy seat, poor thing, she thought. And then, rather meanly: *I hope she isn't sitting next to me . . .*

But the flight was quiet, and as it turned out there was no one occupying the sleep capsule beside her. She was small enough to be able to curl up in it comfortably, and there was a little fixed side table for drinks where the steward promptly placed a mimosa cocktail. Orange juice to hydrate you, cheap champagne to relax you. By the time the glass was cleared away as they got ready for take-off, she had swallowed its contents, together with a sleeping pill, and was curled up in a nest of pillows. And as the plane levelled out, she extended her bed as the steward had shown her, covered herself with her pashmina and then the airline blankets, strapped the seat belt over the entire bundle, and lay down to sleep, doing her absolute best not to think about what the next day held.

They landed on time, at nine a.m. Italian time. Day flights were better for jet-lag, but the passport had come through yesterday at four in the afternoon, and they had immediately made a booking on the first flight to Rome that she could possibly manage, paying with India's credit card to avoid leaving any kind of electronic trail. The rest of the trip Lola would pay with cash or traveller's cheques, and the amount of both she was carrying was enough to send waves of panic through her every time she thought about it.

After the first-class passengers had left, she was the first off the plane. She'd have loved to be in first-class too, but it might have raised too many flags if Evie Lopez had been travelling in that kind of style. Behind her, she could hear the fat woman in the kaftan wheezing as she wheeled her bag down the walkway. Nerves caught

at her stomach, twisting it tight, as she slid her passport underneath the small slot at the base of the perspex to the uniformed
man sitting behind the counter. They were very careful in Italy,
Lola noticed; in New York the passport officials, stone-faced and
imposing though they could be, didn't feel the need to put a whole
panel of clear perspex between them and the people they were
intimidating.

The man was running her passport over a reader, checking something on his computer screen. His eyes lifted to hers, professional
and cold, comparing her face to the one on the passport: blonde
hair, pulled back in the identical style to the passport photograph.
Brown eyes. Small, pretty features. Even the silver earrings from the
photograph. A match, surely.

Stay calm, she told herself. *No one knows you're here. No one
could possibly have put a block on this passport. Stay calm.*

And, sure enough, the man nodded, sliding the passport back to
her through the gap at the bottom of the perspex, and his expression cracked into a distinctly non-professional smile, the smile of
appreciation that Italian men reserved for pretty blondes.

'*Benvenuta in Italia, Signorina Lopez,*' he said.

She had done it. She was in. Through the green channel, round a
corner, down a corridor, glass doors sliding open, the roar and bustle
of the arrivals hall. She paused for a moment, reading the various
signs carried by the throng of men in cheap suits, surnames marker-
penned on sheets of paper. She was searching for her own.

A woman pushed past her, very Italian-looking: hair piled up on
top of her head, dangling gold hoop earrings, enormous bosoms
that she carried in front of her like inflated airbags. Packed into
tight jeans, she was unusually tall, obscuring the view for a few
moments as she sashayed down the aisle between the barriers, the
high, obviously fake shelf of her breasts drawing glances from every
single man she passed. She followed slowly in the woman's wake,
her own chest drawing considerably less attention, still checking
out every sign. And at last, she saw 'LOPEZ' on a piece of paper, and
above it, a round, balding head with dark eyes behind rimless

glasses. Late forties, early fifties, in a rather better-quality suit than most of the drivers here. Tubby, but he carried himself well. And his smile was friendly.

He darted forward, pulling at the strap of her Vuitton bag, indicating he would carry it for her, but there was no way she was letting anyone else take control of that bag, with all its precious contents. She shook her head, clinging tightly to the strap, and he danced back immediately, lifting his hands in apology.

'Excuse me, I only try to help! Evie, yes? Miss Evie Lopez? I am Mario, Mario Piciacchi. A distant, very distant cousin of George Goldman. By marriage only, but still, a relative. He is very important in New York, George, they tell me? Big lawyer. It's good to have a big lawyer in the family, even if you never meet him. And now he sends me you, to look after. I am a guide, you see.' He puffed up his chest. 'The best in Rome, I assure you.'

'Hi, Mr Pi—'

Her tongue twisted over the hard, unfamiliar consonants of his surname.

'No, no, Mario! You call me Mario!' he insisted. 'Is much more easy for the Americans! Always, call me Mario. Is much more easy.'

He looked at her, taking in her appearance, the dark circles under her eyes that she had tried to camouflage with Touche Eclat on the plane.

'You are tired, it's clear. I take you to a hotel now, so you can rest. A nice place, I make a reservation already.'

'No,' she said, shaking her head. 'I need to go here.'

She produced the piece of paper, crumpled now from the journey, handing it to Mario. And she watched in consternation as his expression changed in a split-second from benevolent to deeply concerned.

'No, no,' he said, shaking his head. 'No, I cannot take you here. Impossible!' He handed the paper back to her, pursing his lips and shaking his head. 'It is a very, very bad area where that place is. No police will go. There are guns, drugs—'

His eyes widened as something occurred to him. He darted a glance from side to side, checking out their surroundings.

'Come, we go to the bar,' he said, leading the way across the arrivals hall to a wide curve of white marble. He ordered cappuccino and brioche for both of them, and carried them to a small, breast-high marble table.

'You don't understand,' she said urgently, sipping the coffee, which was rich and loaded her up with energy. 'There's someone I have to talk to who lives there.'

He rolled his eyes.

'Look, *signorina*. I may call you *signorina*, yes? Now in Italy they say, "All ladies must be called *signora*", if not it is *maleducato*, not polite, because you say that maybe a lady is not married. I don't understand, frankly, but that is what they say. But you, so young and pretty, it seems wrong to call you *signora!* You understand?'

'Yes. Fine. You can call me anything you want.' She took a bite of brioche, eggy and sweet. 'But I have to go to this address and talk to the man whose name is on that paper.'

Mario's distress was extreme: he tamped his brow with the flimsy paper napkin, even though the terminal was air-conditioned and cool.

'Look, *Signorina* Evie,' he began, leaning across the table, lowering his voice. 'George Goldman, he says to take very good care of you, and this I want to do. Do you need drugs? Is that it? I myself have nothing to do with this kind of thing, but maybe I could ask. I don't want to, please understand me.' He wrung his hands. 'But if you need it – are you in, *come si dice*, a fall? Do you have pain?'

'No! Of course not!' she exclaimed, eyebrows rising to her hairline. Her surprise was so obvious that Mario relaxed immediately.

'Good! Good! So why do you need to go to this terrible place?'

'There's someone there – this man, Giuseppe Scutellaro, but they call him Joe—' she pointed to the name. 'I need to talk to him. He's told lies about – about a friend of mine, and she'll go to prison if he doesn't tell the truth. I need to convince him to say what really happened.' She lowered her voice. 'I'm supposed to pay him to tell the truth,' she explained. 'Someone paid him to lie, and now if I pay him more—'

'I see, I see,' Mario nodded quickly, appreciatively. Italy ran on bribes, Lola knew from Jean-Marc, whose family had textile factories here. It would be commonplace to give money to a witness; from Mario's response, she could see the truth of that.

'He's holed up here.' It was her turn to point to the address. 'Keeping quiet till he has to go back to New York to testify.'

'So we have to go here,' Mario said, with deep resignation. 'This is very bad. One of the worst *periferie* – suburbs, you would say – in the city. And believe me, there are many bad suburbs here. This is a *quartiere povera, una topaia*. A very poor place. We say, where the mice live. Only there are no mice, because the cats eat them all.' He finished his coffee and furrowed his brow, deep in thought; his cup was still in his hand, suspended in mid-air. 'My son, he knows some people who have the nightclubs. We will take someone from the nightclubs with us. A *buttafuori*. Bouncer, I think you call it.'

Mario set down his cup and pushed it to one side. He steepled both his pudgy hands on the table, fixing her with a business-like stare.

'Excuse me, *signorina*, but I must ask this now. To go to this place for me, perhaps to have my car broken or stolen, to take this risk and to find a *buttafuori*, to pay him, none of this will be cheap. You say you will pay this man, this Scutellaro, much money to tell the truth. So for my expenses too, there will be enough money?'

It was no time for bargaining. Lola's life, effectively, was on the line. She met his stare full-on, nodding in a way that convinced him she was serious. In the Vuitton bag was a small fortune in traveller's cheques, and she could certainly spare plenty to pay Mario Piciacchi to take her to this rathole in the worst suburb of Rome.

'Whatever it takes,' she told him.

Four hours later, Mario picked her up from her hotel, a charming place in Trastevere, built around a small central garden in which a fountain played soft water from a statue of Neptune holding his trident, and deep pink roses were starting to bloom from the bushes planted on each side of the marble paths across the square courtyard.

Mario was waiting in the courtyard, his face grim. But not as grim as that of the man standing a pace behind him and slightly to one side, his hands clasped across his chest.

'This is Leo,' Mario said. 'He will come with us.'

She nodded at Leo, and received a short nod in response. About five feet ten, with a long, bony shaved skull, his nose, in true Roman fashion, was long and hooked and looked as if its arch had been broken a couple of times. The hands clasped over his chest were equally bony, the knuckles swollen and knobbed. Leo had been in plenty of fights. She just hoped he'd won most of them.

'Right, so now we go!' Mario announced. 'I will be positive,' he added rather bleakly. 'It is important to be positive.'

They piled into a small, battered Fiat, which sagged noticeably under Mario and Leo's weight. Mario was driving.

'This is my mother's car,' Mario informed her. 'She had had it for fifteen years, she will not change it. Of course, mine is much better. A Mercedes. For the clients I drive. But we do not take it to this *quartiere*. No, no, no. The animals who live there, they have never seen anything so beautiful as my Mercedes. They will destroy it at once.' He translated this for Leo, who nodded agreement.

Negotiating out of the centre of Rome, with its endless road-works and architectural digs slowing traffic down to a crawl, took a while; but by the time they were on a main road leading out of town they could have been in any poor Italian city. Endless apartment blocks made from slabs of crumbling concrete, sad little strings of washing pegged across the shabby balconies. Advertising hoardings, tattered at the corners, as if no one had bothered to change them in years. It was hard to believe that, just a short while before, they had been in Rome itself, the Eternal City, with its exquisite marble buildings, its narrow, enchanting streets, its moneyed, stylish occupants. They had rounded the Colosseum on their way out and she had gasped, its high colonnades so beautiful that even Leo had nodded in approval of Lola's reaction to one of the wonders of the world.

And now the landscape was going from bad to worse. The graffiti on the stone was becoming thicker and more frequent, the apartment blocks in a worse and worse state of decay. Kids lounged on corners, staring at every car that passed in challenge, or piled onto battered bicycles, one riding, one standing behind with his hands on the rider's shoulders, one sitting behind him, legs out wide, maybe even a fourth perching on the front mudguard. Refuse of all kinds littered the streets. And everywhere, there were the cats. Skinny, feral cats, slipping along crumbling walls, darting across the streets, rummaging through overflowing bins down dark alleyways.

Finally, the car braked with a squeal, backed up, shot right down a narrow street, and halted with a groan of its entire engine.

'We are here,' Mario announced unhappily.

They climbed out and surveyed the territory. On either side of them rose the concrete apartment blocks they had seen from the main road, ten storeys high, built in the 1970s and aging very badly. Dark water stains marked almost every join of the concrete, which was visibly crumbling and filthy; bird shit and graffiti were struggling for dominance, and it was hard to tell which was winning. It was a hot late-spring day, which only made the smells even stronger. Big steel dumpsters of rubbish were overflowing everywhere, reeking, and a cat fight was in progress in a bin behind them – high, unearthly screams and hisses.

But the worst smell was of drains. The lower note was the musty, unhealthy odour of damp, but above that, richer and more powerful, was the stink of faeces and urine. It was as if this entire area had been built on an open sewer. Lola did her best not to gag.

Mario was locking the car, squaring his shoulders as if about to go into battle. Leo was looking around him, and in turn they were being surveyed by many pairs of eyes. Men leaning on the stone walkways that ran around each storey of the apartment blocks. Kids, scruffing around the pavement, kicking battered old balls, seemingly aimless, but their dark eyes sharp and alert. A group of young men, smoking unfiltered Camels, clustered around the dented steel entrance door to the apartment block where Joe Scutellaro lived, their hard stares directed straight at Mario, Leo and herself.

They were all males, she noticed. Even the kids. It was more than a little unnerving.

Leo gestured to Mario and her to remain by the car. Smoothing down his jacket, he walked past the kids, along the short cement path, and straight up to the young men who were guarding the entrance door.

'What's he saying to them?' she asked.

Mario shrugged, and she saw Leo was pointing at her. They stared at her appreciatively; one of them whistled, another laughed. Leo's dour expression almost cracked into a smile. He put his finger next to his head, swivelling it. They all laughed. A young man at the centre of the group said something. From the way the others fell aside, deferring to him, as soon as he spoke, he was clearly the leader. They were all wearing jeans, much tighter than their American gangland equivalents would be caught dead in, light denim, with bright, equally tight T-shirts. 'PRISON CAMP SEX', read the slogan on one. '69 4-EVER', read another. 'ROCK, ROLL, REV', a third. Near-meaningless texts, printed probably in China and sold here cheaply at local markets for a few euros, bought by people who barely understood the words but liked the Americana they thought they represented.

Leo turned back to the two waiting by the Fiat and beckoned. They were in.

'*Santo Dio, proteggimi,*' Mario muttered, crossing himself.

Lola was used to men staring at her, but this was something else entirely. She could almost believe that Leo had sold her to the young men, the way they were looking at her. In her jeans and three-quarter-length sleeve T-shirt, a sweater knotted at her waist, she was pretty well covered, but she might as well have been wearing a string bikini and four-inch perspex stack heels. They leered at her, laughing in her face, saying things that were clearly meant to taunt her but which, mercifully, she couldn't understand. One of the young men flung open the steel door with a mocking smile, and she passed through to a stream of whistles and catcalls, Leo and Mario following. Inside it was dark, dank and stunk like a cattery.

Mario winced in horror. There was a lift ahead of them, but they didn't take it; Leo indicated a set of concrete stairs instead.

That ascent of the stairs she would always remember as one of the worst experiences of her life. The vials on the floor that their feet crunched over, the pools of piss and vomit in the corners, the stench everywhere, the dried bloodstains, the streaks of human excrement, like children's finger painting, on the concrete walls. It seemed an interminable walk. None of them spoke: all of them were too busy breathing through their mouths, to avoid, as much as possible, smelling the odours surrounding them. By the time they reached the sixth floor, Mario was moaning audibly.

Number 45 was halfway down the walkway. Its front door had been painted a jaunty turquoise once, but was so peeled and sun-faded now that only a few bright chips remained to indicate its original colour. Leo approached it, but Lola tapped his arm, shaking her head, and stepped forward instead.

Heart in her mouth, she knocked on the door.

To her surprise, it was opened almost immediately. But the young man who stood there had clearly been expecting someone else. His eyes bugged out when he saw her small figure and Leo, standing behind her. She could see the cogs in his brain whirling as he worked out why her face was familiar to him, and who she was.

And then he started to shut the door in her face.

Leo was very fast. He had one hand past her and pressed flat against the closing door before she even realised what he was doing. And he was strong, too, because he held the door at that exact angle very easily, even as Joe Scutellaro pushed, with his whole slight weight, against him, trying to get it shut.

'Look, I just want to talk to you,' Lola said urgently. 'Please can I come in?'

Joe Scutellaro closed his eyes momentarily.

'Just you,' he said finally. 'Not your animal.' He added something rude in Italian, directed at Leo, who didn't react.

'We must check it inside,' Mario said anxiously. 'To see there is no one else, who could hurt her.'

Joe let out a bitter laugh.

'Sure, knock yourself out,' he said, throwing the door open wide as Leo took his hand away. 'You can practically check it out from here.'

Lola went inside. It was so sparse, so pitiful, that her heart would have broken for him if she hadn't known how much money of Carin Fitzgerald's he must be sitting on. A front room with an old stove and small, whirring refrigerator, two wooden chairs and a chipped Formica-topped table; a blue-and-white checked piece of cloth hung over a row of wooden shelves with a few scanty provisions on them. Beyond was another small room, with a mattress on the floor, an orange plastic crate turned upside down to serve as a bedside table, and some clothes on hangers suspended from nails on the walls. The bathroom was a sink, toilet and open shower all in one narrow cubicle, so that in winter, without the sun to dry off the tiles, the whole room would be perpetually damp. The grouting was already rotten, lying in dark grey worms over the tiles.

She came out into the front room after thirty seconds.

'There's no one here,' she said to Leo, who nodded, understanding that much English, and closed the door.

She was alone with Joe Scutellaro. Slowly, Lola crossed the room to the table and sat down on the further chair, indicating that he should take the other one. His big dark eyes never leaving her face, he sat down too.

'How did you find me?' he asked.

'I can't tell you that.'

'Carin would never had told you. Nor anyone who works for her,' he said. 'They're all too well-paid. And too scared.'

He was very handsome; with his tight dark curls, liquid dark eyes and full red lips he might have walked straight out of a Caravaggio painting, where he would have been depicted as a faun, or a young Bacchus, holding a full bunch of grapes to his mouth. His eyelashes were ridiculously long and thick, his jawline smooth as silk.

'Whatever she gave you, I can top it,' Lola said, her dark eyes boring into his. 'Name your price.'

'I can't! You must be crazy! She's gone so far with this thing. Making me hide out here. "Bury yourself alive," were her exact words, if I remember right. "Somewhere shitty. They'll look for you in the nice places, not the shitty ones."' He gestured around him. 'This is my cousin's place. Nice, isn't it? A real palace. I gave him a bunch of euros and told him to fuck off for three weeks. You can bet he was glad to go.'

She cleared her throat.

'Well then,' she said tentatively, 'doesn't that tell you something? I mean, you're making all this money from her – she must have paid you tons – and still, this is where you've ended up till she needs you again? Somewhere as shitty as this? She doesn't care about you at all! She's just using you!'

'I know she's using me,' he said impatiently. 'It's all about the money, OK? For her and for me.' He looked around him once again. 'You can see the kind of thing I come from. I mean, not as bad as this. Nothing's as bad as this, it's one of the worst fucking places in Italy. Unless you're down in Naples, living on a rubbish heap.' He spat over his shoulder. 'But yeah, we come from nothing. I needed to set myself up, you understand? It wasn't' – he wouldn't meet her eyes – 'it wasn't anything personal.'

He fumbled in his pocket, pulling out a pack of Marlboro Lights.

'I've got to give you points,' he said, still not meeting her eyes. 'Managing to track me down here. Jesus, just getting into this place. It's like Fort Knox. The dealers don't let anyone in they don't know. Heroin,' he said, answering her unspoken question. 'Straight up from Africa. *Roba.* My cousin shoots up every Friday night, just for shits and giggles. Works all week and spends the weekend in a coma. I tell you, if I'd grown up here I'd be a junkie myself.'

He tapped out a cigarette, stuck it in his mouth, and then offered her the packet.

'Thanks,' she said, taking one.

He lit hers and then his.

'Look, there's nothing I can do for you,' he said, blowing out a cloud of smoke. 'Nothing. I'm all bought and paid for. Sorry, but that's just how it is.'

'Like I said, anything she gave you, I can give you more,' Lola insisted. She hadn't come this far to give up now. 'She's got money, but I have the Van der Veers behind me, and they're much more powerful than Carin.'

From the way he looked up at her, she knew she'd found a chink in his armour.

'The Van der Veers have interests all over the world,' she insisted. 'You could be set up wherever you want, with whatever you want. Right here in Italy, if you like. You know about their textile factories. You could have an interest in them. I mean, you need a lot of money to be set up for life nowadays. A *lot*. I doubt Carin's promised you that much. But I will.'

'How do I know you're good for it?' he asked, staring at her. 'This could all be a lot of hot air. I mean, Carin's got her hands on her fortune already. You've got nothing for now.'

She fished in a pocket of her bag, extracting an envelope. 'Fifty thousand euros, in cash, for starters. Yours to keep, just for listening to me.'

'You're kidding!' he exclaimed, his eyes widening.

He snatched at the envelope with such instant, immediate greed that she felt her heart pounding with excitement as she reached into another compartment of the bag and pulled out a stack of papers and a fountain pen.

'Here,' she said, extracting a cheque that was paper-clipped to the top of the pile, and holding it up so that he could read it. 'Made out to you. A hundred thousand euros. Already signed, by Jean-Marc van der Veer.'

She tapped the stack of papers.

'I've got a contract in here for you to sign. Drawn up by my New York lawyers. Really simple language, no loopholes or escape clauses. We get an acquittal, you get a cool million. Read it. It's unbreakable once you and I sign it. I've got copies here for me and for you.'

She was deliberately using the most neutral language possible.

The man sitting before her had colluded in a murder, had committed perjury already, and was planning to do it again to send an innocent woman to prison. He was a nurse, who had helped to kill the patient whose life he was supposed to preserve. She didn't think she'd get very far with appeals to his conscience.

And making him feel guilty, taking the moral high ground, would probably anger him so much he'd throw her out and refuse to enter into any more negotiations. The last thing she wanted to do was provoke any resistance. So she was treating this as if it were a straightforward business deal, where the highest bidder would win out.

She just hoped that it was working.

Joe was reading through the copy of the contract that she had slid across the table to him, poring over it slowly, taking his time. That was a good sign. The tension was unbearable; she wanted to beat her feet against the floor, to pace up and down the room, anything to let off some steam.

But she couldn't. This was a business negotiation, and you never showed weakness if you wanted to win. Her entire body fizzing with nerves, she limited herself to lighting another Marlboro Light off the butt of the first.

Minutes passed, and he was still reading. She stubbed out the second cigarette in the crumpled piece of foil he was using as an ashtray. A light tap on the door made her jump.

'You get that,' Joe said. 'It'll be your animal, checking that you're still in one piece and breathing.'

She opened the door and let Leo and Mario see she was OK. Leo was as impassive as ever; Mario looked on the verge of tears. She raised her hand in front of her, crossing her fingers, then shut the door again, turning so her back was to it, watching the back of Joe's head as he pored over the contract.

'Any bank account in the world?' he asked eventually. 'I can get this paid in anywhere I want?'

'Of course. It says so right there.'

She came forward to put her finger on the sub-clause.

'I like Brazil,' he said. 'I have a lot of friends there. But—'

Just as her heart was leaping into her mouth with excitement, he sighed and pushed the contract away.

'I've committed perjury. You know? This would never work. They'll arrest me as soon as I step off the witness stand.'

'No, they won't,' she said confidently, sitting down opposite him again, fully prepared for this. 'You'll cry. You'll say Carin threatened to frame you if you didn't go along with her. You'll say Rico threatened your family. And it was only grand jury testimony.'

'I was still under oath!' he protested.

'Yes, but if you tell the truth at the trial you'll be fine. Simon Poluck – the criminal lawyer – he says that no one ever gets prosecuted for perjury unless it's a Mafia trial or something to do with organised crime. You break down on the stand, you say your conscience is killing you and you have to tell the truth, and no one will come after you. Guaranteed. Because they'll see you did the right thing and told the truth in the end.'

He nodded, slowly, heavily.

'And you *will* be telling the truth, won't you?' Lola said, leaning forward, taking his hands in hers. 'You'll be telling the truth where it matters. And that means that for the rest of your life, you won't have to live with me on your conscience. Look at me. You're seriously going to send me to prison for killing my own father? When you know I'm innocent? How do you think you're going to live with that?'

He shuddered, but he didn't pull his hands away.

'Besides,' she finished, moving onto her last argument, 'you'll be safer on our side.'

'Safer?' he mumbled.

'You're joking, right?' she said. 'Carin's already killed her own husband. Don't you think she might want to tie up all the loose ends, after she's got the conviction she needs to inherit all her husband's money? Don't you think she might want to make sure that you can't have a crisis of conscience in five years' time and go to the DA to tell the truth?'

Still holding his hands, she made him look at her through sheer force of will, her brown eyes boring into him until he raised his head and returned her gaze.

'You'll never be safe from her,' she said. 'Like you said yourself, you're just a hired hand. It's about the money. She doesn't expect any loyalty from you – she's bought your testimony, that's all. What's to stop you having an accident a couple of months after you've testified, just to make sure you don't change your story? I'm sure Rico's arranged plenty of accidents for people over the years.'

His eyes widened so much that she could see the whites all around his irises.

'If you take our side, you'll be safe,' she insisted. 'We haven't killed anyone. And you know how powerful the Van der Veers are. They can protect you. Anything it takes.'

His hands relaxed under hers. And she knew then that she had him.

'Sign the contract, Joe, come on,' she coaxed, her voice soft, gentle, a total contrast to Carin, her enemy. 'A million euros, for telling the truth. And powerful people to protect you for the rest of your life. Please. Do it. Sign the contract.'

He drew his hands away from hers, and she thought with horror that she had read him all wrong, that he was going to say no.

And just as she thought she would burst into tears of frustration and despair, he reached for the fountain pen, picked it up, and scrawled his name at the base of the first contract.

Chapter 32

'We celebrate, Evie!' Mario said joyously as they tumbled back down the stairs, so jubilant that the stench and the pools of liquid barely bothered them. 'I take you to the best restaurant in Rome! You like the *carciofi*, the artichokes? We are famous in Rome for the artichokes. Raw, with Parmesan cheese and to drink a *prosecco*, or a Vermentino wine from Sardinia – very fresh and dry – and then a dish of *pastasciutta*, maybe with truffles . . . It is not the truffle season, sadly, but under oil they are still very good, very tasty. And then—'

They were on the ground floor now, approaching the entrance door. Leo shouldered forward to open it. A burst of laughter came from the young men outside as they saw who was exiting the building.

The leader, smoking a joint, gestured with it to her, and the young men on either side of him laughed even harder, shoving their hips back and forth at her in the universal gesture of fucking. For a moment they were surrounded, and she felt a jolt of fear. One of them shouted a question at Leo, who answered shortly, and there was even more laughter. The questioner pressed himself against her, his hand to his crotch, shoving it into her, his sweaty face alight with lust, and Lola tensed up in panic, smelling cheap aftershave and unwashed male skin.

Then Leo, clearing a path for them, yelled something loudly and the leader seemed to second it, because the men hemming her in pulled back reluctantly, and Mario was shoving her from behind so hard she nearly stumbled as she followed Leo down the path towards the car. Nearly there, nearly there . . . The men were falling back, still laughing and catcalling in their wake. The group of kids were kicking their ball in a bored, desultory manner up and down the road. And there was a group of women now on the far side of the street, waiting at a bus stop, staring over at the three people walking towards the Fiat, which, mercifully, was still there and seemed to have all its windows intact.

Or *were* they women? She blinked, her heart still racing, trying to clear her vision.

'The *prostitute* – prostitutes of this zone,' Mario said disapprovingly behind her. 'Going to the motorway stops, for the *camioniste* at lunch time. The drivers of the big trucks. They have lunch, they make sex. Disgusting for all decent people. Poor black girls from Africa, *trasvestiti* from this country. Please ignore, *Signorina* Evie.'

That was why she'd been confused: some of the women in that small group were much too tall to be Italian, a country whose women were rarely taller than five foot seven. With their wigs, their big fake breasts, their painted faces, the transvestites towered over the smaller African girls, but all were dressed in the same gear: shiny miniskirts, ra-ra boots, cropped bra tops.

Leo had almost reached the car when one of the women shouted something across the street. It hung in the air for a moment, a cue to action. And suddenly there was the sound of running footsteps, and the ball that the boys had been kicking was bouncing away down the road, discarded, as they came after a new target.

One kid came flying at her, a blade flashing as he tried to slice her bag strap, and before she knew what she was doing she had swivelled on one heel and landed a perfect side kick on the little fucker, as she had done so many times on the weight bag at kickboxing classes. Her legs were strong enough from all the exercise, God knew. The kid emitted a squeal of surprise and pain as he went flying through the air and smacked into another one, who went down under him. Barely eleven, and coming at her with a knife. Maybe Evie, the real Evie, had seen this kind of feral child before, but Lola certainly hadn't. It was like she'd been pitched into a nightmare, a documentary of the kind she'd turn off immediately if she saw it on TV. She was so sheltered. She'd never really believed that people lived like this, and now she was faced with it. A kid, with a knife in his hand. Ready to wound or kill someone he didn't even know.

Instinctively, Lola grabbed the bag to her chest with both arms as she felt another pull on the strap from behind her. It had the signed contract inside: they'd have to kill her to take it from her. Mario yelled something in Italian, a warning, maybe, and she ducked instinctively as Leo's fist flew past her face, catching a kid who was jumping towards her. Some little bastard grabbed at her ankle and she kicked out as hard as she had before, managing to dislodge him, but only for a moment: next second he, or another one, was back, pulling so hard she nearly tumbled over. Small fingers were scrabbling at her bag, trying to drag it out of her hands, and she couldn't free them to defend herself; she writhed wildly, trying to shake the kids off and not succeeding.

Crack! Crack! Two shots rang out overhead, snapping through the air, making everyone scream. The women by the bus stop crouched to the ground, hands over their heads. The kids' shrill voices buzzed around her for a second more, till a third shot rang out and the hands on her ankles let go, and she heard the footsteps again, this time sprinting away.

'*Si! Correte via, pezzenti!*' someone was yelling, and as her ears adjusted after the shock of the pistol shots, she realised it was Leo, standing a few feet away, a wicked-looking gun in his right hand, held up into the air.

'*Oh, mio Dio, mio Dio . . .*' Mario, slumped against the car, was moaning, his face so completely drained of colour his skin looked grey. '*Mamma mia, siamo tutti fottuti . . .*'

'Mario!' She ran over to him. 'Mario, are you OK?

'Is OK, I am OK,' he managed. 'And you, Evie? You have your bag still?' He saw it, still clutched to her breast. '*Oh, Dio sia ringraziato . . .*'

'*Nella macchina! Tutti nella macchina! Via, andiamo!*' Leo shouted, still holding his gun above his head as he strode towards them.

'He say, get in the car, we go,' Mario gasped, fumbling for the car keys.

Leo tore them out of his hand, unlocked the car and practically threw her in, jumping into the driver's seat himself. The car started up and Leo threw it into gear instantly, screeching away from the curb. The kids, who had regrouped further down the road, screamed insults, windmilling their arms to throw stones at them. A couple hit the car, but didn't manage to shatter any windows. Still, Mario yelped in fear.

Swivelling around, Lola looked out the rear window: the kids were slowing down now. The young men stationed outside the apartment building, who had hit the ground when Leo started firing, were standing up, dusting off their clothes and yelling at the kids, waving their hands furiously. A *motorino*, one of the small Vespa-type scooters so popular in Italy, had chosen a bad time to buzz down the road in their wake. Its rider, looping around the kids in the road, was doing its best to dodge the stones lying on the tarmac.

'*Fuck*,' she said, sitting back down. 'What the *hell* just happened there?'

'One of the prostitutes,' Mario said, still gasping. 'She calls out to say your bag is real. That it's worth a lot of money. She says it means you are rich.'

Lola's eyebrows shot up.

'She's right,' she admitted. 'But how the hell did she spot that from way across the street?'

'Who knows, who cares,' Mario said. 'All I know is, never never never do I want to go to that bad place again. Not even if you beg me, *Signorina* Evie. Not even for you.'

'I promise, Mario,' she said in heartfelt tones. 'Look, what did Leo say to those men so they'd let me into the building?'

'I did not understand all he say,' Mario answered, 'but more or less, he say that you are American, you have a lover in America but he leave you and come back here and you are in love so much you come to find him and implore with him to be with you again.'

'You're *joking.*'

'No no. The men there, of course, this makes them happy that an Italian man is so *virile*, so, um—'

'I got it,' she assured him, eager to spare Mario's blushes.

'You understand, yes? That only an Italian man can satisfy an American woman. They enjoy this a lot. They ask if you want more Italian men, of course. That is the problem with this story he tells. When we come out, they ask if you have – um – with him—'

'I got it!'

'—and they ask, of course, how it is, if you want more. They say that – ahem – anyway, it is bad, a bad situation. He should have talk with me, I would have found a better story,' Mario finished disapprovingly.

'Never mind. All's well that ends well,' she said, breathing out a great sigh of relief, feeling her muscles relax for the first time in what felt like weeks. 'I got what I came for. Hey, Leo.' She wasn't sure if she should touch him, so she just leaned forward, her head between the two front seats. '*Grazie, molto grazie*, OK? You were amazing. *Fantastico*, if that's even a word.'

Leo's impassive features cracked into a smile.

And then her phone rang. A withheld number, but that meant nothing: caller ID never worked overseas. She flicked the phone open and said:

'Yes?'

'Lola!' It was Evie's voice, and she was panicked. 'Lola, you've got to get back here as soon as possible! Somehow they've guessed you left the country on my passport! They'll be watching for you at all the airports, the cops have been to the apartment already, trying to see you – well, *me*. Suzanne's being amazing, she's been telling them I'm sick and they can't come in, but they're getting really pushy about it and we can't hold them off forever. George says they'll get a search warrant, because they suspect you've jumped bail!'

Evie took a breath, finally. '

'Lola, you've got to find a way to get back into the States without showing my passport! If you come in on mine, they'll arrest you and throw you in jail!'

From exhilaration to total panic in one short phone call. Lola took slow, deep breaths, doing her level best not to freak out completely. Her mission to Italy had been a complete success: she'd got what she needed from Scutellaro, the crucial contract that she had fought off knife-wielding feral kids to protect. But how on earth was she going to get herself back to New York undetected? The plan for her to travel on Evie's passport had been a brilliant one, taking the uncomfortable fact of their resemblance and turning it to her advantage. Evie had sneaked into the Plaza apartment and was living there as Lola, smuggled out at night to do her burlesque show but present during the day so the maids wouldn't report her absence to tabloid reporters prepared to pay huge sums for any new stories on Lola.

A perfect plan, it had seemed when they hatched it barely two days ago. But now it seemed as if someone, somewhere, had found out what she was up to and reported it to the police. Who could possibly have done that? Lola trusted everyone in her inner circle implicitly!

Lola pushed the question away. She could deal with that one later. Right now, she had a much more pressing problem.

How the hell was she going to sneak herself and her precious contract back into the Plaza before the police got a search warrant and arrested Evie for impersonating her?

Chapter 33

*A*s Suzanne had predicted when she shut the door in their faces that morning, the two cops came back later on that day, around six in the evening. And this time they were determined not to be fobbed off.

'Mrs Fitzgerald?' said the first one, his jaw set. 'We're hoping your daughter will have recovered enough by now to be able to talk to us.'

'We just need to verify her presence in the apartment,' finished the other one. 'If you let us see her, we can be out of your hair in no time. If not, our lieutenant says to say we'll be back first thing tomorrow with a search warrant.'

'My God, this is ludicrous!' Suzanne protested furiously.

Evie and India, listening further down the corridor, exchanged glances of approval with each other at Suzanne's command of the scene. Her English accent had suddenly become much more pronounced and intimidating, and she had dressed up, expecting the return of the two detectives. In the black crepe suit she had worn to the funeral, pearls at her neck, and high heels to make sure that she towered over the two men, she reminded them both that she was recently bereaved, and also that she was Suzanne Myers, who had been a supermodel well before that word was even coined, and was still dazzlingly beautiful.

'*First* of all, I told you before when you came here at the crack of dawn this morning that it's Mrs Myers, not Mrs Fitzgerald,' Suzanne was correcting them.

'It was nine a.m.,' the lead cop muttered hopelessly. 'Not exactly the crack of—'

'Oh boy, I know who you are!' exclaimed the second cop. Balding, sallow-faced, his leather jacket stretching over a larger stomach than it had been made for, he nudged his colleague in the ribs. 'Jerry, you know who this is? It's *Suzanne Myers!*'

'Jeez, the Sunsilk girl?' Jerry asked. 'No kidding! I thought I'd seen you before somewhere—'

'In your dreams!' the balding cop sniggered. 'That's where you've seen her!'

Jerry cleared his throat.

'Look, Mrs Myers, we do need to see your daughter. Like I said this morning, we've received a tip-off that she's left the jurisdiction. Which means that she's skipped bail, which is an arrestable offence. If we could just make sure she really is here, we'll leave you in peace—'

'We don't even both have to go in, if she's sick,' the balding one volunteered. 'Just one of us, if he gets a good look at her face. Five minutes, tops.'

'I'm really sorry about this, ma'am,' Jerry said unhappily. 'But we got our job to do. Like Detective Garcia says, five minutes is all it'd take. Or we'll be back in the morning with a search warrant.'

Evie and India sneaked back down the corridor, into Lola's bedroom, Evie climbing under the covers.

'How do I look?' she asked.

India squinted at her face.

'Horrible,' she said cheerfully. India dabbed her fingers in a glass of water standing on the bedside table, and ran them quickly through the locks of Evie's hair hanging round her face. 'Nice and limp,' she said with satisfaction. 'OK, you're as ready as you'll ever be.'

Nipping across the room, she drew the heavy curtains, plunging the room into near-total darkness; the only light was a lamp across the room, on the dressing table, and India sat down in an armchair next to it, picking up a book. Footsteps were coming down the corridor, and the next thing they heard was a tap on the closed bedroom door.

'India? How is she?' Suzanne's voice came. 'The policemen are here again, and they insist on seeing her – it's *too* upsetting—'

'Come in!' India called quietly.

As the door swung open, India was putting down her book and rising from her armchair, haloed from behind by the glow of the lamp, the picture of a nurse watching quietly over her patient.

'She's been sleeping,' India said. 'I think the antihistamines finally kicked in and knocked her out, thank goodness.'

'What's wrong with her?' Jerry, half-concealed behind Suzanne, asked anxiously. 'I didn't realise she was, y'know, *sick*. She infectious?'

'We hope not,' Suzanne sighed. 'She's *very* sensitive. Ever since she was a little girl, she's been highly prone to catch anything that's going round, poor child. We'll call the doctor if she's no better in the morning,' Suzanne said.

Evie decided this was her cue.

'Mummy?' she said in the croaky voice of someone just woken from sleep, turning over in bed. She put a hand up to shield her eyes from the light, careful not to touch her face. 'Mummy, is that you?'

'Darling!' Suzanne rushed over to her bedside. 'You're awake! Oh God, we woke you up!' She darted a furious look at Jerry over her shoulder.

'My face hurts,' Evie whined in her best English accent. 'And my head.'

'Is it any better than before?' Suzanne rested her hand on Evie's limp golden curls. 'Oh dear, you're all sweaty—'

'Hot,' Evie croaked.

'I wonder if we *should* call the doctor now—'

'I just want to sleep, Mummy,' Evie said fretfully. 'Who are these people?'

Sitting up, she looked over at Jerry. And as he got a good look at her face, he recoiled with an audible gasp.

'Jeez, is she OK?' he exclaimed. 'She looks terrible!'

'We think it's an allergic reaction, Detective,' Suzanne explained, managing successfully to keep the triumph out of her voice. 'Lola has always been sensitive. And you can imagine, with what she's been going through at the moment—'

'Um, sure. Yeah. Tricky time,' he mumbled, still staring at Evie's face.

India had done wonders. Not just the skin of Evie's face, but her neck, and the part of her cleavage that could be seen above the neckline of Lola's silk pyjama top, was a series of pink welts, made from Benefit liquid blusher mixed into skin mattifying cream, which had dried into a dull, chalky paste.

From a distance, it was very effective. But the paste was a little grainy, and India had worried about it beginning to break away round its edges as Evie moved, leaving tell-tale pink crumbs on the sheets. Evie's instructions had been to sit up once, slowly and carefully, and stay propped up against the pillows until – hopefully – the cops left again, satisfied. For extra effect, India had dabbed dark blue eyeshadow circles under Evie's eyes to make her look haggard. Staring plaintively at the detective now, Evie read nothing but concern in his eyes: certainly no doubt that she wasn't Lola Fitzgerald.

'Can I go back to sleep now, Mummy?' she asked plaintively. 'I'm *so* tired!'

'Uh, sure you can,' Jerry mumbled, waving a hand at Suzanne, who crossed the room to Evie's side. 'Get better soon, Miss Fitzgerald! Sorry to disturb you when you're not feeling well.'

Suzanne saw the cops out and then rushed back down the corridor excitedly.

'They've gone!' she said excitedly. 'It worked!'

'Oh, thank *fuck*,' Evie said, rubbing furiously at her face and neck. 'This stuff is so itchy, it's been driving me crazy! Nice job, India,' she added. 'Did you *see* his face when he caught sight of me?'

'He actually backed away,' India said complacently. 'It was perfect.'

'This won't hold them for ever, though,' Suzanne said, crossing the room and throwing open the curtains again. She stared out, at the first shadows of dusk falling gently over Central Park. 'He'll go back and say he saw you in a darkened room, with stuff all over your face. And that'll make them wonder. Don't forget, they've got an idea Lola has a double, because they suspect she's travelling on Evie's passport.'

'How on earth is she going to get back into the country, with them watching the airports?' India asked.

'Fly to Canada, hire a car and drive down to New York?' Evie suggested. 'They don't check the Canadian border half as much as they should.'

'With her own driving licence and credit cards?' India said gloomily. 'They're probably running checks on the cards – they'll spot her as soon as she tries to use one.'

'She said she had a plan,' Suzanne said quietly, still staring over the darkening park. 'I just hope to God it works . . .'

Apart from a week or so when the variations in the dates of summer time mean that the United States and Continental Europe aren't evenly synchronised, the European mainland is always six hours later than the east coast of America. So, at six-thirty in Manhattan, as her mother stared into Central Park and prayed for her safety, Lola Fitzgerald was sitting in a first-class seat on the night train from Rome to Milan, at twelve-thirty a.m., doing her best to get some sleep.

Everything depended on this final gamble. If they arrested her on her return to the US, Evie would be implicated too. No one would believe that Lola had somehow managed to steal Evie's passport. Evie, as well as Lola, would be arrested. And if Lola protested that she had only jumped bail and gone to Italy to track down Joe Scutellaro and make him tell the truth – well, not only would the Van der Veers have to pay a cool $5 million for her bail costs, but she would have to admit that she had bribed Scutellaro.

Right now, the plan was for Scutellaro to break down on the stand, to admit that Carin Fitzgerald had put so much pressure on him to lie that he had gone along with it at the grand jury hearing, but that now, with Lola herself directly before his eyes, sitting at the defendant's table, he was unable to keep perjuring himself to frame an innocent woman. It would be plausible, dramatic and, after all, mostly true; the only lie would be why he had changed his story, and George Goldman was confident that no court would be able to trace the payment that Lola had already made to Joe Scutellaro, nor the one that would be made after the successful outcome of her trial.

'Once a case is over, that's it,' George had explained to Lola. 'The DA's office is always more strained and has way fewer resources than private attorneys. No way they'll put their forensic accountants on the job of tracing a payment that happens after a trial. He's got nothing to worry about.'

So it was absolutely crucial that she manage to get herself back to New York, up into the apartment at the Plaza, before the police came back and discovered their deception. With all of this on her mind, Lola had been sure she wouldn't be able to sleep, but the rocking movement of the train was more lulling than she had expected. With her pashmina rolled up to support her neck, her seat tilted back, she went out like a light for five hours straight as the train sped up the backbone of Italy. Florence, Bologna, Modena, all flickered past, their white-on-blue station signs illuminated briefly in the glare of sodium lights before disappearing into the dark Italian night.

She only awoke because the conductor was walking down the carriage calling: '*Milano! Milano Centrale!*' so loudly that her eyes snapped open, blinking in the pale morning light, and instinctively she grabbed at her pashmina and the bag which she had wedged behind her back as she slept, to ensure no one could steal it.

Trying not to breathe in too much diesel from the huge train engines, she made her way to the central part of the station, where the platforms met the concourse and gigantic buffers held each engine at a stop. There she drank an espresso at the bar, checked the timetables, and under an hour later she was jumping down off the local train at the station for Lake Como, dawn breaking overhead in a delicate explosion of pinks and blues and gold. There were still clouds overhead, but in a few hours the sun would have burned away the haze and be gleaming down over the lake.

There were taxis outside the station, and she hesitated, wondering whether to take one. A woman behind her, who had also got off the local, was doing much the same. She was the classic badly dressed tourist, in a big floral dress with a dropped waist that did nothing for her tall lumpy figure, and Birkenstock sandals worn over socks. The straw hat, pulled low over her face despite the early hour, was the final touch; only tourists ever bought the straw hats that were sold at every Italian market. Italians had no prejudice against exposing their faces to the sun.

In the distance, Lola could see the lake for which Como was famous, glittering already in the early-morning sun. She had been on the lake before, visiting friends, staying in a suite at the five-star Grand Hotel Villa Serbelloni at Bellagio. Always, of course, they had taken speedboats, private launches, to whisk them wherever on the lake they wanted to go, swimming, picnicking, once even to a party at George Clooney's villa, though the film star had barely shown his face, much to the disappointment of the *jeunesse dorée*, the golden young people who had been invited to party with him. And though she had always been on a private launch, you couldn't help noticing the hydrofoils and the ferries that took the common folk back and forth across the lake.

That's what I'll do, she thought. *I'll take a boat to Bellagio. Watch the sun come up.*

So she walked past the taxi rank, crossing the street, in the direction of the lake. It was easy to find her way down to the marina; she bought a ticket and walked down the pier to board the ferry, taking a seat right at the back, in the open air, where the view was already stunning.

She was pretty much alone, this early in the morning. The

woman from the station boarded – Lola couldn't help noticing her, in that drab frock and wide-brimmed hat. A typical tourist, she fished in her bag for her camera and took some photographs of Como behind them, the beautiful panorama of the town stretching round the little marina. And then she went back inside and sat down in the cabin, leaving Lola the outside deck quite to herself.

The faint mist still hanging over the lake was like a delicate veil, pulling back slowly, its edges fading and drifting downwards as the gradually strengthening rays of the sun dissolved it away. Lola twisted in her seat to watch the pretty town of Como receding slowly as the ferry puttered away, its pale pink and white buildings, which curved in welcome round the bay, fading in the distance as the ferry picked up speed. The villages on the lake passed, one by one, each a cluster of cream and pink and ochre houses around a white-painted pier. Beautiful white villas, with terraces over the water, and paths leading down to their private jetties, each set in its own grand hillside site, slipped by, most with their turquoise or emerald shutters still drawn, their occupants not yet awake at this hour. A cluster of swans swam beside the ferry as they pulled out of Varenna, circling in its wake. Seagulls cried overhead, swooping and ducking in whirls of activity, and a shoal of ducks gathered at the shore, an old lady standing there, leaning on an umbrella she was using as a walking stick, throwing stale bread to them and shooing away the seagulls that came flying down to claim some of the food.

By the time they docked at Bellagio, Lola felt as collected and as calm as she had ever been in her whole life. The hour-and-a-half aboard the ferry had been like a meditation, a clearing of all her doubts and fears. She had redone her make-up, and now she surveyed herself in the little mirror of her Guerlain compact, approving her work. She didn't look like an international fugitive who had arrived in the country less than twenty-four hours ago, been attacked by a group of feral kids, had a long journey practically from one end of Italy to the other, and survived on a few hours of sleep snatched here and there. She looked, instead, like a Marie Laurencin painting: big dark eyes, full pink lips, pale, glowing skin, her blonde hair pulled back in a twist at the nape of her neck, over-sized Dior sunglasses propped on the crown of her head, scented with roses from her Stella perfume.

Lola was the last person off the ferry, but the openly appreciative stares of the captain and crew, the uniformed man waiting for her to walk down the wide gangplank, showed nothing but approval for her appearance. On dry land again, she headed up the main street of Bellagio village towards the Grand Hotel Villa Serbelloni, where she got the doorman to call her a taxi. Above them, a helicopter buzzed noisily, flying over the lake to the hills beyond, like a huge dragon-fly, so low she could almost see the markings on its undercarriage.

'Villa Aurora,' she said to the driver as he pulled up.

The doorman jumped to open the door for her, and the driver raised his eyebrows, impressed at her destination. The cab swung round the small turning circle outside the elegant frontage of the Villa Serbelloni, climbing the hill behind the village, describing a few steep curves descending on the far side before taking a narrow, unmarked turn and stopping just a hundred yards later in front of a high metal security gate set in a hedge so thick that it was quite impossible to know what lay beyond. There was no sign, nothing to indicate that this was indeed the Villa Aurora, but certainly all the cab drivers from here to Como knew how to find the entrance to one of the grandest and most expensive private residences on the whole of Lake Como.

Lola was already climbing out of the car. Heart in her mouth, she walked up to the intercom button set in the wall next to the gate, pressing it. When it buzzed to life, she said clearly:

'It's Lola Fitzgerald. For Mr van der Veer.'

Above her head, a security camera swivelled, angling down, get-ting a good view of her as she stood there, the fingers of her left hand in her jeans pocket, the index and middle fingers clamped so tightly together she could barely feel them any more.

There was no answer. No request for her to repeat her name. Just a long, long silence, so prolonged that Lola began to fear that they would just make her stand out there while endless time passed, while the sun climbed higher in the blue sky, till she realised that she would never be admitted to Villa Aurora.

And then, finally, just as she really was giving up hope, the gate mechanism whirred into motion. Her heart surging in excitement, she stepped back, hoping she hadn't misheard.

But no, it hadn't been a mirage. The gates were sliding away from her, opening up.

She was inside.

Chapter 34

'*Mamma mia*,' muttered the driver, who knew where Villa Aurora was, but clearly had never seen it before.

This isn't even the best part, Lola reflected. *This is really only the back of the villa. The front gives onto the lake; these houses were all designed to be approached from the water.*

But even the rear of Villa Aurora was enough to take your breath away. As a hotel, it would have been superb; as a private residence, it was stunningly impressive, a Palladian villa. With its white marble colonnades, its high gracious windows, it was like something out of a fairy tale. The drive was immaculately groomed, the gravel glittering like mica in the sun, bordered by perfectly clipped hedges and miniature formal Italian gardens on each side. In the centre was a turning circle, its grass sleek with daily watering, and a huge marble fountain, in the centre the goddess Pomona, pouring out water into a marble basin as big as a bathtub, surrounded by attendant nymphs.

The cab stopped in front of the wide marble staircase that led up to the main door, and the driver was already jumping out with alacrity to open the door for her. She tipped him well, for luck.

A wrought-iron bell-pull hung beside the big carved door, and she tugged on it, hearing an old-fashioned bell clang dully somewhere deep within the villa. Eventually, she heard footsteps approaching, and not in any great hurry. One of the double doors swung open gradually, and beyond it stood Villa Aurora's housekeeper, a middle-aged woman in a black dress, with nicely groomed hair and very good gold jewellery, staring at Lola with utter and absolute disapproval in her beady dark eyes.

And suddenly, it all came flooding back to Lola. The last time she'd been here, with Jean-Marc. And the time before. Both with groups of friends, all party animals, all determined to live life to the full, no matter how many drugs they had to take, or how much chaos they created for the staff. Skinny-dipping off the pier, drunken excursions in the speedboats. Chopping up lines in full view of everyone who worked at the villa, on the polished travertine tables meant only for displaying the exquisite collection of Buhl candelabra that Jean-Marc's family had assembled over centuries. Bed-swapping, orgies; Lola hadn't participated in those, but she'd known about them and laughed at the stories. Roaringly loud music, crates of vintage champagne emptied in an instant as Jean-Marc yelled for more, glasses smashed everywhere. Some incredibly valuable vase had been broken, she remembered. Two crazy Swiss girls had surfed down the main staircase naked, sitting on trays, and then had a cat fight in the swimming pool and nearly drowned; hadn't they had to call a doctor? She knew a doctor had been called for *someone* . . .

They must have left the staff with weeks of work just to clear up after the mess they'd made.

'Um, Maria?' Lola began, not even knowing how to apologise for what she'd done.

'*Marta*,' the woman corrected, folding her hands in front of her, her glare intensifying.

'Marta. *Sorry.*' Instantly, Lola was wrong-footed. '*Really* sorry I got your name wrong. And I'm so sorry too for – for all the mess we made when we visited before—' Lola attempted.

'That is your affair,' Marta said coldly. 'It is not my business. My business is to look after the family.'

She gestured beyond her, to the main living-room that led onto the spectacular terrace.

'Mr Niels is waiting for you,' she said.

How could I have forgotten about the parties we threw here? Lola thought guiltily as she walked across the entrance hall, her shoes echoing on the marble floor. *Because I was off my face most of the time. Too off my face to wonder why Jean-Marc and I never ended up sleeping together.*

Huge, priceless embroidered silk tapestries hung on either side of the hall, depicting Perseus fighting the sea monster to rescue Andromeda; on the left, Perseus was swooping down on the monster, sword in hand; on the right, he was unchaining Andromeda, who was swooning into his arms, her bosoms falling out of her dress in relief. They were 15th-century, truly priceless, and Lola had a horrible flash of memory associated with them: some girl at one of the parties grabbing the deep gold silk fringe that hung below each tapestry and trying to swing on them.

And had Lola done anything to stop her? She didn't think so. She'd probably yelled some laughing encouragement and poured more champagne down the back of her throat.

I must have been loaded the whole time, she thought in shame. *No wonder Marta made it very clear she didn't want to let me in.*

'What the *hell* are you doing in Italy?' Niels demanded the moment she crossed the threshold into the main reception room. 'I seem to remember us laying down a considerable sum to guarantee your bail! Five hundred thousand, wasn't it? And you had to surrender your goddamn passport! What the *hell* are you doing out of America? Do the authorities know about this?'

God, nothing gets past Niels, Lola realised. *Jean-Marc sorted out my bail. I didn't even realise Niels was involved. He must check on everything Jean-Marc does nowadays . . .*

She stood in the doorway, looking at Niels. His back was to the terrace, to the sun, so his face was in shadow, and she couldn't see his expression. But she didn't really need to. She was sure he was glowering at her. He was dressed more casually than she had ever seen him, in jeans and a long-sleeved black T-shirt, rolled up to just below his elbows, revealing his muscled forearms, while the jeans showed off his slim hips and strong thighs.

She gulped. For some reason, the thought of Niels's thighs always sent her into temporary paralysis.

'Hello! Wake up!' Niels actually snapped his fingers at her, which was so annoying that it did have the effect of bringing her out of her momentary trance. 'Are you going to explain yourself, or are you just going to stand there gaping like a goldfish?'

Oh, thank God. He'd made her angry. At least this way she could talk back to him.

'I am *not* gaping like a goldfish!' she said crossly. 'I'm just trying to get a word in edgewise!' She cleared her throat. 'I did jump bail,' she admitted. 'I'm not supposed to leave the States. But it was for a really good reason. I—'

Niels strode across the room to the terrace, flinging open the doors.

'*Five million dollars!*' he exploded. 'You realise that's what we'll have to pay for this little exploit of yours? Five million dollars, because you got bored in New York and thought you wanted to pop over to get a little Italian sunshine! You're not even a member of the family any more, now that you're not my brother's future wife! But somehow, we've ended up covering your legal fees, your living expenses—'

'Actually, *Jean-Marc*'s doing that,' Lola retorted furiously. 'Out of his trust fund, which has nothing to do with you. And he's doing it because he's my best friend in the world, and also, frankly, because he completely humiliated me by getting engaged to me and sneaking off to have sex with boys in a tranny's drug den. Which if it had happened to a sister of yours, you'd be absolutely *furious* about!'

Niels stood with his back to her, staring out over Lake Como, his shoulders bunched with tension.

'You and Jean-Marc,' he muttered. 'I don't understand it. I don't understand why you got engaged. I don't understand how you could possibly have considered marrying each other.'

'It seemed like a good idea at the time,' Lola said rather feebly.

'So are you going to tell me what you're doing here?' he asked eventually, still not turning to look at her. 'How did you even know how to *find* me, for God's sake! I only arrived half an hour ago myself!'

'I rang your office and said I was calling from Cascabel, Jean-Marc's rehab centre,' Lola admitted. 'I said I needed to talk to you when you were in a private setting, not the office or travelling, and eventually they gave me this number and said you'd be here after nine, and I worked out it was the area code for Como. So I knew you must be coming here, to the villa.'

'Very super-spy,' Niels said sarcastically. 'Well, at least I don't have to worry about that call I was expecting from Cascabel any longer. Why didn't you just say who you were, instead of going through that elaborate pretence?'

'Because,' she said frankly, 'I didn't think you'd want your office to give me any information about where you were. I thought you'd have told them to hang up on me if I said who I was.'

Niels raised a hand and rubbed his forehead as if he were trying to get rid of a headache. Then he stepped outside, onto the terrace. Lola watched him walk away, admiring his strong, muscled back, his firm buttocks taut in the faded jeans. God, ever since she'd met Niels – or, to be honest, had sex with Niels – she'd turned into some sort of sex addict.

No! she told herself firmly. *No no no! I mustn't think about having sex with Niels when I'm talking to him . . . I'll get all embarrassed and distracted and forget what I need to say . . .*

Niels was leaning on the balustrade of the terrace, looking over the waters of the three lakes below. Villa Aurora was exceptionally placed, high up at the tip of the Bellagio promontory, affording it panoramic, sweeping views over the lake. Beyond, high wooded hills rose steeply on each side of the water, rich and lush.

'So,' Niels said finally, still not looking round at her.

He's barely looked at me since I came in, Lola thought forlornly. *He must really hate me.*

'You'd better tell me what's going on,' he continued. 'Obviously something is, and obviously I'm not going to get away without hearing it. So let's get it over with, eh?'

It wasn't a promising start, but beggars couldn't be choosers. As succinctly as she could, Lola told him everything, in the way she had been rehearsing on the whole long train and boat journey up from Rome. The story of what had happened the day of her father's death, how Joe had manoeuvred her into touching the syringe and the insulin. His accusation, which had caused her arrest. Her lawyers' concern that with the fingerprint evidence and his testimony, she was in real danger of being convicted for a crime she hadn't committed – the murder of her father, no less.

And her own determination to track down Joe and confront him, to plead with him and convince him to tell the truth.

There was a wrought-iron table on the terrace, four matching chairs around it, padded linen covers tied over them, a big parasol standing in the centre, its white canvas umbrella opened already to provide shade from the morning sun. Lola walked over to the table and set her bag down, pulling out from it the contract that Joe had signed, anchoring it under her phone so that it wouldn't blow away in the light breeze.

'There it is,' she said. 'Read it. You'll see.'

Niels turned around at last, resting his arms along the balustrade. The breeze caught his dark-blond hair, ruffling it up, and she thought he looked as if he had been somewhere hot in the past couple of weeks: his skin was tanned, the golden hairs on his arms glinting in the sun.

I must not *stare at his forearms,* Lola told herself firmly. *I must* not.

'Lola,' he said wearily, 'all that contract proves is that you paid some corrupt little man a lot of money, and agreed to pay him a small fortune if he lies for you on the witness stand.'

Angry words burst from Lola's mouth, but Niels held up a hand to silence her.

'Or tells the truth for you, OK,' he continued. 'But all it proves to me is that this Scutellaro is corruptible. Not what he did, or didn't see you do the day your father died.'

Lola's eyes flashed fire.

'Right,' she said with icy coldness. 'Fine. If you really think I'm capable of killing my own father, there's nothing more to be said, is there?' She snatched the contract off the table and forced it back into its folder. 'I don't know why I bothered to even try to convince you in the first place!' she snapped. 'What was the point? If you really have any doubt about whether I *killed my own father* for *money*, then I'm completely wasting my time here.'

She put the folder back in her bag and slung the whole thing over her shoulder.

'I know I've got a bit of a sordid past,' she said bravely. 'I know Jean-Marc and I were spoilt idiots who partied much too hard and haven't done a day's work in our lives, either of us. But believe me, we've both learned our lesson. Jean-Marc's at Cascabel, and I haven't touched drugs since that night at Maud's. And I won't be going near them any more. We're both cleaning up our acts. You can believe that or not, as you want. I don't give a damn what you think of me.'

She ticked points off on her fingers.

'Yes, I was a spoilt party girl. Yes, I lived off the money that my father made and didn't lift a finger to try to earn any myself. Yes, I cared much too much about getting my picture in the glossies and sitting in the front row at fashion shows and being famous for doing nothing at all apart from wearing the latest clothes. All of that's pretty pathetic. I get it. But *none* of it makes me a murderess. Particularly someone who'd kill her *own father*! Your own brother's been supporting me ever since I got arrested! Do you really think he'd do that if he thought I'd killed my father? Do you really think he's such an idiot that he can't tell I'm innocent?'

She was almost out of breath by now, she was so angry.

'So you know what, Niels van der Veer? Go to hell. Fuck you, if you can't see what kind of person I am. Fuck you and the horse you rode in on.'

She turned on her heel.

'And now, if you'll excuse me,' she said over her shoulder, 'I'm walking out of here, if you wouldn't mind telling Marta to buzz the gates open for me. Don't bother to call me a cab. The walk back down to town will do me good.'

Lola had failed, completely failed. She was going to have to get herself back to Milan, head to Malpensa airport, and board a plane with Evie's passport, knowing that she was sure to be arrested as soon as she stepped back onto American soil.

But strangely, as Lola walked away across the terrace, the heels of her boots clicking loudly on the marble floor of the reception room, she was full of a sense of triumph that she had barely ever experienced before. Her head was buzzing with excitement. All her life, she had done what her father said, lived the carefree, society-girl existence he had chosen for her. She'd never said no to him, never done anything he didn't want, never made a single real decision of her own. There had been nothing to rebel against, because Ben Fitzgerald had wanted only the best for her.

Lola had achieved more in these past two days than she had managed in her entire over-indulged, rich-girl life. And standing up to Niels van der Veer, telling him to go to hell, was the culmination of it all. He was the strongest, most powerful, most intimidating man she had ever met; and still, she had managed to tell him exactly what she thought of him, and done it, too, in a way so articulate that she could be really proud of herself.

She was so high on her own success that she didn't even hear Niels coming after her, had no idea that he wasn't still standing on the terrace, until his hand grasped her arm and he said:

'Lola – Lola, don't go. I'm sorry. I really am sorry.'

She stopped, but she didn't turn around. She made him come to her, walk around her till he was looking down at her. And she shook his hand off her arm for good measure.

'I deserve that,' he said, grimacing.

His silvery eyes were softer than they had ever seemed before; their expression was almost pleading.

'Don't go,' he repeated. 'Tell me what you need. Tell me what you came here for.' He swallowed. 'I'm sorry, Lola.'

*

The sound of her name on Niels van der Veer's lips was so power-ful that she would have given him anything he wanted, just to hear him call her by her name again. She realised that she had hardly ever heard him say it: he had always been snapping at her. '*You*,' said with contempt in her direction, was probably the best she'd ever got from him until that moment just now.

When he'd said 'Lola', three times, almost – for him – implor-ingly, it had melted her as if she'd been made of wax, and Niels had been holding a blowtorch.

But at least she hadn't let him see. That was the key, she was real-ising as she grew up. You could feel anything in the world you wanted, as long as you could disguise it when you needed to.

So, eventually, she had consented to follow him back out to the terrace, and he had asked what she needed, and called Marta to organise her breakfast – whatever she wanted, everything they had that she might like – and gone off to make a series of phone calls. And now she was sitting here, in the shade of the umbrella, watch-ing the shining waters of Lake Como ripple gently in the breeze, sipping freshly squeezed blood-orange juice, and picking at the feast that a maid had carried out on a silver tray and arranged on the table.

There was a whole salver of the sweet pastries Italians ate for breakfast: almond croissants, dusted with a matt covering of icing sugar; brioches golden and shiny with egg-yolk glaze; little fruit tarts, rich with pastry cream and dotted with bright red berries; pains au chocolat, drizzled with zigzags of dark confectioner's chocolate. And of course, a cup of cappuccino, the milk thick and perfectly foamed.

But in case she preferred to eat something savoury, there were platefuls of tempting little morsels. Bright green broad beans, podded, mixed in with tiny cubes of pecorino cheese, placed on slices of prosciutto and rolled up into little packets, drizzled with extra-virgin Tuscan olive oil; slices of *torta salata*, the Italian version of the French quiche, made with spring peas and new-season chives; a mousse of radicchio, sitting in a pool of savoury cream, toast fingers on the side to dip into it; a dish of smoked salmon and swordfish, sliced so fine she could see the pattern of the china below, arranged in the centre of a circle of lemon wedges and feathery silver-green fennel leaves.

Everything simple and elegant and of the best quality, nothing showy.

I should send Marta a really nice present, she thought. *Something from Fendi. She's very classic, she'd love Fendi. Even if I never come back here again, I should apologise properly for all the trouble we caused.*

'Lola?'

Niels appeared in the open doors to the terrace.

'I've arranged everything,' he said. 'The plane's refuelling now. Have you had enough to eat?'

She nodded, standing up and reaching for her bag. Niels looked at the table, still brimming with food.

'You've hardly touched anything!' he said. 'Did you not like the breakfast?'

Oh, for God's sake, Lola thought, rolling her eyes. *I had a pro-sciutto parcel, some smoked salmon, some salad and half a croissant! I ate so much I feel sick! Do you not know women like me barely eat anything to keep ourselves as slim as we are? Do you think I'm a size two because I have a really, really fast metabolism?*

Men, she sighed. *They don't want you to be fat, but they hate it when you tell them how much you diet. Bloody hypocrites, all of them.*

'I'm fine, really,' she said, smiling at him.

He looked away.

'Come on,' he said, turning and plunging down the stone staircase to the side of the terrace.

Niels was leading her down a gravel path, along the side of the house, past what, in a month or so, would be a spectacular rose garden, when the flowers that were budding now started to bloom. He was walking so fast, taking such long strides, that she had to trot inelegantly to keep up with him. The path began to rise again, taking them through a thickly grown tunnel of boxwood planted steeply up round the side of the villa. And then the hedges rose on either side to a topiary arch, the ground levelled out, and they emerged into a clearing cut into the woodland, a big circle of poured grey concrete, painted with the unmistakeable markings that identified a helicopter landing pad.

Not that Lola needed to see them. The Sikorsky helicopter sitting in the centre of the concrete was indication enough.

As soon as the pilot saw Niels come through the arch of hedge he started up the engine, the blades spinning in a whir of noise. Niels crossed to the open door, climbed in and held out a hand to Lola, helping to swing her up. They took the two back seats, strapping themselves in, donning big padded ear protectors, as the co-pilot checked that they were settled and told the pilot they were clear for takeoff. A few seconds later, they were lifting off the ground in a constant blur and hum of noise, Lola craning her head sideways to watch as the beautiful Palladian lines of Villa Aurora were gradually obscured by the surrounding fir trees. The Sikorsky dipped down, back over the Villa Serbelloni, to cross the lake once again.

This was the helicopter she had seen coming in when she was outside the Grand Hotel Villa Serbelloni, she realised. This was how Niels had arrived at Villa Aurora. *Oh God, poor Niels just got here himself.* He'd probably visited Bellagio for a few days' rest, swimming in the pool, sunbathing, fishing on the lake; and here he was, dragged out again because she'd turned up on his doorstep like a bedraggled waif, begging for his help.

Still, he'd just load her onto the Van der Veer jet at Malpensa and then he could jump right back into his helicopter again, return to Villa Aurora, and keep going where he'd left off before she interrupted his peace and quiet . . .

But that didn't seem to be at all what Niels had in mind. At the foot of the steps leading up to the jet, she turned, holding out her hand to shake his goodbye. She didn't feel remotely comfortable enough with him to kiss him on the cheek, as she normally would have done. She was scared that if she got that physically close to him, she wouldn't be able to control her attraction to him.

'Thank you so much,' she said in heartfelt tones. 'You've saved my life, you really have.'

'You're a bit premature, Princess,' he drawled.

The sun was behind her now, and she could see the fine white lines around his eyes as he narrowed them against its glare.

'What do you mean?' she said nervously.

'I'm coming with you to New York. To make sure everything goes OK,' he said nonchalantly. 'I'll probably take the jet on to Houston afterwards. I've got meetings planned there for next week – I can get my office to move them forwards.'

'You're coming to New York too?' Lola heard her voice go up a whole register, suddenly higher and squeakier than her dignity would like.

'What, don't want my company?' Niels said, raising his eyebrows. 'Too bad. I'm not spending a fortune in fuel to take this plane across the Atlantic without seeing some business benefit from it.'

He glanced at his watch.

'Come on, Princess, we have a tight flight slot to make. It took all the pull I had to get us cleared for takeoff now. Get your bottom up those steps before we miss it, eh?'

Behind him, a *Vogue* model dressed in a stewardess's uniform designed by Giorgio Armani tapped him on the shoulder, smiling. She was tall and blonde and the way she was looking at Niels made Lola's fingers curl into claws.

'Mr van der Veer? I hear we're boarding,' she said flirtatiously.

'Hi, Lesley,' Niels said, returning her smile so appreciatively that Lola's nails sank into her palms. 'We are, you're not. How do you feel about an all-expenses-paid stay in Milan for a few days?'

Lesley's big green eyes widened.

'I feel very good about that, Mr van der Veer,' she said enthusiastically. 'Nice of you to ask.'

'I was hoping you'd say that. Talk to Nazario in the office, he'll organise everything. And Lesley?' He held out his hand. 'That's not quite all I need from you . . .'

Lola wasn't going to stay and watch Niels flirt with his stewardess.

She climbed the stairs to the jet, sighing with happiness as she took in the familiar, luxurious surroundings, the enormous pale beige leather seats, the pristine white carpet, the door to the large (by airplane standards) bathroom at the back of the plane.

She put down her Vuitton bag, stretched to the ceiling, cricking out her back, and sat down in one of the ridiculously comfortable leather seats, buckling herself in.

And then her eyes widened as she finally realised something that should have been obvious to her already.

Niels had just told the stewardess she wouldn't be needed onboard this flight. Surely that meant he wanted to be alone with Lola?

Oh God. She felt an instant, automatic rush of heat between her legs. Alone with Niels, miles up in the air. Was it really a good idea?

Yes! God yes! answered the lower part of her body immediately. *I mean, he's insanely hot, and what else are we going to do for the next eight hours?*

Lola consulted an organ rather higher up her body. But even her brain wasn't much help.

After all, it pointed out, *you must have had some idea that this must happen when you tracked Niels down in Como. I mean, you generally don't seem able to be alone with each other without something of the sort happening, do you? Admit it – you've been fantasising about seeing Niels again, haven't you?*

Niels came up the steps into the plane and, without looking at Lola, ducked into the cockpit to say something to the pilots.

'We're cleared for takeoff,' he said gruffly as he emerged, taking a seat next to hers across the aisle, and buckling himself in. 'Not too much turbulence expected. Might be a couple of bumps as we go over the Alps.'

Lola nodded. Shyly, slyly, she looked sideways at him as the plane began to move, at his long legs in faded old denim, sprawled out in front of him. At his profile, as craggy and intimidating as the Alps themselves. And at his big hands, with their strong, inelegant fingers, as they picked up a *Financial Times*, burying his face now behind a sheet of pink newspaper. Golden hairs on the back of his hands, running up his forearms.

Oh God, she was looking at his arms. At his wide powerful wrists, at the cords of muscle in his forearms, at the veins running round the muscle . . .

That did it. She was going to have sex with him in the next eight hours, whether he liked it or not.

Chapter 35

Niels, however, seemed to have suddenly turned into a Trappist monk. The only responses he made to Lola's attempts at conversation were in grunts, as if he had taken a vow of silence. He practically covered his face with the *Financial Times* as if he had also taken a vow never to look at a woman again. It was entirely baffling to Lola: why had he insisted on accompanying her, why had he sent away the stewardess, if he hadn't meant to try something?

Maybe he was in a mood. Or tired. Men weren't always desperate to jump your bones, after all; maybe he had a headache. She should rest for a couple of hours, try to sleep; perhaps he'd feel more friendly in a while.

But her brain was racing, and not just her brain. Sitting so close to Niels, so close she could smell his cologne, was much too distracting for her to be able to close her eyes and relax.

'You can unbuckle your seat belts now, guys,' the pilot said over the intercom. 'I'll holler if we've got anything bumpy coming up, but right now we're cruising nice and comfortably. Should be pretty smooth all the way over.'

Lola unbuckled hers and turned to Niels.

'I'm going to take a shower,' she informed him.

'Go ahead,' he grunted without looking at her, still buried in the newspaper.

She walked to the back of the plane, sitting down and taking off her boots with huge relief: with only two-inch heels, made of softest suede by Ferragamo, they were as comfortable as boots could possibly be, but they had been her only footwear for three days straight now, and her feet were getting pretty sore. Behind the curtain that separated the bathroom and the galley area from the main part of the cabin, she stripped off all her clothes and dived into the shower. It was fully stocked with Chopard body products, and a few minutes later, slathered with Chopard body lotion, she wrapped her hair in a small towel, herself in a larger one, slid her small feet into a pair of slippers that were much too big for her, and emerged from the bathroom in a cloud of perfumed steam that must, surely, be very attractive to the man sitting in the main cabin. And he must be aware, too, that she was quite naked under the towel . . .

'Would you like a glass of champagne?' she asked, padding back down the aisle.

Niels looked up, briefly, and nodded a grudging acceptance. He had moved onto the *Economist* now, she noticed.

'There are robes on the back of the door,' he mumbled gruffly.

'They're too big for me,' she said, favouring him with her best smile. 'I trip over the hem and go flying.'

But he wasn't even looking at her; he'd buried his head in the magazine again. Furious, she went over to the fridge and pulled it open, retrieving a bottle of Krug and two chilled glasses. What could she possibly do to get his attention?

Well, I could hand him his glass of champagne, smiling at him, and let my towel fall open over my leg while I'm doing it—

But Niels's Trappist monk impression even survived the sight of Lola's bare thigh peeping temptingly through the borders of the white towel. His eyes slid away from her immediately, taking the champagne flute with a grunt of thanks and setting it down on the table next to him.

Sighing, Lola set hers down too and looked around for an ice bucket. There was probably one in the galley, but she didn't feel like going to hunt for it, not with Niels busy pretending that she didn't even exist. She padded back to the fridge, put the bottle in the door, and slammed it shut petulantly.

Then she let out a yelp of surprise. In her annoyance with Niels, she hadn't been watching what she was doing. The closing door of the small fridge had caught the edge of the towel that was wrapped round her, trapping it, and as the door slammed shut, it had dragged the towel right off her.

She was naked. Apart from the slippers.

Lola clamped a hand over her mouth in an automatic gesture of shock as Niels, alerted by her yelp, lifted his head from his magazine and, finally, looked straight at her. Before that moment, she had been visited with the urge to laugh; it was pretty funny – she must look like a complete idiot . . .

But the way Niels was staring at her, his grey eyes silvery and hot, instantly dried up any instinct she might have had to giggle.

With one hand, he reached down and unsnapped his seat-belt buckle, a loud metal click that had never seemed remotely erotic before to Lola, and from now on would always be associated for her with sex. Niels was on his feet in a second, striding towards her, and instinctively, almost scared of what she had started, her hands flew to cover her breasts. It was too much to be naked in front of him when he was fully clothed, too much of a power imbalance. And she realised suddenly that she had never seen him naked. Her mouth watered at the thought of it.

Niels was upon her now, and there was nowhere to go. His hands were in her hair, dragging off the damp towel she had wrapped around her head, tangling in her wet hair, pulling her head back roughly, tilting it up to his: his mouth came down on hers, hard and demanding, and she moaned as his tongue slid past her lips, filling her mouth, hardly letting her breathe.

His body was forcing itself against her, the rough denim of his jeans, the buttons of his swollen fly, hurting her soft bare skin, and she pressed against him even more, wanting to feel every inch of him, even if it hurt her. One of his hands left her hair and shoved between their bodies, his fingers diving into her, making her come up on tiptoe, finding her so wet already that he groaned against her mouth, biting at her lips as he fingered her. His palm rubbed against her mound, his fingers curled around her, and she screamed into his mouth as she started to come, so ready for him that it made her blush with embarrassment and pleasure as she clung round his neck with both her arms. She was lifting herself up for him, his other hand twined in her hair, pulling it, as she came hard against his hand, came again and again till she was begging him to stop, that it was too much, she couldn't take any more for now.

The next thing she knew, still in a haze of such pleasure that her legs were buckling and wouldn't bear her weight any longer, was him spinning her round and bending her over the back of an armchair, his hand still in her hair as the other one unpopped his fly buttons and pushed down his jeans and his boxers over his distended cock. The next second he slammed into her with such force that she cried out; the hand that was twined in her hair pulled her up painfully, the other one came round and clamped over her mouth.

He pounded her against the chair, the leather sticky now with her own sweat, his cock slamming into her, her back bent upwards, tugged by the rope of her own hair that he was using to pull her, position her, exactly where he wanted. She screamed again, and he just pulled her hair harder.

'Don't make a sound—' he groaned in her ear, sliding in and out of her so hard and fast she saw stars.

She was melting, dissolving away. He was fucking her so hard she was melting into the chair, her arms flung out along its back for balance, his T-shirt sticking to her spine as his hips pounded against hers. She could feel the big muscles of his thighs, the hair on them scratching against her, the hair at the base of his cock, and the sensations were so exquisite that she closed her eyes to savour them more, to feel everything she possibly could. For a moment, she thought she would overload on pleasure, that she would faint, as his cock drove up inside her so high that, despite his instructions, she couldn't help moaning again.

Niels's hand left her mouth. Biting her own lip, she wondered what he would do next, and in a second, she knew: he smacked her on the bottom with a crack of his palm against her skin, soft with body lotion, damp with both their sweat, and she bit her lip harder not to cry out. Even when he did it again, she didn't make a sound, agonising though it was not to cry out with sheer pleasure at how much she enjoyed it.

She couldn't believe the depths of perversity they were finding in each other, how perfectly they were matched; somehow everything Niels did to her was what she had been craving without even realising it. It was incredibly risky; it relied on an absolute understanding, an absolute parity between them, and dimly, with no experience of this kind of sex at all, she thought that it must be incredibly unusual, too, that they could communicate so well physically without a word being exchanged.

And then she realised that she could feel Niels's breath, hot on her nape. He was licking at the join of her neck and shoulder, kissing it, the hand in her hair pulling her head up, keeping her hair off the nape of her neck; and then his teeth sank into her, just where he had kissed, a sharp, exquisite pain as he bit her gently, enough to make her feel it up and down her body, to buck against him as he drove into her, arching her back, showing him how excited he was making her.

His mouth left her neck, his hand her hair. Her neck was no longer being pulled up, and her head flopped down gratefully to rest on the soft leather of the armchair. But it was only for a second. Then Niels's hands closed around her hips, pulling her even tighter against him, away from the armchair.

'On the floor,' he said, and she crumpled her legs underneath her as he sank to his knees too, somehow managing it without ever coming out of her, and then she was lying on the carpet, her head cradled in her hands, moaning into her arms as Niels, still holding her hips, drove himself into her so hard that her body slammed into the thick pile of the carpet with every thrust.

He was close now, she could feel it from the way his cock was swelling, hear his breath hissing between his teeth as he gasped in anticipation. And she cried out in disappointment when she felt him pull out, arch and then spurt a stream of hot sticky come into the small of her back. He was right to pull out, of course he was. But God, she'd wanted to feel him coming inside her. There would have been a triumph in that, a sense that fucking her had made him lose all control.

One day, she thought, her eyes closing, her body still throbbing with pleasure. *One day I'll make him come inside me.*

Niels was reaching for something over her – one of the towels. He chucked it on her back and collapsed on top of her, no strength left in him, flattening her to the carpet.

It was wonderful. She lay there, spreadeagled under his heavy weight, not wanting him ever to get up, the sweat on their bodies cooling slowly. His head was close to hers, and eventually he turned it, and with a rush of happiness she felt his lips on her hair. Kissing her. A smile flooded her entire body. Somehow, she knew not to say anything, to let this moment just be, and she drifted off into a half-sleep, so perfectly happy that, despite having a big muscular man lying mostly on top of her, she felt as light as if she were floating on a cloud.

Eventually, Niels stirred, and she floated back to consciousness again slowly, feeling his weight lift off her, his hands wiping up her back with the towel, then reaching down to help her up. She stumbled as she found her feet, her legs still unsteady, and saw him smile the smug masculine smile of a man who has just had such good sex with a woman that she's as weak as a kitten afterwards.

'I'm sorry,' he said, looking embarrassed.

'*What?*' Lola couldn't believe he was apologising for having had sex with her.

'You just showered . . . and now I've got you all, um, messy again . . .' he mumbled.

Giggling, she went down the aisle to the bathroom.

'You'd better hope there's enough water to wash me off,' she called over her shoulder.

There was, just about. She put on a robe this time, holding it off the ground so she didn't trip, and brought him the other one, enjoying watching him pull off his T-shirt and stand, for a moment, completely naked. Then she picked up her full glass of champagne and handed him his own.

'I didn't actually do that on purpose,' she said, sitting down in the chair next to the one he had been occupying and patting his to indicate he should sit next to her.

Niels obeyed, looking awkward. She clinked glasses with him, and they drank some champagne.

How funny, she thought. *Just now, during sex, it was him who decided everything. And now he's looking almost hang-dog, waiting for me to tell him what to do.*

'The towel falling off,' she clarified, seeing that he wasn't going to ask her what she meant. 'I really didn't mean to. Though' – she blushed – 'I expect it's perfectly obvious that I did want to have sex with you.'

Niels was back to avoiding her gaze again.

'I really am sorry,' he mumbled eventually. 'Not, you know, for the getting you messy part. For the . . .' His voice tailed off, and he finished the glass of champagne in one gulp, jumping up and crossing to the fridge to retrieve the bottle.

'For the what?' she prompted.

'For' – he filled his glass again, and topped up hers – 'for the – you know. The—'

He couldn't finish the sentence. Lola tried to fill in the gap.

'You mean, because you like it a bit rough?' she said, drinking some more fizz herself, because she wasn't wholly unembarrassed about the entire situation herself. 'The spanking me, pulling my hair, all that kind of thing?'

He went as red as a tomato.

'I never did before!' he protested, taking another gulp of

champagne. Too fast; he choked on some bubbles and Lola had to pound his back.

'What do you mean, you never did before?' she asked.

She was not looking at him now either, sensing that this conversation was difficult enough for him without her eyes boring into him. Directing her stare instead to the window next to her, she looked out into the sky, waiting for his answer.

'Well, not like that!' Niels sounded very confused. 'Not, you know . . .' He cleared his throat. 'I don't mean this to sound rude,' he started. 'But it's something about you. You sort of . . . bring it out in me.'

'Me too,' she said with great surprise. 'I mean, I never liked anything like that before. But' – it was her turn to blush – 'I never really liked sex that much, believe it or not. I wasn't that keen on it. Even when Jean-Marc and I fooled around, which we hardly ever did—'

'Please!' He raised a hand. 'Can we never, ever mention that you and Jean-Marc—'

'No, sure. Right. Absolutely.' Lola downed the rest of her champagne and reached for the bottle. 'God, this is a *weird* situation.'

'It is, isn't it?' he agreed fervently, turning to look at her.

She glanced up at him shyly from under her lashes.

'Niels,' she said, unable to stop herself asking the question, 'why are you single? Or' – she was struck with horror – '*are* you single? I mean, I assumed—'

'Yes, of course I am!' Niels blurted out. 'I would *never*—' He cleared his throat. 'My mother asks that question a lot,' he admitted. 'Why am I single? And I never know what to say. I mean, I've had relationships, but they've never really come to anything more. I'm good friends with most of my exes.'

Which means things weren't that passionate, Lola deduced. *Like me and Jean-Marc. If there's real passion, I can't imagine that you'd be friends afterwards – it would all blow up like an explosion, not just fizzle out, like Niels is describing.*

Niels was refilling his glass, obviously embarrassed by the conversation.

With those exes, he didn't have sex with them like he just did with me, Lola realised. *He said it was me that brought it out in him.* Her heart leaped, then sank immediately as she understood what that meant:

He thinks I'm just a tart. The kind of girl you have filthy amazing sex with, not the kind of girl you take home to your mother. Not the kind of girl you even mention *when your mother asks why you're single. The kind of girl you dismiss when you're done with her, because there are the 'good' girls you have passionless relationships with, and then me, who he despises but, maybe because of that, he feels free enough to have the kind of sex with me that he really wants to have . . .*

Nothing more. This is all there'll ever be between Niels and me. Just the sex.

She looked over at him, hoping to see something in his eyes that would contradict her gloomy process of deductive reasoning. But he was drinking his champagne and looking down at the Alps below, not even glancing in her direction.

'I think,' he said, 'we had better finish this bottle, put our seats back, turn the lights off and try to get some sleep.'

'OK,' she said a little sadly. 'I think sleep's a great idea.'

He looked hugely relieved.

'And don't worry about anything when we land,' he said quickly. 'I've got Lesley's passport for you. So you won't have to show the one you're travelling on. They never give the passports anything but a quick glance anyway, but just to be on the safe side, I thought it was a good idea to take the precaution. The plane'll be going back to Milan in a couple of days, and Lesley'll be fine there till she gets her passport back.'

'Oh,' she said, a bit flattened.

He stared at her.

'What?' he said, raising his eyebrows haughtily, back to the bossy, rather scornful Niels that she had first met in the hospital. 'You don't think my arrangements are good enough, Princess? What about thanking me for the foresight of having an American stewardess who looks vaguely like you, let alone the considerable inconvenience to me of having to travel with someone who's completely useless as a stewardess! You can't even close a fridge door without managing to lose all your clothes!'

Lola blushed. It was her turn to mumble.

'I just thought you'd left her behind because . . . um . . . because you wanted to be alone with me.'

'Oh,' he said. 'Well.' He looked away. 'I had absolutely no intention of being alone with you at all, in that way. If you want to know. Because of – ahem.'

Lola wasn't going to let him get away with that.

'But you're glad you were, aren't you?' she challenged him. 'I mean, you're not sorry it happened!'

Look me in the eye, Niels van der Veer, and tell me that you're sorry we just had totally amazing sex, she thought. *I dare you.*

Niels' face was the visual definition of a man caught between a rock and a hard place. There was no way he could deny that he had thoroughly enjoyed himself. And she remembered him lying on top of her afterwards, kissing her hair. There had been tenderness too, even though he'd be loath to admit it. He finished his second glass of champagne in one gulp, the rising colour in his cheeks, his inability to answer her, all the response she needed.

'I'm not very good at talking about this kind of thing at the best of times,' he mumbled eventually.

'That's OK,' Lola teased. 'At least you're very good at doing it.'

Niels was even redder now.

'We should both try to get some sleep,' he said, setting down his glass. 'You've got a lot ahead of you when you get back to New York.' He hesitated. 'I'm very sorry about your father. I knew him. Not that well, but I knew him. He was a good man.'

'He was,' Lola said quietly. 'Thank you.'

She was sure Niels hadn't deliberately mentioned her father in order to stop her talking about sex, but that was the effect it had had, all the same. The fizz of exhilaration from orgasms and champagne began to fade as she remembered the last time she'd seen Ben Fitzgerald alive, lying in his huge bed, hooked up to beeping monitors.

And then she thought about what lay ahead of her in New York. It was a more than sobering picture.

'Here,' Niels said, pulling down a couple of blankets from the overhead locker and handing them to her. He followed them with some pillows and a sleep mask. 'Time to have a rest now. You'll need your energy soon enough.'

Propping a pillow behind his own head, he reclined his seat and shut his eyes. The conversation, clearly, was over.

Chapter 36

'Mrs Myers? Mrs Myers? Mrs Myers, we have a search warrant here. You have to let us in!'

Suzanne, panicking, turned to Evie and India for help.

'What do I do?' she mouthed.

'Stall them,' India said quickly. 'I'll get Evie into bed. We'll just hope that they still think she's Lola.'

'It'll never work!' Suzanne wailed.

India's grimace showed that she knew that too, but she wouldn't say it.

'It's all we've got,' she whispered, herding Evie back down the corridor to the bedroom.

Suzanne waited as long as she could, until the door was almost bouncing off its hinges as the police banged on it, before she put the chain on and slowly pulled it open. In the gap, she could see the detectives who had visited yesterday; and, standing behind them, a redheaded woman in a cheap suit, her mouth set in a tight line.

'Mrs Myers, the front desk rang up, I assume,' the woman said. 'I'm Serena Mackesy, an Assistant District Attorney from the DA's office. We have a warrant to search the apartment. We're checking that your daughter, Lola Fitzgerald, is on the premises. I'm here because I've met Ms Fitzgerald at the DA's office, and can identify her.'

Bowing to fate, Suzanne nodded and closed the door just enough to slip off the chain. A door banged further down the apartment – maybe a signal to say that India and Evie were ready for them. There was nothing more Suzanne could do. And Evie really did look a lot like Lola. The same build, the same colouring, very similar features – maybe, without having them both there, standing next to each other, this woman wouldn't be able to tell one from the other—

Serena Mackesy was first through the door, the detectives standing back to let her through.

'I should let you know, Mrs Myers,' she said, patting her briefcase, 'that I have photographs here of Ms Fitzgerald and of Evie Lopez. Our office contacted the publicist of that burlesque place where Ms Lopez performs and got a publicity shot of her. If it's Evie Lopez you have in this apartment, pretending to be Ms Fitzgerald, I'll know. Detective Morgan' – she gestured at the cop who had seen Evie yesterday – 'has been shown the photographs, and he's pretty sure it was Ms Lopez he saw in here yesterday, not Ms Fitzgerald.'

Jerry pulled an apologetic face at Suzanne.

'Uh, it's down that corridor,' he said, pointing the way for ADA Mackesy.

Suzanne watched hopelessly as they trooped off down the hall in the direction of Evie's bedroom. She supposed she should follow them, but her feet refused to move. All this stress ever since the news of Lola's arrest, the rush to organise the feeding of the animals, because Neville, bless his heart, had offered to come with her for the funeral, so they'd had to scrabble around to find someone in Whitstable to look after her whole animal family while he, too, was away. Neville was back in Whitstable now, of course, and thank God he was, because one of the llamas had contracted a bad head cold.

Suzanne couldn't wait to rejoin him. This wasn't her world any more, and she couldn't believe she had ever lived in it. She hated the ridiculous over-consumption. She hated the luxury apartment so high up in the sky you had to go down in a lift to reach Central Park and feel the earth under your feet again. Most of all, she hated the drama that Carin Fitzgerald, that terrible woman, created with everything she touched. Drama and destruction. She was like a plague in human form.

And now Carin had somehow managed to set up Lola, Suzanne's beloved daughter, for murdering her father. Lola would be arrested again, and this time she wouldn't get bail. She might even be convicted.

It was no wonder that Suzanne couldn't manage to move from where she stood, leaning hopelessly against the wall of the foyer, staring unseeingly at her own reflection in the gilded mirror hung above the table opposite.

They were all emerging again. Suzanne watched them walk back down the corridor, and she could see that something had changed; they had been pumped up, alert, when they came in. Now it was as if the energy had been drained out of them through the soles of their feet. Serena Mackesy was first, carrying her briefcase at the same angle; it didn't look as if she had pulled it out to check any photographs at all. Then Detective Garcia, rubbing his hand over his bald scalp, and finally, Detective Morgan.

'I'm sorry to have bothered you, Mrs Myers,' ADA Mackesy said politely. 'You understand, we had to check.'

'Just doing our job, ma'am,' Detective Garcia mumbled. 'We won't be bothering you again.'

Suzanne's heart leaped. Had it worked? Had this Mackesy woman, *and* Garcia, really all been fooled by Evie with the pink cakey cream blotches on her face?

'Um, Mrs Myers—' Detective Morgan had halted in front of her. 'I took the liberty of bringing this—' He was extracting a photo from his pocket, what looked like a printout from the internet, folded in two. It was her as the Sunsilk girl, in full colour, wearing the wretched blue swimsuit that had made her famous, her blonde hair streaming down her back.

He held it out to her with a pen. 'I wasn't going to ask if, you know, things didn't go so well. But since everything's OK – would you mind signing it for me?'

Her brain racing with speculation, her heart high, she smiled at him as she took both pen and paper and quickly rested the photo on the hall table, signing her name.

'Oh boy, that's the smile right there!' he crowed. 'You don't look a day older, ma'am!'

'Detective,' she informed him, 'this smile is murder to hold for hours. Believe me, I'm very glad not to have to do that any more.'

'Oh, wow—' He was reading what she had written. *'With love, Suzanne.* Jeez, Mrs Myers, thanks so much – that's real nice of you, considering—'

She closed the door on the three of them and sprinted back down the corridor faster than she had thought possible at her age. As she tore into Lola's bedroom, she stopped dead in astonishment.

Her daughter was sitting upright in bed, a sheet held up to her shoulders.

India was collapsed in an armchair, clutching her head as if she had a migraine.

And Evie Lopez, her ex-husband's mistress, was crawling out from under the bed, her face now a smeared mass of pink cracking make-up.

Suzanne stared at the scene in front of her and started laughing so hard her eyes watered over.

'When we landed at Teterboro, Niels had a helicopter waiting already,' Lola was explaining. 'It shot me over to the East Side helipad and then I grabbed a cab over here.' She pulled a face. 'It took longer to get across town in a cab than the helicopter journey, believe it or not.'

'Cross-town traffic's a bitch,' Evie said sympathetically.

'But at least I spent the drive working out how to get back into the apartment without being spotted!' Lola's eyes were bright with enthusiasm: she was really pleased with herself. 'I worked out where the service entrance was, just round the corner from the garages. I'd noticed it because they always have big laundry bins there, rolling out all the dirty sheets and towels and things. So I got the cab to let me off there, and sneaked in. All the maids have pass-keys, you know. It still works like a hotel if you want, they'll change your linen every day. And if you look at the corridor from the outside of the suite, you can see there are a couple of extra doors for the cleaners, so they don't bother you by using the main ones. I just slipped one of the maids a twenty to let me in further down.'

She giggled.

'It was like something out of a farce, really. I mean, if it hadn't been so serious. India saw me come in – I was just opposite my bedroom – and she grabbed my arm and pulled me in and started ripping off my sweater, like she wanted to have sex with me or something.'

'You should be so lucky!' India, overhearing this, called from the dining-room.

'And she practically threw me into bed – I was getting in while Evie was scrambling out the other side and crawling underneath it. And about two seconds later, this DA and two cops all piled in, and I had barely got my sweater off, so I grabbed at the sheet to cover me like I was shocked—'

'Which was the perfect finishing touch,' India called.

'—and poor things, I did feel sorry for them. They looked *so* embarrassed,' Lola said with great satisfaction. 'Both the guys just *goggled* at me. And then the DA said to one of them, suspiciously, "Is this the woman that you saw before, Detective?" and he went all pink and said he thought so, but I'd been looking pretty bad last time, and then he said, "Wow, Ms Fitzgerald, your skin has really cleared up!" and I had no idea what he was talking about, because I'd barely seen Evie's face yet, but I just said, "Thank you," because I didn't know what else to say. And then they all left with their tails between their legs.'

The doorbell rang, and Suzanne went to answer it.

'Hey everyone!' carolled another voice from the hallway.

'David!' Lola cried joyously, running out to greet him. 'I didn't know you were coming! No one tells me anything!'

David looked very well. His blue eyes were bright, their whites very clear, and he exuded the health and poise of a gay man who's spending every evening at the gym after work. He wore a tight blue T-shirt over cream chinos, and his dark hair was cropped short.

'Darling!' He enfolded her in a hug. 'It's *lovely* to see you! My goodness, this must be your gorgeous mama! How beautiful she is!'

'Mummy, this is David – Jean-Marc's boyfriend,' Lola introduced him. 'And David, this is India.'

'I know *exactly* who you are,' David said, shaking India's hand. 'Lola's very best friend. She's *so* lucky to have you.'

India went pink with pleasure.

'Well, how nice to find a little party!' David exclaimed. 'I just dropped by to give you news about Jean—' He looked at Lola. 'He's doing *fantastically*. Really, it's from night to day, if you think about how unhappy he was at Desert Springs. Not that it was Desert Springs' fault, of course, they did me the world of good, but poor Jean just wasn't ready to come out *and* clean up his act at the same time! And now he's doing so well that they let him ring me every week. He'll be out in a fortnight, tops. Maybe even less.'

'Oh, that's great!' Lola exclaimed, hugging David again. 'I'm so happy for him! And you, of course!' She tried to make her voice light as she asked: 'Does Niels know? Have you been talking to him?'

'I haven't, but Jean has,' David said. 'That man scares the life out of me. In a mainly good way, but *still*—' He rolled his eyes at India. 'Jean-Marc's brother,' he explained, probably thinking she might not know who they were talking about.

'Oh, I met him once,' India said, going even pinker. 'He's *gorgeous*. But very – grumpy.'

And he hasn't been in touch once since we landed at Teterboro, Lola thought rather sadly. *He didn't even kiss me goodbye. I mean, he'd sorted out the helicopter and everything, which was nice of him, but then he just went on to Houston, I suppose. And I remembered him saying that the plane was going back to Milan in a couple of days, so he probably just took his meetings in Houston and then got on the jet again and went back to Milan, and back to Bellagio and the Villa Aurora as if I'd never even turned up there in the first place.*

As if we'd never had amazing sex on the plane. He gave me a ride back to New York, and he got paid for it. End of story. Who needs him, anyway?

The doorbell rang again, and Lola went to answer it.

'Thai, Japanese and Italian,' she said, lugging in the bags of food. 'We couldn't decide what to get, so we ordered a bit of everything.'

'It's the New York way!' David said cheerfully.

'David, do stay and eat with us,' Suzanne said, pulling up another chair to the table. 'There's so much food, really.'

'Love to,' David said happily. 'Lola, darling—' He patted the chair on his other side. 'Tell me everything! What's going on with your trial? When does it start?'

'In two days,' Lola said, sitting down.

'Oh, *darling*—'

'Sometimes I manage to forget it's happening for hours at a time,' she said, trying to smile but, from David's expression, not doing a very good job. 'And sometimes, I don't. Before I went to Italy – while we were waiting for Evie's passport to come through – I had several sessions with a sort of coach Simon Poluck hired. She questions you as if she were a lawyer, and you give your testimony, and then she tells you you're doing it all wrong and what you should be saying instead. I have to start again first thing tomorrow morning.' She shivered. 'It was really horrible, just going over the same thing again and again till you want to scream. And then she pretends to be the prosecution, and she's really hostile, and you have to keep calm and not let her anger you, but it's OK to get upset as long as I don't get angry, because if I'm angry, the jury will think that I'm possibly a killer, because killers have bad tempers.'

She managed a smile now, a bitter one.

'I have to be careful not to get wound up by anything she says, even when she pounds the desk and storms around the room. I just have to sit there looking upset and helpless and like someone who couldn't possibly kill anyone at all, let alone my own father.'

Tears sprung to her eyes. Her mother jumped up and came to stand behind her, massaging her shoulders.

David clicked his tongue.

'I mean, we *all* have tempers,' he muttered. 'And *I'd* be cross if someone were shouting at me, telling me I'd done something awful.'

'Exactly!'

Lola was really crying now. 'I'm sorry—' she stammered through her tears. 'I'm trying to be brave, but sometimes it just gets too much. I mean, I'm freaking out at the thought of starting those sessions again, and if I hated *them*, the trial's going to be a hundred times worse.'

'Oh, *darling*—'

Suzanne was embracing her, India was looking anxious and David was pouring her a glass of water and handing her tissues. Lola was surrounded by people who cared about her, people who didn't think for a moment that she had killed her father.

But Lola was incapable of being consoled. Sympathetic as they were, none of them could really help her. When she went into court, wearing one of the simple, restrained, not-too-expensive-looking dark outfits that the jury consultant had approved for her, she would sit there at the defence table all alone. Oh, Simon Poluck, and two other lawyers (one for the forensic evidence, one a medical expert) would be there with her, plus the jury consultant and the testimony coach. But none of them would be convicted if the case went against her. They'd all be paid – not the bonuses they would get if she were acquitted, but they'd still all be paid. They would all be able to walk away.

Only she would go to prison. If Joe Scutellaro didn't change his story after all.

Only she would be serving twenty-five to life in a maximum-security prison, if she were convicted.

Lola put her head down on the table and sobbed her heart out in absolute terror.

Chapter 37

'*L*ook at her!' Joshua Greene bellowed, as best he could in his light tenor voice. He lowered it even further for his next line, which he delivered while still pointing accusingly at Lola.

'*Look* at her, ladies and gentlemen,' he insisted. 'Butter wouldn't melt in her mouth, would it? But don't be fooled by her appearance. Before this trial is over, you will have heard clear and certain evidence that Lola Fitzgerald – this pretty, fragile girl – murdered her own father in cold blood. When he tragically slipped into a diabetic coma, her stepmother, a woman of great principle, shocked by the reports of her stepdaughter's decadent and debauched behaviour, decided that it was time to take a stand. Courageously, she did what her husband had been wanting to do for some time, but had been too weak to act upon. She carried out his wishes in cutting off her stepdaughter financially, hoping against hope that the shock would bring this young woman to her senses. Little did she know that Lola Fitzgerald would be unable to envision a world in which her father's money did not ease her every need.'

Joshua Greene turned on his heel and paced away from Lola and the defendant's table.

'What did she do?' he demanded, in a voice trembling with the magnitude of what he was about to say. 'She came to visit her father, the father who was lying, helpless, in a coma. The father who could not raise a hand to defend himself against her. Then' – he drew in a breath – 'she made an excuse to send away the nurse who would have been his security. And, ladies and gentlemen, this depraved young woman took a syringe from his bedside table, and a vial of insulin from the fridge below, and injected her father with a lethal dose.'

He swivelled dramatically, facing the jury full on.

'She knew that as long as her father lived, her stepmother Carin would have control of his money. She had been told by her step-mother that access to her trust fund was blocked for the foreseeable future, in the hope that she would start to earn her own living, to build a more worthwhile life than the shallow, drug-obsessed exis-tence she had been living up till that point. She knew that her only hope of regaining access to her father's extensive fortune was to have his will executed, a will in which he left his beloved daughter half of everything he owned. And so, ladies and gentlemen of the jury, Lola Fitzgerald killed her own father for the most sordid, heinous motive in the world. Money.'

Don't react, the testimony coach had said. *Whatever the prosecu-tor says in his opening statement, don't react. Above all, don't look angry. Keep your face as calm and impassive as you can. Remember, you're innocent.*

Well, Lola had got one thing right. She was definitely saddened. As Joshua Greene had pronounced the words 'beloved daughter' with such sarcasm, such contempt, she had felt a tear begin to roll down her cheek.

Don't look down if you can help it, the coach had said. Lola realised that she was staring down at the table and jerked her head up again. God, it was so hard to remember everything she had said, not to be natural for a moment, in order to present an image of yourself that the jury would read as innocent.

And she was already all too familiar with the courtroom. The waist-high wooden panelling, the faded old oil paintings of nautical scenes, the gilded inlaid words carved and painted into the marble slab behind the judge's bench, reading 'IN GOD WE TRUST'. The judge was different, though, a wizened little woman with a heavily lined smoker's face and bright beady eyes, looking like a wise little dwarf in her black robe with its white collar.

The judge intimidated Lola; she looked over at the jury instead. That was OK, apparently. *Don't be afraid of turning to look at the jury on occasion,* Juliet had said. *If you do, always meet their eyes otherwise you'll seem shifty. But don't be defiant, or angry. Remember, you're in mourning.*

'You will hear,' Joshua Greene was saying, 'that the defendant made sure to ask the nurse, Mr Scutellaro, all the questions she needed to ensure that she injected her father with enough insulin to kill him. You will hear that she then sent him away on an errand that even at the time seemed meaningless to him, in order to make sure she had enough time to carry out the act. You will hear—'

Do they believe him? Lola wondered, looking at the jury. Selection of these twelve people (well, fifteen if you counted the alternates) had taken days. Joshua Greene had wanted to get as many women as possible on the jury, respectable middle-aged ones who would disapprove of everything that Lola stood for. Simon Poluck, naturally, had pushed for men, men who would find Lola so attractive that they wouldn't be able to entertain for a moment the thought that this pretty, fragile blonde could have done something so heinous – as Joshua Greene, who seemed to have swallowed a dictionary that morning, would put it – as murder her own father for money.

Lola didn't see condemnation in the expressions of the jurors. Apart, perhaps, from one thin, rather drawn-looking woman in a baggy beige sweater, whose eyes narrowed ominously when they met Lola's. They looked avid instead. Greedy for the inside scoop. Hugely curious about the window this trial would open for them onto the lives of the rich and famous. A girl in the front row was staring at Lola voraciously, assessing her black Marc Jacobs dress with its wide, Peter Pan collar, her yellow diamond earrings, her hair, which was smoothed down and drawn back into a coil at the back of her head.

Don't try to look poorer than you are, the jury consultant had advised. *They'll spot that straight away and they'll be insulted. Dress well, and soberly. But no big statement handbags – nothing that cost upwards of four figures. Or you'll see yourself on the front of the* Post *the next day with a big tag hanging off your handbag, with the price printed on it. For some reason, expensive handbags drive them nuts. I don't know why, but they do.*

Further down the defendant's table, Simon Poluck stirred, pushing his papers together in one neat stack. Joshua Greene must be reaching the end of his speech.

'She's guilty!' he was declaiming. 'I am sure of that, and by the end of this trial, you will be too. The evidence against her is overwhelming, ladies and gentlemen. Once you have heard it, you will be as convinced by it as the State of New York is. Once you have heard the evidence, you will have no choice but to convict Lola Fitzgerald of the worst crime there is. Patricide.'

It was an awful word. Lola flinched and looked away, to the rows of spectators' benches behind the prosecutors' table. She saw Evie and Lawrence, who had promised to attend the trial as much as they could, to support Lola. And then she spotted Carin. Her stepmother, wearing a black hat with a little veil, like something out of a 1940s movie, was sitting there with a tiny smile on her face as she heard Lola accused of the crime she herself had committed. A black widow spider, at the centre of the web she had woven, enjoying tremendously the process of watching Lola be slowly eaten alive.

Now Lola realised why she had been warned not to look angry. She ducked her gaze, not caring for a moment if she wasn't supposed to; it was the lesser of two evils. Because right then, she had enough rage in her eyes to make the jury, if they saw it, be convinced that she was capable of anything.

Simon Poluck had planned his strategy with the next witness very cleverly, his intention clearly being to wrong-foot the prosecution. After Joshua Greene had declared that he had finished questioning the fingerprint expert, Simon Poluck stood up, saying:

'I have just a couple of questions for this witness, Your Honour. We are happy to stipulate that my client did indeed touch the syringe, the insulin vial and the fridge in which the latter was kept. As we will be demonstrating, my client has a perfectly innocent explanation for the fact that her fingerprints appear on these three items. My first question is simply this.'

He swivelled to stare directly at the fingerprint expert.

'Can you confirm for us that the pattern of Ms Fitzgerald's fingerprints on the syringe do not indicate the position in which one would hold it when one was using it for the purpose for which it is intended – i.e., you didn't find the classic thumbprint on the plunger, or the fingers gripping the syringe as if to position it for an injection?'

'Um, no, they don't,' said the fingerprint expert cautiously. 'As I said in my testimony, there is considerable blurring, but the only prints of Ms Fitzgerald which I can identify as twelve-point matches indicate that she was holding it from below.'

'As you would hold a pen, for instance, if I handed it to you and asked you to hold it for a moment?'

'Possibly.'

'Thank you!' said Simon Poluck triumphantly, looking at the jury. 'And my second question: you found no fingerprints of Ms Fitzgerald's *at all* on the sharps container in which we have been told that the syringe and vial were found?'

'None whatsoever,' said the fingerprint expert.

'How very significant,' Simon Poluck said, never taking his eyes off the jury. 'How *very* significant.'

Joshua Greene was on his feet, about to object, but Simon Poluck was already raising his hand and walking back to the defence table.

'I have no further questions for this witness, Your Honour,' he was saying.

'Mr Greene?' the judge said to the ADA as the fingerprint expert stepped down off the stand. 'I'm sensing some sort of confusion in your general vicinity. Are you calling your next witness?'

'Your Honour—' Joshua Greene, flustered, was leaning back over the prosecutor's table now, conferring urgently with Mackesy. 'Your

Honour, we were not expecting to call our next witness until tomorrow at the earliest. We have been experiencing some difficulties in contacting him – he was due to arrive in the country yesterday on a flight from Rome, but he was not on that flight. The Italian authorities have been contacted and are investigating this with extreme urgency, but he is the last name on our witness list, Your Honour, and his testimony is very important to this case—'

'Who is this witness?' the judge asked, flicking through a sheaf of papers on the desk in front of her.

'Your Honour, his name is Giuseppe Scutellaro, commonly known as Joe – he is the nurse who was attending Mr Fitzgerald on the day he died – his testimony is, frankly, *crucial*—'

'Did you know about this?' Lola leaned over and whispered to Simon Poluck, her heart beating fast. If Joe Scutellaro wasn't coming, what did that mean? Had he decided to go back on their deal? Was he trapped between her and Carin now, and thinking that the best plan of action was to stay in Italy and avoid testifying at all?

'I heard they were having problems,' Simon Poluck muttered. 'Knew Scutellaro wasn't here as of this morning. So I speeded things up to catch them off guard. It worked better anyway – made us look very confident. Like this is an open-and-shut case.'

Just then the door at the back of the courtroom swung open and practically every head in the room turned to see if it was the missing witness, Joe Scutellaro, making a dramatic, last-minute entrance. Lola recognised the man who walked in immediately: it was Detective Garcia, followed by Detective Morgan, who remained standing by the door as Garcia bustled down the centre aisle and ducked down behind the prosecutor's table, muttering swiftly to Serena Mackesy.

Her face went white and she gestured to Joshua Greene to listen to what Garcia was telling her. His reaction was as intense as hers: he fired out a couple of questions at Garcia, then shook his head vehemently, as if trying to deny something he knew to be true. Serena Mackesy just sat there, shaking her own head in an unconscious echo of her boss's mannerism.

Garcia's mouth downturned, he headed back down the aisle again.

'Mr Greene?' the judge prompted.

Joshua Greene pushed back his chair slowly, reluctantly, and stood up again.

'Your Honour,' he said. 'I'm very sorry to say that I've just been informed that our witness, Giuseppe Scutellaro, was murdered last night in Rome on his way to the airport.'

Chapter 38

'Silence!' the judge said crossly, pounding her gavel, as gasps of surprise echoed around the courtroom.

The jury was openly gaping, like spectators at a play that had just revealed a huge twist in the plot. Lola saw, with a cynicism she couldn't help, that their predominant emotion was enthralled enjoyment. The key witness in the prosecution case had been killed – in a foreign country, no less! How much more dramatic could things get?

The sound of Simon Poluck's chair shooting back as he jumped to his feet focused all eyes on him.

'Your Honour,' he said with barely repressed triumph in his voice, 'the prosecution's entire case rests on the testimony of this unfortunate young man. Since he is no longer able to share his story with us' – the delicate contempt in his tone made it quite clear what he thought of the story Joe Scutellaro had been going to tell – 'it is clear that there is no case to answer against my client. We ask the court to dismiss all charges against her immediately and without prejudice.'

'That would mean that you can't be retried,' the second chair muttered to Lola.

Could it really be that easy? Lola's heart leaped; she couldn't help turning to look at Suzanne and India, sitting just behind her, whose faces were as filled with excitement as her own.

But who had killed Scutellaro? It must have been someone paid by Carin, but why would Carin kill him, when it meant an automatic acquittal for Lola? Had she decided to throw in her hand?

Lola glanced over at Carin, who was staring straight ahead, her lips set in a tight line, her entire body drawn up into a taut, thin black column. She looked as if she were concentrating very hard on something, putting all her will and determination into making it happen.

She hasn't thrown in her hand at all, Lola realised in rising panic. *Not at all. In fact, she's playing her most important card.*

'Your Honour!' Joshua Greene, not about to see victory be snatched from him in a case that would make his career if he secured a conviction, sprang to his feet. 'Your Honour, due to the unusual circumstances of Mr Scutellaro's death, we request that his Grand Jury testimony be read into the record of this trial!'

Simon Poluck sneered at him.

'Your Honour,' he countered, 'the Assistant District Attorney is all too aware that grand jury testimony can only be read into the record under very specific circumstances—'

'If you killed the witness, or someone did it on your behalf,' whispered the second chair to Lola, 'then they could read it in. But usually they don't have a hope in hell of pulling this off.'

'—which clearly do not exist in this case,' Simon Poluck was finishing. 'A tragic murder in a faraway country – I fail to see any connection at all—'

'Your Honour,' Joshua Greene interrupted, 'we have a clear chain of circumstance which may well form a connection between Mr Scutellaro and the defend—'

'In my chambers! Now!' the judge said angrily. 'And I hope this is the last time in this trial that I hear you two shouting over each other like kids in a school debating society!'

'Oof,' winced the second chair.

'Is that bad?' Lola said anxiously. 'Going into her chambers?'

'I was more wincing because of the school debating society crack,' said the second chair. 'That's *harsh*. But—' she shrugged. 'Odds are in our favour. Sit tight and cross your fingers.'

But when the two attorneys re-emerged twenty-five minutes later, and the bellow of 'All rise! Court is now in session!' caused everyone to stand as the judge resumed her seat high above them, Lola could tell immediately from Simon Poluck's glum face that the conference hadn't gone the way he wanted.

'They're going to read in the testimony,' he muttered grimly. 'With the proviso that if certain facts don't emerge during the rest of the trial that can connect you to Scutellaro's death somehow, it'll be struck from the record.'

'You can't strike a whole testimony from the record!' the second chair protested.

'Exactly. We're looking at a mistrial, hopefully.' He looked at Lola. 'That means they can retry you, technically, but with Scutellaro dead they'd never do it. Could be worse. Could be a lot worse.'

And when Detective Garcia was summoned back to court to read the Italian police's summary of Scutellaro's murder – stabbed to death by a group of kids outside the apartment building in which he was staying, as he left to go to the airport – it seemed even less likely that the prosecution would be able to make any connection between Lola and what Simon Poluck, cross-examining, called a 'senseless, brutal murder'. Scutellaro's bag and wallet had both been stolen. The police had been able to find no witnesses; the only confirmation that it had been kids who had killed Scutellaro was the prevalence of lower-body wounds on the corpse, and the fact that the area was rife with gangs of shockingly young children armed with knives.

Lola shivered, thinking of Joe Scutellaro, stabbed to death on that concrete walkway. It might have happened to her, if she had been alone. If Leo and his gun hadn't been with them when the kids came after her.

She should have given Scutellaro Leo's number, she thought with black humour.

The testimony itself, read aloud, was very plausible, and very damaging to Lola. She didn't need anyone to tell her that. She could see how the jury were looking at her as they listened.

As if, for the first time, they believed that she might be guilty of killing her father.

'*ADA Greene: When you left the defendant alone, how long were you gone for?*

Scutellaro: About ten minutes. Maybe fifteen.

ADA Greene: And when you returned, what did you find?

Scutellaro: The patient – Mr Fitzgerald – was clearly having difficulty breathing. His colour had changed for the worse.

ADA Greene: Did you suspect foul play immediately?

Scutellaro: I wondered, yeah. I checked the insulin vials as soon as Ms Fitzgerald left and sure enough, there was one missing.

ADA Greene: Did you later find an insulin vial in an unusual place?

Scutellaro: Yeah, I did. In the sharps container in the bathroom. So I knew straight away something was up. I sure as hell hadn't put it there.'

Even read out in the leaden tones of one of the court officers, it was damning testimony.

'You'll be on the stand first thing tomorrow,' Simon Poluck said to Lola as they left the court. 'Get a good night's sleep.'

'Wear the black suit,' instructed the jury consultant. 'With your hair back, but loose behind. Earrings, no necklace. Light on the mascara, and no lipstick. Medium heels.'

'Have a good breakfast,' the second chair added. 'Lots of protein. Not too much coffee, though. You don't want to be too buzzy.'

So the next morning, as they walked back up the steps of the courthouse, amidst the constant buzz of television cameras, reporters shouting questions, the generators of transit vans loaded with satellite dishes and aerials, Lola could at least hold onto the security of having done exactly what the very expensive team of lawyers and consultants had told her to do. She was in a very demure Armani skirt suit, her hair brushed smooth and pinned at the back of her head, wearing Jean-Marc's yellow diamond earrings, her make-up light. She had run through every instruction she had been given, eaten eggs and oatmeal for breakfast, and limited herself to one cappuccino. Her nerves were jumping, but she kept telling herself that she had followed all the instructions, and that her team knew exactly what they were doing.

They were as early as ever, so Lola was able to follow her usual routine: she slipped off to a women's toilet she had found, right down the far end of the first-floor corridor, tucked away round a corner and opposite the janitor's closet; she would never have known it was there if she hadn't been pacing restlessly and stumbled across it. It was in such an inconvenient location, with no offices or court-rooms anywhere nearby, that Lola had never seen anyone else use it.

As always, it was empty, and she chose the furthest stall, sitting inside for as long as she could. It calmed her down to have some time alone, away from the worried gazes of her mother and India and David. And after spending the days of her trial with an entire roomful of people staring at her, reading things into every tiny move she made, being alone was the greatest luxury she could imagine.

She was all too well aware that if she were found guilty, it was a luxury she wouldn't have for the next twenty-five years.

When she eventually unlocked the cubicle door and exited, the sight in front of her was so unexpected that she didn't take it in at first. She was crossing to the row of sinks to wash her hands, and the person leaning against them, smiling at her, was so incongruous that Lola took a couple more steps in her direction before her brain fully clicked into gear, and she realised who it was.

'Well, hello, Lola,' said Patricia, in her rough smoker's voice, smiling a big, toothy smile of a crocodile that's about to swallow its prey. 'Fancy meeting *you* here!'

Lola stared at Patricia in such absolute shock that she felt her lower jaw actually drop.

'Didn't expect to see me again after our little contretemps, did you?' Patricia said affably. 'Thought that now you've got Johnny all packed off to his cosy little rehab clinic, you'd shut the door on nasty old Patricia for good?'

She waggled a long bony finger at Lola.

'Well, you were wrong, weren't you?' she said. 'What a silly girl you are! I warned you, don't you remember? I told you not to make an enemy of me, and you didn't listen.'

And suddenly, Patricia wasn't smiling any more.

'You stupid little bitch,' she hissed. 'You should never have fucked with me. But you'll get your comeuppance now. And I'll be there to watch every minute of it. I've got the best seat in the house. You haven't noticed me there yet, have you? Believe me, there have been a *lot* of times that you haven't noticed me.'

Lola stared at Patricia, who was dressed as if she was doing her best to look as conventional as possible, in a dull brown trouser suit with a black sweater underneath. The jacket lapels disguised the size of her breasts, and she was wearing flat shoes so she didn't tower over everyone. Her poorly dyed hair was drawn back in a stubby ponytail; the collagen-plumped mouth was de-emphasised with a matt lipstick, and she had even managed to alter her over-plucked eyebrows by drawing them on in light feathery strokes so they looked – well, normal.

Presenting herself as she did now, you would never have passed Patricia in a corridor and thought: transsexual, or transgender. You would think: *not* an attractive woman. But that was all. Certainly, she didn't look remotely out of place in the women's bathroom.

'You've overlooked me a *lot*, you silly girl. Underestimated me and overlooked me. I've been watching you for days. I knew exactly where to find you this morning.' Her eyes glittered.

Lola had stood there gawping at Patricia long enough. Recovering her dignity, she stalked the last couple of steps to the sinks and started to wash her hands.

'If you've got something to say, you'd better get on with it,' she said coldly. 'Or are you just hanging out here to get make-up tips? I'd be more than happy to give you some if you want.'

Patricia reared back, looking as if Lola had just slapped her across the face once again. As Lola stared into the mirror above the sink, Patricia's face hove into view next to hers, the black beady eyes glistening.

'Take a good look at me now,' Patricia hissed, and Lola recoiled from the stench of her breath. She remembered the smell from before, the hot breath with its heavy, ingrained smell of menthol cigarettes, seeming to reek from Patricia's pores. And below that, something rotting, sweet and rancid: the odour of decay.

'I can't believe you haven't realised yet,' Patricia said as Lola instinctively pulled away. 'Too busy looking at your own pretty face, I suppose. Oh, they're going to *love* you in prison. That pretty face's going to make you a whole lot of fun new friends.'

She watched Lola in the mirror as the latter crossed the room and dragged on the hand towel, wanting now nothing more than to get away.

'I was with you on your little Italian jaunt,' she said happily. 'On the plane – business class, very nice. You barely glanced at me. Well, why would you? I was just a fat woman in a kaftan, wheezing away. *These*' – she cupped her football-sized breasts – 'aren't that easy to disguise, you know! I have to pad up the rest of me sometimes, make it look like I'm big all over. Then the boobs just look like they belong to a big old fatso wobbling along.'

The crocodile smile was back now as Patricia watched Lola digest this information. Lola was unable to conceal her horror.

'I changed on the plane,' Patricia continued, gloating. 'Tarted myself up in denim and big gold earrings. I knew you'd think I was just some Italian slut in high heels. And I shot through Customs because of my British passport. Easy-peasy. I was out there in plenty of time to see who you were meeting, and follow you.' She grinned wider. 'You know my *favourite* disguise? Oh, go on, guess!'

Lola had finished drying her hands, but she couldn't leave now. She stood there, frozen to the spot, as the cigarette-ravaged vocal cords croaked on triumphantly:

'The tranny hooker waiting outside the building for you!' Patricia crowed. 'Oh, that was *fun*! I did my best to get you mugged. Called out that your Vuitton was the real thing, and sent all the kids running after you. Nearly got your pretty face cut up.' She pouted grotesquely. 'Well, you can't have everything you want, can you? I jumped on my Vespa and followed you up to Como – not on the Vespa, of course—'

'You were the tourist at the station, getting off the train with me. You boarded the ferry, too. Wearing the straw hat and the awful flowered dress,' Lola said slowly. She was having flashes of memory as Patricia spoke, seeing every incarnation, every disguise that Patricia had worn.

'Exactly!' Patricia crowed. 'You're catching on! Fun game, isn't it? I saw you head into Mr Moneybags's luxury villa and I reported back. He played some trick with the passports, didn't he? He's smart, isn't he, Johnny's older brother? Very smart! I had people at Teterboro airport looking out for little Miss Evie's passport, but she never showed up. Well, *I* didn't have people, of course. My employer did.' Patricia looked at her watch. 'Ooh! Almost time to go back inside and see the next thrilling instalment!'

Lola had to ask the question, even though she already knew the answer.

'Your employer?' she said.

'Your darling stepmother, of course!' Patricia said. 'Now, *that's* a woman I respect. I went to have a little talk with her, a couple of days after you and I had our fight. You'd made me very cross, Lola. Very cross. I took some time to think it over and it finally occurred to me: who else doesn't like you? Doesn't like you *at all*? I thought I was tough, but *Carin* – well, let's just say that she takes no prisoners. And she's *very* generous when she wants to be. Plus, she's very careful. Carin saw her trainer sneak into her study and go through her things. Worked out that he'd found Joe's address for you. *Naughty* boy. There are cameras everywhere in that house, didn't you know? Obviously not. It's lucky for him he never went back to train her. She had a nasty surprise all waiting for him.'

'Lola! Have you finished in there?' India pushed open the door. 'The court officers are calling you—'

India saw Patricia leaning against the sinks, and did a double take as she grabbed Lola's arm and hustled her out of the bathroom.

'Who *is* that woman?' she asked Lola as they hurried back down the hall. 'She's really odd-looking, but sort of familiar . . .'

'She's Jean-Marc's drug dealer,' Lola said. 'Look—'

'Oh my God!' India gasped. 'What's she doing here?'

The court officer was waiting outside the doors for Lola, looking furious.

'I'm so sorry,' Lola gasped, 'bathroom emergency . . . *Look*,' she hissed to India, 'grab one of Simon's team, OK? Pull them out and tell them that there are cameras in Dad's house and they saw Lawrence find Joe's address—'

India's soft brown eyes went wide as saucers.

'*Shit*,' she breathed.

A second later, Lola was dashing into court and sliding into her seat at the table, as India, following, tapped on the arm of the lawyer who was Simon's second chair, gesturing to her to come outside.

'What's going on?' Simon Poluck was saying urgently to Lola.

'Carin knows I went to Italy and saw Joe!' she hissed back.

'*Fuck*,' Simon Poluck muttered. 'Can they prove it?'

'They've got photographs. And a witness.'

'Who's the witness?'

Lola smiled bitterly.

'Jean-Marc's old drug dealer. She followed me the whole time.'

'Well, that's not exactly the most reliable testimony—' Simon Poluck's eyebrows had shot up. Swiftly, his brain churned through all the options available to them. 'But *fuck*, that's the least of it. You were on a plane, you stayed at a hotel – they can find plenty of people who saw you, people who aren't drug dealers—' He took a deep breath. 'We can't deny this. We're going to have to get this out on the table now, so they can't slam you with it in cross.'

He looked at her straight on.

'This is going to be tough, Lola. We'll fight as hard as we can, but this is going to be tough. I'll come out with this right at the start. Then we'll go to your testimony, like you rehearsed, OK? Simply: you went to Italy, you skipped bail. None of us knew anything about that, you've just told me this moment. You want to be completely honest, so we're telling the whole story.'

He grimaced.

'It might just work.'

But his tone of voice didn't sound particularly optimistic.

Chapter 39

'Ladies and gentlemen of the jury,' Simon Poluck began. 'This is a terrible case. A terrible tragedy. And the person who has suffered most of all has been, without question, my client. Miss Fitzgerald.' He pointed at Lola, small and delicate, sitting at the defence table. 'She has seen her life destroyed before her eyes. Her father slipped into a diabetic coma, which not even the most malevolent of prosecutors could argue was in any way her fault. And the very day her father became comatose, her stepmother, instead of calling her stepdaughter to break the sad news and to commiserate with her, assumed control of her trust fund, blocked her credit cards and had her locked out of her own house. Can you imagine what Miss Fitzgerald must have been through? Her father in a coma, her entire life – her finances, her house – all maliciously removed from her at one fell stroke.'

He shook is head, pantomiming disbelief at how badly Lola had been treated.

'Miss Fitzgerald and her father had always had an extremely close, loving relationship. Many people might well envy their bond. Like any caring father, Ben Fitzgerald wanted his daughter to have every benefit that he could afford to give her. Perhaps he spoilt her. That is his fault, not hers, if you can really consider it a fault for a loving father to lavish care and attention on his beloved only child, to make sure that she would never want for anything. He made clear, with every action towards her, that her well-being was one of the most important focuses of her existence.'

Lola swallowed hard in an effort not to cry.

'Miss Fitzgerald begged and borrowed funds to get her to New York, to see her father. She had to go through her lawyers to be allowed to visit him! Incredible, isn't it? But it's true, sad to say. Miss Fitzgerald had to use the weight of the legal system to force her stepmother to allow her to visit her comatose father. And when, eventually, a visit was arranged, Miss Fitzgerald found herself at the centre of an appalling plot. Not content with having cut off her stepdaughter's access to the trust funds her father had established for her, Mrs Fitzgerald—'

He gestured to Carin, who returned his stare of loathing with a small, contemptuous smile—

'Mrs Fitzgerald and the nurse she had engaged to look after her ailing husband plotted to frame Miss Fitzgerald for the murder of her father. Because, ladies and gentlemen, the prosecution had one fact right. It is undeniable, from the levels of insulin in Mr Fitzgerald's body, that he was indeed murdered from an overdose. But it was not my client who killed him. It was his wife.'

Lola heard a gasp from someone in the jury box, but she was looking at Carin as the allegation was made, not at the jury members. Carin barely changed expression; her eyes narrowed fractionally, but that was all.

She should have shaken her head, Lola thought. *That's what an innocent person would do when they were accused of killing their own husband.*

'With the co-operation of the unfortunate Mr Scutellaro, murdered overseas in a freak incident that can have no possible bearing on this case whatsoever,' Simon Poluck continued, 'Mrs Fitzgerald planned and executed the murder of her husband. My client will testify that she only handled the hypodermic needle in question, of which we have heard so much, because the nurse Scutellaro handed it to her. *That* is why her prints are on it, and *that* is why those prints are not the ones of a person holding the hypodermic in the way they would if they were injecting someone, but simply as if they were holding it for a moment, as you would a pen.'

He smiled triumphantly, with the air of a man who had made a crucial point.

'Ladies and gentlemen,' he concluded, 'there is really no case for Miss Fitzgerald to answer. She had no motive to kill her father: we are prepared to bring an eminent witness who will testify that she knew she would win her case against her stepmother and regain control of the trust funds that were rightfully hers.'

Lola knew he meant George Goldman, who couldn't be present as a spectator because he was on the defence witness list.

'Miss Fitzgerald adored her father, and he adored her. Losing him has been one of the most painful experiences she will ever undergo. Please, don't compound her suffering by taking this charge remotely seriously. She is not guilty. The idea that anyone could ever have thought she was guilty is so ludicrous that it is only under-standable by the fact that she was framed by the unreliable testimony of a dead witness in the pay of her stepmother, who has demonstrated all too clearly her dislike of her stepdaughter. After you have heard the testimony for the defence, I am more confident than I have ever been in my entire career that you will have no hes-itation whatsoever in finding her' – he paused, momentarily, for full effect – '*not guilty.*'

'That was pretty good,' the second chair, who had returned in time to catch his opening statement, muttered to Lola. 'He made the best of things.'

'More confident than he's ever been in his entire career!' Lola whispered back, encouraged.

'Oh no, he says that every time,' the second chair hissed, deflat-ing her immediately.

'Calling Lola Fitzgerald to the stand!' the court officer said.

Heart pounding, Lola rose, smoothing down her skirt, walked over to the witness stand and was sworn in. She stared across its wooden rim at Simon Poluck, her eyes wide and dark and full of apprehension.

'Miss Fitzgerald . . .' Simon Poluck was looking very serious. 'I was planning to start by talking to you about your father. About your love for him, and the bond between you, as shown by the care he took to make sure you would always want for nothing. And then to move on to the events of that terrible day when he passed away, and you realised that your life would never be the same.'

'Your Honour, if there's a question here I'm not hearing it!' Joshua Greene piped up.

'He's right, Mr Poluck. Fewer speeches, more questions,' reprimanded the judge.

'I apologise, Your Honour, members of the jury,' Simon Poluck said. 'But – quite simply – I had a shocking piece of news from my client just before I stood up to make my opening statement. I'll come straight to the point, Your Honour.'

Everyone was now agog in the courtroom. You could have heard a pin drop.

Lola, sitting in the witness box, had a bird's eye view of them all. The jury, ranged to her left in two lines of seats, were staring at her avidly, taking in every detail of her appearance. The girl in the front had started to copy Lola's outfits; her pale-brown hair was scraped back, her stud earrings were pale yellow and large enough that they had to be cubic zirconia, and her simple dark dress had a wide collar not unlike the Marc Jacobs dress that Lola wore in rotation with the other outfits that had been approved by the witness expert. The girl's eyes were fixed on Lola, eating her up: Lola sketched a little smile at her, and saw her eyes go even wider in amazement at having been noticed by her goddess.

Joshua Greene, resuming his seat, looked wary. Carin, who was sitting a couple of rows behind the prosecutor's desk, looking spectacular in huge, dangling, sapphire earrings that caught the pale blue of her eyes, had raised her light-blonde eyebrows at Simon Poluck's words, but showed no other signs of being affected. India had slipped back into the courtroom, and was sitting by Suzanne, whispering to her, Suzanne blanching as she heard the bad news.

Simon Poluck said:

'Miss Fitzgerald, you just gave me a disturbing piece of information, knowing that as an officer of the court I am duty bound to ask you about it on the stand. Would you tell us first why you volunteered this information to me?'

Lola's voice was very small at first. She cleared her throat and tried to make it louder.

'Because I was about to swear an oath to tell the whole truth,' she said. 'And I realised that I had to be completely honest.'

Simon Poluck nodded.

'And can you please tell us what it is that you have to confess?'

Everyone leaned forward, as if choreographed, irresistibly drawn by the word 'confess' used in the context of a murder trial. Even the judge swivelled in her seat to look fully at Lola.

Very clever of him, Lola thought approvingly. *Now that he's put the idea in their heads, anything I say that isn't a confession of murder is going to come as an anticlimax.*

'I left the country a few days ago,' she admitted. 'I went to Italy to visit Joe Scutellaro.'

Maybe it hadn't been such an anticlimax after all. The judge had to pound with her gavel again to quiet down the exclamations of surprise in the courtroom.

'Miss Fitzgerald, you are aware that you skipped bail by leaving the country, even though you duly returned for this trial?' Simon Poluck thundered over Joshua Greene, who was already on his feet and practically shouting.

'I just wanted to talk to him – to beg him to tell the truth about what really happened to my father—'

'I demand that her bail be revoked *immediately*!' Joshua Greene was yelling, pointing accusingly at Lola. 'And forfeited!'

'Agreed,' the judge said, looking sternly at Lola. 'Miss Fitzgerald, your bail is revoked with immediate effect. You're on remand from this moment.'

Suzanne started to sob on India's shoulder.

'Miss Fitzgerald,' Simon Poluck was saying loudly, to cut through the hubbub, 'can you tell us more about your meeting with Mr Scutellaro?'

'I begged him to tell the truth,' Lola said. 'I didn't kill my father, and he knew it.' She stared angrily at Carin. '*She* did,' she said, pointing at Carin. 'My stepmother. She killed him for his money. And Joe Scutellaro was going to tell the truth at this trial.'

There were gasps heard round the courtroom at this accusation. Carin didn't move a muscle, but sat there, stony-faced, as if even to react to Lola's words would be beneath her.

'You mean he lied in the grand jury testimony that we heard read out yesterday?' Simon Poluck demanded.

'That's right!' Lola said defiantly.

'Miss Fitzgerald,' Simon Poluck said challengingly, 'it's a very convenient story that you're telling the jury, isn't it? After all, Mr Scutellaro is sadly no longer here to contradict what you're saying. Haven't you just jumped on the opportunity presented by his death?'

'No, it's the truth!' Tears started to form in Lola's eyes. 'That's why I went to Italy – to make him tell the truth! I didn't kill my father – *she* did, and he knew that!'

'Your Honour—' Joshua Greene objected.

'Yes, yes,' the judge cut in. 'The jury will disregard that last statement. You can't tell us what Mr Scutellaro knew, Miss Fitzgerald. This entire line of questioning is skirting much too close to hearsay, Mr Poluck. I've given you some latitude because I allowed Mr Scutellaro's grand jury testimony to be read into evidence, but we're crossing a line here and we're going to have to pull back.'

Simon Poluck nodded.

'Miss Fitzgerald, I have to ask you this question,' he started, his tone of voice very grave. 'When you illegally – as you have yourself admitted – jumped bail and travelled to Italy, did you offer, or pay, Mr Scutellaro, any money at all to change his testimony?'

'Not a penny,' Lola said, her chin high, staring directly at Carin.

And there's no way you can prove I did, you bitch, she thought vindictively. *If you produced that copy of the contract I gave him, it would incriminate you.*

And the mere fact that he'd signed it would mean that no one would believe a word of his grand jury testimony.

'So your intent was not to bribe him,' Simon Poluck prompted.

'No! Not at all!' Lola said. 'I just wanted him to tell the truth! I didn't kill my father!'

Tears started to form in her eyes, and she wiped them away. As she did so, she found herself making eye contact with Joshua Greene. He looked like a cat who's got a mouse between its claws and is about to tear it limb from limb; his eyes were glinting, a little smile played on his lips, and as he tilted his head sideways to whisper something to Serena Mackesy, Lola saw with rising fear that Mackesy's expression was exactly the same.

Panicking, she darted her eyes sideways at the jury. No one would meet her gaze: they all looked away.

Even the girl who was dressed like a cheap copy of Lola wouldn't meet her eyes. Lola had heard that when the jury was filing back in with a guilty verdict, they wouldn't look directly at the prisoner. And this was just the same – only earlier. It was as if they had already decided on a guilty verdict.

As soon as she had confessed to skipping bail, they hadn't believed a word she said.

From the grave, Joe Scutellaro's lies were going to convict her.

She looked back at Greene and Mackesy, both of them glowing with smug satisfaction.

They're going to eat me alive in cross-examination, she realised.

'We should seriously consider taking this plea,' Simon Poluck said, his thin dark features concentrated into a knot of tension.

Lola couldn't speak. She could barely breathe.

'It's not looking good, Lola,' the jury consultant said quietly. 'I'm sorry, but I've been watching the jury for the last two hours and their body language is very, very negative.'

They were sitting in a small room in the bowels of the court-house, its walls painted a fading pale yellow, peeling and stained. Outside the closed door waited a court officer, ready to take Lola back to her cell when this meeting with her lawyers was over. At the end of the day, she would be on a prison bus, going back to the Tombs, with all the other prisoners on remand who were currently on trial.

And now Simon Poluck had come to tell her that Joshua Greene, scenting victory, had come to offer a plea bargain. Fifteen years, if she confessed to killing her father.

'It's really not a bad deal,' Simon Poluck said unhappily. 'A hell of a lot better than twenty-five to life. I'm sorry, Lola. But we're all looking at that jury and reading the same thing.'

Nods from her legal team were silent confirmation.

'They're going to convict,' the jury consultant said. 'Inasmuch as you can ever predict these things, I'm reading conviction. My advice is absolutely to take the deal.'

'I won't do it,' she said, swallowing hard, her voice thin and frail. 'I won't take the plea.'

Simon Poluck's frown deepened.

'It's really not a bad offer,' he said. 'I doubt Greene'll make one this good again. You're up against a big machine. I'm trying to get you out of the way as best I can before it rolls right over you.'

'I won't!' she said, her voice higher now, more determined. 'I won't admit to something I didn't do! I *didn't* kill my father!'

The jury consultant sighed.

'Unfortunately,' she started, 'it's about what other people believe—'

'I don't care!' Lola pushed back her chair and stood up from the table. 'I didn't do it, and I won't say I did! It's my *father* we're talking about here, and no one, *no one*, is going to make me admit to killing him, when I didn't do it! They can convict me if they want—'

'They will,' muttered the consultant.

'—but they *can't* make me say that I killed him!' Lola overrode her passionately. 'Because I didn't! And nothing in the world will ever, *ever* make me say that I did! Even if I rot in prison for the rest of my life!'

She turned on her heel and went to the door, wrenching it open. 'Can I go back to my cell, please?' she said to the court officer.

'Lola – please, just think it over—' Simon Poluck called to her as she strode off. 'Just do me a favour, and think it over—'

'I won't!' She stopped in the corridor, swivelling back to face him, hands on her hips. 'You can go right back to him and tell him that there won't be a deal, *ever*. I'll do twenty-five years in prison if I have to. But I'll never, *never* admit to killing my own father!'

As she turned back to follow the court officer, she caught the glance he threw at her. He had seen everything in his time working for the New York State judicial system; he looked world-weary, his uniform straining at the seams, his movements slow. Like a corrections officer or a cop, he had heard everything there was to hear, every protest and excuse and attempt at evasion that a defendant could try to pull.

Which made it even worse that Lola had seen what she had seen in his eyes.

It was pity.

Even the court officer knew that she was going to be convicted of patricide.

Chapter 40

'*M*iss Fitzgerald, once and for all: *did you kill your father?*'

'No!' Lola leaned forward, holding onto the edge of the polished wooden witness stand, turning so that she could look directly at the jury as she answered Simon Poluck's question with so much fervency that her voice throbbed and broke as she reiterated:

'No, I did *not!* I *loved* my father! I could never do anything to hurt him!'

Simon Poluck's narrow dark face was drawn tight for a moment, as if he were listening to what Lola had just said, taking it in. And then he nodded, slowly, as if he had heard the truth in her words, and decided to believe her.

'Your Honour, I have no more questions for Miss Fitzgerald,' he said dramatically, turning on his heel and striding back to the defendant's table with a theatricality that suggested clearly that there was obviously no need to ask her anything else.

His abrupt end to Lola's testimony had the courtroom in turmoil, exactly as he had intended. Joshua Greene and Serena Mackesy were exchanging stares of shock, Mackesy ruffling frantically through the stack of papers in front of her, Greene twisting to look at the clock hanging behind them on the far wall. Two-thirty p.m. Hopefully, much too early for the judge to do anything but insist that the prosecution start their cross-examination this afternoon.

'I'm going to throw Greene a curve ball,' Simon Poluck had muttered to Lola before her trial resumed after the lunch break. 'He'll be expecting me to keep you on the stand for a day, at least. Building you up, going over all the allegations, establishing a strong defence. So I'm going to make him start his cross before he's ready. Just a few questions, then I'll say we're done. I can always come back to you after Greene's done, if it's necessary. I want to throw him off-balance, so he doesn't come on with all guns blazing from the get go.'

Casting a quick stare of dislike across the aisle at Simon Poluck, Joshua Greene heaved his small round body to his feet. His balding head was damp, his glasses and his suit cheap and badly made by comparison to the expensive accoutrements of Simon Poluck and Lola's whole defence team, who charged huge fees and as a result could dress much better than anyone on a paltry ADA's salary. The defence attorneys and jury consultants were razor-sharp in DKNY, Armani, and Michael Kors; the closest the DAs could get to those labels was on deep discount, rifling through the packed sale rails and dodging sharpened elbows in the crowded, fluorescent-lit surroundings of T.K. Maxx.

But as Joshua Greene stood up, tugged his jacket down to hang as best it could, and fixed Lola with a cold hard stare from behind the lenses of his hundred-dollar glasses, he assumed the authority of the whole of New York State. Suddenly, he was no longer a tubby little man in a shiny grey suit from Men's Wearhouse, but a prosecutor with the weight of the Manhattan District Attorney's office behind him.

'Ms Fitzgerald!' Joshua Greene said sternly, and Lola jumped. For a moment her eyes met her mother's – Suzanne was pale with worry, clinging onto India's hand – and Suzanne tried to paint a smile of reassurance for her daughter.

Lola quickly averted her gaze. If she looked at her mother for more than a second, she'd burst into tears out of sheer fright.

'You've already admitted to this court that you defied its orders when you skipped bail, isn't that so?' Joshua Greene said.

'I didn't actually *skip* bail,' Lola said weakly. 'I mean, I did, but I came back. I wasn't trying to run away.'

'We'll talk more about the circumstances under which you left the country later,' Joshua Greene said with relish. 'Obviously, you had help in *skipping*' – he emphasised the word – 'bail.'

Oh my God, Evie! Lola realised in panic. She had been so caught up in her own desperate situation that she hadn't thought how badly this would reflect on her accomplice. Evie had lent Lola her passport – well, Lola could always say that she'd stolen it. But Evie had covered for Lola when the police came by the apartment – that was undeniable. Evie could be prosecuted too.

Through a huge force of will, Lola kept her eyes fastened on Joshua Greene's face. She wouldn't look to the far right of the courtroom, where Evie and Lawrence sat in the last row, discreetly, in order to avoid the scrutiny of the many reporters present. Evie had pulled her hair back under a beret, and was dressed in dowdy layers of sweaters over a pair of jeans, managing to look nondescript enough so that no one would recognise her as Diamond the showgirl, or Evie Lopez, Ben Fitzgerald's scandalously young mistress.

If they know she's here, they might arrest her right away! Lola thought frantically, determined not to give away Evie's presence.

'So tell me, Ms Fitzgerald,' Joshua Greene was saying with undisguised relish, 'since you've already shown yourself utterly contemptuous of the rules and regulations of this court and the State of New York, why should anyone here believe a word you say from now on?'

Lola opened her lips to answer, but Greene pressed straight on.

'Were you really going to Italy to convince Mr Scutellaro to change his story?' Joshua Greene demanded. 'Or were you travelling there to engineer the circumstances by which Mr Scutellaro met his tragic death?'

Lola gasped in shock.

'*Your Honour!*' Simon Poluck leaped to his feet so fast Lola heard his chair bounce back against the wooden divider behind it.

'Mr Greene!' the judge snapped. 'You try that once more, you'll have an automatic mistrial on your hands!'

'I'm sorry, Your Honour—' Joshua Greene started.

'The jury will disregard the entire last question by ADA Greene,' the judge said, turning to the jury box, her forehead so crinkled with annoyance that it looked like corrugated cardboard. 'That is a line of speculation which does not enter into this trial in any way.'

'Duly noted, Your Honour,' Joshua Greene said.

But the damage had been done. Lola could see it in the jury's faces. They thought she was a double murderess. That she had killed her father, and then gone to Italy to arrange a hit on the man who was going to testify against her.

She was going to be found guilty of murder.

Across the courtroom, Evie's big brown eyes were wide with fear. Like Lola, she had been petrified that Lola would give her away somehow, that she would be arrested on the spot for having helped Lola leave the country. And just because it hadn't happened yet didn't mean it wasn't coming.

Evie wasn't sure what the penalties were for helping someone accused of murder skip bail, but she sure as hell didn't want to find out.

Heart racing, she eased herself out of her seat, motioning to Lawrence to stay put; someone needed to stay, to hear what was going on in the courtroom. Evie was too agitated to sit still. She slipped out through the doors at the back, her heart racing, as the prosecutor thundered at Lola:

'You killed your father, didn't you? You stuck a needle full of insulin in him, knowing that it was sure to kill him!'

It sounded as if Lola had started to cry. Evie couldn't stick around for that, either. The doors swung shut behind her and she stood there for a little while in the wide echoing corridor, staring straight ahead of her but seeing nothing, not the long sweeping shiny marble staircase, the panelled walls. Nothing but Lola's face on the stand, crumpled with misery and desperation.

And the stony faces of the jury, who seemed all too clearly to have made up their minds already that Lola was guilty as charged.

That bitch Carin is going to get away with murder, Evie thought bitterly, bile rising in her throat, so sour and acrid that it gagged her and made her cough. She looked around for a water fountain, her eyes watering, and crossed the hall to the nearest one, drinking deeply.

She straightened up, wiping her mouth, and then her head jerked back in shock.

Because, standing right in front of her, leering down at her slight figure, was Rico, his hands shoved in his pockets, his crotch pushed forward, his black eyes hard and full of menace.

'Well, hey, babe,' he said.

And his lips slid back from his teeth in a predatory smile.

'Get the fuck away from me,' Evie said between clenched teeth.

Despite herself, she took a step back. Even with his hands safely in his pockets, Rico's aura was aggressive. His stare was horribly familiar: she found herself remembering with vivid, skin-crawling clarity the way he had stared at her naked body in the bedroom of her penthouse after he'd pulled the towel off her.

Rico was like the worst type of client she'd ever had to deal with in the Midnight Lounge. Only there, she'd had bouncers looking out for her to some degree. Making sure, at least, that she didn't get knocked around so badly that she got marked, or so beat up that she couldn't get back onstage for another dance.

Alone with Rico, without even a bouncer at the door, Evie wouldn't put money on her chances of avoiding either or both fates.

She swivelled around, looking to see if she could get past him.

'Oh no, babe. Don't you walk away from me,' he said, smiling as if he wanted to sink his teeth into her. 'Wait till you see what I got in my pockets for you.'

'Eeww,' Evie said. 'I've got *no* interest in your disgusting—'

And then her voice tailed off as his hands, the skin bluish and stained with the fading jail tattoos, emerged slowly from his trouser pockets, and Evie saw the glittering diamond pasties dangling between his fingers.

She stared at him, lost for words, as his smile deepened.

'Cat got your tongue?' he said, grinning now. 'You want these back, don'tcha?'

He stepped towards her, and this time she stood her ground. It was all she could do not to grab for the pasties and try to run.

'You worked *hard* for these little babies,' he said, sneering at her. 'Jeez, when I think of the state of Mr F before he kicked the bucket . . . he was gross, man. Really gross. Should be a treat for you to take on a hot stud like me.' He winked at her. 'Hey, when I think about it, you should be paying *me*, babe.'

Evie rolled her eyes.

'So here's the deal,' Rico continued. 'I got these off Carin. The stuff I got on her, she owes me big time. And she didn't *want* these. I mean, with all her money? What's she gonna do, break 'em down and make 'em into earrings or somethin'? So I got 'em as a bonus.'

He put one of the pasties back into his trouser pocket, keeping the other one wrapped through his fingers.

'I saw you come out, and I grabbed the chance,' Rico said. 'So here's what's gonna happen. You come into the men's room with me now' – his free hand made an unmistakeable gesture towards his crotch – 'and you do what I tell you to do. And you get *this* one.' He held up the small twinkling circle of diamonds. 'Then, in a few days, I call you, set up a meet. You come over, we have a big party. I mean, big. All night long, whatever I say. You dance, you sing, you fucking stand on your head if I say so. And then you get number two.' He patted his pocket. 'You get your pair. They're worth way more together than apart, Carin says.'

Evie's eyes were fixed on the shine and twinkle of the diamonds, the way they caught and refracted the light in gleams of red and blue and clear pale green.

'How do I know I can trust you?' she asked, her voice sharp.

He grinned.

'You don't. But look at it this way.' He nodded down the corridor. 'You come with me now, it's gonna be a quickie. And then, you get this for being a good girl. So you figure, hey, maybe Rico's a man of his word, and when I call you up, you get your ass over to where I tell you.' He licked his lips. 'Believe me, Carin's a money pipeline. You play your cards right, you'll make a shitload of dough from me. I like the idea of ploughing Mr F's fields, you know what I mean? Having me a pricy whore just like he did.'

He grinned at her.

'I'll check there's no one in the john. You wait outside till I call you in, OK?'

He walked off down the corridor, his wide shoulders rolling, his legs slightly apart because his over-pumped, steroid-swollen thighs were rubbing against each other.

And Evie followed.

It's just a few minutes, a voice in her head was repeating. *Just a few minutes. You've done worse. If you get both of those pasties – they cost Benny a hundred grand, so you could maybe get forty for them – I mean, forty grand! That really is a deposit on an apartment! With what you're pulling in from Maud's, you could have a decent place to live that isn't a rat-infested illegal loft in Bushwick!*

Forty grand, Evie. Forty grand.

Somewhere you don't have roach motels in every corner. Where you don't hear the rats scurrying behind the walls as you go to sleep at night.

Don't think about what you're doing. Just think about the forty grand.

Rico had cased out the men's room. He stood in the doorway, beckoning. And Evie's feet were moving. It was with a weird, out-of-body sensation that she felt herself propelled towards him. She watched, as if she were floating above herself, as she walked through the open men's room door.

Rico was in the last stall, standing in front of the toilet seat, his trousers dropped to reveal a tight shiny pair of briefs. As she reached him, he hooked his thumbs in the waistband of the underpants, pulling them down.

'See?' Rico leered triumphantly. 'He likes you already! You're lucky, bitch.' He looked down complacently at his crotch. 'He don't just go for everyone, you know.'

OK, if he's hard already that means he'll come faster, Evie told herself. *This'll be over before you know it. And what's the worst that can happen? So you do what he wants and he doesn't give you the diamonds. It won't be the first time you got shafted by a guy.*

Hah. That'd be funny, if it were happening to someone else.

She took a good hard look at Rico, as if he were a john in the club and she were assessing his spending power. His custom-tailored suit had clearly been very pricy. Ditto his shoes. So more than likely that Rolex dangling from his wrist, clearly visible as he wrapped his hand round his penis, was actually real, rather than the Canal Street knock-off she'd thought it was. Rico was rolling in money. Being Carin Fitzgerald's hatchet man must pay very well indeed.

Remember what he said about wanting a pricy whore, just like Benny had? He likes that he's paying a lot for this. He's getting off on paying you a ton of money to humiliate you by making you suck him off in the men's bathroom.

When you'd worked in the Midnight Lounge for a couple of years, you learned how to read the kind of man who paid for female services. Evie looked into Rico's beady dark eyes and knew that he wouldn't try to cheat her after she'd done what he told her to do. This was all about his ego, about his taking over Benny's girl and paying what Benny had paid for her. This was him trying to take Benny's place.

Forty grand, Evie. Think what that'll buy.

Rico snapped his fingers and pointed to the tiled floor directly in front of him.

Evie's hand was still on the scratched Formica-covered door of the disabled stall. She hesitated for a moment. All she'd need to do was turn and walk out. Back to the safety of the corridor, the courtroom, her seat beside Lawrence.

Lawrence, who she wasn't even seeing any more, who she didn't even have to feel guilty about . . .

'Good girl,' Rico purred as she sank to her knees. She winced at the cold hard tile, which was already cutting into her kneecaps.

Have to make this fast, she told herself grimly.

'Do it just like you did Mr F,' Rico instructed, as Evie pushed her hair back from her face. 'I got a billionaire's whore, I wanna billionaire's blow job! Here.' He pulled one of the pasties out of his pocket and dangled it in her face. 'See that? You make it worth it, bitch, and it's all yours.'

Don't think about it, Evie. Just do it, said the little voice in her head.

And Evie reached out and took hold of Rico's cock, guiding it to her mouth.

Chapter 41

'Miss Fitzgerald? Do you need to take a break?'

The judge was leaning sideways, swivelling her head to get a full-on look at Lola, who was sobbing into a tissue which by now was patchy with damp sooty blotches. When Dior had been testing its high-tech Diorshow Black Out waterproof mascara and guaranteeing it as 100 per cent smudge-proof, it clearly hadn't given samples to defendants on trial for murdering their own parents.

'I don't, thank you,' she said to the judge, and saw Simon Poluck, seated at the defendant's table, give a little nod of approval at the courtesy. He had been stressing all along that the better manners she showed, the less likely it would be that a jury would believe that she was a killer.

Lola looked over at the jury.

'I can keep going,' she said firmly, suppressing the little catch in her voice. She was scared that if she asked for a break from Joshua Greene's cross-examination, it would only be worse when he started up again. For the past forty-five minutes he had been worrying her as relentlessly as a dog with a bone full of marrow, finding new ways to ask her the same questions, trying to break her down.

No matter how many times Simon Poluck barked: 'Your Honour,

this question has been asked and answered!' Joshua Greene would come at Lola from a different angle, his eyes glinting menacingly from behind his glasses, taking her through every detail of that last visit to her father, throwing in comments about her extravagant lifestyle, doing what even she could see was an utterly successful job of painting her to the jury as a depraved, money-hungry socialite desperate enough to do anything, anything at all, to ensure that her 'money tap', as he called it, was turned back on.

'Miss Fitzgerald?' Joshua Greene snapped. 'Are you ready to answer the question now? I'll remind you of it, shall I?' he said, striding back towards the witness box. 'I was asking you where you went after you were forced to settle your hotel bill at 60 Thompson? When the manager effectively made it clear to you that, without a functioning credit card, you would no longer be welcome to stay there?'

'She didn't quite say that,' Lola said weakly.

'So where *did* you go, Miss Fitzgerald?' Joshua Greene persisted.

Lola opened her mouth to say that she had packed her bags and gone straight to the Plaza. And then she met the prosecutor's eyes, and the lie died on her lips. From the triumph in his stare, like a cat about to pounce on a mouse that has just made the fatal tactical mistake of going left rather than right, she realised suddenly that the prosecution knew about her brief, abortive attempt to sneak into Madison's apartment, the bribe of her beautiful lemon sable wrap to Mirko.

This was going to make her look *terrible*. Bribing a doorman with the clothes off her back. Nothing could make it so clear that, before her father's death, Lola had been utterly and completely at her wits' end. This pathetic little story would demonstrate with merciless clarity that Lola had really had absolutely nowhere else to turn besides the charity of a former fiancé who might decide to withdraw it from one moment to the next.

It was the biggest motive possible. Financial desperation.

She darted a frantic glance towards Simon Poluck, hoping against hope that he would have some objection that would save her from having to answer the question. Joshua Greene, watching every fleeting emotion that played across her face, scanning it with the experience of years spent in courtrooms, cross-examining reluctant defendants, smiled nastily, his round chubby features contorting into a grimace of satisfaction.

But Simon Poluck wasn't looking back at her. He was huddled over to his second chair, who was squatting down by the side of the table, whispering something to him, her eyes wide and staring, one hand tapping convulsively on the leg of the table for emphasis.

Joshua Greene's smile deepened as he saw Lola floundering, hoping for a rescue that wasn't going to come.

'Miss Fitzgerald, I'm going to have to press you! Will you please answer the question – *where did you go when you were forced to leave the 60 Thompson hotel?*' he thundered.

'Your Honour!' Simon Poluck jumped to his feet. 'We have just been presented with new evidence that is so explosive that I couldn't wait a moment longer to bring it to your attention—'

Joshua Greene threw up his hands.

'What, *more* grandstanding from Mr Poluck?'

'Enough!' said the judge sharply. 'Both of you, approach the bench immediately!'

Simon Poluck and Joshua Greene bustled up to the bench, Poluck whispering away so urgently that everyone in the courtroom was agog.

'My chambers, *now*,' the judge said grimly, rising to her feet.

As Poluck and Greene duly followed her, Lola was escorted back to the defendant's table. Swivelling around, she exchanged stares of incomprehension with her mother and India. David's blue eyes were saucer-wide.

Then, beyond them, Lola noticed the man standing just inside the courtroom doors. Chunky and square-built, he had a head shaped like a big bullet on his short muscular neck. Though he had to be in his sixties, he looked strong and energetic, his wide arms folded over his chest, his big upper torso encased in a dark blue suit that was so well-cut that it must have cost several thousand dollars.

She would have assumed that he was a policeman, because the way he was standing, completely comfortable waiting there, was very reminiscent of the cops she'd been forced into contact with over the past few weeks. But the quality of his suit contradicted that. She was wondering who he was, and why the court officers were letting him stand there, when the door at the back of the courtroom opened, the bailiff calling for everyone to stand as the judge bustled back in, followed by the four attorneys.

Joshua Greene looked livid, Lola noticed as she turned to face the courtroom, rising to her feet. Serena Mackesy was biting her lips in fury as he whispered to her what had happened. And Simon Poluck was taking his place beside Lola, his eyes bright, his entire body seeming to be surrounded with an aura of triumphant golden light.

'What—' Lola hissed to Simon Poluck, but he shushed her, grinning, as they resumed their seats and the judge began:

'This trial has, without question, been full of surprises. Having heard what Mr Poluck has had to tell me about a defence witness who has just come forward, I must agree that the nature of the testimony is such that it does indeed justify his taking the extreme step of breaking into Mr Greene's cross-examination of the defendant. Normally, I wouldn't allow the testimony to be given at this time. But because of the very unusual nature of the decisions I have already had to make during the course of these proceedings, I am going to allow the defence witness to testify – with the proviso that it may be necessary to declare a mistrial if events do not proceed exactly as Mr Poluck has assured me they will. And—' she stared severely at Simon Poluck – 'if the witness's credentials do not prove to be absolutely as impeccable as I have been assured that they are.'

'Duly noted, Your Honour,' Simon Poluck said as demurely as a lawyer with the glint of victory in his eyes can ever manage.

'The defence calls Marco Ranieri to the stand!' called the court officer, and Lola saw the Latino man in the very well-cut navy suit walk past her down the aisle. As he passed Lola, he turned his big bald head in her direction, looking at her directly, and there was something in those black, flat eyes that Lola would have given a great deal to be able to read.

Marco Ranieri settled his heavy body into the witness stand, shot his cuffs, and swore the oath with the blasé air of a man who had gone through this kind of proceeding many, many times before. Lola stared at Simon Poluck, her eyes wide, pleading to have her curiosity satisfied: but he shook his head again.

And then he winked at her.

Simon Poluck, a man whose tie always co-ordinated with his silk pocket square, whose shoes were perfectly shined and whose shirts cost more than most people's entire outfits, winked at his client.

Lola felt a terrible hope swelling inside her – terrifying, because how could she dare to hope, when things had been going so badly for her? But as Simon Poluck, taking his time, rose slowly to his feet, with the air of a matador about to strike a killer blow, she could hardly suppress the excitement she was feeling.

'Mr Ranieri, will you please tell us your profession?' Simon Poluck began.

'I'm a PI. A private investigator,' Ranieri clarified in a gravelly voice, turning to nod at the jury.

A buzz of interest ran round the courtroom at this information. The jury, already highly stimulated by Simon Poluck's dramatic interruption of Lola's cross-examination, sat up even straighter in their seats.

'And before you were a private investigator—' Simon Poluck prompted.

'I was on the job for twenty years. A cop with the NYPD,' Ranieri explained.

So she had been right about him, Lola realised. And that explained his ease in the witness box: he must have had to give testimony countless times during the course of his career.

'Ended up as a detective on the Major Case Squad,' Ranieri was saying.

'And during the twenty years you served the city of New York, you received several commendations, and a medal, I believe—'

'Racked up three commendations, plus the Medal of Honour,' Ranieri agreed casually.

'Which is awarded for—'

'Your Honour,' Joshua Greene said between his teeth, 'the prosecution will stipulate that ex-Detective Ranieri had an exemplary career with the NYPD, and that he has since collaborated with my office on a couple of occasions.'

'Leading to successful prosecutions,' Ranieri added nonchalantly.

'Thank you, Mr Greene,' the judge said. 'Mr Poluck, I think we can move forward with the understanding that this witness's character and credentials have been thoroughly established.'

Simon Poluck dipped a little bow in her direction.

'Mr Ranieri, the story you have to tell is a very dramatic one,' he began, 'and in order to lay it out fully we need to go back to January of this year, when you were contacted by a new client. Will you please tell us the name of this client?'

'It was Ben Fitzgerald,' Marco Ranieri said. 'The dead guy.'

The jury leaned forward almost as one, sensing that some really good dirt was about to be dug up.

'And what did Mr Fitzgerald ask you to do?' Simon Poluck inquired, with the nonchalance of a poker player who knows that he's holding a Royal Flush.

'He wanted me to upgrade his house's security system.' Ranieri grinned, and it was like watching a shark swim up behind an unsuspecting shoal of fish and open its mouth. 'Well, that was the official version. You know, what we said we were doing when I sent my guys in there.'

'And the unofficial version?'

'He wanted a master feed of all his house's security cameras.'

'Can you explain that for the jury, Mr Ranieri?'

Ranieri swivelled in his seat, his grin deepening, as he crossed one leg over the other.

'OK, this is how it works,' he started leisurely. 'You have security cameras already installed in your house, say, like Mr Fitzgerald did, God rest his soul. You know, you got them there so you can check your staff aren't going through your personal shit they got no reason to be in,' he added over his shoulder. 'You and your wife are the only people who get to watch the footage, obviously. But then, like Mr Fitzgerald, maybe you start to . . . have concerns.'

He paused, enjoying the cliffhanger moment.

'What kind of concerns?' Simon Poluck prompted.

'Well, about his wife, of course!' Marco Ranieri said, leaning back in his chair, his eyes gleaming. 'I mean, who else? She's the only one who sees the footage, apart from him! She's the only one who could wipe stuff off so he doesn't see it! So when a guy asks you for a master feed' – he looked at the jury – 'that means all the footage, *everything*, goes to this kinda online website that only he can access. Raw, unedited. When a guy asks a PI for that, it means he don't trust his wife. No other explanation possible.'

Joshua Greene was on his feet.

'Your Honour—'

'Yes, yes, Mr Greene,' the judge said. 'Mr Poluck, this had better not be speculation on the part of the witness—'

'Mr Ranieri,' Simon Poluck asked, 'did Mr Fitzgerald inform you of these suspicions, or are you merely making assumptions?'

'Oh, I've been round the block a few times,' Ranieri said cheerfully. 'Believe me, I know how a courtroom works. I got emails from Mr Fitzgerald, printed out right there.' He nodded to the defence table.

Simon Poluck picked up a clear plastic folder containing several sheets of paper.

'Defence exhibit number sixty-seven, Your Honour,' he said, putting it back on the table. 'Email correspondence between Mr Fitzgerald and Mr Ranieri . . . So, did Mr Fitzgerald engage you to acquire evidence he would use in divorce proceedings?'

Ranieri's eyebrows shot up in surprise.

'Well, sure,' he said. 'There was a big prenup. Mr Fitzgerald showed me. If the wife cheated, she got nothing. Nada. Zippo. Bye bye, babycakes, and don't slam the door on your way out.'

For the past few minutes, the stares of practically everyone in the courtroom had been darting back and forth between Marco Ranieri and Carin Fitzgerald. The two of them could not have presented more of a contrast.

Ranieri was relaxed, charismatic, enjoying to the full the drama of his testimony.

And Carin Fitzgerald, who, since Ranieri had mentioned the words 'master feed', had been as still as if she were carved from bone. The white mink collar of her black silk-and-cashmere sweater didn't even tremble with the rise and fall of her breast, nor did her sapphire earings; she might not even be breathing, so motionless was her body. Any colour had faded completely from her face, which was as pale as the marble tombstone at the head of her husband's grave; apart from her Siberian-husky blue eyes, whose pupils were dilated to large black dots. The fuchsia lipstick she wore made the rest of her face look blanched.

Lola sneaked a glance over at the jury. They were all riveted on Carin now, greedily observing every detail of her appearance.

'So you proceeded to set up this master feed?' Simon Poluck was asking Ranieri.

'Sure. It wasn't a tough job. We set up the website with streaming feeds, Mr Fitzgerald plugs in a password and bingo! Simple enough.'

'Now, let me make this clear,' Simon Poluck said. 'When you say that Mr Fitzgerald plugged in a password—'

'It's his own. That's how he wanted it,' Ranieri explained. 'He's the only one that can access that website. We set it up but then we got out of the way. We don't watch it, we don't have any way to see that footage. Just Mr Fitzgerald.' He looked at the jury, his expression serious now. 'Which is why I haven't come forward before. My company, we don't fool around with this stuff. Mr Fitzgerald wanted top-level secrecy, and he paid a ton of money for it. When he died, and his daughter was arrested, I mean, obviously I knew straight away that I could be sitting on crucial evidence. But we got a client confidentiality agreement that's rock solid. If I go to the DA with this, I could be sued seven ways to Sunday by Mr Fitzgerald's estate. And, you know, would clients trust me again? My reputation – well, it speaks for itself. I was back and forth on this for a long time, believe me, trying to figure out how to handle it. Plus – and here's the kicker – the password-protection on that site is shit hot. I've got the best guys in the business working for me. You enter the wrong password more than twice, it wipes *everything*. All the footage. Fragments it so you'd never be able to get it back in any recognisable form.'

'And you didn't have the password?'

Ranieri shook his head.

'Like I said, no way. That was the whole point.'

Simon Poluck strode across the room so that he was directly in front of the witness stand.

'But, Mr Ranieri,' he said softly, 'you have brought us today crucial footage of events at Mr Fitzgerald's house the day that he died which utterly contradict the prosecution's case! How did you manage to access this completely private master feed that you set up for Mr Fitzgerald, if you didn't know the password?'

Ranieri's shark eyes were inscrutable as he answered:

'I got an anonymous tip.'

'You can't be serious.'

'Believe me, I got an anonymous tip. Last night. Some guy rang me from a payphone on First Avenue. Eight letters, which was the length of Mr Fitzgerald's password. I figured, I got three goes, I'll try this and see if it works.'

'And it did?'

Ranieri's laugh was short and dry.

'Oh yeah. It worked all right.' He coughed. 'We burned off a couple DVDs of the really crucial stuff. One for the day Mr Fitzgerald went into his coma. One the day the poor guy died.'

'Your Honour' – Simon Poluck was back at the defence table now – 'these are the DVDs in question, if the court officer has set up the monitor for us to play them on—'

'Go ahead, Mr Poluck,' the judge said, waving her hand. 'And yes, Mr Greene, I'll pre-empt you. Your objection is noted for the record, OK?'

As Simon Poluck slid the DVD into the player, as the lights in the courtroom were dimmed slightly, as Poluck fast-forwarded through footage of Ben Fitzgerald in bed, asleep, Lola thought her heart would beat right out of her chest.

And then Simon Poluck hit 'Play', and Joe Scutellaro walked onscreen.

Despite the grainy black-and-white video, he was instantly recognisable. It was the first time Lola had ever seen someone she knew, someone who was dead and buried, come back to life in this bizarre way, walking so easily, so unaware that a mere few weeks later he would be hiding out in a sleazy apartment in a crumbling tower block in one of Rome's most dangerous slums, and shortly after that would be stabbed to death by a group of kids paid a handful of euros to kill him and leave him to bleed out on a concrete slab.

Her father, sleeping, and Joe in his white nurse's uniform, moving to the foot of the bed, standing there, watching him. Her father was snoring, despite being propped up on a mound of pillows to facilitate his breathing: you could hear it in the video, a low rumble, unhealthy, less like a purr than an ancient motor trying, and failing, to catch into life.

Lola's arms were wrapped around each other, the fingers sinking deeply into the flesh of the opposite forearms, hurting her. Good. She dug into her skin even harder, needing the pain to keep her from screaming with the tension.

Joe was rolling up the sleeve of her father's pyjama top now, baring the flesh to above the elbow.

And then Carin Fitzgerald, her hair cut so short that you could almost see her scalp, wearing a white velvet robe belted tightly around her long slim body, walked into the bedroom from the adjoining bathroom.

'He's still asleep,' Joe said, his voice thin.
'Good,' Carin replied. 'Just as we planned. Is it ready?'

Gasps from the spectators in the courtroom were hushed by the court officers, and, spellbound, everyone watched Joe reaching down to the small metal trolley that stood next to the bed, coming up with a syringe, his hand shaking.

'I'll do it,' Carin said, taking the syringe from Joe.
'Are you sure?'
'Absolutely. My hand's much steadier than yours.'

There were more gasps as Carin leaned forward to inject her husband, then handed the needle back to Joe.

'Good,' she said, smiling at him. 'That was easy.'

'Your Honour,' Joshua Greene cut in, 'all this proves is that Mrs Fitzgerald administered to her husband his regular insulin shot—'
But his voice tailed off, his mouth dropped open, as Carin's clear, lightly accented tones, were heard saying:

'Now. Take your clothes off, and fuck me.'

'*Oh my God!*' exclaimed a viewer on the back benches, as Carin took off her robe, as Joe fumbled with his trousers, and as Carin added:

'And make it quick. I've got a long list of things to take care of today.'

Simon Poluck reached for the 'Pause' button, but fumbled it deliberately, long enough so that the image that was frozen was Joe and

Carin, by now naked and joined in what was very obviously sexual congress.

'Again, Your Honour—' Joshua Greene attempted feebly, but Simon Poluck cut through him with:

'Goes to motive, Your Honour. With the condition in the prenup that Mr Ranieri mentioned, and which we can easily establish—'

'The DVD is in,' the judge said immediately.

'I'll just play the other one . . .' Simon Poluck said, and as he took out the first one and inserted the second Lola looked up at the judge, and saw that even she, as much as she was trying to hide it, was agog to see what the other DVD contained.

It was Lola herself. She realised this was the footage after the fatal injection, after Joe and Carin had set her up, when she had been left alone with her father. And she watched herself kneel down beside the bed, take her father's hand gently, watched her shoulders move as she cried; saw herself climb onto the bed beside him and cuddle up next to him, and realised that tears were pouring down her face as she remembered what it had been like to be so close to him, to hold his hand, to embrace him, and know that he would never open his eyes and see her again.

She didn't know how long the clip played for. But when Simon Poluck eventually paused it, she knew that the atmosphere in the courtroom had completely changed. She could hear people crying, moved by the sight of her with her dying father; someone a few rows back whispered: 'Oh my God, that *poor girl*,' to murmurs of approval. Though the light was dim, she looked over at the jury, wiping the tears off her face, and saw that they were all staring at her now, their expressions soft with sympathy. One woman in the front row was wiping her own eyes; another was rustling in her handbag for tissues: and Lola's little clone had pressed her palms to her cheeks, her mouth an open 'O' of disbelief and excitement.

'Mr Poluck, this is *not* the clip that you briefly showed us in my chambers,' the judge snapped angrily. 'If you've pulled a bait-and-switch here—'

'No, no, Your Honour, I assure you. Nothing could be farther from my intentions. I played that briefly to establish the bond between my client and her father—'

He clicked on the remote he was holding, and a new scene filled the monitor: Lola standing next to Joe, by her father's bedside. 'Here we are. Twenty minutes earlier. Mr Ranieri's technicians have actually spliced together footage from two different cameras, to show simultaneous versions of the same time period. You can verify that from the date stamps. One camera was in the bedroom, and one was in the master bathroom. I think the reason will be self-evident.'

In the total silence before he pressed 'Play' again, everyone heard a noise from where Carin Fitzgerald was sitting. It was a sharp hiss of fear, breath drawn in between fuchsia-painted lips that were so tightly clamped together that only the thinnest sound of terror could be caught in between them.

While, on the screen, Joe was saying to Lola:

'Perhaps you'd like to help?'

The spectators watched, as Joe handed Lola the syringe to hold. As he asked her to get the vial of insulin from the small fridge built into the bedside table. As he injected her father. As everything happened exactly as Lola had just recounted to the court.

And then the screen split, to show Carin Fitzgerald in the bathroom, clearly watching the scene in the master bedroom through the crack in the hinge of the half-open door.

The spectators exclaimed now, despite the reprimands of the judge. They muttered frantically to each other as Joe Scutellaro crossed the room, as he went into the bathroom, as he placed the vial and the syringe carefully down on a marble shelf and as Carin Fitzgerald patted him on the shoulder in approval as he gave her the thumbs up sign before heading back into the bedroom. And their mutters rose to gasps of disbelief as Carin Fitzgerald sat down on the upholstered chaise longue at the foot of the bath, smiling, reached for a brimming martini glass on a low table beside her, and raised it in the direction of the master bedroom and her comatose husband, before drinking from it in a silent celebration.

'*Silence, or I'll have the court cleared!*' roared the judge, pounding away with her gavel, the sparkle of utter enjoyment in her eyes completely belying the reproving tones of her voice.

The lights snapped back on: the courtroom was fully illuminated.

And everyone's heads were turned in the same direction. To Carin Fitzgerald, who had risen to her feet, gathering her shaved-mink coat around her shoulders, her Gucci bag in her hand, hoping to flee the courtroom in the semi-darkness. Rico, beside her, was trying to shoulder a way along the row of seats to the side aisle; but, despite his menacing appearance, the other spectators were blocking him. The woman next to him was shaking her head furiously at Rico.

'Don't you push me!' she was exclaiming. 'That murdering bitch isn't going anywhere!'

Applause broke out. Someone yelled: 'Arrest her now! Why aren't you arresting her?' and a woman's high-pitched voice screamed: 'Stay strong, Lola! Your dad's in heaven now!'

'*Silence in court!*' the judge bellowed, as the bailiff strode forward to calm the crowd. 'Mr Greene?' she prompted. 'Are you going to make an application to the court?'

'The prosecution withdraws all charges against Miss Lola Fitzgerald,' Joshua Greene muttered angrily.

'That means you're clear on the bail-jumping too!' Poluck's second chair whispered excitedly to Lola.

'Miss Fitzgerald, since all charges against you have been withdrawn, you leave this court today a free woman,' the judge said cheerfully. 'Let me stress that this means you have no stain on your character whatsoever. Occasionally, a prosecution will be made in error, but in good faith, and the State of New York can only regret your recent ordeal and wish you a happy life now that you no longer have this extremely distressing charge hanging over your head. Ladies and gentlemen of the jury, we thank you for your service and release you from jury duty for the next ten years. I'm sure the drama of these proceedings has more than compensated for the time we've taken up. Court is dismissed! Bailiffs, *please* clear the court!'

Lola had cried out every tear she could possibly cry: she was probably completely dehydrated.

So she fainted instead.

Or rather, she collapsed. Every bone in her body seemed to dissolve simultaneously. Jelly-like, she flopped forward onto the desk, and it was only Simon Poluck's quick reflex in catching her shoulders that saved her from hitting her head on its unyielding surface.

Someone was shoving her head between her legs and telling her to breathe. Someone else, across the room, was saying loudly:

'Carin Fitzgerald, you are under arrest for the murder of your husband, Benjamin Fitzgerald. You have the right to remain silent, as anything you say can and will be used against you in a court of law. You have the right to have an attorney present—'

'She'll make a deal,' Simon Poluck was saying to his team. 'No way she won't make a deal. That DVD evidence is cast iron. Ranieri knows his stuff backwards, it'll stand up to any forensic tests they run it through—'

Lola raised her head, the world spinning around her. Suzanne was crouched by her side, sobbing, holding Lola's hands for dear life. India and David were hugging tightly, both of them crying with relief. Beyond them was Carin, whose arms were being handcuffed behind her by a police officer. He was raising his voice to make sure she heard the last words of the Miranda warning.

'Do you understand the rights I have just read to you, Mrs Fitzgerald? With these rights in mind, do you wish to speak to me?' he yelled doggedly over the hubbub in the courtroom.

Suddenly, Suzanne jumped up, striding through the crowd, which parted immediately to let her through. As tall as Carin, and as beautiful in her own very different way, even with her face stained with mascara, Suzanne was utterly compelling.

'You stole my husband, and you *killed him!*' Suzanne accused, pointing her finger dramatically at Carin. 'And you tried to frame my *daughter!* What the hell is *wrong* with you, you evil bitch?'

'Yeah! You tell her, Mom!' yelled one over-excited woman.

'Suzanne, I love you! Marry me!' called a guy from across the room.

'You know, when you moved in on my husband, when you convinced him to leave me, when you *married* him, I knew you were a *gold-digging bitch*,' Suzanne continued magnificently. 'But I had no idea you were truly evil! What are you, some kind of *psychopath*?'

'Right, that's IT. Let's take this show outside! Go, go, move this out, *MOVE THIS OUT!*' yelled the bailiff in a big booming voice. 'Everyone *OUT OF THE COURTROOM NOW!*'

'Fucking *get away from me*!' Carin screamed back into Suzanne's face. 'You couldn't keep your fucking husband, so get out of my fucking face!'

'At least I didn't *kill* him!' Suzanne retorted superbly.

'Mrs Fitzgerald, we're taking you out now—' the police officer started.

'Take your hands off me!' Carin screamed, out of control now, wrestling her shoulders away from him so that he grabbed hold of her harder.

Rico barreled into him from the side, knocking the officer off-balance.

'Show Mrs Fitzgerald some respect!' Rico shouted. 'You can't just pull her around like she was some cheap hooker!'

Carin, incredibly, managed to wriggle free of the police officer and, staggering up to Suzanne, spat in her face. Suzanne slapped her, a ringing slap that echoed right round the courtroom and sent Carin sprawling back against Rico. As he caught her, Lola, who was craning her neck to see the scene unfold, saw Evie slip up to him from behind.

What is she doing? Lola wondered.

Evie was pulling at Rico's jacket, her hands swift and deft as they reached around the bulk of his body, slipping into his left-hand front pocket, lifting out a handful of something that sparkled brightly for a second or two before her hands disappeared again, burying themselves in her bag. Another second later, she was sliding back through the crowd, her small body easily weaving away towards the door. Rico was totally unaware that anything had just been stolen from him: he was understandably distracted by the fact that he was being grabbed by two burly NYC cops, his arms wrenched behind his back as they yelled at him that he was under arrest for assaulting a police officer.

'Fuck you!' Rico yelled back, as they dragged him out through the courtroom doors. 'Fuck you!'

'You should be arresting that woman!' Carin screamed over her shoulder. 'She just assaulted me! She *hit* me! There are *witnesses!*'

'Very impressive, Mrs Myers,' said Marco Ranieri, strolling up to Lola's mother. 'That was a great right hook.'

'*Thank you,*' Suzanne said fervently, reaching out to grasp his hand in both of hers. 'You saved my baby! Thank you so much!'

'Well, I never turn down an embrace from a beautiful woman,' Ranieri said, enfolding Suzanne in a long hug, 'but I can't claim most of the credit—'

'People! We need to *clear the courtroom!*' yelled the bailiff, shepherding everyone towards the doors.

'We'll be making a statement on the courthouse steps,' Simon Poluck said to Lola. 'Feel free to speak if you want, or we can schedule a press conference later—'

But as they pushed their way through the doors, hearing the screams of journalists, the roar of the spectators gathering at the foot of the steps, the hum of the TV vans parked below, engines going, an endless series of flashes popping in Lola's face, Lola was sure she couldn't say a word. She felt completely drained, limp as an old piece of lettuce. She had been trying so hard to stay strong, to summon up as much energy as she could, and now she had nothing left. She clung to her mother as the fresh air hit her, a free woman, the wide marble portico of the courthouse, held up with its huge marble pillars, the most beautiful sight she had ever seen in her life.

And then adrenaline raced through her veins, the strongest and most powerful drug in the world. Her blood pounded so hard it was like a physical pain, an explosion of excitement and shock; because she had just spotted the last person she had ever expected to see here. He was leaning against one of the pillars, hands thrust into the pockets of his sleek grey suit, staring straight at her, unsmiling.

It was Niels van der Veer.

Chapter 42

*L*ola had thought she was burned out. That if another huge surprise hit her today, she would just stand there, blankly, unable even to process it, utterly exhausted by the sheer volume of crises that she had just had to confront. But clearly, the rollercoaster ride wasn't over; she was still strapped into her seat, and the last drop was the steepest of all.

With a wild, rising thrill, she stared at Niels, her eyes huge, colour rising to her cheeks as she speculated frantically about what he was doing here—

And then two more figures emerged from round the side of the pillar, and Lola's heart melted as one of them squealed with excitement and started running towards her.

'*Lola! Darling!*' cried Jean-Marc, his golden hair blowing in the breeze, his blue eyes sparkling with health as he dashed towards her, picked her up and spun her around, laughing with happiness. 'You're free! You're free!'

Looking down at Jean-Marc's ridiculously handsome face, laughing herself as she took in the truth of his words, Lola rested her hands on his shoulders and let herself be twirled in a huge circle of celebration. Jean-Marc was holding her round the waist; she let her head go back, and then she took her arms off his shoulders too, trusting his grip, and spread them wide, laughing louder and louder, her hair coming loose from its clasp and tumbling onto her shoulders, the two of them, golden and beautiful, like the couple they had thought they were, once upon a time.

They were so gorgeous, Lola and Jean-Marc, so seemingly perfect together, that none of the spectators could resist a sigh of appreciation. And one photographer, who had managed to sneak up past the cordon of police officers keeping the media penned together halfway down the steps, snapped a couple of photographs of them, Lola raised high in Jean-Marc's arms, their clothes sleek to their slim figures, their golden heads thrown back in triumph, that went round the world. They made the cover of the *Herald*, the *New York Post*, and most of the weekly gossip magazines from Europe to Asia.

'*FREE TO LOVE!*' blared the *Herald* the next morning. Which, as David observed on reading it, was at least technically true.

'Oh, darling,' Jean-Marc said, finally lowering Lola to her feet and enfolding her in a tight hug, 'you've lost weight, you poor thing . . . you're just skin and bone . . .'

'Exaggerating as always,' Lola scolded him. She squeezed his back under his suede jacket, feeling a new layer of muscle there. 'And you've been *working out*? You feel fit!'

'It's Cascabel,' Jean-Marc said proudly, pulling back to get a good look at her face. 'They have an exercise facility. With cute trainers. I've been *pumping iron*, believe it or not.'

'I don't,' Lola giggled, remembering the Jean-Marc she had been engaged to, who thought raising a martini glass to his lips counted as exercise. 'I don't believe it.'

In her turn, she took in Jean-Marc's face: the smooth skin, the clear whites to his eyes, the air of health and stability that he exuded now. He looked more relaxed and happy than she had ever seen him.

'Jean?' came a hesitant voice from behind Lola.

'Oh, *David – angel*—' Jean-Marc exclaimed ecstatically.

David, with exquisite tact, had come up behind Lola and waited there patiently. Jean-Marc, his eyes blazing aquamarine with happiness at the sight of his boyfriend, opened his arms wide, as did Lola, and David flew into them, the trio hugging each other tightly, as they had done so many times in Jean-Marc's apartment, cuddling together, remembering the time when it had been just the three of them against the world.

And then, gently, Lola detached herself so that Jean-Marc and David could wrap their bodies together, dark and blonde curls blending, their builds so similar they fitted perfectly. Over their heads, she met the steady gaze of the third person who had emerged from behind the pillar: Frank, the sober buddy who had escorted Jean-Marc to Cascabel, a bare fortnight ago. Solidly built, his balding head shaved, wearing a scruffy old sweater that sagged over his bulk, and an equally baggy pair of jeans, Frank nodded calmly at Lola in acknowledgement.

'We just flew in to be here to see the charges against you dropped,' he said, with the raspy voice of a recovering addict who has replaced his previous addictions with a minimum of two packs a day. In fact, a Marlboro dangled from between the fingers of one of his meaty hands, and he raised it to his mouth now, taking a drag. 'Special dispensation. We're turning round and heading back for the West Coast as soon as Jean-Marc's had an hour or so of visiting time.'

Lola gaped at him in bafflement.

'To see *the charges against me dropped?*' she exclaimed, taken completely aback. 'But you'd have had to leave hours and hours ago – how could you have the faintest idea—'

Frank didn't do anything as unprofessional as grin on duty, but a light of amusement shone in his deep-set eyes.

'Mr van der Veer seemed pretty sure,' he said laconically.

'Jean-Marc seemed pretty sure? But how—'

'No, Lola,' Jean-Marc said from over David's shoulder. 'Not *me*, silly! Niels!'

'*Niels?*' Lola's mouth dropped open.

'He rang up and busted me out of prison' – Jean-Marc grinned playfully at Frank, to show he was only teasing – 'God knows how he convinced them, but I'm doing so well at Cascabel, it was so sweet of them to let me come to see you walk out of that horrible place a free woman—'

'*Niels?*' Lola repeated.

And now she wasn't looking at Frank any more, or Jean-Marc. She was pivoting on her heel, her whole body feeling as if it were moving through water, every gesture a slow, deliberate effort. Until she was face to face with Niels, who didn't look as if he had moved one iota from when he had first come round the corner of the pillar. He was still leaning against it, his hands shoved in his pockets, an inscrutable expression on his hard features; they might have been carved out of stone, so little did they move. His mouth was a straight firm line, his eyes the colour of steel. The only softness to his stance at all was the breeze lifting his dirty-blond hair, playing with a lock of it, moving it back and forth over his forehead.

Lola longed to go over and smooth it down for him.

'This was all Mr van der Veer,' Marco Ranieri explained, smiling at Lola. 'He found me, and convinced me to try opening the site with your father's master feed.' Ranieri pulled a face. 'I don't mind telling you, I had my balls in a wringer about that one. I knew your dad wouldn't want me just telling the cops about the site without checking exactly what was on it first, but there's no way I could ever have guessed his password. But then Mr van der Veer' – his black eyes glanced over at Niels – 'tracks me down. Finds out I did some work for Mr Fitzgerald, tells me he knows you didn't have anything to do with this, and what can I do to help? So I tell him about the master feed – I was pretty damn glad not to be alone with that one any more – and he says, OK, I can tell you right now what that password is.'

Ranieri grinned.

'I didn't believe it. No way. But like I told 'em in court, we had three tries. So I say, well, go for it, we got nothing to lose. And I get my guys to pull up the website, and he types it in, and—' He threw his hands up in the air theatrically: 'Bingo! We're in!'

He looked around him, at his audience. Lola, Jean-Marc and David, India and Suzanne, all hanging off his words.

'What's the name of that Shakespeare play?' he asked. '*All's Well That Ends Well?* Here we are, eh?'

Lola was staring at Niels, whose silvery eyes were fixed on her. Everything else was dissolving away, going fuzzy at the edges, while Niels was as clear and in focus as if he was the last thing left in the world, the only thing she had to hold on to. His square shoulders, his broad chest – she felt the colour hectic in her cheeks as she remembered the rest of his body, tried and failed to resist picturing him naked.

He had been there for her all along.

'What was the password?' she asked in a tiny voice, her eyes never leaving his.

Niels's lips curved, just slightly, as he reached into the breast pocket of his jacket and extracted a pale calfskin notebook. Flipping it open, he slipped out the pen held in its spine and scrawled eight letters on the top sheet of paper, ripping it off and handing it to Lola.

She took it wordlessly, her eyes widening as she saw what Niels had written.

And then she turned, scanning the wide stone terrace of the courthouse, looking beyond Simon Poluck, who was shaking hands with the jury consultant, talking animatedly, beyond Serena Mackesy and Joshua Greene, who were huddled together, conferring urgently, to a small slender figure in jeans and a baseball cap, who was stretching her arms above her head and rotating her neck.

'Evie!' Lola called. 'Come over here!'

Evie, her hands linked above her head, met Lola's eyes across the distance and mouthed: 'Are you *sure?*' her expression pantomiming disbelief.

Lola nodded vehemently. Shrugging, Evie started over to Lola's group, followed by Lawrence. 'Hey,' she said a little shyly.

Now that everything was over, now that Lola was free, Evie found she couldn't meet Suzanne's eyes. She had been buoyed up by the excitement while she was living in the unimaginable luxury of the Plaza apartment, standing in for Lola; and besides, she had spent most of the time with India, watching TV, hanging out. India, Evie had quickly realised, was the least judgmental person ever. There was no side to India about Evie having been Lola's father's mistress. India, seeing the best in everyone, had accepted Evie from the start, because she was trying to help Lola, and Evie had instantly felt comfortable with her.

Suzanne, of course, was a different story. Suzanne and Evie had avoided each other as much as possible, which, in that enormous apartment, hadn't exactly been difficult. And then the drama of the visits from the police, living on high alert, had proved an effective distraction from the awkwardness of their respective relationships to Ben Fitzgerald.

Suzanne had been long gone when Evie started her affair with Ben; Evie hadn't done anything to injure Suzanne; and her resemblance to Lola, after all, wasn't exactly Evie's fault. But this wasn't a situation where logic could be relied on to predominate. Evie had seen, from Suzanne's whole demeanour towards her, that Suzanne was very uncomfortable with her ex-husband having kept a mistress of her daughter's age, who looked so like her, and Evie had done her best to keep out of Suzanne's way.

And now Lola was calling Evie over to join the family group. Practically every single person here had been born into riches and privilege – apart from the PI, of course, and she knew exactly what ex-cops like him thought about strippers like her. They'd all been polite enough to her while they needed her, but now she was surplus to requirements. If Lola kept her word, Evie would walk away with her apartment and the kind of kiss-off that said *thank you nicely now please disappear from our lives for good so we can forget we ever needed help from someone as scummy as you.*

So that was what Evie was expecting. Thank you, goodbye and don't let the door hit you on your way out.

Then something else occurred to her.

'Am I in trouble?' she asked, concerned. 'Are they going to arrest me for pretending to be you when the cops came round?'

She was asking Lola, but it was Niels who answered, nodding at Evie in greeting. Evie's eyes widened when she realised who he was.

The James Bond guy from Maud's! Wow, who'd have thought it? No wonder he wasn't interested in me. She couldn't help sighing. *Jeez, Lola Fitzgerald, you definitely landed on your feet. Rich, beautiful and a hot millionaire looking out for you. Some girls have all the luck.*

'Don't worry,' Niels reassured her. 'If they've dropped all the charges against Lola, they won't bother with you. They can't let her off for skipping bail and charge you as an accessory. It's impossible.'

'Phew!' Evie said, miming wiping her forehead in relief.

'Evie, do you know Niels—' Lola began awkwardly.

'Met him at the club,' Evie said, winking at Niels.

Then she saw Lola's horrified expression, and added quickly:

'At Maud's. He's a partner there. You know, Lola. The night you – ahem—'

'I'm a big fan of Miss Diamond's act,' Niels said, his eyes glinting silver as Evie smiled back at him flirtatiously.

Lola felt a wave of jealousy rise in her, so strong and powerful that her hands suddenly twitched with the effort to not slap Evie in the face. She looked behind Evie, at Lawrence, whose pure, handsome features were such a contrast to Niels's craggy, hard ones, and wondered angrily why Evie was flirting with Niels, when she had someone as sweet and gorgeous as Lawrence at her side.

She's just a flirt, Lola told herself firmly. *There's nothing in it. She's done more to help you than anyone . . .*

'Evie, look,' Lola said, handing her the piece of paper. 'It's the password Dad chose for his secret files. I wanted you to see it.'

Evie's pretty forehead wrinkled into a frown as she took the paper, not seeing why Lola was sharing it with her. And then she read the eight letters Niels had written on it, and she knew.

'Oh, *Lola,*' she whispered, stepping towards the girl who looked so much like her.

'I know,' Lola said, as the two girls embraced for the first time. They could have been sisters. Both blonde, both beautiful, both dark-eyed and slenderly-built, with the same delicate features and pale skin. As they pulled apart a little and looked at each other, they took in fully the strangeness of the bond between them, the daughter and the mistress.

'I really cared about Benny,' Evie said bravely. 'I know it looked like I was just gold-digging, and of course I wouldn't have got together with him if it hadn't been for the money. But he was a good man. He was always very kind to me. He took care of me, he really did.'

She looked over at Suzanne.

'I know this must be tough for you,' Evie continued. 'We've never talked about it—'

Suzanne shuddered.

'I'd really rather not,' she said firmly.

'I just want to say, there was nothing weird about—' Evie cleared her throat. 'I mean, Benny was a really nice guy, and I feel sorry for your loss—'

'Evie, that's more than enough,' Lawrence said gently, to everyone's great relief.

'Sorry,' Evie said, embarrassed. 'As long as we're good,' she said to Lola and Suzanne wistfully.

To Evie's amazement, Suzanne stepped forward, taking her hand.

'You were there for my daughter,' Suzanne said, looking straight into Evie's eyes for the first time ever, 'and that's what matters to me.'

'I did it for money, Suzanne,' Evie admitted guiltily. 'It wasn't out of the goodness of my heart. I'm not some heroine, you know? I came to Lola because I thought I could make some money out of her being in trouble.'

'It was a fair deal,' Lola said. 'I attacked you onstage, after all. Besides, my father promised you stuff, and you were entitled to it.' She smiled at Evie. 'And you didn't have to lend me your passport, or pretend to be me, and put yourself in danger of getting arrested. That was above and beyond anything we agreed on. You really helped me when I needed you.'

Evie's eyes were watery, but she managed a brave smile.

'You mean I'm not just a crappy little gold-digger?' she said.

Lola shook her head.

'You're a good friend,' she said.

Hearing the truth of her words, Lola was amazed at how far she had come. This was the girl she had loathed and resented for being her father's mistress, the girl whose face she had wanted to claw off just a few weeks ago! And now, not only was Lola calling her a friend, she was actually reassuring Evie that she was a good person.

Wonders never cease, Lola thought.

'Thank you,' Suzanne said to Evie, smiling at her as she released her hand. Evie swallowed hard, and Lawrence put his arm round her.

'I'll find the title deed of your apartment and make it over to you, like we agreed,' Lola promised. 'And you'll be getting a big lump sum as well. It's the least I can do.'

'Make it an investment in her company,' Niels advised. 'That way it won't look suspiciously like a payment for services rendered.'

'But I don't have a company!' Evie protested, bewildered.

'You will soon, when Maud's builds you up into a major burlesque act,' Niels promised. 'Personal appearances, endorsements—'

'Oh *wow*,' Evie breathed, seeing all her dreams about to come true.

Lawrence reached out and took the piece of paper from Evie's hand, reading the two words written on it.

LOLAEVIE.

He nodded quietly to himself and handed the paper to India.

'He loved you both,' Lawrence said to the two girls, who looked at each other again.

'Can you forgive me?' Evie whispered, grasping Lola's hand.

'It wasn't your fault,' Lola answered, and the calmness that flooded through her as she said it told her that she meant the words completely. 'Evie, you were really poor, and you were just doing what you needed to do to survive. My dad's the one to blame for being a dirty old man.'

'Try to forgive him too,' Evie pleaded.

'I have, pretty much,' Lola reassured her. 'I mean, I'm not saying I'd have been that keen on you as a stepmother, for instance' – she grinned ruefully – 'but *anyone* would have been better than Carin!'

'You think?' Evie said, and they both started to giggle. In their laughter was a huge release of tension, a sign that they could finally put to rest any lingering dislike or resentment.

'Well, isn't this lovely and cosy!' exclaimed a voice as rasping and hoarse as a crow. 'Everyone just having a friendly little love-in! And look at *you*, Johnny! Don't you look bright-eyed and bushy-tailed!'

Every muscle in Lola's body tightened as she recognised the speaker. She glanced immediately at Jean-Marc, whose expression had changed from happiness to fear in the split-second it had taken him, too, to realise who was croaking behind him. He reached out instinctively grabbing onto David's hand for support as he turned to confront his nemesis.

'Hello, Johnny!' Patricia drawled. 'Fancy seeing *you* here! Back in New York, are you?' She smiled her big toothy crocodile smile. 'All ready to come out and play with me and the boys?'

Chapter 43

*I*n her brown trouser suit and the black high-necked sweater that concealed her Adam's apple, with the cheaply dyed dark hair and pancaked make-up, Patricia looked almost average. As a result, no one but Jean-Marc and Lola realised initially who she was. The impact on both of them was instant and powerful. Lola's brow furrowed with concern as she saw Jean-Marc go pale as death. The colour drained from his skin, the suntan he had acquired in California suddenly looking yellowish, jaundiced, rather than healthy and glowing.

'Come on, Johnny, don't look so grumpy!' Patricia cajoled, her dark eyes gleaming with pleasure at seeing Jean-Marc so affected by her presence. 'We had lots of fun together – don't you remember the good times?'

David began to register who this unattractive, oversized woman really was. He looked at Jean-Marc, horror dawning on his face as he saw his boyfriend's reaction to Patricia's presence.

'Jean-Marc!' he hissed. 'Tell her to get lost!'

'If he won't, I will,' Lola said angrily. '*This*' – she pointed at Patricia, loading her voice with scorn – 'is how Carin knew I'd gone to Italy. Patricia followed me and took photographs for Carin, and Carin gave them to the prosecutors. They were going to spring it on me. Only Patricia' – Lola gave the name a derisive spin – 'couldn't wait. She wanted to do it herself, didn't you?'

She glared at Patricia, feeling her anger rising even more strongly. 'It's all about power for you, not money, isn't it? You wanted to punish me for throwing you out of the apartment, breaking up your party with Jean-Marc. And now you don't have any control over me, do you?' she said triumphantly. 'They're not going to charge me for skipping bail. And Carin's been arrested. You've got no power over me at all any more.'

'Fuck you, you spoilt little bitch,' Patricia hissed. 'I'd have *loved* to see you get what was coming to you in prison.'

Niels took one furious step forward, his fists clenching. Patricia laughed, a short cawing rasp that had no amusement in it whatsoever.

'You're going to hit a woman?' she said. 'Really? In front of all these witnesses? Go ahead. It'd be lots of fun to sue you for assault.'

'You're no woman,' Niels snapped. 'You're *dirt*.'

Patricia's eyes narrowed, and, deliberately, she looked away from him, focusing on Jean-Marc.

'What do you say, Johnny? This is all so boring, isn't it?' she cooed at him, softening the rasp of her voice as much as possible. 'We were never bored, were we? I never asked you for anything, except to have a good time, remember?'

She extended her hand to him.

'I've got a suite waiting in a lovely hotel, with the boys all dressed up and ready to go . . . we'll have a party, just like the old days! And don't worry.' Her smile was as wide and toothy now as Lola had ever seen it; she looked as if she could eat Jean-Marc in a couple of bites. 'I know we went a bit over the top before, didn't we? But I'll take care of you from now on. Nothing too hard.'

She was cajoling now, horribly persuasive. Niels was chafing to get rid of her, Lola could tell: his mouth was an even thinner, harder line, his jaw was set so violently that a pulse was throbbing along it. Lola's eyes flashed to Frank, Jean-Marc's sober buddy, asking wordlessly what they should do. But Frank, watching the scene intently, his tired, experienced gaze taking in every detail of Jean-Marc's reaction, shook his head. Lola knew what Frank was saying: that Jean-Marc had to be left to handle this on his own, if at all possible.

'I'll take care of you, Johnny,' Patricia was continuing. 'No one else is taking care of you, are they? They're giving you a hard time, aren't they? Making you talk about all sorts of nasty stuff at that clinic . . . not letting you even have a little drink or a little fun every so often! So mean of them! They can't stop you if you choose to come with me, Johnny. You're a grown man, and you can make your own decisions . . . and what's going to make you happy right now is to come with me back to my lovely hotel suite and get all nice and relaxed and send all your troubles floating away . . .'

Jean-Marc was still gripping onto David, but his other hand was free, and Patricia had secured it by now. Caressing his fingers with her own, she fixed her dark beady eyes directly on his.

'You know it's what you want, isn't it?' she coaxed. 'You know it is!'

'No!' Jean-Marc gasped, pushing Patricia's hand away, jumping back from her as if she were Typhoid Mary. 'I won't come with you! You're *disgusting*!'

Patricia gasped.

'Johnny, you don't mean that . . .' she began.

'Oh yes I do!' Jean-Marc said, his voice high and carrying. 'You don't want to look after me – you want to drag me down!' He shuddered. 'And it's not true that I was happy with you! I loathed every minute of it!'

'That's right, Jean! You tell her!' David chimed in, unable to stay silent any longer. But Niels's deep voice cut through both of them.

'That's enough,' he snarled. 'My brother's told you to get going, and now I'm giving you your marching orders. Get the hell away from me and my family, and stay the hell away. Or you'll wish you'd never been born.'

'Ooh, very butch.' Patricia managed to smile, her Adam's apple bobbing over the neckline of her sweater. 'I see why Johnny's so afraid of you—'

'You heard him!' Lola cut in sharply. 'He told you to go. Now do it, before I call a cop and have you arrested for pimping.'

'*You little bitch!*' Patricia, out of control with frustration now, raised her hand and dived towards Lola, aiming a slap at her with the considerable weight of her body behind it.

Lola saw the blow coming towards her, but she was paralysed, not knowing whether she should duck or jump back, sure that her worn-out reflexes would make the wrong decision. As she hesitated, a split-second before Patricia's palm slapped across her face, a big male hand, glinting lightly with a sprinkling of golden hairs, smashed onto Patricia's wrist and grappled her arm behind her back, twisting her around.

'You stay away from her too,' Niels said between clenched teeth. 'Or I won't be responsible for my actions.'

He threw Patricia away from Lola so hard that Patricia staggered a few steps across the marble paving, nearly stumbling into a pillar.

'And don't even *think* about suing me,' he finished, so menacingly that Patricia's shoulders sagged in defeat. 'Or I'll have you deported so fast you'll be on a plane back to the UK tonight, in handcuffs.'

'Or we could send her to jail here, before we deport her,' drawled Ranieri, stepping up to flank Niels. 'Won't be hard to find that hotel suite you were talking about. And I bet there's enough marching powder in there to send you away for a nice long stretch. You been to jail in America, Patricia? It ain't so much fun.'

'Fuck you all!' Patricia hissed over her shoulder as she walked away. 'Fuck you and the fucking horses you rode in on!

'If I had a dollar for every time I've heard that . . .' Ranieri said lightly.

'Jean-Marc! You were *wonderful!*' David sighed, cuddling up to his boyfriend.

Frank stepped up to Jean-Marc's side, throwing one meaty arm over his shoulders.

'Well done, buddy,' he said.

'I feel so dizzy—' Jean-Marc said, still looking white as a sheet. 'That was so scary, I can't believe I managed to do that—'

'We're gonna get you straight home to Cascabel,' Frank promised. He looked over at Niels. 'Plane refuelled and everything, Mr van der Veer?'

Niels nodded.

'OK then, say your goodbyes,' Frank instructed Jean-Marc. 'Boy, are you gonna crash on the flight back!'

As Lola hugged Jean-Marc tightly, his body already felt limp as a rag doll, drained from the effort it had taken to say 'No' to Patricia for the first time in his life.

'I love you, Lo,' he murmured in her ear.

'I love you too, Jean-Marc. Be well,' she said, swallowing hard, as he was hugged by Suzanne, then India, and finally fell into David's arms.

'Time to break it up,' Frank said, and Jean-Marc and David reluctantly detached themselves.

Jean-Marc turned to face his brother.

'Thank you, Niels,' he said. 'For trusting me. For looking after me. For being my big brother.'

The hard lines of Niels's face softened as he looked down at Jean-Marc.

'I'll always take care of you, Jean,' he promised.

'No, as soon as I get all better, I'll start taking care of *you*,' Jean-Marc insisted. 'It's about time.'

He reached up to whisper something in Niels's ear, resting one hand on his brother's wide shoulder. As Jean-Marc pulled away, Lola saw with astonishment that Niels's face was bright red.

'You know I'm right!' Jean-Marc said, with a trace of his old jauntiness, as he looked over at Frank, standing right next to him. 'Time to go,' he said. 'I know. I love you all!'

And he made a grand exit down the flight of marble steps, Frank fielding off the reporters and photographers while Jean-Marc blew kisses at them right till the minute their limo pulled away.

Suzanne took a deep breath.

'Niels, I can't thank you enough for what you've done for my daughter!' she said gratefully. 'Without you finding Mr Ranieri and working out poor Ben's password, I'm sure Lola would be in prison by now. It's so kind of you to have helped out. Especially since you only know Lola as darling Jean-Marc's, um, ex-fiancée . . . well, best friend now, I suppose . . .'

'*Definitely* best friend,' David chimed in, smiling at Lola.

'So why don't we grab Lola's marvellous legal team and all go back to the Plaza and celebrate!' Suzanne suggested.

'I have other plans, I'm afraid,' Niels said rather curtly.

'Oh, but that's impossible!' Suzanne cried, all the beauty and charm that had got her cast as the Sunsilk girl very much to the fore. 'You can't just sweep in here and save Lola from prison and leave again without so much as letting us raise a glass to how wonderful you've been!'

'Yes, you have to come,' India chimed in, staring up at Niels worshipfully. 'I mean, it wouldn't be the same without you!'

Niels shook his head emphatically, like a lion impatiently dismissing some gadflies buzzing round him. His silver stare was fixed on Lola's diminutive, black-clad figure, her smooth golden head, sparks of gold in the sunlight from the yellow diamond earrings glittering in her ears as she looked back at him, her dark eyes wide, her lips slightly parted.

'I've got another plane waiting at Teterboro, scheduled to take off in about an hour and a half,' he said gruffly to her. 'I've hired a private island, in Thailand. Very quiet, very luxurious.' He cleared his throat noisily. 'I thought you might want to come with me – get away from everything – just sunbathe and get some massages and swim in the ocean—'

'You're asking *Lola*?' Suzanne exclaimed, completely bewildered. 'But you don't even *know* her!' She looked at her daughter. '*Do* you?'

Not really, Lola thought. *He's never asked me one thing about myself. All he does is shout at me before we have meaningless animal sex.*

Niels had folded his arms across his chest, staring straight at her. The breeze caught the stray lock of his hair, blowing it across his frowning forehead. The marble pillar behind him couldn't have looked more solid and unyielding than he did, his shoulders set, his legs braced as he waited for Lola's answer.

She didn't say a word: she just started running towards him. He unfolded his arms wide and scooped her off the ground just as she reached him, tossing her high in the air so she squealed in delight and shock before he caught her, settling her high on his chest, her head nuzzled into his shoulder.

'I'll bring her back in a few weeks,' he said over his shoulder. 'Oh, and, um – nice to meet you, Mrs Fitzgerald.'

'It seemed rude to say no after you saved me from prison . . . A fate worse than death!' Lola said breathlessly into his ear as he carried her down the stairs.

'It was purely selfish,' Niels said carelessly. 'It would be a waste to send a girl as pretty as you to jail for the rest of her life.'

'Oh, Niels, admit it. You wanted to fuck me again,' Lola said, throwing caution to the winds.

She looked up at him.

'You've gone red!' she crowed happily.

'I'll make you pay for that—' Niels said malevolently, as a myriad camera flashes and TV lights hit them both full in their blushing faces, the paparazzi literally screaming in ecstasy at the sight of Lola Fitzgerald, society It girl, only just absolved of the murder of her father, swept off her feet by the fantastically sexy brother of her ex-fiancé.

'*Lola! Niels! Are you guys a couple now? Please, say something!*' yodelled a reporter for E! News, hyperventilating so much with excitement that she was reaching for her inhaler even as she yelled the question.

'Miss Fitzgerald is much too busy to talk. And so am I,' Niels said, reaching one big hand up Lola's back, to her head, and pulling it up so that he could reach her mouth with his own.

When he came up for air, Lola was too dizzy to do anything but cling to him, her head buried in the silk and wool fabric of his suit, as he ducked down to place her inside the stretch limo, sliding in after her. The door closed, and the car took off, leaving the journalists running behind, still screeching questions.

'*Well!*' Suzanne said, staring in amazement as Niels's limo pulled away. 'I suppose it's always true that a mother's the last to know about what's going on in her daughter's love life, but *still*—'

She looked at India and Evie.

'Did *anyone* have any idea that this was going on?' she asked.

India and Evie shook their heads.

'Well, that's a relief,' Suzanne commented. 'I mean, at least I'm not the only one to be completely in the dark.'

'Oh Suzanne, *please*,' David said. 'Lola used to blush bright red every time Jean-Marc mentioned Niels's name. You never picked up on that?'

Suzanne shook her head.

'Jean and I had our suspicions all along,' David said smugly.

'I must be a terrible mother,' Suzanne sighed.

'He's so gorgeous,' India sighed. 'Lola's really, really lucky . . .'

Evie and David nodded fervently in agreement.

'And Jean-Marc did amazingly,' India added to David. 'You must be really proud of him.'

'I know,' David said, patting her hand. 'I miss him so, but he was wonderful today. And he'll be back here before I know it.'

He kissed Evie on the cheek.

'You were a good friend to Lola,' he said. 'We're all so grateful. And you know she meant it. She'll take care of you too. You've got your penthouse back, honey. And a glittering career ahead of you. I see real diamonds in your act now, not Swarovski. *Very* exciting!'

Evie smiled at him. 'I can't wait to be famous,' she confided.

'*We* can't wait for you to be famous!' David said happily. 'How I'm going to boast when you're the most famous burlesque star in the world!'

'Evie?' Suzanne said to her. 'Would you like to join us for our celebration?'

Evie smiled back at her.

'Thanks, Suzanne. That's really sweet of you. Maybe I'll come along later.'

Suzanne, Ranieri, David and India descended the courthouse steps to collect Lola's legal team. And then it was just Evie and Lawrence, standing on the marble terrace, blue sky and sunlight behind the heavy marble pillars, a fresh wind from the Hudson river lifting Evie's hair, Lawrence's clear grey eyes looking directly into Evie's.

Below them, halfway down the wide staircase, Joshua Greene had finished his press conference and Simon Poluck was taking his place in front of the massed bank of microphones, ready to give a statement of triumph on Lola's behalf: the journalists were a mob of baying excitement, determined to get the full scoop on what was by far the most exciting celebrity gossip of the year, if not the decade. Disinherited heiress accused of murder! Attacks pole-dancing mermaid onstage at burlesque club! Her ex-fiancé overdoses with a transvestite, comes out as gay and goes back into rehab! Her stepmother caught on film committing the murder! And *then*, the heiress runs off with her ex's brother, an international tycoon!

No wonder grown men and women were shoving microphones at Simon Poluck and pleading, with tears in their eyes, for the full story.

'Evie—'

'Lawrence—'

They both started at the same time, and then broke off, laughing nervously.

Evie looked up at Lawrence, her heart in her eyes.

'I've been spending so much time trying to find a way to say this,' Lawrence said, 'and then I realised the simplest way is always the best. You must know I'm in love with you.'

'*Lawrence!*' Evie squealed, sounding exactly like the kind of fluffy, silly girl she had always despised.

Colour touched Lawrence's high pale cheekbones.

'You must have known, Evie,'

'You never *said* it!'

'I knew you wouldn't want to hear it,' he said soberly. 'You weren't exactly in the right place for a declaration of love.' He swallowed. 'I'm not even sure you're in the right place now.'

The next second, he found himself staggering back as Evie jumped up and threw herself onto him, her legs wrapping round his waist, her arms round his neck, kissing him with abandon.

'I *am*! I'm *exactly* in the right place!' she cried happily. 'I am, Lawrence! I love you too!'

Lawrence's mouth on hers, Lawrence's strong lean body holding her so easily, was like rain in the desert. Evie hadn't realised how much she'd missed him till this moment. She could have screamed from sheer relief; it was as if, ever since breaking up with Lawrence, she'd been holding her breath, and now she could finally let it out.

'I never want to leave you again,' she said, locking her calves round his waist so tightly he'd have needed a pry bar to get her off him. 'I never want to be sleeping downstairs and know you're up there with that stupid bitch crushing on you and being snotty to me – God, I hated her so bad!'

'Evie—'

'Fuck it, Lawrence, you're moving out of that shithole *tomorrow*, we'll be back in my lovely penthouse and live there together and train together and it'll be just the most amazing life *ever*, I'm so fucking happy—'

'*Evie.*'

Lawrence's tone, quiet, controlled, yet carrying absolute authority, cut through Evie's joyous babble like a warm Sabatier knife through butter. She stopped dead, her eyes widening nervously, pulling back so she could see his face.

'What?' Her heart was pounding; she was freaking out.

'There's something very important I need to get straight,' Lawrence said.

'The apartment? You don't want to live there because of Benny?' Evie said in panic, realising how much Lawrence meant to her. 'OK! OK, if that's what it takes! I'll sell it!'

God, I love that apartment so much, I'll hate to leave it! she thought miserably. *But Lawrence is worth it – Lawrence is worth more than an apartment, goddamnit—*

'Or do you not want me to strip any more?' she said desperately, sensing that wasn't enough. 'I won't, then! I won't, if you don't want me to! If that's what it takes to get you back!'

'*Evie*,' Lawrence said, lowering her gently to the ground, her legs unwrapping from their lock on him, as weak as a newborn colt's with fear. She clung to him as he said:

'Of course you can keep the apartment, and of course I'll live there if you want. You know material surroundings don't matter to me. I'll go wherever you want, and live wherever you choose. That's not an issue.'

'Then is it stripping?'

'Evie, you know I believe that everyone has an absolute right to do as they choose with their own body—' he started.

And then he sighed, and shook his head, his handsome face frowning, his eyes dark.

'I'm a hypocrite,' he admitted sadly. 'I must be a hypocrite. Because I say those words, and I mean them. But Evie—'

'Yes?' she said breathlessly, gripping onto the front of his sweater with both hands.

'Dance all you want, with your clothes on or off or flying round your head for all I care,' Lawrence said very seriously. 'But I want us to be exclusive. From the moment you and I first made love, as long as we were together, I've never so much as laid a finger on another woman in that way. I fought the feeling that I wanted you to be the same. I knew you were in a relationship with Benny—'

Evie snorted sarcastically.

'OK, I knew you had an *arrangement* with Benny,' Lawrence corrected himself, 'and I had to respect that for your sake. But Evie, I can't do it again. If we're together from now on—'

'We *are*!' Evie insisted furiously. 'We *are*!'

'—then I need us to be exclusive,' Lawrence concluded. 'No other men. No other women for me. No one else for either of us.'

'That's *it?*' Evie burst out laughing. 'That's what you wanted to say?'

He nodded, his grey eyes searching her face.

'Lawrence, you moron!' she said through her laughter. 'As if I could *look* at another man when I've got you! I want you to travel with me – when this burlesque thing takes off, I'm going to be travelling *everywhere*, all over the world – they book you all over the place, you travel to parties and clubs in London and Paris and Sydney and Tokyo and *Dubai*, where they pay *so much money* – anyway, will you come with me? Will you be my personal trainer and travel with me everywhere? Think of all the different yoga classes you could take – all the other teachers you could meet—'

'Evie!' Lawrence was laughing too. 'You don't need to sell this like crazy! Of course I'll come with you! I'd love to travel the world!'

'Oh, *Lawrence*—'

'But Evie—' Lawrence unpeeled her hands from his sweater and took them in his – 'you know I'll never be rich, don't you?'

He brought her hands to his lips and kissed them.

'I'll never be a millionaire,' he said seriously. 'I'll never make any money, by the standards that you want. I'll never be anything but a yoga teacher and personal trainer. I don't want my own exercise DVDs or TV show or anything but what I have now. All I want is you.'

'Are you kidding?' Evie said happily. 'I'll make enough money for both of us! Look!'

She reached into her jeans pocket and pulled out a shining diamond pastie, flashing it triumphantly before Lawrence's amazed face.

'Isn't that—'

'Yes! That bitch stole it from me, but I got them back!'

'*Them?*'

'Both of them!'

She pulled out the other pastie, dangling them together, watching the sunlight refract off the stones.

'Rico – that's Carin's bodyguard, the hulking one who was arrested with her – he helped her throw me out of the apartment – God, he's a *pig*. He cornered me in the hallway this afternoon and said that if I'd – uh, go into the men's room with him, he'd give me one of them back, and then if I partied with him later, he'd give me the other—'

Lawrence's face was a picture of horror.

'Lawrence! It's OK! I know you're saying to yourself, well, it's Evie's body, she can do what she wants with it, and we weren't exclusive then—' Evie said happily. 'But I didn't do it! I *did* go into the john with him,' she admitted. 'I thought I could go through with it. But at the last minute, I couldn't.'

She shuddered.

'It was so gross. So disgusting. I really did feel like a whore. And Lawrence – I promise this is true – I thought of you. I thought of you, waiting in the courtroom, and I knew I couldn't go back and sit down next to you and have you smile at me, with Rico's—'

With the taste of Rico's come in my mouth, she thought, but didn't say.

'I couldn't do it,' she said instead. 'I jumped up and ran out of there with him bellowing all kinds of shit after me.'

Well, now Rico was under arrest and out of her life. Evie would never have to see him again, never have to hear him calling her foul names or leering at her. She grinned in triumph.

'So how did you get those?' Lawrence asked, hugely relieved, but now bewildered.

'When they were arresting him, it was such a clusterfuck in there, I sneaked up to him and pulled them out of his trouser pockets!' Evie crowed in triumph. 'The cops were hauling him around, they were so furious with him they didn't even notice me, and he didn't either – he'll probably blame them and get into even worse shit as a result! I could have made a good pickpocket, eh?' She smiled demurely. 'Lucky I've gone so respectable now – with a steady boyfriend and a proper career—'

'You *stole* them from him?'

'Lawrence, *they* stole them from *me*! I was just taking back my own property!' Evie pointed out, pulling his head down to kiss him, the pasties still twined between her fingers. 'We're rich! I have my apartment *and* my diamonds back! And *you*! Oh my God, this is the happiest day of my life!'

'Evie, you're a force of nature,' Lawrence said lovingly, wrapping his arms around her and kissing her back.

'Right,' Evie said happily. 'Oh! And I just had a really cool idea—'

She unpeeled herself reluctantly from Lawrence and tilted her head to look down the steps, where Simon Poluck was just finishing up his press conference.

'Wait for me right here, OK?' she said, planting a quick extra kiss on his lips. 'I won't be long—'

She pulled the elastic out of her ponytail, shaking her hair loose over her shoulders, dashed down the steps and wove her way through the mass of people to Simon Poluck's side.

'Hey!' she said into the microphones. 'My name's Evie Lopez, but you all know me better as Diamond, the burlesque dancer. You know – Lola Fitzgerald and I had a catfight onstage during my Mermaid routine?'

Gasps of excitement issued from the journalists as they jostled to get a good view of Evie, so small and pretty, her blonde hair tumbling around her heart-shaped face, her big dark eyes striking against her pale golden skin.

'Since then, Lola and I have become really good friends,' Evie continued, 'and I wanted to say that no one's more happy than me that the justice system has finally realised that she's totally innocent!'

She flashed a dazzling smile at the massed paparazzi, tossing back her hair, a phalanx of cameras going.

'And Lola's come to be such a huge fan of my act,' Evie continued, 'that she's going to finance me to take it to a whole new level! I'll be continuing my residency at Maud's, but I'm working on a completely new act where I'm going to be *covered* in diamonds, and

I'm going to take it on a world tour. With my signature look – real diamond pasties!'

And, with a performer's instinct for the killer theatrical moment, Evie whipped out the pasties and held them up so that every journalist and TV camera present could get a good look at them.

'They're worth a hundred grand!' she said recklessly. 'And I'll be wearing them at special performances!'

She beamed as the cameras whirred and clicked frantically, the journalists ecstatic at this extra twist to the biggest celebrity story of the year.

And if someone tries to mug me before I get these back to the safe in the Plaza, she thought fervently, as the diamonds glittered blindingly in the sunlight, *I'll rip their heart out with my bare hands. I worked too damn hard to get these babies back to ever let someone take them away from me again!*

Chapter 44

Everything in my life is changed, Lola mused as she floated face down, naked, on a lilo drifting gently on the huge infinity pool of the villa. Occasionally, the warm sea breeze would ripple over the bright blue water of the pool, nudging the lilo along till it bumped gently against one white stone edge, and then Lola would stretch out with an infinitesimal movement of a French-manicured toe or finger and send the lilo out again into the centre of the pool. That was pretty much the entire extent of her exercise for the day, apart from having energetic sex with Niels that morning. She smiled into the cushion of the lilo, remembering. And then they had wrapped themselves in robes and gone outside to sit on the white stone terrace to feed each other fresh mango and papaya, so soft and sweet it had been like eating melting ice cream from fruit shells.

Everything in my life is upside down, she reflected, turning her head to the other side, away from the rays of the sun.

Barely six weeks ago, I was on my hen night, and now I'm best friends with my ex-fiancé and his boyfriend.

Barely six weeks ago, I thought Madison and Devon and Georgia were my best friends, and India was just a sweet girl who tagged along with us. And now, I've dumped Madison and Devon and Georgia for being traitorous cows, and India's been a total rock of strength. None of my friends are who I thought they were.

Barely six weeks ago, I had no idea my father had a mistress, let alone one my age . . . ugh . . . And now I'm not only friends with her, I'm giving her a ton of money to put together the most extravagant burlesque show ever . . . which I'm flying back to New York to see in a fortnight . . .

Barely six weeks ago, my mother and I were hardly on speaking terms. And now we're closer than we ever were.

Barely six weeks ago, my father was alive.

Lola lay there, the lilo revolving slowly in the soft sea air, letting memories of her father flood into her consciousness. It was one of the ways she had been spending most time here on the island; it was lavishly stocked with books, plus the latest copy of every magazine and DVD they could conceivably want, but she had hardly even picked up a newspaper. Her head had been so full of everything that had happened to her since her hen night – Jean-Marc's hospitalisation – her father's coma – that it felt as if she had no room to take anything else in, not a single story, real or invented. She had spent the past week swimming, having massages in the open-air spa, with its covered gazebo trailing fragrant white jasmine and delicate yellow ylang-ylang flowers, eating fresh fish, having phenomenal sex with Niels, but mostly just lying here by the pool, listening to the waves lapping the beach and the waterfall that cascaded into the pool from a pond above, rich with floating pink and purple water lilies.

Lola was remembering Ben Fitzgerald, and though from time to time the memories made her cry, mostly she found herself smiling, full of the love that she would always feel for him, and the love she knew that he had felt for her. She had even managed to be glad that he had found Evie, someone who had brought some happiness into his last few months.

And she kept telling herself consolingly that her father had known nothing about what Carin had done to him. At least the video proved that. He had been asleep when Carin injected him, and after that had been in a coma, never aware of his wife's treachery.

Niels had kept Lola, at her request, almost completely isolated from the outside world; but he was checking messages regularly, working on various projects, and reading all the main financial papers, and Ranieri had rung him to tell him that Carin had been indicted for the murder of her husband. A plea deal was already being discussed. There was no way Carin was going to trial, not with that damning video evidence to show the jury.

Lola still couldn't believe how successful Niels's efforts to save her had been.

'Why didn't you let me know you were trying to help me?' she had blurted out as soon as Niels put her in the limo outside the courthouse.

Niels looked embarrassed.

'I only tracked down the PI yesterday,' he said. 'We were watching the video footage all night and into this morning . . . and then you were in court . . .'

'No, I mean before!' Lola said. 'You just disappeared after we flew back from Italy—' she went pink, thinking of what had happened on board the LearJet. 'I thought you didn't want to be in contact with me any more. I mean, what was I supposed to think?'

Niels looked genuinely amazed.

'But you must have known I wouldn't leave you to be convicted!' he said indignantly.

'*No*, Niels,' Lola said patiently, realising that she was going to have to do a lot of training him in women's thought processes. 'How would I know that? You never even rang to ask how I was doing! I'm not psychic.'

'But—' Niels ran a hand through his hair: 'how could you think I would just walk away and not take care of things? I got a whole team of private investigators on the case immediately!'

'So why didn't you let me know?' Lola persisted.

'Because—'Niels looked baffled. 'Because I'm not used to having to tell anyone what I'm doing, I suppose. Not until something produces results. I've never sent back bulletins on my progress . . .'

He looked at her warily, and Lola thought that he resembled

nothing so much as a large jungle animal backed into a corner, being made to apologise for having gone off hunting without telling his mate beforehand.

'It would have reassured me so much to know you hadn't just vanished into thin air,' she explained to him, 'and that you were on my side . . .'

Niels nodded abruptly.

'I get it, OK?' he said, which Lola supposed was the closest he could manage to an apology.

We're really going to have to work on his communication skills, Lola thought ruefully. *But it's amazing how quickly everything's happened. Barely six weeks ago, I didn't even know Niels. I knew who he was, of course. Jean-Marc told me he had an older brother who ran everything, and was much too busy to do anything like come to our engagement dinner, and he sounded like such a bore I barely even remembered his name.*

And now . . . now, every time I think of Niels, every time I say his name to myself, I get wet. Every time I look at him, all my insides melt. I've never been so infatuated with anyone in my entire life. I didn't even know that I could feel like this.

Lola was spinning off into a vivid recollection of the way she had woken up that morning, with Niels's head between her legs, his stubble grating deliciously on her skin, so that the first thing that had issued from her lips that morning had been a scream of pleasure, when she was interrupted by Niels's deep voice saying:

'Aren't you going to go for a swim?'

She looked up, but couldn't see him. Paddling with her hands to bring the lilo round, she swivelled to find him, standing by the edge of the pool, hands on his hips, damp with sea water, his swim shorts dripping onto the white stone edge of the pool.

'I'm feeling really lazy,' she said, shading her face with her hand and smiling up at him. 'I can barely even be bothered to turn over.'

Niels grinned devilishly.

'Well, let me give you a hand with that—'

'No! Niels, *no* – I don't want to get wet yet, I'm sunbathing—'

But Niels had already jackknifed and dived into the pool. He came up under the waterfall, shaking his hair back, his eyes gleaming and his skin lightly tanned from a week of sun. Niels's fair Scandinavian skin needed a lot of sunblock, and Lola had found a great deal of pleasure in carefully applying it to the tips of his ears, his nose, the back of his neck, as he grumbled and pushed her away and pretended to be annoyed, while actually enjoying tremendously having her minister to him.

'So,' he said, wading towards her with evil in his eyes, 'you need some help turning over—'

'No! Niels, *no!*' Lola screamed with such relish that the butler and maid on the terrace above could hear her squeal even over the tumbling waterfall below. The two members of the villa's extensive staff had been arranging orchids along the marble table in the shade of the veranda where Niels's and Lola's lunch would be served; but now they looked at each other, rolled their eyes, and retreated back inside the villa again to give the couple privacy.

'At least they're not doing it inside this time,' the maid said in relief. 'I've had to change the sheets once already this morning.'

'*No!*' Lola protested happily, wriggling back on the lilo as Niels approached, grabbed the rubber rim, and dragged it high in the air.

She had a glorious view of his flexing biceps, and then he twisted the lilo and, despite her efforts to hold it flat, she spun off it, flying into the warm, soft water, coming up giggling and pummelling him as he caught her and held her, pretending to fight him, letting him catch her hands and hold them behind her back with both of his while he kissed her so hard it took her breath away.

She tasted salt on his mouth from the sea. Her naked body was pressed tight to his, and even though they had spent the past week mostly naked together, being underwater gave it even more of an erotic charge; she could feel how hard he was already, his cock pressing insistently up between her legs, fully erect, and she went limp in his arms with pure desire, kissing him back with everything she had, trying to get every inch of her body in contact with his, floating in the water, wrestling her arms free from him so she could wrap them round his neck and twine herself around him and kiss him forever.

And then Niels was spinning her round, pushing her against the side of the pool, his hands leaving her momentarily to strip off his swim trunks and throw them impatiently onto the pool edge. She braced herself, so ready for him she could hardly bear it, moaning in excitement as Niels's feet caught hers and nudged them apart, her eyes closed to feel the sensations better, suddenly so desperate for him that if he didn't fuck her then, that instant, she knew she would explode with frustration.

She felt his cock behind her, parting her buttocks, and then she screamed in surprise as Niels eased it up inside her, the first time he had done that, one hand guiding it slowly, the other one coming round to finger her so she writhed in pleasure even as the shock of him doing what no one had even tried with her before made her cry out again, not knowing whether she wanted it or not.

'Is it all right?' Niels said in her ear, the first time he had ever asked her permission for anything, and she opened her mouth to say that she wasn't sure, knowing that if she expressed any doubt at all, he would stop instantly. But just then his clever fingers made her come, and simultaneously his cock slid up her another inch, hurting her, but somehow so exciting, so forbidden, so shocking that she found her body pushing down on it, trying to take him in even further, amazing herself with her own abandon, and Niels groaned against her, biting her earlobe, making her moan with sheer delight as he kept going, licking and biting her ear, driving his cock still higher inside her till she could feel his balls pressed right up against her bottom, fucking her slowly but surely, making her come again and again, till by the time he cried out and slammed into her with a series of fast hard finishing strokes, she was crumpled on the edge of the pool, overwhelmed with sensation, unable even to stand up any longer, the combination of pain and pleasure like a drug that had sapped every ounce of strength and will from her, everything but her ability to feel ecstasy.

Niels collapsed on top of her, breathing heavily, the weight of his torso pressing her down, hot and wet, water trickling down from the sides of his body, his damp head pressed into the nape of her neck, his hips still jerking slightly from the aftershock of his orgasm.

'That was *amazing*,' he said fervently.

'Mmm,' Lola agreed, barely able to talk.

'Were you—' he cleared his throat. 'Was that OK?'

She smiled drowsily, her cheek pressed against the warm stone. 'That was the first time anyone ever did that,' she admitted.

'Really?' Niels sounded unbearably smug.

'You love that,' she accused him. 'You *love* that you're the first man ever to do that to me.'

'First and last,' Niels said possessively, biting the back of her neck and making her shiver under him. 'Will you marry me, Lola?'

'*Niels!*'

She got her hands underneath her and, with every trace of strength she had left in her body, she managed to shove herself upright, pushing him off her, backing him away till he slid out of her. He grabbed for his discarded swim trunks to clean himself up as she turned to face him and said indignantly:

'Did you just *propose* to me while you were still *inside my*—'

'I'm sorry!' Niels raised one hand in the air in apology, the other still wrapped round his cock. His tough, craggy face wore such a hangdog expression that she burst out laughing at the sight of him; he looked more ashamed of himself than she had ever imagined he could be. 'That wasn't how I planned it at *all*—' He was bright red now. 'It was supposed to be tonight – I had a special meal arranged, the ring was going to be floating on an orchid in your champagne glass . . . It's full moon, I was going to wait till the moon was up and do it then—'

Lola was still giggling at the sight of Niels van der Veer, international tycoon and multi-millionaire, one hand wiping off his penis, the other flailing in the air helplessly. He came towards her, bunching up his swim trunks and throwing them by the pool again, taking both her hands, looking down into her eyes with such sincerity, such love, suddenly, that the laughter dried up in her throat; her mouth went dry as she met his gaze.

'Lola, this wasn't how I planned it at all, please believe me. It just – it just came out, I couldn't hold it back,' he was saying. 'And that's why I want to marry you. Do you remember in the plane coming back from Italy, when you asked me why I was single? This is why. You're the only woman who ever does this to me. You're the only woman who's ever made me lose control, do the things I really want to do, say the things I really want to do. I'd built a life for myself that was so controlled, so regimented – you're the only woman who's ever made me feel free.'

He looked imploringly at her.

'I don't know how you do it, but you've set me free to be myself. Please, say yes. I need you, Lola. I need you more than you can possibly imagine.'

Niels's words were so beautiful, so heartfelt, that Lola was temporarily tongue-tied with sheer happiness. She wanted desperately to remember every word he had just said, to save this moment forever, never forget the way he was looking at her with his whole heart in his eyes.

Niels misunderstood her silence, and panicked.

'Lola—' he said urgently, 'if you're not sure because of Jean-Marc, all of that, believe me, Jean-Marc knows – he's happy for us—' He swallowed. 'He told me on the courthouse steps, remember, he whispered in my ear? He said, "Let Lola take care of you." God knows, I've spent my life making sure no one ever needed to take care of me. But somehow I actually *like* it when you look after me – Lola, *please* say yes!'

'Of course I will!' Lola said, finding her voice, watching his expression turn to sheer joy. 'Of course I will, you big *idiot!*'

And then she screamed as Niels picked her up and threw her high in the air, catching her as she splashed back into the water, hugging her tightly to him, her face buried in his neck, kissing and kissing his salty skin, her arms wound round him, her fingers twisted in his hair.

'Niels?' she said finally, lifting her head.

'Anything,' he said fervently. '*Anything* you want.'

'We go through the whole thing tonight, just like you'd planned,' Lola said firmly. 'Full moon, ring in orchid, everything. And you propose again, OK? And I pretend to be surprised.'

'Well, sure,' he said, frowning in bemusement. 'But why?'

'*Because*,' Lola continued, 'when people ask me how you proposed, I am damn well *not* going to tell them the true story of what you were actually doing to me when it happened, OK?'

Niels grinned.

'I think,' he said, lifting her out of the pool and setting her on the edge, 'I have been more embarrassed in the brief time I've known you than in the whole rest of my life.'

He vaulted out himself and stood up, reaching down a hand to pull her to her feet, crossing to the pale teak loungers on which lay a pile of white fluffy towels. Picking up one, Niels enfolded Lola in it.

'I love you,' he said, looking down at her seriously. 'You make me human, Lola Fitzgerald.'

Lola went up on tiptoes so she could plant a kiss on his lips.

'And you saved my life, Niels van der Veer,' she said. 'So I'd say we're even. Just promise me one thing.'

'Anything, Princess,' he said, smiling down at her.

'That you never tell anyone the story of how you proposed to me,' she said firmly. 'Just *imagine* Jean-Marc using that in his best man's speech!'

And she laughed so hard at Niels's appalled expression that he grabbed her with one hand, pulling her in for a kiss, and smacked her bottom hard with the other.

'Start as you mean to go on,' he murmured against her mouth.

'I should have married Jean-Marc,' Lola sighed naughtily. 'I can tell that you're going to be much harder going as a husband.'

'You'd better get used to it,' he said, sweeping her up into his arms and starting to carry her up the stairs to the terrace of the villa.

'I'm not going to be just a socialite wife, either,' she told him. 'I've had a fantastic idea – I'm going to manage Evie's burlesque act. If I'm investing in it, I should have a stake in it too, don't you think? I might not be any good, but I won't know until I try!'

'Nice to hear you're planning to make youself useful, Princess,' Niels said.

'Don't call me that!'

The butler and maid, who had re-emerged onto the terrace where they were setting out a bottle of champagne in an ice bucket, next to a pitcher of freshly pureed mango juice, rolled their eyes and retreated back inside.

'I'll have to change the sheets *again*,' grumbled the maid.

'You never know,' the butler said consolingly. 'The way he's looking at her, they might not even make it to the bedroom . . .'

POCKET
BOOKS

Jackie Collins
Married Lovers

Three high-powered Hollywood couples, two hot affairs,
one underage Russian ex-hooker, a passionate murder –
and the players' lives are changed forever.

Cameron Paradise, a stunning twenty-four-year-old personal
trainer, flees Hawaii and her champion-surfer husband, Gregg,
in the middle of one of his abusive tirades and makes her way
to L.A. Tall, blonde, with a body to die for, it doesn't take
Cameron long to find a job at an exclusive private fitness club
where she encounters L.A.'s most important players.

Although she could have any man who walks through the
club's doors, she is more focused on saving money – so that
she can open her own studio one day – than getting caught
up in the L.A. scene of wild parties and recreational drugs.
Until she meets Ryan Lambert, an extremely successful
independent movie producer.

Ryan is married to pampered Mandy Lambert, the daughter of
Hamilton J. Heckerling, a Hollywood power-player son-of-a-
bitch mogul. Ryan has never cheated on his demanding
Hollywood Princess wife . . . until he meets Cameron.

ISBN 978-1-84739-448-4
PRICE £7.99